# The Wet

## Paul Kane

*(The First Novel Paul Ever Wrote,
Never Published… Until Now!)*

## A HellBound Books LLC Publication

Copyright © 2024 Paul Kane
All Rights Reserved
Cover and art design by Tee Arts for
HellBound Books Publishing LLC

### www.hellboundbooks.com

No part of this publication can be reproduced, stored in a retrieval system, or transmitted by any form or by any means, mechanical, digital, electronic, photocopying or recording, except for inclusion in a review, without permission in writing from the individual contributors and the publisher
All contents in this novel are works of fiction. Names, characters, places and incidents are imaginary. Any resemblance to actual persons, places or occurrences are coincidental only.

www.hellboundbooks.com

Printed in the United States of America

## Praise for Paul Kane:

"Paul Kane is a first-rate storyteller, never failing to marry his insights into the world and its anguish with the pleasures of phrases eloquently turned."

>(**Clive Barker** – Bestselling author of *The Hellbound Heart*, *Abarat*, *Mr B. Gone* & *The Scarlet Gospels*)

"Paul Kane's lean, stripped-back prose is a tool that's very much fit for purpose. He knows how to make you want to avoid the shadows and the cracks in the pavement."

>(**Mike Carey** – Bestselling author of the Felix Castor series of novels and *The Girl With All the Gifts*, *Fellside* and *The Boy on the Bridge* as MR Carey)

"Kane finds the everyday horrors buried within us, rips them out and serves them up in these deliciously dark tales."

>(**Kelley Armstrong** – Bestselling author of *Bitten*, *Haunted*, *Broken*, *Waking the Witch*, *Spell Bound* and *Thirteen*)

"An artistic visionary for our times. A deft and daring writer, Paul is equally accomplished at editing, filmmaking, illustrating, and painting, and in all these forms he asks a set of probing questions about life, destiny, meaning, and 'something else'."

> (**Nancy Holder** – Bestselling and award-winning author of *Crimson Peak*, *Buffy The Vampire Slayer: The Book of Fours*, *Wonder Woman* and *On Fire*).

"Paul Kane is a name to watch. His work is disturbing and very creepy."

> (**Tim Lebbon** – *New York Times* bestselling author of *The Cabin in the Woods*, *The Silence* and *Among the Living*)

"His stories not only, at his best, put him neck and neck with Ramsey Campbell and Clive Barker, but also in the company of greats like Machen and MR James. You don't rest easily after reading a Paul Kane story, but strangely your eyes have been somewhat opened."

> (**Stephen Volk** – BAFTA winning screenwriter of *Gothic*, *Ghostwatch*, *Afterlife*, *The Awakening* and *Midwinter of the Spirit*; author of *Whitstable*, *Leytonstone* and *The Parts We Play*)

"He stands out as one of the better writers I've read."

> (*Eternal Night*)

"Wonderfully dark and satisfying."

(*Dark Side* Magazine)

"Kane is best when taking risks with his bizarre flights of imagination."

(*SFX* Magazine)

"Kane is a highly regarded author whose influence can be felt across the genre, with a large and notable body of work behind him."

(*Starburst* Magazine)

"The hype is very real... Fall under the thrall of the new king of horror."

(*Mass Movement* Magazine)

"Paul Kane is up there with James Herbert as one of the greatest British horror authors, not only today, but ever!"

(Encyclopocalypse)

"Paul Kane is a superb author."

(The Horror Channel)

"A legendary horror writer."

(*This is Horror*)

**Other Books by Paul Kane:**

**Novels**
Arrowhead
Broken Arrow
Arrowland
Hooded Man (Omnibus)
The Gemini Factor
Of Darkness and Light
Lunar
Sleeper(s)
The Rainbow Man (as PB Kane)
Blood RED
Sherlock Holmes and the Servants of Hell
Before
Deep RED
Arcana
The Red Lord (Robin of Sherwood)
Her Last Secret (as PL Kane)
The Storm
Her Husband's Grave (as PL Kane)
The Family Lie (as PL Kane)
The Gemini Effect
The RED Trilogy (Omnibus)

**Novellas & Novelettes**
Signs of Life
The Lazarus Condition
Dalton Quayle Rides Out
RED
Pain Cages
Creakers (chapbook)
Flaming Arrow

The Bric-a-Brac Man
The P.I.'s Tale
Snow
The Rot
Beneath the Surface (with Simon Clark)
Blood Red Sky
Confessions (as PL Kane)
Corpsing (as PL Kane)
Coming of Age (as PB Kane)
Murder on the Golden Sands Express (as PL Kane)
The Communion (as PL Kane)

**Collections**
Alone (In the Dark)
Touching the Flame
FunnyBones
Peripheral Visions
The Adventures of Dalton Quayle
Shadow Writer
The Butterfly Man and Other Stories
The Spaces Between
Ghosts
Monsters
The Dead Trilogy
Shadow Casting
Nailbiters
Death
The Life Cycle
Disexistence
Kane's Scary Tales Vol. 1
More Monsters
Lost Souls
The Controllers
White Shadows (as PB Kane)
The Colour of Madness (official movie tie-in)

Traumas
Darkness & Shadows
The Naked Eye
Tempting Fate
Nailbiters – Hard Bitten
Zombies!
Even More Monsters
Dark Reflections

## Editor & Co-Editor
Shadow Writers Vol. 1 & 2
Terror Tales #1-4
Top International Horror
Albions Alptraume: Zombies
The British Fantasy Society: A Celebration
Hellbound Hearts
The Mammoth Book of Body Horror
A Carnivàle of Horror: Dark Tales from the Fairground
Beyond Rue Morgue
Dark Mirages
Exit Wounds
Wonderland
Cursed
Twice Cursed
The Other Side of Never
In These Hallowed Halls

## Non-Fiction
Contemporary North American Film Directors: A Wallflower Critical Guide (Major Contributor)
Cinema Macabre (Contributor)
The Hellraiser Films and Their Legacy
Voices in the Dark
Shadow Writer – The Non-Fiction. Vol. 1: Reviews

Shadow Writer – The Non-Fiction. Vol. 2: Articles & Essays
Leviathan – The Story of Hellraiser and Hellbound: Hellraiser II (contributor)
Hellraisers
War is Hell: Making Hellraiser III: Hell on Earth (Contributor)
Stuart Gordon: Interviews (Conversations with Filmmakers Series) (Contributor)

*For my dad, who got me into horror.*

## Acknowledgments:

My thanks to James H Longmore and HellBound Books for taking a big leap with this one. Much love, hugs and thank yous all round to the editors and publishers who've ever published my work.

Plus, all my friends in the writing and film/TV world, for their continual help both now and in the past. You all know who you are! Lastly, a massive thank you to my "couldn't ask for better" wife and best friend Marie. Love you so, so much.

## The Wet
### An Introduction

Picture the scene...

A shy, overweight kid at school; always the weirdo, the odd one out. Bullied mercilessly. You probably know the story already, you'll have heard it from dozens of genre writers in the past. Who, like me, also retreated into the world of TV, film and books as an escape. In my case, it just happened to be the scary stuff that came first. I was watching horror movies like *Alien* long before I should have been. My late parents, God love 'em, let me watch films like *Invasion of the Body Snatchers* (the '70s version!) – actually showed them to me! – when I was only knee-high to a grasshopper. That led eventually to so-called Video Nasties, flicks like *The House by the Cemetery*, *Deep Red*, *The Exorcist* and *The Evil Dead*.

At break times I'd take myself off to quiet corners, empty classrooms or down on the playing field and lose myself in the latest King, Barker, Herbert, Brite, Campbell, Masterton, Rice... On holidays at the coast, I'd curl up in the caravan or car with a Guy N. Smith or Shaun Hutson. Was it any wonder that I used to write horror stories for English classes or try my hand at bashing out pulps on my mum's old, battered typewriter. I've said this before in a lot of interviews, but one of the first longer pieces I did in my teens was something called *Night Beast*. I thought I was writing some kind of "balls to the wall" horror novel, but it ended up being just about novella length and was more like Garth Marenghi than Stephen Laws or Stephen Gallagher. Needless to say, it's never seen the light of day.

So, there I was.

Life got in the way, as it always does, and I ended up at art college with some kind of half-arsed notion of becoming a painter or photographer, but just wasn't good enough. Then at uni, I started writing articles and reviews, which got me a foot in the door as a self-employed journalist. But those dreams of someday writing horror tales, or even – imagine it! – a novel never left me. And even before I began submitting my short stories to small press magazines, meeting other horror writers like Simon (*Blood Crazy*) Clark and Paul (*Stalkers*) Finch, I set out on a journey to try and write an actual horror novel myself.

Inspired by those weeks by the sea in places like Cleethorpes, Bridlington and Scarborough, and especially trips to see the local lifeboat stations, I decided to set it in a fictional place, similar to those (I did the same when creating Golden Sands more recently for *Her Husband's Grave*); probably because it was more exotic than setting it on the midlands housing estate where I grew up (little did I realise back then, that this location was perfect for all kinds of other kitchen sink horrors – as evidenced by my short novel *Of Darkness and Light*). I did lots of research, into the RNLI (the Royal National Lifeboat Institute) and just life in a seaside village in general. But I was still stuck for a "big bad". Now, I've always been into body horror (myself and my better half, the author and editor Marie O'Regan, even edited *The Mammoth Book of Body Horror* years later), and I began to think about what the coast has a ton of. How that could be used in a body horror type situation. There was probably also a smattering of one of my favourite movies, *Jaws*, in the mix too.

So, there I was again.

A *wet*-behind-the-ears horror writer trying to write a horror book about water. I did more research, science this time – stuff about cloud seeding and the weather – and suddenly I was off and running. Without any kind of idea how to structure a novel, other than what had gone in through osmosis by reading a massive amount of them. The first draft, which I think took me a couple of years or more, was a mess. And I mean, a *real* mess. I carried on trying to sort that out all through those years of doing the journalism and short stories, then eventually just started focussing on the shorts. Written off, if you'll pardon the expression. Another novel project abandoned, in favour of something a bit slicker and more serial killer-ish in the form of *The Gemini Factor*. For the story of that one, you'll have to pick up the tenth anniversary edition of the novel from Encyclopocalypse.

Anyway, fast forward almost three decades, which I packed full of writing, editing and all kinds of other good stuff. My first mass market books came out, I started to be eyed for awards, and there was even TV and film interest in my work – the two most high-profile things so far being the Lions Gate/NBC episode of *Fear Itself*, *New Year's Day* (based on "Dead Time") and the movie *Sacrifice* (based on "Men of the Cloth") starring one of my childhood horror heroes from *Re-Animator*, Barbara Crampton. I've worked with lots of cool people, in lots of cool franchises (one highlight was the audio of *Robin of*

*Sherwood*, a TV show I used to be glued to in the '80s), and some much more talented folk than me have said nice things about my stuff.

When you get to a certain age, though, you start looking back. We moved house a little while ago and various old manuscripts and such came to light. I've been trying to include old shorts – that I wrote back in the day but never got published – as extras in my collections for some time. "Bounty", for example, I found on a hard drive and tickled up – it's just about to be reprinted in a collection, along with the script of the audio adaptation by Brennan Storr. In that same book is a handwritten tale I never even typed up from the 1990s, included as a bonus for readers: "Echoes". And I recently put together a book of my short scripts from projects that were filmed, including a rare one I wrote as part of my screenwriting module for my BA, along with a storyboard I drew for yet another thing that never happened. I used to love finding that kind of material in the back of books by my favourite authors, like hidden treasure in a cave, so hopefully I'm now paying that forward – and at the same time getting things out into print before they disappear forever in a skip or something.

And yes, you guessed it, I also came across the manuscript for what I eventually called *The Wet*. I hadn't thought about it in many years, but as I sat reading through it, I said to myself: *You know what Kane, this isn't quite as shit as you remember it being.* It was at that point the germ of an idea about tidying it up and perhaps presenting it in book form – as a curiosity if nothing else – struck me. After all, if it's good enough for Clive with *Maximillian Bacchus*, or Ramsey with *The Inhabitant of the Lake*…

So, here we are.

You're about to read the first longform novel I ever wrote, back when I was in my early 20s and knew nowt.

I'm still not sure I do! Is it the book I would write today? Most definitely not, although I might do something else with the idea at some point. Something I *would* write with all that experience under my belt – I've had thoughts, let's put it that way. Is it well written? I'll let you be the judge of that, I'm probably a bit too close to it. But I do think it rattles along at quite a pace, even if it does riff massively off some of my favourite genre movies like *The Blob*, *Village of the Damned*, *Dawn of the Dead*, *Lifeforce*, *Rabid*, *The Fog*, *From Beyond*, *The Thing*, *The Abyss* and on and on… It's entertaining enough, and a fun read, so I'm hoping people will enjoy it for what it is. Please don't compare it to any of my later novels though, because it will almost certainly suffer. In fact, it'll be torture – and, trust me, I know all about that.

The thing I find most interesting about it, and I'm praying it will be the same for you, dear reader, is you can see the seeds of other things in here. Someone once said that writers are like carrion, circling a body and picking at the same bits over and over. Therefore, you can absolutely see the template for characters like Wendy Douglas, the artists' agent for Ellis Blare ("Facades"), Andrew Croft ("Yin & Yang") and more recently Gavin Hale (in "Stigma"), or the titular "Keeper of the Light" in the much older Stanley Keets. The loss of a child crops up, both in my ghost story "Wind Chimes" (which was turned into a poignant but shocking short film by Brad Watson based on my script) and then much later formed the basis for my crime novel *Her Last Secret* for Harper/HQ as PL Kane. Some of the events that take place in here mirror *Sleeper(s)*, my version of *Sleeping Beauty* by way of *Quatermass* and *The Andromeda Strain*, plus there's the possible origins of my shady Corporation from "Reflections", "Planet of the Dead" and "Mortis-Man: Legacy". There's more than a whiff of the army-trained "have a go hero" Keegan from *The Storm* in Rob Woodhead – hell, just look at the title of that monster-fest and tell me it wasn't influenced by *The Wet*! When two of the protagonists here get to know each other, it mirrors a certain scene in a pub in *The Gemini Factor*. In the mysterious "Colonel" and "interrogator" you can see the first inklings of one of my most famous characters (star of stage and screen), The Torturer. And those extremely familiar with my back catalogue will spot ideas like "the circle", which is a crucial ingredient in possibly my favourite novel of mine, *Before* – not to mention the Biblical stuff.

Even the legendary St August puts in an appearance… Sort of.

I could go on all day, but I won't; I'll get out of your way and let you get stuck in. With, as Columbo might say, just "one more thing" to add. Remember that shy, overweight kid from school, the weirdo who was bullied, the one who used to take himself off and hide away from the world, retreating into fiction written by his heroes? He's still in here, always will be. I hope you'll take into consideration how brave it is to let the world see this one, his first baby steps into what would become some sort of career in fiction.

And, most importantly, I hope you'll be gentle with him.

Paul Kane

# The Wet

## Prologue
### Stormbringer

<u>Sable, Mid-1990s</u>

A stone was cast into the water on Friday, causing tiny ripples to form. Disturbing an otherwise still and peaceful plane.

This is how it began...

\*\*\*

At first it was just a scarlet pinprick on the horizon. But Jacob Rand heard the sound of the motor long before he could see the vehicle itself. He'd always had superb hearing, and it was still acute in spite of his advanced years.

Jacob took a bite out of his cheese and pickle sandwich and screwed up his eyes. From his perch atop the tractor, he watched this blur turn off lower Haven Point

Road and careen up the narrow dirt track near the very edge of his land.

As it got closer, Jacob could make out the shapes more clearly: a red Land Rover, pulling a large metal trailer behind. The oblong appendage was almost as big as the four-wheel drive towing it. They rattled along the path at ridiculous speeds, a cloud of dust billowing in their wake like a dirty parachute.

Once or twice, they threatened to skid off and plough right into the grassland on either side, but the driver would always straighten up just in time.

Jacob swore under his breath. Bloody tourists; he wished Sable could manage without them. But then, this *was* a seaside resort after all, and the revenue it screwed from these idiots between the months of April and September helped keep the village afloat. It wasn't as if the fishing industry alone was going to do that. Or the farming industry either for that matter.

Hell, he'd even been known to rent a field or two out himself, to touring caravans, tents and the like, so it would be more than a little hypocritical of him to complain. That didn't mean he had to like the situation, though. And anyway, he hadn't done it since Annie passed away. Nowadays, he much preferred to be left alone.

Obviously, whoever this was didn't know that. Well, they would soon enough. They might not – probably did not – realise it, but they were trespassing.

Jacob hoped that wasn't camping equipment in the trailer. Because, if it was, these people would be very disappointed indeed.

He watched the mini-convoy zoom down the track a little way further, heading towards the cliff-tops, then slammed his lunch down.

"Right!" said Jacob to himself. The tractor engine started on the second go, and soon he was guiding the heavy beast across his field in the direction of the intruder.

It took him quite a while to catch up, and if the Land Rover hadn't parked just shy of the precipice, he probably wouldn't have intercepted it at all. A man in jeans and a pullover stood next to the vehicle, gazing out over the ocean. Jacob could only see his back, but he appeared to be mesmerised by the scenic view. As far as he could tell, the man was alone.

The farmer brought his own transportation to a halt, and killed the growling engine. He leant out of the clear glass case to yell at the stranger.

"Oi. Oi, you!" He was no more than twenty feet away from the bloke, but his calls went unanswered.

"Are you deaf or somethin'?" bellowed Jacob, his cheeks bulging red. "This is private property."

Still no acknowledgement.

Jacob clambered out of the cabin, his boots connecting with the hard ground beneath. He tried again.

"Hey, I'm talking to you, mate!"

The man continued to stare out into the distance. Jacob sighed. This was going to be tougher than he'd thought. At his age he didn't relish confrontations, but he hated uninvited guests even more – especially ones as pig-ignorant as this.

Slowly, he walked towards the Land Rover. The man didn't so much as twitch as Jacob approached, and the farmer started to think something might be very wrong here. He scratched his chin and wiped his hands on his overalls; for some reason they were unusually clammy.

"Didn't you hear me? I said—"

"It's beautiful, don't you think?" The fellow's voice started him. Deep and gravely, it communicated authority without the need for shouting.

"I... What the hell are you talking about? Listen, this is my land and right now you're trespassing, so if you wouldn't mind..." said Jacob, effecting his most intimidating tone.

"The sea. It's *so* beautiful."

Jacob gaped at the man's back. He wasn't getting through in the slightest. This moron was some kind of nature freak or something, and probably high on drugs too. Or maybe just plain drunk. Perhaps more drastic measures were called for.

"I haven't got time for this. Either you clear off, or I'm going to fetch my gun from the tractor. I don't want to use force, but I will if I have to." Actually his 12 bore was back at the farmhouse, about half a mile or so behind him (and he never kept it loaded anyway). Jacob hoped the threat of violence would be enough.

"Such a wide expanse of water. Can't you see the beauty?" was the only reply he got.

Jacob wasn't a patient man, as Annie constantly reminded him throughout their marriage, and this fellow had just crossed his very narrow tolerance line. All feelings of unease vanished, replaced by a sudden and overwhelming anger.

He stepped forward and put a hand on the man's shoulder. "Now you turn around when I'm speaking to you, boy!"

The figure spun with the precision of a ballet dancer and grabbed Jacob's wrist. He wasn't particularly forceful, yet the farmer found himself dropping to his knees.

"Wha—?" spluttered Jacob. His head was spinning, and it felt like someone had unleashed an entire aviary inside his stomach.

Jacob looked up at his arm where the assailant still gripped him. To his astonishment it was swelling up, the skin around his wrist and forearm inflating like a hot air balloon.

Then it started to spread along the length of the entire appendage until it reached his shoulder. His shirt sleeve bulged and ripped, exposing the bloated flesh beneath, like the bodybuilder back in the TV show of that green comic book character.

His eyes watered. At first he thought it was from the intense pain, but these were unlike any tears he'd ever shed – not even when he'd fallen out of his tree house, aged ten, and broken two limbs in the process. No, the salty deluge had a mind of its own, cascading down his cheeks and forming a puddle on the floor. Jacob didn't know tear-ducts could produce such a tidal wave.

And his mouth was salivating at an alarming rate. Jacob found himself drooling like a baby. He tried to swallow the liquid, but there was simply too much. It broke through his teeth and forced his lips wide apart.

Inevitably, the skin on his arms began to split. Blood mixed with water on the ground, producing surreal patterns in the dirt. He could feel his chest undulating now, and his stomach expanding to twice its normal size.

Through sodden eyes Jacob saw the man bend towards him. He spoke softly to the farmer. "And God said to Noah, 'I am going to send a flood on the earth to destroy every living being. Everything on the earth will die.'"

It was hard now for Jacob to make out the man's features, but he could see the smile: the broad, beaming grin of a madman. Jacob attempted to reply and choked on his own juices.

There was one last excruciating bout of agony that seemed to wrack his whole body, and then Jacob was gone.

His murderer let go and watched the body keel over. As it struck the ground more rips appeared in the flesh, this time on the neck and face. Thick, crimson pulp spilled out. There was nothing left in the eye-sockets but fluid, which continued to pour, and the nostrils flared to accommodate the watery mucus emerging.

The stranger cocked his head, and stooped to gather up the corpse. With his fingertips he pulled the handle on the Land Rover door and deposited the – now unrecognisable – farmer in the back.

"Wait here," he whispered. "I won't be long."

He reached under the passenger seat, pulled out a black briefcase, then slammed the door to. The man strode round the back of the metal trailer, taking a key out of his pocket as he went.

The locks popped open easily and the large door dropped at his feet, forming a ramp. He lay the case on the ground and disappeared inside for a moment. When he returned, he was carrying a thick piece of rope.

He yanked on the cord and a gigantic white cone poked out of the trailer. He pulled again, much harder this time. It looked for all the world like he was playing tug of war with this unseen monstrosity.

At last the light aircraft came rolling down the ramp, nose first; the wheels of its trolley squeaking under the pressure of the move. He set to work assembling the thing: unfolding the wings and tail section. It took him no more than five minutes from start to finish, and then he was ready to push it into position.

He swung open the cockpit door and placed his briefcase inside. As he put on his headset, he enjoyed one last look out at the sea.

The engine turned over the first time, its whining voice sounding like a mass of angry bees in a bag. The plane taxied past the tractor and Land Rover, and up the grassy pasture serving as a runway.

The man coaxed more speed out of his vehicle, pointing it in the direction of the cliffs. Just as it seemed like the craft would go sailing over the edge into oblivion, it began to lift off the ground.

Higher and higher it rose into the sky, leaving the nonsense of gravity far behind. It wasn't long before both the plane and its pilot had disappeared into the cotton wool clouds, out of sight.

Absorbed by the white and blue heavens.

# Part One
## The Rain Circle

"O Lord, methought what pain it was to drown,
What dreadful noise of waters in my ears,
What sights of ugly death within my eyes!"

*Richard III: Act 1, Scene 4*, William Shakespeare.

## Chapter One
### The Maelstrom

It was safe and warm where he was.

Jason Harding turned his face towards the sun and smiled. He closed his eyes, the light from that yellow giant illuminating all the veins and blood vessels in his lids. He was content to lay there forever if he could.

A giggling to his left roused him, and he looked at his son, Alex. A laughing, happy youth with ginger hair (on his mother's side), his face was full of promise for the future. The promise of all the things he'd do over the course of a lifetime.

Harding watched him play, as he often did, and thought how truly lucky he was to be a father. Alex would kick the leather football across the field, run and fetch it – his tiny legs propelling him forward – then repeat the whole process again in the opposite direction. It made Harding long to be a child again himself. To be free of worries like work, tax and death.

Something was brushing against his ear. Whatever it

was tickled, and he tried to knock it away with the back of his hand. He heard yet more laughter, a woman's this time, and turned to see Christine with a blade of grass in her fist and a cheeky grin playing across her face.

He feigned indignation and pretended to be mad with her. She played along and proceeded to blow in his ear to compensate. He liked that a lot better. Then she began to kiss his lobe, occasionally nibbling the fatty tissue that dangled there.

Christine worked her way round his face, brushing his cheek with her mouth, until finally she found his own lips. And when they connected it was like an electric current passing through him.

Eventually she broke off, and reared herself up on one elbow.

"Happy?" she asked.

Harding smiled once more. "You know I am."

They looked into each other's eyes as she took his hand: two souls at peace, now and for always.

Alex's cries distracted him and Harding rolled over to see what all the fuss was about.

"Dad, Dad!" Alex was hopping up and down on the grass with excitement, his football cast aside near a tree. "The man's come back from lunch. Can we take a boat on the lake now?"

Harding blew out a breath. "I don't know, champ. Maybe later, yeah?"

Alex frowned. "Dad, you *promised*."

That's right, he remembered now. He had mentioned something about a lake to Alex. "You know I'm not keen on the water, Al."

"Please, Dad. *Can* we?"

Harding looked back at Christine, hoping for some support. "Would you like me to take him, love?" she said.

It was a tempting offer, but Alex wanted his old man

to go with him. It was understandable really; they spent little enough time together as it was.

"No, no. It's all right."

Except it wasn't all right. Everything was all wrong actually. The sky that had been so bright a minute ago, was now cloudy and dark, with no trace of the sun. Harding felt a chill wind on his skin and shivered slightly.

Then he realised he could no longer feel Christine's hand. Nor could he see her face. Alex had disappeared too, and Harding looked around frantically for them. He heard screaming, but couldn't make out the source.

The vista surrounding him had become faint, blurry almost, like an out of focus photograph. The colours began to run into each other until they became a dark, murky mess.

There was a second noise in the distance, like the rattling of sheet metal. Harding began walking in that direction, using it as a beacon. He could still see nothing in the gloom.

"Christine? Alex, where are you?" His voice echoed into the black, but there was no answer for him. Harding tried to call out again, only this time nothing emerged from his mouth. It was as if his larynx had shut down completely.

A sudden wetness on his skin made him shudder. Tiny arrows of rain were bouncing off his body. *That's it*, he thought, *we must be having a spring shower*.

But the downpour had targeted Harding alone. And as the droplets came down with more force, it hurt when they struck, causing cuts and bruises along his arms and across his face.

Harding wanted to cry out but couldn't: it was becoming difficult enough just to breathe, let alone shout. And he felt like he was flying – there was no grass, no ground beneath him and his hands were flailing around in front.

Yes, he *was* flying. Or at least that's what he thought, until he saw the bubbles coming from his nose.

The rain was gone and somehow he'd wound up underwater. That's why it was so hard to catch a breath.

Finally, he could fight it no longer. His body expelled the last remnants of air from his lungs and desperately searched for more. But there was no oxygen around to supply him, only the filthy liquid he was submerged in. It gushed up his nostrils and violated his throat, regardless of his protests.

Harding wrestled around, trying to break the surface of the water. It was no use. There didn't even appear to *be* a surface. He swallowed more water, and felt the ghastly flood choking him, pressing down on him.

He panicked.

Harding thrashed around, legs kicking, arms reaching out for some kind of purchase.

Strangely, he could still hear the booming noise of the thunder, as if the sheet metal were inside his head rumbling away, tattooing an insane rhythm on his brain.

Harding knew that death was just around the corner. There was no escape from this place now.

His systems were shutting down, one by one. He could no longer feel his legs, arms or hands, and his head began to loll onto his shoulder.

But before he passed out for the final time, he saw something in front of him. It wasn't very clear because of the foggy water, yet he could see an image. A face maybe, in the corner of his field of vision, grinning coldly as it watched his demise.

Then it was over.

This was the end...

# The Wet

Harding opened his eyes and shot forwards in bed, breaking his intense link with the dream-world. He was still gasping for air, but it came more readily to him now. Almost as soon as he sat up, he started dry retching, coughing up the non-existent water he'd "swallowed".

The sheets around him were saturated with sweat, despite the coldness of the room, and his hair was plastered to his scalp. It was still dark, and Harding rubbed his eyes in a vain attempt to read the glowing digits on the clock: 4.30 am, it informed him cheerily.

"Shit!" he mumbled as he cast the soggy bed-linen aside. Harding grabbed his robe, but before putting it on he dried his face on its coarse surface.

In the half-light of the bedroom he staggered to the open door, tripping over his discarded shoes as he went. Once he was in the hall, he made a sharp left turn and entered the bathroom.

The light was almost blinding when he pulled the cord, and he stood there shielding his eyes for a moment. He caught a glimpse of himself in the mirror and groaned. The bags under his eyes were much darker than they'd ever been; deep worry lines burrowed into his forehead with abandon. What little hair he had (less than two thirds left now) was going grey, and there was at least five days' worth of stubble clinging to his chin.

He looked like a man of seventy something, yet he was only half that age. The events of the last few years had certainly taken their toll.

Harding felt sticky and unclean, so instinctively he went to turn on the shower. The head spat out its first load and the droplets pattered noisily on the plastic floor. The sound took him back to the dream – the nightmare – of being pelted with razor-sharp rain. Quickly he turned off the spray again.

He decided instead to have a strip-wash in the sink,

filling the porcelain bowl with steaming water.

***

The light in the kitchen was just as unforgiving as it was upstairs. Harding went to the wall cupboard to get the coffee jar, but on the way noticed the half-empty bottle of whiskey on the work surface – a casualty of the previous night's drinking binge. He made a U-turn and grabbed a glass tumbler out of the sink.

Harding tipped a copious amount into the glass and took a gulp. He winced as the light-brown alcohol burnt his – already tender – throat on the way down. It didn't stop him picking up the bottle and bringing it with him to the living room. He wandered in and pulled on a side light.

The first thing that greeted him in here was his painting. It loomed over him, a square of half-filled canvas propped up by an old wooden easel. His oils were strewn over the table beside it and a filthy mug of turps balanced precariously near the edge.

Harding looked the piece up and down, a frown materialising on his face. He took another swig of whiskey and approached his work.

It was a promising start, there was no denying that. The brushstrokes were so broad and swift. And the colours: aqua-marine, cyan, sapphire, navy; all evocative of the sea, swirling maniacally around in a semicircle with splashes of white highlights here and there.

He stared at the maelstrom and brief fragments of the nightmare came back to him again. He was definitely on the right track.

Harding edged towards the nearest armchair and collapsed into it, never once taking his eyes off the image.

# The Wet

He sat, quietly cradling his drink, until his eyelids were just too heavy to hold up, and the shroud of sleep fell over him once more.

There were no dreams this time, but Harding did hear the booming sound again. It woke him just after 8:30, drowning out the usual noise from the seagulls. That same sheet metal rumbling from his nightmare, except it was very real and very loud.

And it was coming from outside.

He set down the bottle and glass, then went to the window to peek through the blinds. Although he put his hand to his eyes to shield them from the inevitable daylight, it still took him by surprise, and he was temporarily robbed of his vision. When the mists cleared, he saw it.

There, over the cliff-tops, in the middle of the ocean, was the strangest storm-cloud he'd ever seen in his life. It was dense and jet-black, like a solid ball of smoke. Harding could see tiny flashes of lightning both inside and out.

Rain was falling like a curtain. It punched the churning froth beneath and obscured the view beyond. But the strange thing was, it appeared to be falling in one particular spot. Harding had never seen anything like it; never would again probably.

It made him think of those comical storm-clouds you see in cartoons, the ones that follow miserable characters around and drench them wherever they go – even indoors. It was crazy, but that was the closest thing he could compare it to.

However, there was nothing even remotely funny about this one at all. If anything, it was overtly terrifying.

Harding's jaw dropped and he felt the perspiration break out again on his forehead, then down his back and along his arms.

Where the hell had he put his camera? Harding raced around the room looking for it, finally discovering his Pentax in its bag behind the settee. He attached the telephoto lens, but cursed when he looked through the glass square at the back of the camera. It was empty. Harding scuttled into the kitchen and ransacked the drawers, looking for 400 speed film.

When he found one, he dashed to the back door of his cottage. Harding clicked off the Yale lock then undid the door. Like a man possessed, he charged out into the garden in his robe and started snapping away with the single lens reflex.

As he looked at the isolated storm through the viewfinder, he got the distinct feeling it was looking right back at him. He shivered, but put it down to the cold sea breeze. Deep down, though, he knew it was much more than that.

This was the storm from his dream. An unmistakable, brutal thing with no remorse or pity. That was what really scared him.

It was as if his very inner demons had been given form; the maelstrom was here, and it was alive.

## Chapter Two
### Appointments

From somewhere that seemed like a million miles away came the sound of a rock band reciting their incomprehensible lyrics. At first the music was muted, almost as though they were playing underwater. But the nearer to consciousness he swam, the louder their twanging chords became. Until, finally, Rob Woodhead was aware of the radio alarm clock blaring away in his ear from its home on the bedside table.

Still half-asleep, he reached over and banged the top of it with his fist. The row stopped. With the effort of a Titan, he roused himself, rubbing his face and attempting to open his eyes.

There was a blurry shape perched on the end of his bed.

As he blinked, it slowly came into focus. The figure of a young, dark-haired woman pulling on a pair of faded jeans. He observed her silently for a moment, first slipping one leg in and then the other; only standing at the very last minute to do them up and tuck in her purple top. Rob's vision trailed over her body, that beautiful body he so adored. He felt something akin to sadness that he'd missed the first part of this ritual.

"I didn't know the alarm was on," she said without turning. "I was going to let you have a lay-in."

"S'okay. I set it myself. Work to do," Rob murmured, then slid his tongue over his teeth in an effort to clean away some of the overnight crust.

This time Dawn did look round at him. "Working? Not today. You promised you'd keep the weekend clear."

"I know, I know. It's just that I told Mike I'd have a look at his van. He needs it for a job on Monday."

Her eyes narrowed. "This is because of Dad, isn't it? You knew we were meant to be going up there at noon."

*A weekend up at the lighthouse with bloody Portland Bill,* thought Rob. *Why ever would I want to miss that?*

"Look, he only asked me yesterday down The Seagull. What was I supposed to say? Anyway, I should be done by lunch-time," Rob lied, having no idea what time he'd be finished.

"Well you'd better be, Rob Woodhead. You know how much this means to me. I want you both to get on."

"Hey, I get on with everybody. It's in my genes." He grinned, that same schoolboy grin which had attracted her to him that night six months ago. She could never stay mad at him for long. Rob beckoned her over with his finger. "Here, let me show you. I still have a little time before I have to meet Mike."

Dawn's frown merged into an expression of mischief. "A *little*?"

"Enough."

Rob propped himself up in bed, urging Dawn to come and sit next to him. Her fingertips explored his naked torso, stroking the firm muscle. Rob leaned forward to kiss her hard on the mouth, then gently brought his lips to her neck, butterfly kisses making her squirm with delight.

His hands found the button on her jeans, and quickly undid it – the zip descending a little of its own accord. Dawn moaned softly as he caressed her. She made no protest when he pulled her over onto the duvet. In seconds her top was untucked again, and the jeans were being removed. Rob tenderly kissed the inside of her thighs as the trousers came off. He looked up to see the desire in her eyes, and his own hunger reflected in those pupils.

*What would Daddy say if he could see you now, Miss Keets?* Rob absently mused as he discarded the jeans and set to work on the T-shirt...


One sniff at the milk told him it was off.

The putrid aroma offended his senses and he poured the contents of the carton down the sink. Rob rinsed the lumpy globules away, which swirled around in clear-white torrents. No cereal this morning, then.

He wandered over to the bread bin in search of a loaf. It was empty. No toast either.

Rob switched on the kettle. Black coffee for breakfast again, it would appear. He really ought to make a bit of an effort now that Dawn was staying over more often. No wonder she couldn't wait to get back home. Back to Haven Point.

But he thought then of the grin she'd flashed him just before she left, turning and waving with one hand in the air.

He loved that smile, the dimples it caused in her cheeks. He loved Dawn. For the first time in as long as he could remember, Rob was truly happy. He'd never expected to be when he returned home after all these years – especially considering the circumstances which had brought him back.

Rob took a sip of the dark, steaming liquid in his cup. He swilled the bitter taste around in his mouth before finally forcing it down his throat. He went to the cupboard in search of sugar. All out. What a surprise.

Reluctantly, he drank again. Rob shuddered and tipped the rest away. Maybe he'd grab something in his mid-morning break, if he had time. No, he'd make time. It wasn't as if he was going to eat much later on, not with Dawn's father giving him the evil eye.

Snatching his key-ring from the hook where it always hung, he dashed to the door. Had to get a move on. Dawn would skin him alive if he didn't get his work out of the way and show up at the lighthouse for lunch.

Rob walked round to his garage. The thick padlock wasn't really necessary, not in Sable (which seemed to have dodged the crime wave sweeping the rest of the country; the rest of the world, even). But Rob felt better with it on, seeing as his pride and joy resided in that garage.

He swung open the door and was greeted by the wonderful sight of a 1952 Vincent Black Shadow motorcycle, eagerly awaiting its owner's return.

"Morning, baby. Fancy a spin?"

With the utmost care, Rob wheeled her out into the daylight. The sun bounced off her sleek black form and he couldn't help patting the side of the fuel tank, the way other people might stroke a favourite pet.

He'd spent innumerable hours working on her, fixing her up, hunting for spares, restoring the bike to her former glory. Taking her back in time to the day she'd come off the line at Philip Vincent's factory in Stevenage, Herefordshire.

The bloke he'd bought her from, some poncy executive in the midlands, had inherited the "item" when his uncle died and had let her get in an awful state. Not even worth selling for scrap, he'd said, betraying his lack of knowledge about bikes in one sentence. Rob had nearly wept when he clapped eyes on her for the first time. He'd seen much more than the rusted up old heap the twat was desperate to get rid of (so desperate he'd let it go for a song). Some people had no soul, no respect.

That was then. Now, with new – well, almost new – parts (including twin 7" drum brakes at the front, a replacement of the alloy cylinder barrels and their cast iron liners with cast iron barrels, and giving her 19" wheel rims in place of the original 20 inchers to make tyre-replacement that much simpler) and a lot of loving care, she was a dream machine. A classic to be proud of again. The second most important lady in his life.

Rob hastily locked up again, and was sat on his steed in an instant. He slipped his helmet on, smoothed down the leathers he'd donned, and kick-started her up.

He listened to the revving engine, rising and falling as he twisted the throttle. It was a symphony to his ears. Slowly, he rolled her out through the open gates and onto the rough dirt track which ran alongside his house.

Soon he would be on the open road, a feeling like no other. Rob Woodhead grinned once more under the helmet and rode his very own Black Beauty onwards.

\*\*\*

Dawn Keets giggled to herself as she maneuvered round the bend, her pink Suzuki jeep (courtesy of a certain mechanic she knew) handling like a dream. Her "Love Mobile" as Rob called it.

Her grin broadened as she thought of him again. She was still flushed from their early-morning love making.

The sensation of his arms around her, squeezing harder and harder, had left an impression like a footprint in the sand.

Things were getting very serious between them, she could feel it. Nothing had been said, nothing needed to be said: she could simply tell. That was one of the reasons why she wanted Rob and her dad to get along. It wasn't too much to ask, was it? Except that Stanley Keets seemed determined to ruin any chance of happiness she might find. He'd already put off several boyfriends in the past and had attempted to ruffle Rob's feathers on more than one occasion – her birthday do was a prime example. So in a way she could understand Rob's reluctance to come along today.

Yet she could also understand her father's motivations. She was still his little girl, and ever since her mother had left them, he'd looked to her for support. Dawn was all he had, compensating for the fact her mum was shacked up with some bloke ten years younger than herself. He was frightened of losing Dawn, just like he'd lost his wife.

Which was why Rob had to be the bigger man in this equation. He could do it; she knew he could. Dawn felt sure that if her dad had spent as much time with him as she had in the last few months (all right, not *quite* as much), he might come to like and respect him. This lunch was the first step along that lengthy highway.

If it didn't work, she'd just have to lock them in a room together and see which one came out alive.

Dawn chuckled at the mental picture forming in her mind, though she knew all too well it was no laughing matter. She couldn't stand to think of the two men she loved constantly at each other's throats. And she didn't relish the thought of having to make a choice. She wouldn't – couldn't – let it come to that.

But what if—

# The Wet

The flow of Dawn's reflections was suddenly stemmed by an unusual scene up ahead on her left. Old farmer Rand's tractor near the cliff-top, parked on the angled grass. It waited there, a forgotten sentry guarding the treacherous sheer drop on the other side.

The further along Haven Point Road she went, the closer she came to the vehicle. There was no sign of Rand anywhere. Curious, Dawn pulled up and clambered out of the jeep. She took her pocket binoculars from their cubby-hole in the jeep's door and scanned the area for traces of the aged landowner. She could see the tractor quite clearly now, its door hanging open, the cabin empty. But the subject of her search was still unaccounted for.

Dawn didn't know Jacob Rand that well; nobody really did because he kept himself to himself, but from what little her father had told her she gathered he was a miserly sort. The kind who would sit all winter in a freezing house just so he didn't have to pay the fuel bills. Not the kind of man to abandon an expensive piece of equipment without a good reason.

Maybe he'd had an accident? He could have tumbled out of the tractor and crawled round to the other side where she couldn't see. Possible, but hardly likely. If he'd fallen out of any side at all, it would have been the one with its door ajar.

For the second time she surveyed his estate with her glasses.

Nothing.

She pondered what to do. Ring for help on her mobile, which she had for emergencies? But if it all turned out to be a false alarm, if Rand came rushing across the fields after having taken a leak or something, she'd look like a prize idiot. Not to mention an interfering busybody. On the other hand, she couldn't simply drive off. How would she feel if something serious had happened?

Before she knew it, Dawn found herself back in the jeep, heading for the dirt track just off the "main" road. It was trespassing, she was fully aware of that, but Dawn had to ease her conscience somehow. So what if she did receive a mouthful of abuse for her trouble? At least she'd know Rand was alive and well and ready to take on all-comers.

Besides, if she explained why she'd ventured onto his terrain, he'd understand. Wouldn't he?

Dawn swayed left and right as the track passed under her. It was times like these she was glad she owned a jeep, and not something like Rob's bike. He wouldn't stand a chance on this surface.

It wasn't long before she came upon the tractor. Dawn braked alongside its thick rubber wheels, and anxiously thrummed her fingers on the steering wheel.

The first thing she did was check underneath and around the other side of the vehicle, half expecting to discover a body. Thankfully her suspicions were unfounded. She'd guessed correctly back on the road. Jacob Rand was not here. Nor was he shouting warnings at her from the field, threatening to unload the contents of his shotgun into her if she didn't get back in her jeep, turn around and get the hell off his property.

So where was he?

Slowly, she turned to look at the edge of the cliff, rearing up, taunting her to step closer. Dawn swallowed hard. Rand's wife had died a few years ago, hadn't she? The pair of them had lived like a couple of outcasts on the farm for decades, never visiting the village, never going to the pub or the shops; apparently all they needed was right here. It stood to reason that he'd be feeling lonely now. Perhaps it had finally caught up with him, the realisation that he would never see his beloved partner again, unless he did something about it that was.

There were easier, less painful, ways of taking one's own life. But still...

Dawn moved forward, up towards the peak, hardly noticing the tracks to her right – or the dark patch on the ground. Because something else had gripped her attention. She forgot all about Jacob Rand's "suicide" and his mysterious abandoned tractor. Because Dawn could see it now in all its glory: a single black thunder cloud over the water with a sheet of violent rain issuing from its innards.

The only dark spot in an otherwise perfect blue and white sky, it seemed expectant, anticipating something. Dawn mentally chastised herself; it was silly to think of that as a living thing. It was just another aspect of nature like the cliffs, the sands, the sea.

Nevertheless, it hung there, as if waiting for someone to explain that it shouldn't exist.

## Chapter Three
### SOS

Rob pressed his foot down on the back brake. He was coming up towards the bend which would take him into Sable proper, and sure enough that familiar "SLOW" sign greeted him by the side of the road. 30 mph maximum here.

But he was in no hurry to get to work. Rob gently squeezed the right handle brake, easing her down to a sensible 20, just to make sure, the huge 5" diameter speedo confirming this change. His premises weren't that far away now, anyway.

Along each side of the road were patchwork houses, made from every colour brick imaginable: a big draw for the tourists. Small homes, some brown, some grey, some tan – but all with the same white windows – were stacked side by side like fillings in a vertical sandwich.

Rob drifted by the church, one of two in Sable. This was the traditional sort, ancient-looking with arched doors, a mammoth cross on its roof, a clock on the tower at the front and an elongated section being dragged behind it.

# The Wet

And then, of course, there was the graveyard. Spread over two patches of grassland on either side of the road and cut off from each other by two thick stone walls, it was where virtually everyone who lived in Sable ended up. Including his parents.

A welcoming sight next: the Seagull Inn. Ironic really that an alehouse should be situated next to a cemetery. What was the line in that ancient poem, "Eat, drink and be merry, for tomorrow we die." What more proof did you need?

Without fail every time Rob popped in for a pint, the landlord, Big Billy Braden, would say to newcomers, "Keep it down, will you. You're making enough noise to wake the dead!" Upon which his regulars would all burst out laughing.

Just down from the beer-garden was the local park, almost hidden from view by weeping willows. Everyone called it a park, but it was really no more than a patch of grass with a pond in it. The round circle of water was separated from the green by a small fence. The parents of Sable had petitioned the council to erect it when a toddler almost fell in a while back.

Diagonally opposite was a white-washed building which housed Graham Cotton's shop. A newsagents slash grocers, slash post office, slash DIY store, slash… well just about everything really. Outside were your typical seaside goods: cheeky postcards on rotating stands, buckets and spades, fishing nets; and in the window Rob could just about make out shell ornaments and miniature models of boats. Graham would probably even sell fish 'n' chips if he wasn't such good friends with Rodney Twain, owner of the Cod-U-Like on the high street.

Rob scrutinised all these as he rode past, places he'd known since he was old enough to scream and fill his nappies, but which he now looked on with new eyes. Each time admiring them as a visitor to Sable might. He waved to people he knew, people he didn't know, and thanked the Lord such a village existed.

Because up until five years ago, Rob thought he would never see any of it again as long as he lived.

He remembered vividly the confrontation before he'd left, almost a decade and a half ago now – where had all the time gone? Rob saw it in his mind as if it had happened last week, even as he rode through the cheery Sable streets.

His dad disowning him because he'd chosen to move away. Rob didn't want to become a fisherman like him, and his granddad before him and great granddad before that, and so on and so on, ad infinitum. Woodheads stretching back further than anyone could remember, every one of them in the fishing trade. And he, Robert William Woodhead, had dared to fly in the face of tradition.

Oh, he'd heard the call of the sea all right, hard not to in Sable. It was just that it called to him from much further away.

"Fine, Robert. You want to go off and see the world," his father had said, "You take a holiday. Get it out of your system. But don't turn your back on your family, your responsibilities, to go chasing a fantasy in the Navy. If you do, then by God you'll never be welcome in this house again as long as I'm breathing."

And sadly, Rob never was.

Though he'd kept in touch, mainly through his mother, informed them of how well he was doing in the Engineers, learning a trade he enjoyed and was good at, he didn't return until that fateful week in late October when he learned of his dad's cancer. His mum had remained silent about it for almost a year – at her husband's request, the stubborn old fool – but she could no longer obey his wishes. Their only son had a right to know and deserved a chance to make peace with his father before the end; or at least try to.

Rob had one last shot at explaining why he'd had to leave and apologised for all the harm he'd done (only now could he see what the effect had been). As he sat by the hospital bed, his mother nearby, he tried to make his dad see he'd had no choice, had to get out of Sable before it drove him mad. The old man, his face like that of a corpse already, had just lay there and listened, not making his feelings plain either way.

But at the very moment of death, he reached out to Rob with one pale, wrinkled hand and the son had taken it in his own, clutching it and weeping as the parent who'd ignored his existence for so long took his final breath in this world.

Rob felt as though a huge boulder had been lifted from his back. But at the same time waves of regret washed over him for the years they had missed out on. So much time they would never get back. Not now. And the knowledge that he let his pop down would gnaw away at him till he lay on his own death bed.

After that came the funeral at the church he'd passed a few minutes ago. Naturally Rob had stayed around to look after his grieving mother, and the days turned into weeks, which turned into months. He had fully intended signing up for the Navy again after his current tour ended, but before he knew it a whole year had passed by and he'd done nothing about this.

It was the damnedest thing. He found himself falling in love with Sable in a way he'd never experienced before. The scenery, the quietness of the surroundings, the slow pace of life – such a contrast to the regimented hustle and bustle he was used to in the forces – all compelled him to stay a little longer, just a little longer. Maybe it was his age, maybe absence really did make the heart grow fonder like the cliché suggested, or maybe he'd seen enough of the world to know it was far better here than anywhere else? Whatever the reason, he was glad to be back.

Even the attentions of villagers that he'd once found stifling, were now comforting. Everyone in Sable knew everybody else and there was something reassuring about that. People bound together in times of joy, but also in times of...

It had been the locals who'd been so kind to him when his mother passed on, too – a year and a half after her "soul partner" slipped away. Rob used to watch her some days, aware that the life was draining out of her bit by bit, yet also conscious that there was nothing he or any doctor could do for the woman. It was a natural process. His folks had been together for almost forty years, and where one went, the other would surely follow – even if it was into the afterlife.

By then Sable was truly his home. Rob had saved up a considerable amount of money during his time in the Navy and he decided to spend some of it on a place he could call his own, a lovely fixer-upper opportunity just outside of Sable centre, but close enough for him to feel part of the community. Then, with the proceeds from the sale of the family house (admittedly not a large abode, but it was located in a prime spot), Rob invested in a small business: a motor shop and garage inside Sable itself. He was doing what he was trained to do, what he enjoyed doing. Fixing engines. There was enough trade in Sable to keep him afloat during the winter and in the tourist season he sometimes had more custom than he could handle on his own. No, he'd never been as fulfilled as he had been these last few years.

And meeting Dawn? Well, that was the icing on a very rich and delicious cake.

At the mini-roundabout Rob turned to his left instead of heading straight across the main street. There was the

Town Hall and then the Methodist Chapel, the newest, cleanest structure in Sable bar none. He was almost at his destination. Rob turned one more corner and saw Mike Croxley, the nearest thing Sable had to an odd-job man, standing outside the garage, glancing first at his watch, then at the battered yellow van he always scooted around in. It looked particularly sorry for itself today, the headlights shedding rusty tears.

The bike pulled up mere inches from Mike's lanky frame.

"Whatchit, Rob!" he exclaimed. "You know, one of these days you'll be doing that and you won't be able to stop in time."

Rob rid himself of his helmet and smiled. Mike's half-hearted anger soon turned to happiness when he saw that grin. *I told her*, Rob said to himself. *I can charm the birds from the trees if I put my mind to it.* He could always rely on that particular facial expression to get him out of trouble. And it worked on both genders.

"Just give me a second to open up, Mike, then I'll have a look at her. Okay?"

"Yeah, fine."

The mechanic undid another lock, hefting up the corrugated metal door of the workshop.

"You want a cup of tea?" called Rob over his shoulder.

"Not if it's too much bother."

"Don't be daft. I'm having one myself. All I've got at home is coffee, and no sugar or milk," Rob said with a laugh. At least he knew he'd be sure of a decent drink at work. He may be lax when it came to his home life, but Rob never forgot to stock up on essential supplies here. Sometimes a nice cuppa and a chocolate Hob-Nob was all that kept him going.

"So, what did you say was wrong with her, Mike?"

The man scratched a bony elbow and contemplated the question. "Er, well, for a start she's making banging noises, you know under the front bit."

"Where the engine is, you mean?" The sarcasm was completely lost on Mike. "All right, banging you say? That doesn't sound good. You might be looking at a complete overhaul here," Rob said sombrely.

"Really? Oh no, and I went and promised Lisa we could get the kitchen done this summer."

"Mike, Mike, relax. I'm pulling your leg. It's probably nothing, and anyway I'll see you right." What else could he do after all the work he'd put in over at Rob's house?

The relief was evident on Mike's face. "Thank Christ for that! You really had me going there for a minute, Rob."

It wasn't a hard thing to do. Mike Croxley was well known for his gullibility. He'd lost the price of many a pint of beer because of some clever trick or another. Rob couldn't help having a go himself.

"But seriously, Mike, you really ought to consider trading her in for a newer model."

Mike appeared mortified. "I couldn't do that; we've been together for so long."

"That's part of the problem, you see— Whoa, what the hell do you think you're doing?!"

The cigarette was hanging precariously from Mike's lips, his right hand clutching the match he intended to strike against the small cardboard box. His eyes were wide at Rob's outburst. "W-What's up?"

"What's up? *What's up?*" Rob shouted, perhaps a little too harshly. "*We* were, very nearly. Look at that sign and tell me what it says."

Mike followed his pointing finger and squinted. Without his glasses he clearly found it hard to make out, "No... sm... no..."

"No smoking! Jesus, do you want to kill us both?"

The Wet

The customer still looked puzzled until Rob drew his attention to the oxyacetylene welding gear, the tanks containing filtered-off oil, not to mention the petrol cans stacked up in the corner. Gingerly, Mike put the match back in its box and took the fag out of his mouth.

"I'm sorry, Rob." His voice was trembling, though Rob couldn't tell whether he was more upset about what he'd done, or the fact that Rob had chewed him out.

Rob nodded. "That's okay. Just remember, there's enough flammable liquid in here to stage a sequel to *The Towering Inferno*. Only there'll be no Paul Newman or Steve McQueen to pull our fat out of the fire. Just a bunch of blokes dressed in white raking over the charred remains."

"Sorry, I—" Mike's apology was cut short by the phone ringing on Rob's cluttered desk.

"I'm never going to get started this morning," complained the mechanic. "Just take a seat while I see to this, Mike. And try not to blow anything up."

Rob grabbed the receiver. "Hello, Rob Woodhead..."

"Rob, it's Phil. I thought it was better to call rather than beep you." Dammit, he knew he'd forgotten something this morning, his bloody beeper! But what with Dawn going on about her father and—

"Listen, you'd better get down to the station right away." There was a grave tone to Phil's voice that made Rob uneasy.

"What is it?" The words almost dried up in his throat.

"Rob, it's the Turners. The Coastguard received an SOS. I figured you'd want to be in on this shout."

"What's happened?"

There was a pause. "You mean you haven't seen it yet?"

"Seen what?"

"You can see out over the coast from the back of your

garage, right?"

"Yeah, but—"

"Go take a look. It's better if you see for yourself. I'll meet you at Angels Landing, we're leaving in ten." Phil Holmes killed the line, leaving a mystified Rob on the other end. Then he was at the back door, hardly in control of his own movements, ignoring the questions of Mike Croxley behind him.

Initially he could spot nothing. Everything was normal enough out at sea. What the devil was Phil on about?

Then he turned and looked south in the direction of Angels Landing and Haven Point.

It was only small from this distance, but it was there. As angry and black as pure evil itself, it was a vision he'd never forget as long as he lived.

## Chapter Four
### Distractions

The BMW flew along wide country lanes and met hardly any traffic coming in the opposite direction. It certainly was peaceful around here.

Though she was a city "girl" through and through, in some respects Lily Palmer could see the attraction. If only it wasn't so far away from civilisation as she knew it – not even a decent wine bar for 100 miles. She'd had to get up at stupid o'clock in order to stand any chance of making it to Sable that morning.

And then she had the prospect of finding the cottage to look forward to, tucked away on top of a damned cliff somewhere. The maps were useless; all she had to go on was a garbled description over the phone. He liked to make life difficult for her, all right.

She came to a junction and consulted the hand-written note, jottings she'd made at the time – peering over the glasses she wore to drive. Turn left, or was it right? God, she could hardly read her own handwriting anymore. A sign she was getting old. Old-*er*, at any rate. Left, yes definitely left...


Lily looked at her watch as she changed down gears. The hands had just crawled past nine, slow but sure. She'd not done so bad for somebody who had no sense of direction whatsoever. There was the fabled cottage, the Holy Grail she'd been searching for. She had to admit it was nice, the kind of place she might consider buying when she retired – *if* she ever retired.

The creamy residence was surrounded by a varnished fence, designed for show rather than protection, and a neatly-cropped garden boasted roses, chrysanthemums and marigolds; the blend of colours was quite breath-taking. Surely not his own work?

Lily parked the car just shy of the gate, putting away her glasses. The first thing that struck her upon leaving the confines of the BMW was the air. Salty and crisp: sea air, no mistaking it. Much better than breathing in car exhaust fumes and the second-hand smoke of nicotine addicts. *Hmm... Not bad at all.*

It was a short trip up the path to the door. She took off her gloves and rapped three times. No answer. She waited a minute or so, then tried again, much harder knocks. But despite her best efforts to attract attention, the door remained firmly shut.

Lily sighed. She hadn't driven all the way up here just to turn round and go back again. He knew she was coming, why wasn't he answering?

"Hello," she called through the letterbox. "Anybody home?" Where the hell could he be?

For the last time she pummelled the wooden obstruction, half wishing it would collapse into the hallway. Lily was just about to go and look through the window when she heard footsteps on the other side, followed by chains and a heavy bolt being drawn back. Whatever he needed all those locks for up here was beyond her. But then, some people felt safer locking themselves away from the world. And not just physically, either.

Through the open gap in the doorway, she saw a gaunt face peering back at her. His eyes were hollow chasms, at once chilling and sorrowful. His were pupils that had seen far too much of the horrors life had to offer. He was dressed very simply in a white shirt and trousers, a choice which took the least amount of thinking on his behalf.

"Hi, Lily," said Harding, opening the door wider and inviting her inside.

The older woman stepped through. "What took you so long, Jason? I've been stood out here ages."

"Sorry, I was round the back." He sounded down again. *Damn, I thought he was finally pulling himself together.*

"Well, I know it's hackneyed to say it, but this is a great place you've got here. Perfect, absolutely perfect!" She made her way through to the living room. The blinds were open only a fraction, but she spotted the piece immediately. Lily clapped her hands together. "Jason, is this the new one?"

Harding nodded, pinching the skin on the bridge of his nose.

"So what's wrong? I think it's marvellous! Much better than anything in your last collection, and look how well *they* went down."

"I had the dream again last night," he mouthed quietly. "I woke up about half past four, coughing and covered in sweat."

Lily ran a hand through her silvery hair. "Worse than the ones in your first year?"

"Much worse. And *different*."

"Jason, I'm so sorry." She dropped down into one of

the armchairs, placing her handbag beside her on the floor. This was bad news, and if there was one thing she hated at this hour in the morning it was that.

"What brought this on? You were doing so well. On the phone you sounded really excited," said Lily, hoping the whole thing had been some big misunderstanding. A joke, yes that's what it was. He was playing with her. But one look at that face told her it was wishful thinking.

"I don't know. Everything, nothing... Maybe I'm feeling guilty about the paintings, the money—"

"Now, you stop right there. That's rubbish and you know it. If the cash makes you uncomfortable, you only take enough to live on. Give the rest to charity or something."

Harding's eyebrows narrowed and he came further into the room. "I never started painting to make money, Lily. It troubles me."

"Look, I understand. Really I do. It was therapy. Something to help you confront what happened to you." And it was such a far cry from his former profession, that of a GP... "But Jason, you've been given a second chance here to—"

"I don't *want* a second chance," he snapped.

"You're good, though. Too good to just sit at home and build up your own private collection. People should be able to see your work, to understand what drives you."

"And of course you're not just saying that because you represent me!' He looked down, obviously regretting the words as soon as they'd strayed from his lips. She'd been very good to him. Lily had put up with a lot: his mood swings, depression, the dreams. Ah, the dreams... She'd been more than just his agent; she'd been his friend. His best friend he'd told her once, and said he valued that more than anything in the world. She didn't deserve this. "Lily, I—"

"You know me better than that, Jason. Or at least I thought you did. Maybe I should leave." She started to rise.

Harding went over to her and placed a hand on each shoulder. "No, Lily. Please stay. I'm sorry. It's just..." The tears came then, and Lily's stern features melted. Instinctively, she put her arms around him and held on tight as it all came out. Harding pressed his face into her dress, weeping openly.

"Shhh," whispered Lily, patting his back. "It's going to be all right, Jason. You'll see. One day it'll all slot into place."

She cradled him till the sobbing ran its course, like a mother comforting her frightened infant. Only then did he feel strong enough to talk again.

"Thanks, Lily. I honestly don't know what I'd do without you."

"I bet you say that to all the old hags." Harding couldn't help himself. A faint glimmer of a smile appeared on his face. She fanned the flames. "You laugh, Jason, but if I was ten years younger—"

"Five, surely."

She let out a soft chuckle. "That's better. There's the Jason we all know and love. Now you sit down, and I'll fix us both a drink. Coffee might be appropriate, judging by your breath."

"Yes. Yes, it probably would," Harding replied.


When Lily returned from the kitchen she found him standing in front of the painting, examining it with an artist's eye. The picture really was quite excellent, or would be when it was finished. Despite herself, Lily couldn't help weighing up its value in her head, based on Harding's previous sales. She was his agent when all was said and done; his counsellor second, perhaps?

He looked at her, finally noticing the woman's presence. She was forced to turn away sharply before she caught his eyes, ashamed of her thoughts, her ponderings – especially in light of her earlier indignation. *Only thinking of money, eh? How* dare *you!*

"Here's your coffee." Lily handed him the mug and he took a quick sip.

"God, that's strong!"

"Yep. Just what you need."

"I won't sleep for a week after this." Harding turned back to the canvas, eyes darting from left to right. A true craftsman.

Lily stepped forward. "I meant what I said, you know. It really is terrific. It's so..."

"Alive?"

Lily nodded. She couldn't have put it better herself. That's what was so exciting about it. There was a verve, a vitality. You expected to see the blue spirals surging round at any minute. She felt sure she could just stick out her hand, plunge it into the very wetness of the vortex and feel the cool rain on her fingertips.

"You want to hear something really crazy?"

"Why not?"

"I think it is. Alive, I mean." Lily looked at him sideways as if to say, "Should I phone for them now, the men in white coats?"

"First I started painting the picture, then I dreamt about it—"

"Wait a second," Lily cut in. "Don't you mean you dreamt about the... this whatever it is, then you painted it? That's what happened all the other times."

"Not with this one. I began sketching this composition over three weeks ago. Don't ask me why. Then I saw it last night in my sleep."

"You said this time the dream was different. How so?"

Harding frowned.

"Tell me, Jason. If you keep refusing to go back and see Dr McKenzie, you'll have to open up to someone. Might as well be me again." Lily pulled him around to face her. "Please, I want to know."

Harding hesitated, and for a moment she thought he was going to clam up completely. Then he put the mug down and spoke, slowly and clearly. "It was the same old story to start with. I was with Alex and Christine at the lake. Alex was playing ball and I was kissing Christine. Anyway, before it got to *that* bit, I found myself inside a kind of maelstrom – I really don't know how else to describe it. A manic storm, just like that one." Harding pointed at the oil-colour. "But there was something else. I felt someone, something, was with me inside it. Watching me. Laughing at me as I..."

Lily finished the sentence for him: "As you drowned."

Harding lowered his head once again. "Yes."

"It's not unusual to dream about something you're working on, Jason. I know how obsessed you can get with a piece," said Lily, having a drink of her own coffee.

"Yes, I realise that. But you haven't heard it all yet. Don't you want to know why I was round the back when you called?"

"I just assumed you were looking out over the sea, perhaps drawing. That is, after all, why you moved here." It wasn't the only reason, but she wasn't going to raise the other matter. Harding's gaze was intense. He fixed her with those deep green eyes of his and she felt her body turn cold. "Jason, you're scaring me. What *were* you doing?"

"Taking pictures," he answered.

"Of what?" Now she really was anxious. Harding didn't say a word in reply. Instead, he set down his mug, took her by the elbow, and led her to the back door. When he opened it she nearly dropped her cup on the step.

"Of that!" His hand was out, as if he was introducing a new stage act at the theatre.

Lily was lost for words. Ahead of her was the most incredible thing she'd ever seen. Horrifying and fascinating at the same time, the storm-cloud was an enigma of the highest order.

"It's been like that since I got up, which is in itself, you have to admit, very odd. It hasn't moved an inch. Just keeps raking up the water, swirling it round and round. I'm only guessing, but I'd say the pattern of the rainfall is circular, same as—"

"That's... It's..." stammered Lily.

"My painting. Yes, I know." The resemblance was uncanny. The same colours, direction of water; everything was identical, barring a certain amount of artistic licence. It was like Harding had been working from photographs he'd not even developed yet.

"I'm thinking of adding the thunder cloud at the top. It's the only thing missing. What do you think?"

Lily hadn't even heard him. "I can certainly see why you were so distressed."

"I don't believe in omens, Lily. But if I did, I'd say that was quite a bad one."

"My dear Jason, I think I might be inclined to agree with you there."

Inside again, Lily was uncharacteristically quiet. She just sat staring at Harding's painting. A fresh perspective on his work had opened up for her.

Eventually Harding broke the silence. "So, what did you want, Lily?"

"Sorry?"

"You said on the phone you wanted to discuss something. Must have been important for you to drive all the way out here."

Lily thought about this, trying to remember what was

happening in the real world; as if the call she'd placed yesterday had been made by someone else, another Lily Palmer. Someone who wasn't going completely insane. "It seems rather inconsequential now."

"Try me. I could do with something to take my mind off all this."

"Okay. There's a small informal gathering at a gallery in Birmingham Thursday week. I wondered if you might like to attend. It's about time you started mingling with people in the business. You're beginning to get a reputation as a bit of a recluse." Lily knew that was what he was, to all intents and purposes. But it saddened her to think of him this way.

"Couldn't you just have asked me that over the phone?"

"Good job I didn't, don't you think? Besides, I wanted to put it to you in person. My powers of persuasion work much better if the victim can't escape by simply slamming the phone down on me."

"You're wasting your time, Lily. I don't do public appearances. You know that." The edge to his voice was returning.

"At the very least it might get you away from here for a while. You said you needed something to take your mind off what's going on. From what I can see it's only making things worse at the moment."

Harding walked over to the window. He parted the blinds wider with his fingers. The menacing shadow of the storm-cloud looked straight at him, just as it had apparently done when he awoke that morning.

"Rhona will be there. She's taken quite a shine to you, Jason."

It was true, Lily's personal assistant had expressed more than a passing interest in him. He closed his eyes. "I can't, Lily. It was very thoughtful of you, but I just can't at the moment. Rhona's nice enough but..."

"She's not Christine, right? Jason, love, no one ever will be. But that's no reason to shut yourself away like a hermit. You need some distractions in your life, otherwise you're never going to forget what happened."

Harding rounded on her and she braced herself for another tongue-lashing. "Drop it, Lily. Please," was all he said. Reluctantly, she did as he requested.

"Listen, do you mind if I use your bathroom, Jason? It's a long drive from the city and my bladder's not what it used to be."

"Sure. Upstairs, straight ahead. You can't miss it."

His agent made for the door and gave it one last shot before she left the room. "At least think about it, Jason. That's all I ask."

\*\*\*

When she was gone, Harding went over to the telephone. He picked up the receiver and stabbed at the buttons. A number he knew by heart; his own number until a few years ago.

Harding waited, desperate to hear her voice.

"Hello..." A man answered. *Shit, it's him!* "Hello? Who is this?"

Harding slammed down the phone, his hands shaking violently. He brought both of them up to his face and covered his eyes. He couldn't go. How could Lily even think of asking him? The old Harding would have been there like a shot. But this was the new and "improved" model.

He had to stay and finish his painting. Get to know his dark friend outside a little better. Something was happening in Sable, something wondrous or frightening – he didn't know which yet.

All Harding did know was he had to see it through.

No matter what the cost.

## Chapter Five
### West's Weather

The helicopter lurched forwards once more and Vicky West felt the remains of her cornflakes and orange juice breakfast sloshing around in her stomach.

She hated flying. Ever since that scare when she'd been going on holiday to Barbados and the plane had run into "difficulties," she'd been inclined to agree with those Luddites who argued that human beings were never meant to be in the air. Leave it to the birds, was her philosophy. But it was part of her job, at least for the time being. What else could she do?

Cameraman Tobe Howell wrenched his neck around in the front seat, his round head and that annoying chirpy expression he always wore (didn't anything get the man down?) reminding her of a clock face with the hands permanently stuck on ten past ten.

"You okay, Vic? You look a bit green," he said through the headset.

"I'm just fine," Vicky snapped using her most

sarcastic tone. *Yes, everything in the garden's fucking peachy, thanks for asking. I'm suspended miles above the ground in a chopper that should have been decommissioned long ago by the station, on my way to some godawful dreary coastal region to film a segment for a show I shouldn't even be working on in the first place! Can life get any better than this?*

Tobe looked hurt. "Was only asking."

"Ignore her." Matt Stark – the pilot and soundman – took his eyes off the controls momentarily. "She never was much of a morning person."

"Fuck you," spat Vicky with enough venom to lay out a dozen snake charmers.

"See?" Matt laughed out loud.

Whatever had she seen in that waste of space? It certainly wasn't his intelligent conversation or his sparkling wit, that's for damned sure. So it must have been a physical thing. Yes, it certainly had been that. He'd been around at a time when she felt lonely and vulnerable. The station had just passed her over for the plum job of presenting a serious primetime weather show, half hour 8.30-9.00 in the evening. And as if that wasn't bad enough, they had something else planned for Vicky.

Honestly, she could have ripped her producer's head off at the time. Richardson had given her the daunting task of roaming the country doing ten-minute pre-recorded reports ("You know, Vicky love. The local angle!") which would go out weekend-mornings and in the middle of the night under the corny banner of "West's Weather". The title alone was enough to have anyone with half a brain reaching for the remote.

It was always the same old story. Ever since she'd joined Creation-Time TV – *The satellite station for the dawn of a new era!* – they'd given her lousy assignments which could have been handled by anyone. She was a trained meteorologist, for Christ's sake! Didn't that count for anything? Obviously not. All they could see was a blonde twenty-nine-year-old who looked good in front of the camera. So, here's an idea, why not have her wandering around on a beach in her swimsuit or roaming over the moors in a tight pair of shorts supposedly assessing the weather situation – make the viewing figures soar! Because Vicky was more of a jeans and sweater kind of girl... Bastards, the lot of 'em!

She'd only accepted the post because it was another step up the ladder and gave her more airtime. What they didn't tell her, though, was that she'd have to get to these places by flying – because that might have been the final straw. And, of course, that had been when she encountered Matt for the first time. She saw him every day in her new job and somehow they'd wound up in the sack together. Vicky had told herself it was a bad idea to get involved with someone at work, but as usual she believed she could handle the situation. Made it clear from the outset that she wanted someone with no strings attached, and he'd said the same thing, or as good as. That was to begin with. When Matt started to come on a little too strong, she'd ended it right away. Vicky's "career" meant too much to her. She needed to be focused on the task at hand, not worrying about Matt all the time. In any event, her attraction to him had been a short-lived thing, little more than a fleeting infatuation. But she never considered the consequences of the break-up on her working life. The coldness, the hostility. It was like sharing the same house as your ex-husband or something. How could she have known he'd be so bitter about it all? Now he was making things difficult, intolerable even.

Vicky gazed out of the window and immediately wished she hadn't. Small green and yellow squares whipped past like a patchwork quilt, sometimes broken up by the occasional hill or a collection of nomadic sheep. Her stomach did a somersault and she sat back in her seat, fingers clutching the squeaking vinyl. She had to stay calm; couldn't let Matt see her getting wound up. He'd love that.

"How much further is it?" Vicky asked, trying to filter the panic out of her voice.

"Not too far," mumbled Matt. "About— Oh shit!" The pilot started tapping the dials in front of him.

Vicky leaned forwards, as far as her safety belt would allow. "What's wrong?"

Matt's hands were moving frantically, wrestling with the pitch stick and flipping switches. Vicky felt a colossal fear rising up from the pit of her abdomen, her half-digested meal forgotten about for the time being.

"I don't know!" Matt shouted back. Suddenly the chopper started to dive and shake. Vicky was thrown sideways, her belt preventing her from hitting the door.

"Matt! MATT!" The second time she called his name it was a virtual scream. This was it, the moment she'd been dreading since she first set foot in one of these contraptions. Her heart was bouncing around in her chest; sweat began to pop at her temples. They were going down with a trained gorilla at the controls and a deliriously happy cameraman sat next to him. Vicky steeled herself for the inevitable crash that was to come.

Then she heard the laughing; a guffawing to be more accurate.

Matt pulled back on the stick and straightened up the 'copter. "Works every time, Tobe." The cameraman giggled like a schoolkid.

Vicky couldn't believe what she was hearing. It had been a trick, an infantile, braindead prank because he knew how much she loathed this piece of crap. She couldn't make up her mind whether to be relieved she was still alive, or enraged at the way she'd been taken in. Vicky soon decided to go for the latter option and lashed out with her fist, punching Matt hard on the arm.

"You fucking moron! I thought we were going to crash."

"Ow, that hurt. Stupid bitch! Can't you take a joke? Oh no, sorry. I forgot. No time for fun, our Vicky. Too busy off trying to become a celebrity."

Tobe's smile faded when he saw the scene turning ugly. "Come on you two. Let's all calm down, shall we."

"Keep out of this," Vicky warned him. "It's between Mr Inadequate and myself." Her face contorted in pure hatred. "He's just trying to play the big man by scaring me half to death. Congratulations, you succeeded." She gave him a few claps of her hands.

"You needed taking down a peg or two."

"Hah! Well that was never your problem, Matt. From what I can recall you were permanently down a peg or two – in all departments."

Tobe couldn't help sniggering at that one, until Matt shot him a vicious glance.

"Your problem was you couldn't cope with a real man, Vic. Got scared and backed away, just like you always do. Just like you did when you were gunning for your promotion."

"Bullshit. You know I couldn't do anything about that. The decision was out of my hands." Vicky fell back into the seat again, suddenly wanting to put as much distance between her and her former "boyfriend" as possible.

"I heard that Richardson thought you weren't ready for the responsibility yet. He might have considered you for the presenter's job if you'd pushed him harder instead of accepting every stupid job they threw at you. He didn't think you had what it took. Didn't have it in you. That's what you're doing here. You've only got yourself to blame."

"Richardson's a dick. And so are you." There it was again, the defence mechanism that kicked in when she felt anyone was getting too close to the truth. The truth hurts, someone once said. In reality she realised Matt didn't have a clue what the top brass were thinking; he was only trying to provoke her further. But there was always the possibility that he might be right, that he'd overheard something when he'd been ferrying a few of her so-called colleagues around. The nagging seed of doubt had been planted and now it was flourishing.

No. She'd done everything in her power to secure that post – hadn't she? If she'd pushed Richardson, questioned his decision, or that of the station's chief, he might have simply sacked her on the spot; plenty more where she came from. And Vicky couldn't risk that, not now she was on television at last. She couldn't do that to her mother. After all she went through to get her here, and how proud she'd been when Vicky delivered her first broadcast. Seeing her daughter, her *only* daughter, on that 25 inch screen in the corner of the room, the same one they used to watch children's programmes on together. She could hear her voice now.

*"From small acorns, Vicky sweetheart. After all, that's how Ulrika started out, and look at her now!"*

She didn't have the heart to shatter her mum's illusions about the TV world, that it wasn't one big happy family and that if you scratched beneath the surface of the glamour you'd find yourself drowning in a sea of back-biting and uncompromising bitchiness, where men ruled the roost like they did with everything else, sadly.

Excuses, excuses. But the more she thought about it, the more she had to grudgingly admit that Matt was right. She did always back away from things. As much as she liked to think she'd changed over the years, that she could take charge whenever she wanted, there was still a shy, timid Vicky inside persuading her not to take risks. Maybe she *didn't* have what it took to make it all the way in this business. Maybe she just didn't have the strength to keep going up against blinkered chauvinists like Richardson and Matt day after day.

Vicky stared at the back of Matt's head. She could imagine his delight in silencing her. Some of their arguments when they initially broke up had turned very nasty indeed. She'd even let him win one or two just to get out of his immediate vicinity. Oh, but the smug look on his face as she left. It made her heave more than any chronic case of air sickness.

Whenever she felt like giving up on herself, on her career, all she had to do was think about people like Matt. About folk who'd been putting her down ever since she could remember. The fighting spirit would always come back, then. Once they returned to base, she might just have a few words to say to "Mr" Richardson, put her feelers out and listen to those in the know. Matt could be setting her up for a fall, she was fully aware of that. The ultimate revenge. Vicky dropped him for work, so he destroys her career by getting her to say something she shouldn't. But perhaps it was time to try another station, or she could even have another go at the terrestrial channels – her ultimate goal. Even if it was only background work in the offices instead of in front of the cameras, it had to be better than this. Maybe she could—

"Jesus, look at that!" Tobe's excited, nervous outburst cut into her thoughts. His finger was jabbing at something through the domed glass at the front.

Vicky peered over his shoulder, straining against the seatbelt. She couldn't see a thing. "What? Tobe..."

But Tobe didn't, or couldn't, reply. His arm seemed

to be stuck in its outstretched position, mouth gaping open.

Reluctantly, she turned to Matt. "What is it? What's going on?"

"There, look! Can't you see it?" As cold as ever, but even he couldn't hide the apprehension.

Vicky was still blind to the sight, so she wriggled over to look out through her side window. She had to put her face right up to the glass, almost crushing her cheek, before she saw it.

The cloud was small and solitary in the distance, but it was impressive nonetheless. Black and thunderous, it hung fairly low over the plane of water running parallel to them. Vicky squinted and could just about make out the sheet of rain being rung out of it. In all her years studying and reading about the weather, she'd never seen anything like this before. And judging by the reaction of her two companions in the cockpit, she wasn't alone.

*No way that's even possible*, she told herself. Storms aren't confined to such a limited area, never had been, never would be. They were not single entities. Rather, storm cells continually erupted as the storms moved, daughter cells constantly breaking out so that the bad weather was spread over a wide area, breaking it up.

Yet this particular one seemed to be going against the documented norm. It was a singular, almost pulsating, thing. You could see it was! The clouds surrounding it were as white as snow, unaffected by the activity of their darker cousin. And it was moving slowly compared with the rest of the sky, almost at a standstill, as though it were taking over any healthy clouds that floated by, transferring its blackness to them so it could remain in that one fixed place. Not only that, it was maintaining the same shape all the time – the characteristic cauliflower-topped cloud which, traditionally, produced the most amount of rain.

There was also a strange confidence about the storm-cloud, if you could even use that word about something like that. It knew its place in the great scheme of things and to hell with everything else. Although Vicky understood that thunderstorms were created over land and drifted out to sea by chance, somehow she felt this one was different. It was only a gut instinct and threw logic right out of the window, but she was almost a hundred percent sure that it had originated out at sea: right in the very spot it now occupied.

"Find somewhere to land." The words were out before she even realised she was speaking.

Matt tore his eyes away from the phenomenon. "We've got another 30 miles to go along the coast yet."

"Just set us down nearer to..." For a moment she didn't know how to describe it. "That *thing*." Sterner now. She was in no mood to argue about this.

"Vicky's right," Tobe chipped in, finally snapping out of his delirium. "We have to check this out. Get some pictures or something. That thing's a goldmine, Matt."

"The station will understand if we make a little pit-stop, especially when they see what we've brought them." Vicky's head was spinning. She could see the possibilities. They were in the perfect place at the perfect time for once and she certainly didn't intend to look this gift horse in the mouth, regardless of Matt's reluctance. He was probably only worried that she'd get a scoop.

Outnumbered, Matt pushed the chopper on, searching left and right for a suitable spot to descend. "Looks like you might get your wish after all." It was said in a snide way, but Vicky found herself smiling. Soon she wouldn't have to worry about Matt anymore. This would pluck her from obscurity. The warmth of a studio beckoned. And, who knows, an anchor job perhaps. It was a sign. It had to be.

Yes, things were definitely going right for her at last.

## Chapter Six
**Angels Landing**

The day was just getting worse and worse.

Rob realised he was pushing the Shadow too hard and eased off the accelerator slightly. She was in good shape for an old bike – and in her prime she'd reached top speeds of something like 122 mph – but he still had to be careful. Besides, he'd be no use to anyone if he ran her off the road and ended up in hospital.

No use to the Turners.

Of all the men to be out there, why did it have to be the Turner family in the thick of things? Rob had known them all his life, had grown up playing with the lads: George, David and Brian. Had considered their father, Lou, to be a sort of uncle; it was a given seeing as Lou was like a brother to his own dad. The Turners and the Woodheads were as close as any two clans could be, or at least they had been until Rob had gone off and deserted them both, ruining his dad's dreams that one day they all might go into business together at some point in the future.

Oh, he'd seen Lou and the boys since his return – hard

not to with the funeral and all. But their relationship had changed markedly. Even though none of them would come right out and actually say it, Rob could tell they were as disappointed as his father had been that he didn't become a fisherman. Like it was a personal attack on their profession or something.

Well, he was determined not to let them, or his father, down again. Rob was in a position to help the Turners and he was damned if he was going to let anything stop him, not even the monstrosity he'd seen from the back of his garage.

Nothing could have prepared him for that first glimpse, though. A Godless, unnatural freak of a thundercloud bearing down on the water. The image in his mind still made him shudder.

Rob had heard tales in The Seagull of storms that had cropped up out of nowhere, proper raging storms that covered the entire length of the horizon. But never anything like this. Not a self-contained cloud which left the rest of the sky alone. Hell, even the blasted sun was up and riding high, just like on any other normal summer's day. How could you explain that? The fact was Rob *couldn't* explain it, so he didn't even try. That was one for the scientists, not him.

His friends were in trouble because of the storm, that was the most important thing, and all he needed to worry about at the moment. That and getting to Angels Landing in one piece.

Ordinarily Rob would have enjoyed negotiating the narrow bends that led to the car park and station at the Landing. They gave him a chance to really test his skills as a biker. However, the sense of urgency drove all such pleasures from his mind, transforming the whole ride into one long blur.

He parked the Vincent on the concrete square and

jogged across to the station hut, an overlarge grey and white corrugated iron affair with an angled roof and blue doors. Over the entrance at the back was a big sign that read "LIFEBOAT". At the front was the steep but functional slipway, running from the front two doors – which were three times Rob's height – down to the beach and sea below. It looked like some huge grey tongue, unfurled so that it could catch a much needed drink of water. Along its length were tracks the boat would travel down, once the special pin at the back was knocked out. The means by which their vessel would reach those who needed it most. In this case the Turner family.

Rob had always been captivated by the RNLI, even as a young boy sat on his father's knee listening to stories of heart-stopping rescues; particularly of the times his own dad had needed their services. It was impossible not to be impressed, really. The lifeboat men were as much a part of life in Sable as shells on the beach.

Yet they were that little bit more. They were heroes. Not comic strip supermen who flew about the place lifting buildings over their heads and came out of fights with hardly a scratch on them. But real people, flesh and blood, many of whom his dad was friendly with. Rob got to meet most of the crews that way, and even took to hanging around outside the station in case a call would come in and he'd see a spectacular launch.

They risked their lives every day, in all kinds of weather and conditions – sometimes even at night when it was pitch-black. And they were ready to sacrifice themselves for others. They went out knowing that they might never return. That was the true definition of hero as far as Rob was concerned.

The other thing that made them so great was the fact that they were ordinary, everyday folk, volunteer part-timers from different walks of life who were paid relatively little for their work. The RNLI was not some exclusive club. Anyone could join up, provided they could stand the pace. Where else would you get doctors, fishmongers, builders, electricians and lawyers working side by side for the common good? It was something to aspire to.

Of course, when things became intolerable at home and Rob was forced to leave Sable, he thought his childhood dreams would never be realised. Who said you didn't get second chances in this life? Little did he know that he'd be back one day, and that the Institute would welcome him with open arms; his surname alone giving him some pull, not to mention his years spent in the Navy.

Naturally he'd had to go through rigorous training (he still did) but luckily for him his return to the fold had coincided with the arrival of a new Arun-class 52 ft self-righting boat, paid for by a lot of fundraising, charity events, and generous contributions from the public. This larger rig replaced the old Oakley boat which had been in commission for an eternity and had saved countless lives.

It was decided that the Arun should be based at Sable and not at the neighbouring town of Hambleton because from that position it could get to most calls quite easily. And anyway, the more experienced people all lived at Sable so it seemed like the wisest choice. The crew nicknamed her "The Jenny" after Coxswain Phil Holmes' niece, who had been diagnosed with diabetes the previous year. The gesture was much appreciated by their chief.

All men in the team had been put through a course at the same time to familiarise them with the new boat – fourteen in total, though only six got to go out on a shout. Here Rob had got to know those individuals he didn't recognise or remember, and since that week he had considered himself to be a fully-fledged lifeboat man, ready to inspire a new generation of children. Hopeful that his own adventures might in time become legend as well.

Phil greeted Rob even before he could get to the hut. A sturdy fellow with a mass of grey-black curly hair, Phil was already kitted out in the familiar yellow waterproof trousers and jacket but was struggling to pull his red life-jacket over his head.

"Rob! Get inside, we're almost ready to go. Just need you to give the engines a once-over."

The mechanic didn't need telling twice. He'd get his own gear on and Phil could bring him up to speed as they went.

Then they could set about heading out to sea.

\*\*\*

It was a perfect spot. It was the only spot, actually: Angels Landing near Sable, according to their map. None of them had heard of it.

The car park was mostly empty, apart from a few cars and one bike. Plus, in contrast to the surrounding landscape, it was mercifully flat. It was also close enough to the storm to get reasonable pictures.

Matt eased the chopper down slowly, blowing away bits of rubbish from the makeshift landing area. The skids had barely scraped the floor before Vicky was out of the back. She ducked down and ran beneath the blades, heading for the edge of the park. She could see the cloud quite clearly now, though it was still some distance away. Tobe would have to get closer, even with a zoom lens. Maybe down to the beach?

As if answering some sort of silent call, the man came trotting up beside her, his weighty camera hanging by his side.

"There seems to be something going on down there." Tobe motioned towards the lifeboat hut. "I've just seen a couple of guys in waterproofs."

"You don't think someone's out in the middle of that, do you?"

Tobe shrugged. "Must be."

"But there's only one way to find out, correct?" Without bothering to wait for Matt, she started off in the direction of the building, dragging Tobe along with her.

\*\*\*

Rob marvelled at The Jenny, the craft that would take him to his friends. It really was a beauty, with its dark blue hull sporting a red trimming and the orange main section on top (which housed a wealth of technical equipment and essential supplies), its windows and handrails picked out in white.

Two of his colleagues, Frank Dexter and Sean Howard were taking off the chains that held the lifeboat in check on the slipway. Phil walked with Rob as he went to put on his gear.

"The Coastguard got Lou's mayday around ten to nine. It was a bit garbled, but from what he could make out the storm came out of nowhere. Hit the Turners' boat pretty hard. Then he lost them."

"And he notified Elliot?" asked Rob. Elliot Chambers was the secretary of the station.

"Who then contacted me, and I... Well, you know the rest."

"So he didn't even get a position?"

"Not really. We're going to have to rely on radar to pick up the boat. That and our own eyes. But at least we know which direction to head in." Phil let out a deep sigh.

Rob stood up and grabbed a cap from the rack. "Aye. Just follow that black bastard outside." He paused for a second to look at Phil. "Have you ever seen anything like that before, Chief? I mean, you've been at this game longer than most. What do you make of it?"

Phil shook his head. "I can honestly say that I've never clapped eyes on anything like it in all my years, and I hope I never do again."

"That's what I thought. Okay, give me a second to look at the engines and we'll be on our way."

***

The doors of the hut swung open, almost knocking Tobe Howell off his feet.

"Careful Tobe!" Vicky's hand kept him steady, her eye on the camera as well as him. If anything happened to that they were screwed.

A bearded lifeboat man emerged from the entranceway. He didn't seem at all surprised to see the pair of them waiting at the door, but he looked them up and down just the same. A tubby bloke with a video camera and a blonde-haired woman wearing a sweater and jeans? Probably tourists.

"Sorry, love," he said. "No tours round today. We're on duty."

"No, you don't understand—"

Vicky was cut off by another man who came to help the first with his task, hooking the doors back as he asked: "What's the hold up, Keith?" He sounded flustered, impatient.

"I was just saying to these visitors, we're not open

today."

"Hold on a sec."

The second bloke turned to face Vicky, fixing her with his chocolate-brown eyes. She took in that face, the strong jawline with just the merest suggestion of stubble running along it, the smooth cheekbones on either side of a perfectly proportioned nose, a few tufts of tousled black hair poking out from under his cap. *God, if this guy ever decided to take up modelling, he'd make a killing,* thought Vicky.

"Haven't I seen you somewhere before?"

In spite of herself, Vicky laughed. "Very original."

He wasn't amused. "No, no. I have." His eyes moved across to her companion, as sharp as any hawk's. They settled on his camera. "Bit big for taking home movies, isn't it?"

"Let me explain. I'm Vicky West, and this is Tobe Howell. We're part of Creation-Time TV's news department." It sounded better than saying they were the weather people. More important.

The man called Keith clicked his fingers. "Ah, that's right. I seen you, too. My wife's a news addict. She'd watch that station twenty-four hours a day if she could."

"It's good to know someone's watching." Vicky proffered her hand which Keith promptly shook, even giving her a surname: Tomkinson. He seemed a touch starstruck. The other man completely ignored this. Indeed, Vicky couldn't help noticing the way he was retreating, stepping back an inch at a time.

"Look, if we could just ask a few questions. Is there somebody in trouble out there?"

"Hey, Miss West. Are we going to be on the telly, then?" Keith asked, full of expectation.

"No. No we're not." Open hostility now from the model-guy. "Listen, we've got a job to do here, lady. Now if you wouldn't mind shifting out of the way."

*Not another*, thought Vicky. *Why are all the good-looking ones such complete and utter arseholes?* "You haven't answered my question, Mr..."

"Woodhead, Rob Woodhead. And I'm not going to answer it, neither. Come on, Keith. Shape up will you, for the love of God!"

Vicky heard footsteps behind her on the path. "There's something wrong with the mobile," Matt's dulcet tones announced. "Can't get through to Richardson. Must be atmospherics or something. I don't suppose we could use their..."

"I very much doubt it," answered Tobe.

"Vicky's been making friends again, has she?"

Woodhead was just about to head into the hut again when he paused, turned around and came back to the group. "Oh, I nearly forgot. Is that your thing up there?" He nodded at the helicopter behind them.

"Yes. So what?" Vicky was trying to keep her temper under control, though this irritating man was making it very hard. Jesus, in some ways he was *worse* than Matt. At least that scumbag had a reason for being the way he was. What was this creep's excuse?

"Just don't be getting any funny ideas, that's all. If you want to take pictures, you do it from here. We've got enough to worry about already."

"Doing what, exactly?"

Woodhead refused to be drawn. Instead, he simply left the trio to it and turned away. Vicky pulled a face at his back.

"So, what did you say to upset *him*?" Matt was grinning like a Cheshire Cat.

"Nothing. I didn't say anything."

"You must have."

"Maybe he just doesn't get on with TV reporters,"

suggested Tobe.

"Or Vic, here. In which case I already like him. Besides, she's not a reporter. She's just eye-candy for the weather nuts."

"Piss off, Matt." The cloud out over the ocean was nothing compared to the thunder in Vicky's eyes. If there had been any sharp implements to hand, Matt may have needed one or two parts of his body stitching back on.

This was not a good start. If she was going to scoop this story – and she would do so if it killed her; now there was a rescue in the offing as well as the cloud – she'd need interviews for the edit. Soundbites. That's what viewers remembered the most. Rubbing these rescue workers up the wrong way would get her nowhere, even if she didn't know why they were so uptight.

Mind you, that Woodhead bloke had given her an idea. Sure, she would have settled for pictures from the beach, but imagine the footage they could snag if they got even closer. Award-winning stuff with an on the spot commentary by Creation-Time TV's very own Victoria West! Her reports might even end up on broadcasts overseas. Imagine how proud her mother would be then! There was nothing illegal about it. They would be doing nothing wrong, despite all the threats and warnings.

No one would be able to stop her. She'd worry about getting interviews and dealing with recriminations later. At this moment in time Vicky was jazzed and ready for action.

"Come on. Let's give them some space."

"Aren't we going to get any shots of the lifeboat launching, Vicky?" Tobe was frowning. He hated the prospect of missing out on a good scene.

"Don't worry," said Vicky, leading them away from the hut and back up the path. "You'll get your shots all right."

Matt's face soured at her sudden perkiness. It clearly frightened him, though he would never admit it. "What are you thinking?"

"I'll tell you on the way to the chopper. Trust me, you'll love it."

Now he looked really worried.

Vicky set off, tugging Tobe along with her, barely waiting for Matt to catch up.

\*\*\*

Rob glanced around and watched the TV people go. Maybe he had been a little hard on them. After all, they were just doing their job and he'd probably have to face a lot more of those cameras before this day was over – though for the life of him he couldn't work out how these three had got here so quickly.

He wasn't his usual self. Ever since Phil had called him up he'd been on edge. There was a fear building in the pit of his stomach. A little voice at the back of his head kept telling him that he was wasting his time, that it was too late for the Turners. But he had to ignore it, focus on what he was doing.

Rob couldn't afford any distractions today. With the doors now fully secured, he went back inside to get on with his own job.

## Chapter Seven
### The Break

The room was small with no windows.

He lay on the bunk looking up at a ceiling he knew to be there even if he couldn't see it, wondering how all this could have happened.

There was no one else he could blame. *He'd* been in charge and *he* would pay the price if anything else went wrong. His superiors would see to that.

He'd come in here to get some rest. To recharge his batteries before it all hit the fan. That was easier said than done. How could he relax knowing what was out there? And he didn't have the faintest idea where to start looking.

The darkness was bleak and matched his mood perfectly. He let it wash over him, absorb him. He became the darkness and the darkness became him.

Wouldn't be the first time.

The man put his hands behind his head in an effort to make himself more comfortable. He'd been sleeping on "beds" like these half his life but somehow it didn't help much. There would be no sleep today, he understood that.

# The Wet

Just how had their guest escaped? That's what he'd like to know. He'd gone over the arrangements himself. Security had been as tight as a drum at the facility. But then, the guy had been working there for some time. He was bound to have spotted one or two ways of slipping past the guards. And, to be fair, no one was expecting a breakout. All the measures he'd put in practice had been based on the principle of someone trying to get in, not the other way around.

Still, he should have seen the signs.

Had there even *been* any signs, though? Apparently not. He'd had lunch with the man just a few days ago and he hadn't noticed anything different about him. Then he goes and does something like this! Just showed you. Never trust anyone, not that he ever did.

He shut his eyes, praying that when he opened them again, he'd be on some Caribbean island somewhere, living out the rest of his days in the sun, getting massages from pretty native girls. No, not an island. An island is surrounded by water...

There were heavy footfalls outside. Boots, standard issue.

He reached down the bed and curled his fingers around the handle of the gun. He hadn't lived this long without taking precautions. It could be one of his men outside. Then again it might be someone who'd just killed one of his men and stolen his uniform. Or it could be someone else. Someone sent by *them*. If the word was out, he might just be expendable. They'd be looking for scapegoats.

Whoever it was knocked on the door.

He didn't reply. Let them identify themselves first.

"Sir? Sir, are you awake?" A young voice, innocent, natural. *Never trust anyone*, he reminded himself.

The door opened. He raised the pistol until it was level

with the visitor's head. Then he pulled on the light.

He was greeted by the sight of a soldier only just out of his teens. The man's mouth was a wide black hole, his eyes were trained on the firearm pointing at him. All the blood had drained from his face, giving him the appearance of a ghoul in an old horror movie. One hand was on the door knob, the other was by his side, and it was the latter which now shook. With nothing to cling on to, it became a quivering white shape next to the leg of his camouflaged trousers.

At first the older man facing him didn't move, then something appeared to register inside his mind, as if he were accessing data from a computer and had just found the relevant file. Slowly, he lowered his weapon.

"What do you want, Moss?" he asked in a hoarse voice.

"S-Sorry to disturb you, sir, but they thought you should know..."

"Spit it out, boy!"

"We've intercepted a call from the Coastguard, sir. Could be the break you've been looking for."

Now he swung himself round and sat on the edge of the bed, the gun still clenched in his fist. "Where?"

"A place called Sable. Coastal village near Hambleton."

"On the east coast? That would make sense." He wasn't talking to the soldier, rather he was trying to get things straight in his mind. It was the kind of place they'd talked about: remote, secluded. Perfect, except for the fact it was already situated next to a large body of water. "Has the call been isolated?"

"Yes, sir." Moss didn't quite know what that entailed, but he had been told to relay the message.

"Good, good. At ease, Moss, you're not on the parade ground now."

# The Wet

The soldier's idea of "at ease" seemed to involve standing straighter than he had done before. He kept one eye on the man talking to him and one on the glinting metal now resting on his thigh.

"All right, so we won't have any problems with the media. Now here's what I want you to do, Moss. You get back up there and tell them I want the entire area sealed off, tight as a drum. The usual procedure for a Level Five contamination."

"But sir, what about authorisation?" The teenage recruit swallowed hard as the man stood up. This was no time to be questioning his authority, not when he still had the piece, not when he'd come within a hair's breadth of blowing his stupid head clean off his stupid shoulders. A head with a mouth that tended to say things without checking with his brain first.

"Don't you worry about that, Moss. I have enough clout to get you transferred to the fucking moon if I see fit. Now have you got all that?"

Moss nodded; it probably wasn't wise to speak when you had no control over what came out.

"Good." The foot-soldier stood there waiting to be dismissed. "Now go on, get fucking moving! Oh, and contact Fuller. I want to see him before we leave."

This time Moss did go, and he started running the moment he was through the door. The man listened to the *tap, tap, tap* of his boots on the concrete floor, and smiled.

Sable, eh? So that's where this little scenario would be played out. Well, he had been working hard recently.

Perhaps a holiday would be just what the doctor ordered.

## Chapter Eight
### Obligations

The boat rose up slightly as it hit the water, leaving the angle of the slipway in its wake. Coxswain Phil Holmes was piloting the craft from his open-air station at the very top, protected from the elements only by a sheet of curved glass. He swung to the right as they went over a wave crest, the gushing foam sweeping up the sides of The Jenny. His niece's boat. She'd be proud of what they were attempting to do today.

Rob climbed the steps at the back, holding on to the white metal bars which ran all the way up. In jerky movements he came to stand just behind Phil. The view was incredible from up there. Miles and miles of ocean ahead, the clear blue sky, with one noticeable exception: the storm-cloud, eyeing up these intruders, waiting for them to get closer. Daring them to enter its territory.

It was true that navigator Frank Dexter was on radar duty below, handling the sophisticated technology that was part and parcel of any lifeboat today (there was even satellite surveillance if need be) and Wayne Gough, the youngest member of today's group, was out on the deck with his powerful binoculars. But Rob preferred to rely on his own senses. They hadn't let him down in the past and he hoped they wouldn't now. By being up here he would probably be able to "feel" when the Turner boat was around long before anyone saw it. An uncanny ability he'd developed and learned to trust over the years. Many was the time he'd known his parents were coming back from their weekly shopping expedition in Hambleton even before he could hear the sound of their car trundling down the road. Rob never discussed this with anyone, naturally. Never told his friends or family in case they thought he was odd. But it was a fact of life for him, and sometimes a pretty damned handy one at that. With his close links to the Turners it should make things that much easier.

Phil pushed The Jenny harder, and she speeded up. To the untrained eye this orange and blue vessel beneath his feet might appear bulky and cumbersome, yet Rob knew the truth. Its twin turbo-charged diesel engines were capable of up to 500 horsepower, with a top operating speed of 18.5 knots, and could function within a radius of 110 miles. He *should* know; he was the mechanic when all was said and done. But even if he was totally ignorant of schematics and engine capacities, the evidence was there for all to see in the way Rob had to hold on for dear life as this vessel sped over the sea. Faster and faster towards her ultimate destination, the choppy waves little more than a slight annoyance.

Part of Rob didn't want to get there so soon, however. He didn't want to see the potential horrors that lay ahead. He had to fight to clear all thoughts of casualties – of deaths – out of his mind. Lou Turner and his lads were old hands. Fishing was in their blood. Sure, they only had a small trawler to match their business, like his father had once owned, but they were survivors. Just because their message was cut off in midstream, didn't mean—

A hand on Rob's shoulder made him jump. He'd been so caught up in his nightmarish thoughts, he hadn't noticed Phil turning to speak to him.

"Easy, Rob," shouted the Coxswain, a concerned look on his face.

"I'm okay. Just a little on edge, that's all."

"Understandable." It was hard to hear over the engines and the rushing water, so Phil kept it short and sweet. "That was Frank on the mike. At least I think it was... this blasted static's a bugger. He still hasn't come up with anything yet so I've told him to call for an air-sea rescue chopper. That's if he can get through. I reckon we're gonna need all the help we can lay our hands on."

Rob nodded weakly, his world-weary posture speaking volumes. Both men returned their gaze to the horizon, staring out at the storm-cloud which was getting nearer and nearer with every blink of their eyes.

\*\*\*

The car park was gradually starting to fill up as the Creation-Time TV chopper made its ascent. No doubt residents of the overlooking cottages had come down to see what all the fuss was about, mixing with visitors to the area who had already planned to call on Angels Landing and look around the RNLI hut or take snapshots of the cliffs with their automatic cameras. You could imagine the sorts of conversations going on down there:

"What's happening then?"

"So and so says someone's been caught out in that terrible storm."

# The Wet

"Yes, my whassiname's been called up to help with the rescue, you know. So, this is straight from the horse's mouth..."

It was a given.

From her new seat up front, Vicky observed the cars rolling in one after the other. Pretty soon there would be no place left to land again. If it carried on like this people would begin parking on the grass verges, along the tops of cliffs, across the pathway. Anywhere that would afford them a decent view of the strange cloud or the lifeboat as it returned from its rescue mission. Matt would have to cross that particular bridge when he flew to it. They'd find somewhere else to set down when they returned.

At least the mobile burger van which had just parked itself at the head of Angels Landing would do a roaring trade. He probably thought it was his birthday when he arrived at his usual pitch this morning. *You can't stem the tide of free enterprise*, Vicky mused.

In a sense, that was all they were doing too. Just as the crowds in the car park would become hungry for underdone meat crammed between two thin baps over the course of the morning, so audiences around the globe were clamouring for their news fix to fill that gaping hole in the day. It was only normal to take an interest in what was going on in the world. But when something like this came along – a once in a lifetime thing – there was almost an obligation to report it. And, if they could further their careers in the process, that was simply a bonus.

"I still can't believe we're doing this," said Matt. "You heard the man. He told us to stay put."

"Grow a backbone, will you." Vicky was not going to retreat this time, like she had on so many occasions in the past. Matt knew deep down this would be good for all their futures, even his. She never would have persuaded him to get in the helicopter otherwise. He just wanted to bitch about it as usual. "You know as well as I do that this could be huge. And we're the only station here, have you noticed that? We have a duty to—"

"A duty. What duty?" grunted Matt. "Half an hour ago you were on your way to do a piece about windsurfing. We should let the big guns handle this type of stuff."

"The 'big guns' aren't around. We *are*." Vicky folded her arms, sick and tired of the same old arguments. "Tobe agrees with me, don't you?" She looked around at the cameraman in the back, who was loading a fresh tape into the machine and checking his viewfinder.

"Er..." He found it hard to say anything against Vicky. But on the other hand, he knew Matt could be a real psycho at times and didn't relish antagonising him. "I'll have to pass on that question."

Disappointed by the lack of moral support, Vicky faced front again and took in the scenery below: the cerulean mass skipping along underneath and the tiny lifeboat jigging around on its surface. Tobe was tapping her on the shoulder, offering a microphone like some kind of hi-tech olive branch.

"You're all set," he said.

"Have you plugged the mic in?" Matt asked with a growl.

Tobe didn't answer. Good on him. Matt may be the soundman on the ground, another example of Creation-Time cutting corners by having one man do two jobs, but up here he was the pilot and nothing else. God, he was only flying them because she was supposed to be doing interviews with those windsurfers and that required a "trained" soundman on hand. Hence the equipment on the seat next to Tobe: booms, tape recorders and the like. But Tobe knew what he was doing; he hadn't spent three years at film school studying every aspect of production for nothing. Probably knew a lot more than Matt when it came down to it. Had a fair idea of how to rig up a microphone so that it didn't explode into a thousand little pieces.

"Ready?" checked Vicky.

"Ready," Tobe confirmed.

Vicky twisted round to talk to the camera. She launched into her spontaneous commentary immediately, with all the skill of someone who'd spent most of their life practising in front of a mirror. This was probably because Vicky had done just that, in her bedroom, hairbrush in hand. Now it was the real thing, and she was more than ready. Any rough edges could be tidied up later, the lead-in added and so on; but it was better if she did the commentary for this part right now, while it happened. That way people would know Vicky had been here, staring danger in the face on their behalf.

"These are the quite extraordinary scenes at Angels Landing near Sable today, where a weather phenomenon is occurring. Out across the ocean we see the remarkable sight of what appears to be a freak storm-cloud..." Tobe panned over to the window to illustrate. "As you've probably noticed already, the rest of the sky is bright and sunny, perfectly normal for a day like today. Marred only by this intriguing anomaly. It apparently sprang up out of nowhere, taking villagers and seafarers alike by surprise. Indeed, as I speak the RNLI of Sable are attempting a perilous rescue mission. Plunging headlong into dangerous waters."

***

Harding's hands were shaking as he looked through the fold-up binoculars. Something was wrong out there. It wasn't just the fact that the cloud was still there, virtually immobile. Impossible as that may seem, he was starting to get used to the idea – or as used to it as anyone ever could be. No, there was something else going on.

"What is it?" Lily was by his side in the back garden, a green square that was almost as beautiful as the front. She pulled her coat around her. It might be a warm enough day everywhere else, but on the tops of the cliffs it did tend to get more than a little chilly. Harding seemed unaffected by the biting winds. He was too absorbed in the unfolding drama.

"I can see a helicopter and... the car park's filling up now at Angels Landing. The lifeboat must have launched, but I can't get a good view of that from this angle."

Harding passed her the glasses, letting her see for herself.

"Lily, I have to get down there. See what's going on."

"Mmm?"

"I can't explain it. I feel this is important somehow. Will you take me in your car? Lily, are you listening to me?"

His agent took the binoculars away. "Do you really think that's wise?"

"What?"

"I mean, look, Jason this could make things worse for you. You're still a little shaky after the dream and everything. What if you go down there and, I don't know, see something?"

Harding knew exactly what she was getting at. What if there were fatalities? Could he handle it? *For the love of sanity, what if someone had drowned?* It was a risk he had to take.

He placed a hand on her arm. "Please, Lily. I'll even take my sketch book with me if it'll make you feel any better. Call it research for the picture." There was a persuasive streak to his words he knew she'd listen to. A conviction. There was a connection he knew she wouldn't be able to understand; he wasn't sure he did, either. Harding had to go and he had to go *now*. He knew what she was thinking: why? Why put himself through even more pain?

"You really can play me like a fiddle, can't you Jason?" That worked both ways, it seemed.

Harding kissed her softly on the cheek. "Ah, but a Stradivarius no less, Lily. You're the best, you know that?"

He left her blushing, as he dashed back to the cottage to get ready. Probably hoping against hope that she was doing the right thing.

\*\*\*

Stanley Keets stood at the very top of the lighthouse, a position he'd occupied so many times before in the past. He patted the cold white rail, its smoothness comforting; not a piece of chipped paint to be seen. It was one constant in an ever-changing world.

He'd kept that lighthouse going for half a century or more, as a young man and adult: a torch passed on from his father, as with many professions in Sable. It was his whole life, or had been until they'd made him retire. Bloody government. And, of course, everything was all computerised nowadays. The lighthouse was controlled from miles away to save money and turf good keepers out of their jobs up and down the country. Even if he'd sired a son to pass on the trade to (and he was by no means saying Dawn couldn't do the work, she just wasn't interested), it would have been a waste of time and effort. The whole thing stank, to be honest. It went against the grain. If this was progress, then the world could stick it when the sun had trouble shining.

Mind you, he should at least be grateful that they'd let him stay after the change-over, even though he now had absolutely nothing to do with the running of the shop. They didn't really have a choice, faced with his service record. He would have kicked up such a fuss if they'd thrown him out of his home! The only home he'd ever known. Their home, his and Dawn's. Always had been and now always would be, thank the Lord.

*Not if that bastard Woodhead gets his way*, a little voice inside his head chirped. He wanted Dawn all to himself and now she was spending her nights at his place. Whatever was she thinking, hooking herself up with that lowlife grease-monkey? Goodness knows what her mother would say about this carry on... if she were here.

But he kept his mouth shut, bottled up his real feelings. Had to, for fear of Dawn turning against him. Now that really would make her so-called boyfriend's day if she walked out of the lighthouse altogether. So, Stanley would bide his time, keep digging at the lad just like he'd done with all the other tow-rags, and work away at Dawn in more subtle ways. One day Woodhead would show his true colours, it was only a matter of time. After all, look at the way he'd deserted his own family – devastated them – and waltzed back in when his father was too poorly to do anything about it. He'd then waited for his parents to kick the bucket and flogged their house off so he could set himself up in business, if you please. Yes, he was a bad seed and no mistake! Probably couldn't wait to get his hands on *their* money, either: the nest egg he'd put aside for Dawn. Over his dead body would—

A tapping on the stone steps behind him. Dawn returning from her "outing".

As she rounded the curved wall, he saw a flash of her mother's face and he was transported back decades to when Dawn was little and he'd lived happily here with *all* his family. Dawn really was the spit of Maureen, especially with her dark hair flowing free like that, the strands bouncing over her shoulders.

"Dad? Oh, there you are. I thought I might find you up here."

"Where else?" It was meant in a light-hearted way, but somehow came out tinged with bitterness.

"Have you seen it?"

"What? Oh, the cloud. Yeah, I seen 'im. Been watching for quite a while now. Nasty piece of work." *Just like Woodhead!*

Dawn frowned, probably wondering why he was referring to the thing in that way. Though the more he looked at her, the more he wondered if she thought the same way; that it might be a living thing. She joined him at the rail and rested her arms over the metal, just as she'd done as a girl, escaping up here when her parents were arguing about nothing and everything. She'd spent *a lot* of time up here, he recalled.

"I've been at the Rand farm," she said, "looking for old Jacob. He's left his tractor out, but there's no sign of him. I even tried knocking at the door of the farmhouse and peeking through the windows."

"You're lucky you didn't get a gun barrel in your face. Jacob Rand don't like snoopers on his patch."

"That's the thing. No one answered at all. I mean, he wouldn't just leave something like that out there, would he?" Dawn's brow furrowed again, trying to make sense of the enigma. "With its door open and everything. I even thought for a minute he might've, you know..." Dawn made a diving sign with her hand.

Stanley chuckled. "Jacob, top himself? That's about as likely as me coming up on the pools and moving to Florida. No, he probably saw a trespasser in the thicket and went to see 'em off."

"I don't think so." Dawn shook her head. "Even if he had, he would've locked the tractor up first, surely?"

Stanley shrugged. "What time's this boyfriend of yours supposed to be coming, then?" he asked, changing the subject.

"He has got a name you know. Rob. And he's not supposed to be coming, he *is* coming." Dawn turned to face her father, wagging an accusatory finger in his direction. "You'd better be civil this time, Dad. I mean it. Rob'll be here. He promised. Unlike some people, he knows how important this is to me."

"That's good." Stanley smirked. "Only when I saw the lifeboat pull out of Angels Landing—"

"The lifeboat's gone out this morning?" Dawn interrupted.

"Certainly has. Set off about five, maybe ten minutes ago. Didn't you know?" The look of apprehension on Dawn's face said it all. Stanley was acutely aware of the fact that she hated Woodhead going out to sea, had even hinted that she'd like him to quit. Never said it outright, of course; Dawn understood what the lifeboat meant to him and would hate it to come between them. Ah, now wouldn't that be a shame? Apparently, he'd promised to think about it, but he was probably on that lifeboat right now.

The old man felt not a twinge of guilt about breaking the news to his daughter. He realised what a good job the RNLI did – almost as important as his own work had been – risking their necks for others. But he would use every means at his disposal to stir up trouble between them. Woodhead could carry on playing the hero once he was out of Dawn's life. Indeed, he could bloody well do what he liked, then.

"Rob will be here," Dawn said, gripping the rail again

and chewing her lip. There was very little conviction in her voice when she spoke the second time, though:
"He'll be here..."

## Chapter Nine
### Discoveries

Rob held on with both hands as the front of The Jenny lifted a good two metres out of the water.

The change in conditions from Angels Landing was astounding. It was far rougher than expected at this hour, even taking the storm into consideration. Almost as if the sea itself was attempting to stop them. It was, of course. Every time they came out here it tried to stop them. Rob had a great respect for the ocean, however. It nurtured life, animal, vegetable and mineral, provided a livelihood for the fishermen of Sable, and was one of their biggest attractions in the summertime. But it could also take lives and had done so on numerous occasions in the past. You could never underestimate that.

Being out here, it wasn't hard to see why the Turner boys had run into difficulty. The lifeboat men weren't anywhere near the cloud yet, and Rob had to wonder what it must be like directly underneath the thing. If this kept up, Phil would have to move inside to guide the vessel's path from there.

# The Wet

"We should have seen some sign of them by now, surely. Of the boat at least," Phil bellowed. "And still nothing on the radar."

Rob's vision was fixed on the blue area ahead. "Where's that fucking Search and Rescue chopper?"

"Give 'em a chance, Rob. They've got to come from—" Phil stopped and looked up at the sky. "Wait! I think I see them."

Rob followed his gaze. He had only intended to take his eyes off the sea for a split second, long enough to confirm what his skipper was saying, but what he saw made him freeze like a statue in that position. "That stupid— It's not the RAF 'copter, Phil."

"What?"

"It's that blasted TV crew, Creation-something-or-other. They must have been tailing us from the shore, staying behind so we wouldn't spot them."

Phil squinted. "What are they playing at?"

"Boosting their viewing figures, and getting in our bloody road, that's wh—" Rob stopped suddenly. There was a strange knot building in his stomach.

"Phil! Phil!" Wayne Gough's frantic cries drew their attention away from the chopper. "I've spotted something." He had lowered his binoculars and was waving his arms, flapping them out in the direction he wanted them to look. "Over there!"

Rob hurried down the steps to join him at the front of the craft, desperate to see the alleged spectacle. Wayne passed him the lenses as he came alongside. It was hard to discern at first because The Jenny was rocking so badly.

That knot in his stomach was tightening.

"Where?" asked Rob, but before the young man could point it out again he saw them. A lump rose to his throat and wedged itself there, refusing to budge no matter how hard he swallowed. Wayne had indeed spotted something.

Minute black dots bobbing up and down on the water's surface, buffeted by the hostile breakers. They were too close to the raging torrent for comfort, gathered at virtually the base of the storm. Froth bubbled all around, obscuring some and bringing others to his attention.

"What are they?" Wayne spoke with more than a touch of panic; he already knew, he just needed someone else to say it. "They're too small to be boats or dinghies." His last comment was a first class example of stating the obvious.

Rob lowered the binoculars, his left hand clutching the rail in front to steady himself. He'd seen enough.

"They're bodies," he uttered coldly, dragging Wayne's fears kicking and screaming out into the open.

Now it was real. Now it was all real.

\*\*\*

"They've seen us, and they look pissed."

"Will you shut it, Matt. I'm trying to do a commentary here." Vicky told Tobe to cut the vid and wait until they came closer to the cloud. No sense wasting good battery time.

"Vicky, I'm beginning to think this was a bad idea." Tobe wasn't usually known for voicing his concerns, had a reputation for being one of the most easy-going cameramen in the business. But today was different. Today he was flying towards what looked like a big hole in the sky, and he was upsetting the authorities to boot. By his reasoning this was a pretty crazy thing to be doing.

"Not you as well, Tobe? Look, you don't want to be a Creation-Time cameraman all your life, do you? I know you've got ambitions the same as anyone else. Maybe some foreign coverage, perhaps even work on a film? You're always going on about films. Right, so now this could be your chance. This could mean big things for us all... Okay, maybe not Matt unless he takes that stick out of his rectum." She tried to paste on her most encouraging smile. "Of course there's a risk, but how do you think they get all those pictures of tornadoes and earthquakes? Somebody has to take them. And they usually end up getting paid a bundle, especially when the footage is used in one of those 'When Nature Turns Bad' programmes Creation-Time is always foisting on the viewers. They get all the money, all the credit. Why not us?"

The pep talk was over and Tobe still wasn't convinced. But he could see the spark in Vicky's eyes and so he busied himself with his camera rather than say anything more.

There was silence for all of ten seconds before Matt piped up again. "I hate to be controversial—"

"Yeah, sure." Vicky was getting in the first strike this time.

"—but for once I agree with Vicky." Now that *was* a shocker. "If it means I get a promotion and never have to see Miss Icebox UK here again as long as I live, I'm all for that!" More like it.

"What a crushing blow to my ego," Vicky intoned. "And there was I hoping—"

"Shut up a minute," snapped Matt. Vicky looked set to snap something back when she saw what had grabbed his attention.

"Er, guys, I think we've got company." Tobe flinched as the massive yellow form pulled up alongside them, its side-doors already open and a man wearing a green jumpsuit and yellow helmet standing by the winch. His erratic hand movements were definitely not friendly.

"You think they want us to pull over?" Matt's lame

attempt at a joke was heard by no one.

"Keep going."

"Vicky, I don't know whether you noticed or not, but that's the fucking RAF, love. And they don't take kindly to people yanking their chain."

"I said keep going, Matt," Vicky ordered. "I'll take full responsibility. You just head for that cloud and don't stop till you get there. Tobe," she said, casting a look back at him, "get ready to start shooting again because this is it.

"This is the day we're all going to make television history."

\*\*\*

Wayne Gough stood transfixed, watching the figures in the water. He didn't like this at all. Not one damned bit. There was no sign of the Turners' fishing trawler whatsoever, just those dots he'd spotted being thrashed about by the constantly churning currents.

All right, so he was the youngest member of the crew (didn't he know it, the way the others teased him sometimes you'd think he was still in school), but he was a good lifeboat man. Phil recognised that; it was part of the reason he was here ahead of some of the others. Regardless of his age, or the fact he hadn't logged as much time at sea as Sean, Frank and Keith, he knew when something was amiss. The ocean simply didn't *feel* right. The way that rain was coming down – almost too precisely, so fast you couldn't see through to the other side… Well, you didn't need to be an old Jack Tar with a lifetime on the rolling surf behind you to see that it was strange.

The chief had now gone inside to steer the vessel from there. If the rains suddenly whipped up and into The Jenny,

# The Wet

he needed to be able to see clearly to navigate it closer to the stranded men. That meant being under cover. Meanwhile Rob, Keith and Sean were busying themselves on deck, preparing to hoist some of the men on board. They worked steadily and calmly, ignoring the weather's best efforts to disrupt their progress.

He'd be needed soon enough, as well. But for now, Wayne knew his task, to keep scanning the water for more sailors. Altogether, he and Rob had counted four floating bodies. Lou Turner always hired an additional one or two fishermen in summer to add to his sons, making a possible total of six people in all – same as them. Some might not be visible yet at this range, he told himself. Or perhaps they'd gone down with the boat. The big question was, though, were any of them still alive, above or below the surface? They'd seen no waving of hands, no frantic attempts to swim towards their boat and away from the storm. But that could just mean they were injured or in shock.

Wayne judged the distance to the first victim by sight. It would be incredibly difficult to keep The Jenny steady under these circumstances, but if anybody could do it, it was the Chief.

The hull tipped this way and that like a baby in its cradle. Wayne risked a peek above him at the dark mass suspended up there. He'd never seen anything quite so frightening in his life; big and black, like cotton wool dipped in ink. At this proximity it turned his blood to ice. The way it seemed to be pulsating, expanding, and the fizzles of pure energy that were zigzagging through it, never allowed to escape...

Yes, all things considered, Wayne Gough would rather have been downing a refreshing glass of real ale at The Seagull. Instead, he was out here involved in the rescue mission from Hell.

"Keep your eye on the ball, Wayne," said the faint voice. He now had a job to hear through his helmet and hood. Shaking himself out of the daze – had the cloud somehow hypnotised him? – he gave the thumbs-up signal to Rob Woodhead.

When the lifeboat man turned away again, young Wayne Gough, a lapsed Catholic since he was in his late teens, crossed himself and said a prayer with all the conviction of a bishop at Sunday services.

## Chapter Ten
### Regrets

Flight Lieutenant Anthony Craig – a career Royal Air Force officer who, during his lifetime, had seen action abroad, delivered much-needed supplies to starving regions, drunk most of his colleagues under the table several million times, as well as trouncing them all at poker, had married a red-head called Sharon and fathered two sons, Johnny and Kyle – kept his canary yellow Sea King HAR3 helicopter on a straight course, heading directly for the storm front and the lifeboat ahead.

The S&R team and the lifeboat had become friendly rivals over the years, each one trying to outdo the other in terms of rescues at sea. Their competition had to be limited to the sea, because Craig's squadron was involved in activities covering an area four times that of Wales, on land as well as out here. They ferried sick patients to hospital in cases where transplants and the like were needed, picked up injured climbers from mountainsides or people who had come a cropper on the cliffs. In fact they covered every kind of emergency you could think of.

There was no way the lifeboat could compete with them on that score, "confined", as it was, to the water.

But it was horses for courses, Craig supposed. More often than not it was the lifeboat that came up trumps on the cruel sea, down where all the action was. However, judging by the scene passing in front of his eyes, there would be plenty of work for both of the crews today.

When the call came through to the Search and Rescue unit, some forty miles away, Craig had been sat having a cup of tea in the lounge and wishing he'd not left the house without saying goodbye to Sharon properly. He hated it when they rowed, and they seemed to be doing nothing but lately. This time it had been over a set of car keys, which Craig insisted he'd placed on top of the portable TV in the kitchen and which Sharon equally insisted she hadn't seen or moved. Her comments as he searched for them hadn't helped.

"They'll be in the last place you look for them," Sharon had said, laughing.

But Craig had seen nothing funny about the situation at all and the argument rapidly deteriorated into another slanging match. In the end he'd stormed out, snatching Sharon's keys and leaving her to look for his – knowing full well that she couldn't stand driving his Renault.

He'd always promised himself he'd be the kind of husband who wouldn't lose his temper or argue with his wife all the time. Craig had seen enough of that growing up. Yet here he was, making all those same mistakes; raising his voice and ten minutes later not being able to remember why he was shouting in the first place. Telling himself he'd make it up to Sharon later, except later never came.

At the end of the day he still loved her. Sometimes, when she looked at him a certain way, it was like they were both dating again; him just out of training and her a secretary at a local solicitors. Both passionate about their jobs, but more so about each other. She'd known when she married him that his work would take him away sometimes, though. Perhaps she hadn't realised just how much...

But it wasn't too late. He refused to accept that his own marriage couldn't be rescued somehow. That there was no way back. He was due some leave soon, so maybe they could slip away for a week or so. To the Lake District or whatever. Bundle the kids off to stay with their parents, one lad at each, and try to rekindle some of that youthful passion.

God, he wished he'd said goodbye properly this morning and—

"Just look at those idiots!" The statement came from co-pilot Flt Lt Jim Tucker (whose nickname wasn't too much of a stretch of the imagination), sat to the left of Craig in the cockpit. He was, of course, referring to the chopper running parallel to theirs. "They're going to get themselves into real trouble if they're not careful."

"Yeah, and we'll have to pick up the pieces when they do!" Craig cursed them under his breath. Wasn't their job hard enough without pillocks like that getting in their way? Emblazoned across the side was the cheesy logo: "Creation-Time TV". He was familiar with the name as the rec-room back at the unit had satellite television. It was a station that showed more repeats than all the terrestrial channels put together – most of their material appeared to come from those anyway, which in turn was brought in from the States. Crap, the lot of it!

You had to admire the lengths they'd go to for a news story, mind. Brave. Stupid, but brave nonetheless. They should be back at the shoreline filming this in safety, not out here trying to commit suicide. That helicopter had to be eight or nine years old if it was a day.

Craig had attempted to find their frequency to warn them, but ever since they came within spitting distance of the storm their radio had fed back nothing but static. He couldn't raise the lifeboat either. Hell, those guys were lucky to have got a message back to the unit at all. It must have been the last call they made.

In any event, Craig knew that winch operator Flt Sgt Seth Allen would be trying to "persuade" Creation-Time's lot to turn back before they got hurt. And if they decided to ignore all that and press on regardless, well then there was nothing he could do about it for the time being. Not while they were still in the air. It wasn't as if he was in the pilot's seat of a Harrier Jump Jet and could let off a few warning shots across their bow. *More's the pity*, Craig thought, the makings of an evil-looking grin on his face.

Fortunately for them he was conducting a search and rescue operation. One where the searching had already been done by the looks of things. Now all that remained was the other part.

Turning to Tucker, Craig said: "OK, then. Let's take her in."

***

"Wow, Jesus! Are you getting all this, Tobe?" Vicky was ecstatic with the way things were going. They were as close as they possibly could be to the cloud, and they weren't in anyone's way. Matt had given the Sea King a wide berth and had manoeuvred round to the side where it was still possible to see the rescue taking place. Vicky couldn't bear to miss out on one exciting second of it. "There's a tape in?"

Tobe groaned. "Yes. Look Vicky, we're getting some

terrific footage here. Don't worry."

Her eyes were wide and sparkling, the commentary forgotten about, at least for now. And it was as she glanced over at the storm-cloud from this angle, the torrents of rain pouring down like Niagara Falls, that she noticed something else.

"Hey, Matt. Just pull this thing back a bit, will you? I want to check something out."

"Of course, your highness." Not even Matt's sarcasm could faze her at this moment in time.

"That's it, and yep, if you could swing her round the side a sec... Aha, that's it! I thought so. Quick, Tobe, get a shot of that."

Tobe took his eye away from the lens. "Of what?"

"Of *that*," said Vicky pointing impatiently. "Look how the rain curves at the edges."

"So what?"

"I think it goes all the way round, that's what!" Vicky was smiling like a loon. "Instead of just falling straight down to the sea at random, it's actually forming a pattern. A kind of circle. A... Rain Circle. Do you realise how incredible that is?"

Tobe shook his head, obviously still didn't know what she was going on about. But then, he hadn't understood half of anything on this eventful trip it seemed. Probably better to just keep quiet and take his "award-winning" shots.

Matt was less polite. "This is bullshit. How can rain fall in a *circle*?"

"I don't know," replied Vicky. "But it's no more unusual than having one single storm-cloud open up in the middle of a perfectly ordinary blue sky, wouldn't you say?"

He had to give her that, surely. Nothing made sense about this whole thing.

"I think it's probably—" Vicky began, but never got a chance to tell them her theory.

The chopper started shaking.

"Matt, this isn't funny. I'm not falling for the same gag twice."

"I'm not doing anything," Matt told her with a deadpan expression on his face.

Vicky could see through the front that the drizzling spray from rain was splashing back onto the helicopter, carried by a sudden gust of wind. They were only fine droplets as far as she could tell, but they clung onto the glass bubble just inches away from her face. They were being swept back, too, and some must have landed on the rotors. Vicky knew now that it was no joke. As tiny as they were, those beads must be having an effect on their old rust-bucket. *Let's face it,* she thought, *it wouldn't take much to have an effect on this wreck.*

The slight tremors developed into brutal vibrations. Vicky felt a tingling in her feet, travelling through the leather boots she was wearing and up her calves. She dropped her microphone, metal clanging against metal. Her fingers clawed at the seat.

It was like she was waking up from a tantalising trance. Everything since they spotted the cloud had been like a dream, a well of excitement building up inside her, blinding Vicky to the reality of the situation, to the dangers. Bloody hell, what had she been thinking? *She'd* talked them into coming out here, into facing that freak of a thing! All she could see was a scoop, a way to further their careers. But that wouldn't do them much good if they were...

Her air sickness was back with a vengeance. The breakfast she'd fought to keep down was rising again. She could see it all now; everything was so clear in her mind.

They were in a quaking pile of junk, hovering over

endless miles of angry sea, with an inexplicable grumbling thunderstorm waiting for them to fall from the skies. Yes, this was it. This was the big one.

As sure as eggs were eggs and God created little kittens, they were all going to die.

## Chapter Eleven
### The Sea King

Flt Lt Anthony Craig eased the Sea King down a touch. Below and to his left he could see the RNLI men pulling another soul onto their craft, snagging him with what looked like a boat-hook and bringing him within arm's reach.

Craig and Tucker had positioned the helicopter over one of the victims nearer to them. In the back, winch-operator Seth Allen was guiding them as best he could over the crackling internal mike and his winch man, Flt Sgt Martin Shepherd, was getting ready for the drop, fastened securely inside his strop harness. Shepherd would go down on the winch and collect the figure in the water – who looked to be unconscious from here – while Allen worked the cable dangling from the side of the Sea King.

Craig lowered the chopper down again, slowly, gently, then held it steady. He was too close to the storm-cloud for mistakes. A flash of lightning reminded him just how close.

Usually nothing could shake him. Craig had nerves of

steel, even his flight instructors had said so. It was how he'd won the Air Force Cross for valour two years ago for his part in the rescue of a dozen fishermen during violent storms off the coast of Ireland. (Now Sharon *had* been proud of him that day, when they'd all gone off to Buckingham Palace dressed up to the nines.)

But something about this one particular storm managed to unsettle him. Like it was watching their movements, weighing them up. Ridiculous, he knew, and yet that was how he felt. Judging by the way Tucker's hand kept clenching and unclenching around the controls, he wasn't the only one it was affecting.

"How... longer... hurry..."

That was all Seth Allen could hear through the headset, Craig's garbled message. Was that panic in his voice? Christ, if Craig was unnerved by all this then there wasn't much hope for the rest of them! Allen said that it would be another few minutes, but he doubted whether Craig had heard him. He'd never seen atmospherics like this; powerful enough to disrupt their internal systems as well as outside communications. Even the two month stint he'd pulled in the Falklands not long ago had been less of a headache than this.

Allen bent over the opening in the side of the chopper, looking down at Shepherd below. He swung to and fro like a marionette, or a ball of string dangling over the jaws of a cat. *Bad analogy*, thought Allen, visions of a great roaring sea-monster coming up to swallow Shepherd whole now invading his mind.

Another sudden blast of wind threw him about and the tips of his toes scraped the water. Shepherd wasn't far away from the battered fisherman. If he could just reach out... Allen gave him some more slack on the line, the motor churning away. He wanted to land him safely next to the bloke, not drown the both of them.

*THUNK!*

Allen turned to look for the source of the noise, so loud he could even hear it through his helmet and above the roaring rotor-blades. It had come from behind him, and when he studied the far side of the helicopter he saw there was a big dent in the metal. Allen's mouth was open, jaw hanging. That metal was as tough as a rhino's hide. What could have—?

He had precious little time to ponder this before he heard the unnaturally loud screams coming from beneath him.


Craig glanced back from the raised cockpit at Allen. Tucker was twisting round himself, trying to discern what had caused that almighty row. In the next few minutes both men saw things that would remain with them for the rest of their lives.

The first shock was for Craig.

Gazing down he saw Shepherd suspended above the water. He was as near as he could possibly get to the fisherman, almost a perfect drop in spite of the hazardous conditions. Craig had seen this countless times before. Shepherd would now reach out and draw the man closer, then attach himself to him. After that, Allen would pull them both up and into the safety of the Sea King's belly. That was how it should work.

What actually happened was another story entirely.

Shepherd's hand was out, all set to grab onto the fisherman's jumper, when the fellow seemed to jerk awake. He began thrashing about, spinning this way and that, arms flailing about like a man possessed.

*Damn and blast*, thought Craig. *Another couple of*

*seconds and we would've had him.* Now he was coming to, probably wondering where he was, remembering the accident. It would make Shepherd's job that much more difficult.

Suddenly there were screams coming from the man, so high-pitched he heard them in the cockpit. He sounded like he was in agony, writhing about as Shepherd tried to get a grip. As it happened, it was the man in the water who grabbed Shepherd first.

The fisherman wound the fingers of his left hand around Shepherd's leg and squeezed tightly. A moment later and his other hand came into play. Now it was like the guy was trying to climb up Shepherd, using him as a kind of human ladder. This was more common than people realised, the casualty grabbing their dangling saviour and hanging on for all they were worth.

Craig blinked. No, that wasn't what he was doing at all, the pilot could see that now. This man, the one they'd been attempting to rescue – risking their bloody necks in the process – this stupid fucking lunatic was trying with all his might to drag Shepherd down into the water with him.


This is what Tucker saw: the film of rain coming from the cloud was changing shape, warping like melted glass.

It looked like one small, round portion of it was being sucked inwards, pulled back by an invisible force on the other side of the wall. Tucker couldn't tear his eyes from the strangely beautiful sight. Further and further back the dimple went until it started resembling a tunnel, one which stayed level with the side of the Sea King at all times.

Too late he understood what was happening, and what had caused the loud banging earlier.

A blast of water exploded from the "tunnel". The effect was similar to a catapult being drawn back and then released. Tucker's breath fogged the window as it came in gasping convulsions.

The wall of precipitation let loose its volley, striking the helicopter dead centre with all the force of a battering ram.


Allen heard a second bang, and then the screeching of metal behind.

There was no time to move out of its way, no time to escape its ferocity. The side of the Sea King buckled, its already weakened hull collapsing under the sheer might of the eruption. Flt Sgt Seth Allen's eyes opened wider than they'd ever done in his life.

Then the streaks of water burst through, tearing up the canary yellow metal as if it were no more than soggy tissue paper. Allen felt an oddly serene sensation as the liquid rocketed towards him, the gushing sound relaxing him, calming him. He knew the feeling wouldn't last.

That was when the typhoon ripped into him.

Allen felt his right arm being wrenched off at the shoulder as he fought to stay upright. The pain was indescribable, but as nothing compared with what came next. His legs were knocked out from under him, turning the white bubbles crimson. His consciousness held on for a bit longer in the desperate hope that he might survive this ordeal. However, as more fluid bullets punctured his body, slicing easily through lungs, liver, kidneys, and finally his heart, Allen's mind realised that it would be better for all concerned if it threw in the towel.

Mercifully, Flt Sgt Seth Allen was already deceased before his head was cleaved from his neck in a torrent of moistened fury.

# The Wet

At the other end of the winch, Shepherd was having his own problems.

It was understandable for the fisherman to be scared, to want to get out of the water as quickly as possible. But his mad attempts to clamber up Shepherd's body were yanking them both down into the foam. His arms were around Shepherd's waist, crushing him, forcing the air right out of his diaphragm.

"Ease up, mate!" Shepherd shouted as loud as he could manage. "I'm here to help."

The man took no notice. If anything, his grip was tightening, boa-constrictor style. Shepherd was left with very little option. He had to knock him out, stop him forcibly. The idea held no appeal for him, but it had to be done.

Shepherd brought back his right fist, gripping the man's jumper in his other hand so he wouldn't drop back into the sea. His brow creased as he prepared to strike.

The man looked up at him.

All the power went out of that blow, and it glanced ineffectually off the side of the sailor's head. What Shepherd had seen left him reeling. Something was clinging to the fisherman's face, or what he could see of it. The entire front part of the head seemed to be covered in an oozing, gelatinous slime. His mouth was opening and closing, in an effort to cry out as he had done earlier. But nothing would come. Shepherd wanted to look away, and ultimately to be someplace else. The problem was his eyes seemed to be operating on their own, picking out more and more details of the face – the way that foul stuff was spreading back over the man's ears and hair, engulfing him, almost certainly suffocating him.

Only the whooshing sound above could break the spell. Shepherd was grateful for its intervention, for something else to concentrate on. But when he strained his neck back he had cause to alter his opinion drastically.

A shaft of water several metres wide had speared the Sea King, holding it like cheese on a cocktail stick. But that wasn't all. Shepherd saw an object falling from the sky. At first he thought it was a bag or a sack full of supplies, but as it got closer he could tell it was too big. The object seemed to separate into five or six pieces; it had come apart either in mid-air or before it started its descent. Regardless of what it was, it was heading straight towards them and would land on their heads if he didn't do something fast.

Shepherd attempted to swing himself out of the way, ignoring the aberration hanging from his waist. Whether it was due to his swaying, or the water blast itself, he had no way of knowing, but at that particular moment the winch line went completely slack. Shepherd plummeted into the water, sideways out of the object's path.

Both Shepherd and the mangled pieces of Flt Sgt Seth Allen hit the sea at the same time. Shepherd was spared the sight of his friend's dismembered body landing all around him, but only because the fisherman was tugging him down under the freezing brine. Not even his life jacket could keep him afloat. The sailor still had him in a bear-hug and showed no signs of letting go. He had all the strength of a bear, too, and withstood a couple more of Shepherd's punches.

Saltwater seeped into the RAF officer's mouth at the corners, then shot up his nose with such gusto he thought his brains might actually explode through the top of his head. Shepherd gazed down past bubbles of air. His air. He screamed, allowing yet more precious oxygen to escape.

A silent, doomed scream which no one would ever hear this side of his watery grave.

Craig and Tucker struggled to control the Sea King. Perspiration gathered at Craig's hairline, involuntarily dripping down his forehead with each fresh shudder of the helicopter. He ground his teeth so hard the fillings at the back were almost worked loose.

The water cannon had ravaged most of the main section of their chopper and part of the tail. Craig had seen it emerge from his side of the vehicle, taking with it the remains of Seth Allen. Then, almost as suddenly as it had shot out, the sodden spike was withdrawn, leaving nothing to hold up the lacerated bulk of their flying machine but the damaged rotors above.

The front went into a nose-dive.

Craig had always wondered how his end would come. When you did this sort of job for a living, you couldn't help thinking about such things. But never in his wildest dreams had he ever considered this scenario. He felt cheated. The tragedy that was about to take his life didn't fit with his picture of reality. A watery armature punching through the side of a Sea King helicopter? It was absurd, a cosmic practical joke. Any minute now the Almighty would step out from behind a cloud with a big grin on His face, just like they do in those hidden camera shows; stepping in to put a stop to the proceedings and congratulating them for being such good sports. He laughed quietly to himself, a nervous laugh. A terrified laugh.

Their fate was sealed. No reprieves. The best they could do now was try and crash away from the lifeboat, minimise the casualties.

Craig found himself thinking about other things as well. About life, about death. Asking the questions he'd never had time to ask himself before. Why are we here? What's the purpose of it all? Where do we go...

afterwards? Profound, mind-numbing topics that had been debated and argued about for centuries by some of the finest minds his world had ever known. And he realised this: in precisely one minute from now he would get the answers to those questions, one way or another. He would be the envy of every professor and theologian on the planet. Lucky him!

*Why isn't my life flashing in front of my eyes?* he asked himself. *It's supposed to do that, isn't it?* But still no images from his childhood, no memories of his drinking binges or birthdays or the nights he'd spent with Sharon. Nothing.

Nothing except one mental picture, as clear as a bell. Of Craig coming home from work and tossing his car keys onto the sideboard in the living room before collapsing onto the sofa and nodding off. There they still were on the sideboard – he'd never put them on the sideboard before, always on the portable TV in the kitchen. Why had he done that? *Why?*

Why hadn't he made up with Sharon before he left? Told her how sorry he was? How much he loved her? (And Jesus, he loved her so much it hurt!) Said goodbye properly?

He could always do it later. Always put it off. But all Anthony Craig's laters had just run out.

The sea was approaching fast. Oblivion beckoned.

Craig turned to his co-pilot and said, "Tuck, I just wanted to—"

Tucker nodded. "I know." He held out his hand and Craig shook it, a strong, sure grip as tears started to pour down his face.

Time came to an end. And Flt Lt Anthony Craig, a career RAF officer who, during his lifetime, had seen action abroad, delivered much-needed supplies to starving regions, drunk most of his colleagues under the table several million times, as well as trouncing them all at poker, had married a red-head called Sharon and fathered two sons, Johnny and Kyle, ploughed his canary yellow Sea King helicopter into the raging surf.

Then everything turned yellow and white.

## Chapter Twelve
### Reactions

The explosion could be heard from the shore.

And, eventually, the billowing curls of smoke that rose from the scene became visible as well. They snaked their way up into the air, thick pummels of choking blackness, in part blown along by the gusting wind.

Seagulls flying high above the site turned their heads at the sound, then altered their flight paths to avoid both the smog and the thunderous cloud, squawking at the inconvenience.

Birds nesting in the cliffs acknowledged their warning cries and answered back. All the dogs in Sable looked up at the same time and started to whine loudly. In the nearby town of Hambleton, residents and early-morning shoppers heard the noise and wondered if they were in for a summer thunder storm – blissfully unaware of the storm that already existed miles back, just off the coast.

Lily and Harding looked out of the car window on their way down the north-bound road, her BMW making light work of the winding lanes that ran alongside the beach and sea.

At the lighthouse, even Stanley Keets was roused by what he heard and saw, his daughter slipping a hand into his – the flesh quivering inside his own as she silently prayed for the men out there, one of whom was almost certainly Rob.

And at Angels Landing the people in the crowd turned to each other and speculated about what had happened. Those with binoculars described what little they had seen, stating that they thought one of the vehicles involved in the rescue had somehow blown up.

The man serving burgers dropped a whopper bun on the floor of his decidedly unhygienic van, but picked it up quickly, wiped it with his sleeve and then served it with meat and onions inside to the next hungry customer. Waste not, want not, that was his philosophy.

But standing in the middle of this crowd, and looking on as eagerly as the rest, was a stranger to these parts. As soon as *he* heard the booming sound, distinctly different to the thunder coming from the cloud, he knew that it had drawn first blood. No doubt remained about that. It had only been a matter of time.

No one around him noticed, they were too caught up in their own little worlds, their own private and not-so-private conversations. But if they had looked at him properly they might have seen the way he stared out to sea. Intently, hardly ever blinking. They might have realised too, that he was no ordinary bystander, no ordinary tourist or visitor to Angels Landing. He wasn't there for the thrills, the excitement, the gossip.

He just wanted to look upon the cloud out at sea. That which he had brought – or helped bring– into being. His creation.

And if one person, just one, *had* turned to look at the

stranger, they would have seen the solitary tear rolling down his cheek. But as for whether it was a tear of sadness or of joy, well, only the man himself really knew that for sure.

## Chapter Thirteen
### A Life on the Ocean Waves

The lifeboat men had just finished hauling the fourth body from the water when all hell broke loose above, in front, below and in every direction they cared to look.

Wayne Gough had been the first to spot the Search and Rescue chopper's descent, but he couldn't warn the rest of the crew in time. They were so busy trying to fish those unconscious men out of the sea, they didn't notice the jeopardy they were in themselves; especially Rob, working like a man on speed to pull the fishermen from the water, urging Keith and Sean to check them over. Frank had surfaced, too, ready to lend a hand. Everything had been going well.

Then The Jenny was thrown so far over by the blast, she was nearly called upon to prove her self-righting capabilities.

Wayne was running round to the back when it happened. He was pitched sideways and collided with the white railings running around the side of the boat.

Something snapped with a sound like brittle twigs crunching underfoot in autumn. Wayne saw stars ahead of him, tiny pinpricks breaking up his normally faultless vision. The right-hand side of his body was on fire, but he wrapped his fingers around the railing, panic-stricken.

Debris from the explosion was flung in their direction. Frank barely had time to pull Rob down as something sharp and white-hot flew over their heads. Keith and Sean kept down at the back, huddling over their charges. A little thing like the boat almost capsizing wasn't going to stop them from helping the fishermen they'd dragged aboard.

"Fuck!" This came from Frank. He pointed and Rob looked up in time to see a piece of spinning rotor-blade strike the front of The Jenny. Sparks and shards of glass spilled out onto the front of the boat, and both men knew instantly what had happened.

"Phil," shouted Rob, his eyes moving swiftly from Frank to the cabin at the front. His crewmate lost no time in going back towards the door.

Rob was just about to follow when he saw Wayne lose his grip on the side of the boat. A veritable tidal wave scuffed port-side as Wayne fell. Rob held his breath. *His safety line. Please let his safety line be—*

Wayne was caught by the line at his chest, but the tugging aggravated the ribs he'd broken only moments before. He let out an almighty wail. Below, the water crashed up against Wayne's body, enveloping his legs for a second and pressing him against the hull. Rob was there in an instant. Keeping hold of the railings with one hand, he swung himself over so he could grab Wayne's line. It was like trying to pull up a boulder with a length of cotton. Rob's bicep was taut under his jacket, the tendons in his forearm stretched. He brought Wayne up an inch at a time, grunting with the strain of it all. After a few more yanks he was able to get hold of Wayne's collar. Hooking his arm around the rail, he pulled the youth up with both hands. Rob leaned back and his body-weight caused them both to fall onto the deck. Wayne screamed in agony again. Another blast rocked the boat as they lay panting next to each other.

At the back, Keith and Sean saw to their patients. All four men were completely out of it, Lou and two of his three sons amongst their number. Frank had identified the other guy as Harry Dale, a relative newcomer to the village but a damned good fisherman by all accounts. Who knew if there had been another hired hand, though. They were all absolutely saturated, as was to be expected. But there was something strange about that water. It seemed thicker somehow, more like a kind of translucent mud. It was moulded around their faces, gagging them, fastening their mouths shut. First order of business was to try and clear as much of it away with their hands as possible. Neither Keith nor Sean stopped to consider what it might be (although Sean did briefly wonder whether it was down to pollution – well, you hear so many stories nowadays). There just wasn't the time. Lives were at stake and all that stood between these men and death was their knowledge of first aid.

Keith attempted to give Lou a chin lift, placing his fingers under the front of the jaw and pulling it forward, the best method in case he had a broken neck. There was movement in the chest area, a breath of sorts culminating in globules of liquid bursting from his lips. Keith moved on to the next, putting all thoughts of the crash and the chaos surrounding them to the back of his mind. *Concentrate on what you're doing*, he told himself. It was the only way.

Sean's "invalid", David Turner, still wasn't responding even after a jaw thrust to check that his tongue wasn't blocking the airway. He tried to think; the medical training he'd been given was playing a game of hide and seek in his brain – and the pandemonium going on all around didn't help. *Is this what it's like in a war zone?* he thought. *It couldn't be much worse.*

Was the neck broken? Sean didn't believe so.

What was next? Start mouth-to-mouth, or the kiss of life as it was more commonly – and appropriately – called. Sean tilted the casualty's head up, cupping his left hand under David's neck and pinching his nose shut with the right. Without hesitation he sealed his lips around the young fisherman's own and proceeded to breathe into his mouth until he saw the chest move slightly. The taste was awful, and not just of salt. There was a bitterly sour tang to the saliva, like rotten fruit. Nevertheless, he carried on, the next three breaths coming more quickly. Then he removed his mouth to see if David's chest was falling. It was, so he took another breath for the lad.

Keith let out a howl from beside him. Sean turned to see that George Turner had coughed up a mixture of bile and algae, right into Keith's face. The lifeboat man scraped the foul stuff out of his eyes and held up his hand to indicate he was all right. He'd been through worse traumas in his life than having someone throw up all over him.

It was only then, after he'd had cause to look up, that Sean saw where The Jenny was heading.


The inside of the cabin was a mess. Frank pushed past the tangle of maps on the floor, his own navigation maps, and made his way up to the control deck. There was no sign of Phil at first and it wasn't until he came fully inside that Frank saw the Coxswain lying on the floor next to the driver's seat.

Hands shaking, Frank turned over the body of his old friend. Blood coated his cheeks from a cut just above the eye but it probably looked worse than it actually was – *Yes, that's it. He'll be okay. He will be okay. Oh Lord* let *him be okay*... Frank checked his neck for a pulse. There was a steady rhythmic beat just below the chin.

"Thank God," murmured Frank. Their Coxswain was unconscious but still in the game. Which was more than could be said for the windscreen or the steering column. The wheel itself was more or less hanging off, twisted beyond recognition by a piece of rotor that had taken up residence lengthways across the column.

With a terrifying dread, Frank realised the boat was now out of control. He stepped up to the column and peered through the open gap at the front. The ominous sound of thunder and rain greeted him.

Frank pulled back sharply. No. This wasn't happening. But it was. The boat was on a collision course with the storm.

Full speed ahead.

## Chapter Fourteen
### Harm's Way

"Vicky... Vicky?" Someone's hand was on her shoulder.

But she was back home again, a little girl with pigtails and braces on her teeth. It was Sunday, and that could only mean one thing: the highlight of her week! Sunday dinner with all the trimmings. Her mum had really gone to town this weekend, though, the chequered tablecloth trapped beneath bowls of steaming potatoes, beans, carrots, cauliflowers, mashed spuds, a square of Yorkshire Pudding in a tray – the ends curling so high you might mistake it for a living, breathing organism – and the pièce de resistance in the centre: a slab of succulent beef blessed with a smell that could make a grown man drool in anticipation.

Her mother was standing over the meal, head bowed, saying the blessing while she sat giggling with her sister Becky.

"For what we are about to receive, may the—"

Except it wasn't the blessing at all, it was now the

Lord's Prayer, learned by rote at school...

"—forgive us our sins as we forgive—"

And it was Vicky who was whispering it over...

"—but deliver us from evil—"

...and over, and over, and over, and...

A flash of light. An explosion. Why would there be an explosion in her mother's house? Was the chimney on fire again? Just like that time at Easter when— No, she was starting to remember. A big yellow bird, shot down by those boys at number eleven. Them and their air rifle. She'd tell on those nasty thugs, yes she would. Poor, defenceless creature. Why did they have to go and do something like that to—

Wasn't harming anyone, and they came along and... and...

It was the bird that had exploded, hadn't it? A big bird, enormous. On fire. A bird with no wings, just a silly hat that went round and around and...

"Oh God in Heaven." Vicky mouthed the words, but no sound would emerge. The fantasy bubble was bursting, and she finally recalled where she was, and what had happened to the RAF chopper that had tried to get them to turn back. If only she'd listened instead of being so—

The hand was shaking her shoulder now, harder. "Vicky, Vicky? Stay with us."

She looked at her reflection in the window and hardly recognised the frightened adult gaping back. *Pull yourself together*, Vicky, *you're not a kid anymore.* She reached up and gripped Tobe's hand. "I'm all right. Really. It was just... seeing the helicopter go down, you know."

"Forthcoming attractions," said Matt dryly.

Their own chopper was still shaking, bucking even, and Matt was trying desperately to pull them away from the Rain Circle. "The water's doing something to the engines," he grumbled to nobody in particular.

"Can you get us out of here?" asked Vicky. At least if they made it away from the storm they'd have a chance of swimming back to shore. *If* they survived landing in the sea, that was.

Matt looked at her blankly, as if he'd just misheard what she'd said. "What the fuck do you think I've been trying to do, fly us into the bloody storm?"

"Sorry." Vicky had lost all of her will to fight with him. She felt more than a little guilty for dragging them both into this expedition in the first place. Matt had every right to be angry with her. As did Tobe, although he'd never show it openly. Both had voiced their concerns and she'd just gone ahead and done what she thought was best. Now because of her they might all end up winging their way back to the station in bodybags.

But whatever Matt was doing it seemed to be working. Their chopper veered away sharply, almost too sharply Vicky thought, as if the Rain Circle had found more appetising prey. The engines juddered and clanked, an effort for its ancient parts, but at last found the reserves to carry them away from this nightmare, and temporarily out of harm's way.

As they moved slowly forward, Tobe brought his camera up once more, his nerves steadying somewhat.

"Do you want more footage of the lifeboat?" he asked.

Vicky shook her head vehemently. "Screw it. I think we've tempted fate enough for one day, don't you? Let's be satisfied with what we've got."

*And be honest*, she said to herself, *if we get out of this alive what we've got will be plenty.*


Tobe sighed with relief. He'd snagged some of the best shots this year, probably of his whole life. But there was only so much tragedy he could take in one go. The so-called Rain Circle and helicopter explosion would see him nicely through until he was about eighty, he reckoned. And his only wish at the moment, was to live long enough himself to see the damned stuff played back on TV. That was all. Wasn't asking too much, was it? He'd taken the risks, now let him reap the rewards. It was only fair.

Tobe looked down at the rough seas. He couldn't see any more people floating about on the surface; the lifeboat must have got them all. His eyes roved across to the orange and navy-blue craft being tossed about by the wind. He spotted figures on the deck: some at the back, some at the front. Now their job was finished they'd be making their way back to shore.

*So why are they going* towards *the Rain Circle?*

Alarms began ringing in his ears.

In spite of himself, Tobe put the lens up to his eye. Something was wrong. He could see the front of the boat all smashed in where he assumed the cabin was. He zoomed in as far as he could, picking out the men on board. Even though he couldn't see the look on any of their faces clearly, he knew what was going through their minds. The same thing that was going through his own.

The boat is a runaway and if they don't do something about it quick, they'll run slap-bang right into that storm.

\*\*\*

Every second lost brought them nearer to disaster.

The Jenny was a sturdy enough boat, but there was no telling what would happen if she went sailing into the almost solid curtain of liquid tumbling out of the cloud. There was no evidence to support the fact, but it was obvious to anyone with half a brain that the storm had wrecked the Turners' fishing trawler. It was either on the other side of the rainfall in pieces or at the bottom of the sea waiting to become the latest attraction for scuba-diving fanatics in years to come. Frank didn't want The Jenny to end up the same way. She was self-righting, not unsinkable. Nothing was unsinkable – a famous vessel at the turn of the century had proved that.

He came out of the cabin and hit the ground running. The boat was still lurching from side to side, but nothing would dampen his resolve. Rob was behind him, struggling to keep up.

"What's happening?" he called out.

"No time to explain," Frank shouted back over his shoulder.

He was going so fast his feet nearly missed the steps entirely. Then he was climbing up them, two at a time until he came to the top. An unexpected jolt almost sent him back down and he realised, as incredible as it may seem, that for one stupid moment he'd forgotten about the storm and the cloud. And all the damage it could do.

That thing was a killer. Two fishermen were potentially still out there somewhere, presumably dead by now. And if that wasn't enough, there was the crew of the Sea King to add to its tally. If The Jenny went down as well, then that dark, rumbling son-of-a-bitch would win. The notion put yet more steam in his stride.

The engine was thrumming away, powering them towards their destination. So, theoretically, all he had to do was turn The Jenny around from up here. That was all.

Simple.

Frank took hold of the tiller and pulled with all his might. It was stuck fast.

"Shit!" He beat the wheel with his fist. What the hell was wrong with the thing? It was almost as if it was doing

# The Wet

this on purpose, building up his hopes only to dash them seconds later. Frank had another go, his hands slipping on the wet plastic.

The Jenny continued its suicide run, careering along, about to strike the deluge at any moment. Sucked in by the terrific eddies which now had hold of the boat and wouldn't let go.

Cutting the engines would do no good at this point, he reasoned. Good old inertia would simply carry them into the unknown. Not far away, the last pieces of burning helicopter were sinking under the ocean. The fire extinguished as easily as the lives of those inside it. Frank heaved on the tiller, giving one last almighty do-or-die tug.

It started to move. Frank turned to see Rob standing beside him, his own hands grasping the wheel. Rob grinned as the tiller came round almost half a circle. They moved it together, changing the direction of The Jenny. Now all they could do was wait and see if they'd done it in time.

The boat drove into the rain at an angle, clipping the bow and then the side. That colossal downpour struck her just as she was starting to turn and beat the blue paintwork as hard as it could. They felt the craft tipping over. Rob's rubber-soled boots squeaked against the floor as he was flung sideways, Frank falling on top of him.

The two men rolled down the platform, knocking elbows, knees and shins on the side. Frank came to a stop at the summit of the steps and put a hand out to prevent Rob from flying over them and breaking his neck. Neither man moved. All they could hear was the lashing rain and the sound of the engines.

Frank looked at Rob, he looked back. Any minute now they'd know their fate.

***

The helicopter was dipping over the sea. The further away from the cloud they went, the slower it seemed to crawl, hindering their escape.

"At least the shaking's stopped," commented Vicky. That had to be a good sign.

"Then why are we still dropping?" Tobe asked, as if she could give him a reasonable answer. Not for the first time he thought of the lifeboat men. Had they gone down, too? As the Creation-Time TV chopper had left the scene, they'd been heading right for the Rain Circle. Now the boat was well behind them, out of sight. But not out of mind.

Matt made no attempt to answer Tobe's question about the loss of altitude, either. He couldn't, not without getting out of the helicopter and examining the thing, and he wasn't about to do that in mid-air.

However, if he had been able to he would have found tiny droplets of wetness still clinging to the stabiliser bar on the roof. These droplets had divided, their molecules separating, and had begun flowing down the main rotor shaft and mast, whereupon they found cracks in the shell of the 'copter. Tiny slivers in the panelling eaten away by rust and neglect.

Some even danced down the tail boom, past the horizontal stabiliser that jutted out on either side, and gathered at the tail rotor itself.

Consequently, when Matt pressed down on the foot pedal, he became instantly aware of the fact that he couldn't control the direction of his vehicle. And no matter how much he pulled back on his pitch stick, the chopper just seemed to dip more and more.

Rivulets of the water broke off to run along the front

and into the cockpit. They were so fine that the pilot and his two passengers failed to notice them. In they crept like thieves during the night, seeping into the instrument panel, interfering with vital connectors. But when they made contact with the live electrical parts of the panel they sacrificed themselves to produce sparks. These sparks, in turn, produced flames.

"Matt, look at the panel! I think it's on fire."

"Dammit! Use the fire extinguisher, my hands are a bit full."

"Where is it?"

"There, just—" He took his eyes off the deck long enough to nod with his head, and as he did so an electrical surge blew through the front end of the cockpit.

It appeared to Vicky as though the whole of the panel bowed outwards, liquefying like solder. Then she saw the results of the fire. Matt's right arm was shielding his face, burns boiling away up to his elbow, his white T-shirt smudged black in places, smoke rising from where he'd patted out the blaze.

"Oh no, Matt!" He hissed as she tried to examine his wounds, the controls still sparking away in front of them. A scalding piece of plastic propelled itself at her leg and began devouring the material of her jeans. Vicky flicked it off briskly before it could do the same to her skin.

"Matt, can you hear me? We have to get this thing down now!" Vicky tried to stay calm. Matt was the only one who could fly this chopper but, more importantly, he was the only one who could land it. "I know it hurts, but you have to concentrate. If we can make it to the beach then we can get you to a hospital."

The helicopter touched the sea with one of its landing skids. Vicky examined the amount of water they still had left to cover, chewing on her lip. *If Matt's going to do something, he'd better do it now*, she thought, reaching for the fire extinguisher.

***

They'd done it.

The Jenny was limping her way back to shore, back home to Angels Landing. Rob was at the helm, driving her as fast as he dared. Frank was assessing the situation below. With their Chief still out, he was basically in charge.

But Rob was counting the cost of their mission himself, running over events in his mind like an action replay. Four men saved, but what of the others? Brian Turner being one of the sailors still missing... Maybe when the storm died down another search could be mobilised, but it was far too dangerous at the moment. The dead RAF men and the injured members of his own crew were testament to that, not to mention the state of The Jenny herself. Ah, but she'd done them proud when the crunch came, you had to give her that. As the song went, she'd carried them safely home from the seas.

Idly, Rob wondered what had happened to the TV helicopter. He'd not noticed it since before the accident. Probably got what they wanted and hightailed it out of there. You couldn't really blame them. What they'd seen would've been enough to turn anyone's stomach.

But they were on their way back now too, he reminded himself. Safe.

Yet something told Rob – his sixth sense maybe? – that this was all far from over.

That they were far from being safe.

## Chapter Fifteen
### Good Samaritans

The short cut along Hunter's Pass was beautiful this time of year.

On one side of the narrow road were acres and acres of rolling grassland that one day, no doubt, somebody would turn into a golf course, and on the other were the cliffs themselves which ran all the way up to Angels Landing. Fencing had been placed along the edge of this particular stretch because of the erosion. Numerous people in the past had wandered too near to the tip of the cliffs, getting a better view, only to find the ground beneath their feet crumbling away into nothing, speeding limestone the last thing they saw before striking the rocks below.

Yes, every seaside resort had its horror stories. Some more horrific than others.

Depending on your position, and how far you'd travelled, the sea was quite visible from Hunter's Pass. And it was this magnificent view that now filled the lenses of Harding's binoculars. He'd chosen to sit in the back, just behind Lily, so he could get a good look as they ran alongside the escarpment – his sketchbook tucked away under the front seat.

He could still see the cloud sure enough, the road didn't start to dip until you came almost to Haven's Point, but his small glasses weren't powerful enough to sufficiently magnify the scene out there or tell him what had caused the explosion not so long ago. The lifeboat was simply too far out to see now.

But before they'd arrived at the junction for Angels Landing, he did note something on the horizon. To start with he thought it must be a bird, this black dot. Except as it flew into range he realised it was acting far too erratically to be a seagull or heron, graceful animals that they were.

Harding pressed the button for the automatic window, which drew an immediate look of annoyance from his agent.

"Jason, do you mind? That wind's freezing on my neck!"

He shushed her, cocking his head at the distant sound. An engine. A plane, perhaps? No, a helicopter! RAF Search and Rescue probably, and it was having problems. The droning sound fluctuated between excessively loud and non-existent. Harding watched as it shambled slowly inland, travelling towards the shore on a downward trajectory. It was heading back to the beach but there was no way it would make it to Angels Landing by the sound of things.

"Turn right here, Lily."

"I thought you wanted to—"

"Head down towards the cove off Hunter's Pass." Harding needed to be there when the helicopter landed.

*But there might be injured people on board, perhaps even—* He derailed that particular train of thought even before it left the station. In any event that wasn't the real reason why he was going down there. He needed to speak with the crew. They'd seen his cloud – the maelstrom – up close. He had to know what it was like.

"Why the change of plans?" Lily twisted her head round slightly, keeping just one eye on the road. The big glasses she required for driving made her look like some sort of television agony aunt.

"There's a chopper in trouble. Over there."

"Where? Oh, yes. I see it." He could tell by her tone of voice that she wasn't happy, but now that she'd seen the people in distress Harding knew she couldn't just drive by. Even if she was risking the sanity of one of her most valuable clients.

The road narrowed off even more, if that were possible, and they coasted past a white wooden "To the Beach" sign which was doing its best to hide behind some of the densest foliage he'd ever seen. There would be no one here at this time on a Saturday morning. The small beach off Hunter's Pass was hard to find even if you were looking for it; he was only aware of such places because he'd made it his business to find out before he moved here. Holidaymakers were either just arriving at or just departing from Sable, and neither would have the time to go out exploring the surrounding areas.

Harding just hoped he would be able to handle what he found at the end of this road.

A road that was rapidly becoming a pathway with each kilometre that went by.

\*\*\*

Rob Woodhead left the lifeboat station and began the walk up to the car park at Angels Landing. The Jenny was now inside again, having been winched up the slipway backwards. She'd need extensive repairs, perhaps even a refit, and the crew would be given a replacement while this went on.

As for the "damaged" members of his party, well they were on their way to be looked over, too. At the nearest hospital, halfway between Sable and Hambleton. Rob had tried once more to raise the shore on their way back with no success, so they decided it would be quicker to run the casualties there by car rather than ringing for an ambulance (ambulances?) from the station; not that they'd had much success giving them a heads up from there either. Frank, Sean and Keith had driven the six men off, with the crowds at Angels Landing looking on in awe. Then, just as they were loading up, the throng had burst into a spontaneous round of applause. Rob supposed it was the only way they could express their admiration for such courageous fellows, but somehow he just couldn't get past the idea that they were clapping like they would after a theatre performance or an afternoon at the circus. Rob wondered how many of them realised that this was all real. Did they have a clue what had gone on out there at all?

Did *he*?

Reports would have to be made, of course – God, he didn't envy Frank that task. Investigations carried out, especially in light of what had happened to the RAF helicopter. (What exactly had happened to it, though? He'd been too busy to notice himself, but assumed a bolt of lightning must have struck it. That was more feasible than Wayne's gibbering about "a giant water spear" shooting out of the rain.) But all Rob was concerned about at the moment was tailing the gang to St August's. Being there when Lou came round to explain. He'd left the job of clearing up and contacting the Coastguard to the other volunteers at the station. Most had been on shouts themselves and understood his need to follow this one up.

Some of the crowd from the car park had departed

The Wet

now that the drama was over, leaving residents of the nearby cottages to stand alone. As he walked over to his Vincent, which hadn't been stolen, thankfully (that showed where his mind had been at when he first arrived, leaving his pride and joy up here where anyone could get at her), someone took his picture. Rob spun round to see a small man in a thin short-sleeved shirt.

"Were you one of the rescuers?" he asked, his voice tinny.

"Yes," answered Rob bluntly, straddling his bike.

"Er... I wonder if you could tell me what that explosion was out there?" Rob looked down to see the man was bringing out a notepad. Not another fucking reporter.

"Look, I've got nothing to say."

"At least tell me what happened, can't you?"

Rob looked back over his shoulder at the cloud in the distance, then returned his gaze to the man. "I wish I knew," he said, then slid his helmet over his head.

The Vincent roared into life first time and the little reporter stepped back to avoid being flattened.

Rob wound in and out of the remaining people. He rode carefully in case there were any children still about. And it was because he drove the Vincent so slowly that he happened to notice a lone figure standing at the very edge of the car park like a sentry. His back was to Rob, but as he rode past, the man took his eyes off the water and the cloud. The stare bored right through him, almost causing him to lose control of the bike.

Then Rob turned off to head up the road that connected Angels Landing with the rest of the world. But he never forgot the eyes of that man. They haunted him.

So full of power and intensity it was as if they could actually see into the very core of Rob's soul.

\*\*\*

The chopper came down only about forty or so feet away from them. It had ditched into the sea twice, but finally made it onto the collection of white, round stones which kept the beach and water apart. Its landing skids made a cringeworthy sound as they connected with these miniature boulders worn smooth by time and tide alike.

A few minutes later the rotors ceased spinning, possibly out of sheer exhaustion rather than anything the pilot had done. Harding was already halfway to them before anyone got out. Lily was close behind, putting a hand to her mouth when she saw the state of their cockpit. Tiny branches of black smoke grew out of the doorway, escaping with the blonde woman as she gladly abandoned the craft. A broad smile swept across her face when she saw the man and woman. Obviously she'd been expecting a long walk before she reached civilisation and seeing a car was for her on a par with a thirsty man spying a cool pint of lager in the desert.

She hobbled precariously over the rocks a distance, losing her footing just the once. Her legs looked to be very shaky and the fact that she was waving to the couple wasn't helping her balance any.

"Hey, hello! Can you hear me?" she shouted. "My pilot's injured and we need to get him to a doctor."

"I'm—" Harding dried up. He was going to say the words, habit taking over from common sense: *"I'm a doctor. Or, at least I* used *to be before I went completely round the twist."*

"I'm Jason. Here, let me help you."

Harding hopped over the stones to take her hand. He drank in the sight of her. A breathtakingly pretty woman wearing jeans and a jumper, small handbag over her shoulder. The touch of her hand was warm in his. It felt nice, soft. Alive.

"Thanks, but it's really my friend in there who needs the help." She said the words but didn't withdraw her hand.

"Er... yes, of course," said Harding, releasing her at last. However, he made no effort to move. He wanted to, oh Jesus he wanted to, but his legs were refusing to obey his commands.

"He's burnt. There was a fire in the cockpit."

"Must... It must have been quite an ordeal." *Okay*, he told himself, *you're going to march over there and take a look at that guy. Ignore the sea, ignore the fact that it's only inches away from the helicopter. You're going to get on with it. The bloke needs you, so get your bloody arse in gear!*

This time he did move, slowly but surely towards the chopper.


Vicky watched the man. He looked more shook up than her. It was all she could do to stop herself giving him a hug for comfort (his or hers?). And something had happened when he touched her. She felt it instantly, a connection of sorts, like two battle-scarred veterans meeting up long after some bloody and bitter war.

Vicky guessed he was in his mid- to late-thirties because of his receding hairline, although it quite suited him she thought. He wore a maroon-coloured leather jacket, open at the front, and she could see by the cut of his shirt that he had a fairly lean physique. Probably not one centimetre of fat on his whole body, which stood roughly 5-9 give or take an inch or two. The black trousers looked fashionable without being over-dressy, and – heaven help her – she spent far too much time gazing at the curves of his legs as he walked. She'd surprised herself by this reaction. Even after all she'd been through... Vicky felt her face turning red.

But it was his face that was the most fascinating part of him. It was as if Vicky already knew him. She'd seen untold sorrows reflected in each line on his forehead, at his mouth and around those deep, green eyes. Deep – yes, that was an apt description. They said the eyes were the windows of the soul and if that was the case then this stranger who called himself Jason was one hell of a mystery.

*A mystery you'd like nothing better than to unravel*, a tiny voice said at the back of her mind.


Harding put one foot in front of the other, walking towards the chopper with a newfound resolve. He was drawing strength from somewhere – Lord alone knew where. Maybe from the woman behind him. He could feel her watching every move he made, but instead of being off-putting, he found it strangely satisfying, encouraging even. Burns, she had said. The man had burns. He could cope with that. Could handle burns, no problem.

Couldn't he?

Someone else was climbing out of the back, an overweight chap carrying something. A camera.

"Matt's over that side," he pointed out. The guy was flushed, cheeks filled with blood. *Definitely a candidate for an early coronary*, thought Harding. Even more so after the trip they'd just taken. Harding acknowledged him with a nod.

He opened the pilot's door and steadied the guy as he climbed out, an arm around his shoulders in case he should fall. The sound of foam hissing up over stone reached his ears. Harding shut it out and focused on the pilot's burns.

"Don't worry," he told him, "it looks worse than it is." From what he could tell, "Matt" had mostly first-degree burns, though some blisters were starting to form on his arm. The main thing was that his injuries wouldn't kill him. Harding escorted him over the rocks and back towards the others.

"Bastard helicopter," grumbled his patient under his breath.

Harding risked a glance back at the machine and then addressed the chubby guy ahead of them. "That thing safe now?"

"We... Vicky put the fire out. I-I think it's safe, yeah."

Vicky, so that was her name. It seemed so right, matching the face completely. Harding wasn't entirely convinced about the chopper, though.

The burnt man couldn't have been more than twelve stone, but the way he was leaning on Harding made him feel much heavier. The cameraman didn't offer to help and seemed more concerned with his precious equipment. After what felt like an eternity, Harding caught up with the blonde woman. She was standing next to Lily now, waiting to get in the car.

"Your wife's very kindly offered to take us to the nearest Casualty department," she said as he drew up to her.

"Oh no, she's... That is, I'm not—"

"What Jason is so very tactfully trying to say is we are not married. I'm his—"

"We're friends," Harding cut in.

Vicky smiled. "Oh, right." Her sudden relief was obvious, at least to him. "Well, I'm very grateful to the both of you. And I'm quite sure Matt here is, too, though he'd probably never say it out loud."

"Miss West has just been telling me that she works for a satellite TV station, Creation-Time wasn't it?" Lily was excited and Harding knew why. Publicity. She was probably lining him up for an interview to promote his work. She could forget that for starters!

"Have you ever seen any of our shows, Mr..."

"Harding. But, like I said before, it's Jason. No, I'm sorry. I don't own a television set."

Vicky looked a bit dejected. Harding hadn't meant to upset her or put her job down at all, but what was he supposed to say? He *didn't* have a TV, that was the truth of the matter. Too many distressing images came through that little box in the corner of your room. His life was depressing enough without intruding upon other people's misery.

"I'm sure they're really good, though," he added quickly. Why was it so important to him that she was happy? Why did he long to see that smile again, the one she broke out now, flattered by his attempts to make her feel better? Christ, this couldn't be happening now, could it? He felt like a teenager again bumping into Claire Smith in the corridor outside the biology lab.

Before he could prevent himself, Harding smiled back.

A cough from Lily was all it took to shatter the mood. "Right, let's get everyone in and we'll be off."

A slight groan came from Matt. "The sound equipment," he said. "We forgot the sound equipment."

"We're not going all the way back for that. It'll be safe enough until we return," Vicky reasoned. "Or until Creation-Time can come and collect the chopper. Besides, I doubt whether there'll be room in the car."

Matt came right back with: "But there's room for the camera, right?"

"Yes."

He didn't say another word, he just clambered into the front seat of the car without being asked. Vicky and Harding sat on either side of Tobe in the back. It was a bit of a squeeze, but they made do.

"I didn't see a hospital on the way in, Jason. Where's the nearest one?" Lily enquired, placing the enormous glasses back on her face again.

"Just go up the drive and turn left. I'll show you the quickest way there."

And with that they were off, the BMW retracing its steps up the path masquerading as a road that led to Hunter's Pass beach.

## Part Two
**Ebb and Flow**

"Waters flowed over mine head;
Then I said, I am cut off."

*The Bible.* Lamentations 3:54

## Chapter Sixteen
### Examinations

The ripples spread.
 Repelled from the centre in concentric circles, they disturbed and displaced the tiny creatures, the insects and such, that had, until now, lived peacefully upon the surface...

***

From the outside, St August's Hospital was an imposing sight. The Victorian building was originally built some hundred and thirty years ago at the bequest of a rich landowner and industrialist of the time called Sir Gerald Fairbanks, and for forty of those years it was used as a "modest" holiday home by him and his family. However, scandal struck at the very heart of the Fairbanks dynasty when the head of the household was arrested emerging from a brothel in the East End of

London. Historians suggest that he was probably set up by one of his rivals or enemies in the business world, for he had so many it would have taken a whole day to just sit down and write a list of their names.

Hounded by the press and with their patriarch languishing in jail (it would take him all of a week to pluck up enough courage to end it all), the family retreated permanently to the house near the sea. There they lived until bankruptcy arising from the mishandling of the estate forced them out.

A discharged army officer, who had spent much of his career in India, then bought it quite cheaply. The heat had eventually brought about a rare debilitating illness, and he and his wife moved into the house with the calming country surroundings so he could convalesce. The change in atmosphere seemed to do the trick because they lived out the rest of their long lives here, until the late 1930s. The soldier, being a patriotic sort, and having no children or other family to speak of, bequeathed the property to King and Country.

Unfortunately, both King and Country had more pressing matters to attend to, with the advent of the Second World War. Subsequently, the house lay empty for several years. After Labour's landslide victory in 1945, however, the National Health Service was born and it soon found a use for the place. The old Fairbanks House was perfectly situated between the small village of Sable and the port of Hambleton, so it was able to serve the inhabitants of both in this respect. Plus, there was easy access to town and village alike by the road that joined one locale to the other.

So, the place became a NHS hospital and has remained one ever since; no doubt much to the chagrin of its late beneficiary who was himself a staunch Conservative. It had never closed its doors to patients once, apart from the time when a fire swept through the

# The Wet

halls in early 1975, caused by a poor rewiring job meant to save money, but which actually ended up costing the taxpayers dearly, and would tragically cost three people their lives (two patients and the fireman who tried to get them out). A couple of months – and one renovation – later, St August's was open for business once more.

In its sixty or so years as a medical facility, the hospital had seen many strange and unusual cases, most of which were cured successfully – sometimes thanks to a healthy dose of good luck. From kidney disorders to Malaria contracted abroad, from rashes to astigmatisms, from ingrowing toenails to various foreign objects (some small, furry and alive) wedged "accidentally" in the rectum, from cancer to broken necks... This hospital had seen it all; everything under the sun.

Or at least it thought it had.

Then one Saturday morning in late June, three cars pulled up outside its Accident and Emergency entrance. And St August's would never be the same place again.

Frank Dexter burst in through the double doors and everyone in the waiting room looked round: the parents sat with their young son, who had earlier fallen off his bike; the middle-aged woman complaining of a shortness of breath; the man who'd cut his leg when his garden strimmer went out of control; a DIY enthusiast who'd been a little too enthusiastic with his hammer; and the heavy-set receptionist with her hair tied back so severely it looked she was in a decompression chamber. All in all it had been a fairly quiet morning and most of the patients would be seen to and on their way in no time, for a change.

But, as the staff had come to learn the hard way around here, you just never knew what was round the next corner.

"We need six stretchers, outside. Now!" Frank informed the receptionist. "Tell Ben four drownings, a man unconscious, and another with possible broken ribs."

Then he disappeared again, leaving the patients in the room wondering if they'd just shared some kind of collective hallucination.

Thankfully the receptionist knew better. She went into the back to relay the message. Seconds later, the stretchers were being wheeled outside, metal legs vibrating on the concrete slope. The three cars, one a red Escort, one a silver Proton and the other an Astra estate painted blue, were parked at an angle to the entrance and would block the path of any incoming ambulances should they happen to arrive in the next few minutes.

Dr Benjamin Hopkins, A&E consultant at St August's, came out in time to witness the wounded being loaded up.

"Frank, what's going on? We never got a call to—"

"Check your lines, Ben. We couldn't get through from The Jenny or the station. Figured it was best to bring these fellas straight here."

Ben ran alongside the first of the stretchers. "Isn't that Phil Holmes, and young...?"

"Wayne Gough," Frank completed for him. "Yeah. The others are local fishermen. We managed to get them all breathing on board the lifeboat, but I think a couple have stopped again now."

"Don't worry," said Ben, "we'll do our best for them."

Frank, Sean and Keith followed the trundling trolleys as hospital staff whisked them into the waiting room, but were stopped at the desk by the receptionist.

"You know the rules," she told them strictly. "You've done your jobs. Now let the doctors and nurses do theirs."

Frank felt like answering back, but deep down he knew she was right. They would only be in the way back there. Ben and his team didn't need any distractions from their work; they were the experts here on the land. The only thing Frank and his two friends could do now was move their cars out of the way, then sit and wait to hear any news. It was frustrating, after going through all that trouble to rescue them. But it was just one of those things.

Life or death? Death or life? One way or the other, they'd find out soon enough.

\*\*\*

For quite some time nobody spoke in the car, only Harding as he gave Lily increasingly vague directions. Vicky felt more than a bit awkward, so she tried to spark up a conversation with their new acquaintances. Anything to combat the silence which threatened to drive her loopy. There was too much time to think, and that was the last thing in the world she wanted to do right now.

"So how come you two happened to be down on that beach at the exact moment we needed you? Are you psychic or something?" Vicky looked past Tobe at the man who'd come to their rescue. But it was Lily in the front seat who answered.

"We were heading for... What's it called again, Jason?"

"Angels Landing."

"Yes, that's right. I knew it had something to do with religion. Anyway, we – that is Jason – wanted to get a better look at the storm-cloud."

Vicky saw Harding's cheek twitch at the very mention of the thing. And after coming so close to dying at its hands she knew exactly how he felt.

Harding turned to look back at her. Their eyes locked again, and Vicky couldn't break the contact; didn't want to shatter the link. Yes, she felt as if she knew this man. Certainly the name rang a bell, but it was much more than that. There was an intimate connection; she felt close to him on some other level... But before she could ask if they'd ever met before, Harding broached his own question, one she sensed he'd been trying to force out since they all climbed in the car together.

"You saw the storm up close, didn't you?"

Both Vicky and Tobe nodded. In the passenger seat Matt groaned.

The next question threw her, though. "What was it like?" asked Harding, as if he was trying to find out her opinion about a new flavour of ice cream.

"It was scary," replied Tobe without missing a beat.

Vicky twisted about under her seatbelt. "For a while back there, I thought... Well, I thought we were going to end up like those poor RAF men."

"The explosion?" Lily had been keeping one ear on the chatter behind. "Oh yes, we heard that earlier, didn't we Jason? Do you mean to say a Search and Rescue helicopter blew up out there?"

"Boom," said Matt rather callously, illustrating the crash with an opening of his hand.

"Sadly, yes." Vicky's eyes were mournful. Harding didn't appear at all surprised. Lives had been lost before to such disasters and lives would be lost again. It was inescapable. A certainty, like the changing tides. Nevertheless, Harding respected a moment or two's silence for those men before carrying on with his "interrogation".

"But did you notice anything out of the ordinary at sea?"

"What, you mean apart from the fact there's one solitary storm-cloud hanging there on an otherwise sunny summer's day?" Vicky had unconsciously allowed a note of sarcasm to creep into her sentence and she mentally reprimanded herself. *The man was only asking, that's all.*

# The Wet

*You've been spending far too much time cooped up with Matt lately.*

But she was worrying for no reason because Harding hadn't even noticed. "Yes. Anything to do with the storm itself."

"Vic noticed something about the way the rain was falling," offered Tobe. "She can explain it better than me, though. She's the expert."

"Expert?" Harding's eyebrows were raised.

"A meteriologist. You know…" Vicky couldn't help laughing at Tobe's mispronunciation.

"She's a weathergirl," Matt explained sourly. "Most of the time."

"But I thought you were, that is I assumed you were a reporter. Or a presenter."

"I'm working on it Mr… sorry, Jason."

"I see." Harding scratched behind his ear, if only for something to do with his hands. "Anyway, you were saying about the rain…?"

He'd forced the conversation back round to the storm again in a way Tobe appeared to find most disquieting. His curiosity was starting to border on the obsessive.

"It was falling in a circle," Vicky disclosed.

"A rain circle? I've never heard of that before."

"You and the rest of the known world. Every once in a while, nature likes to surprise us."

"And the rain was actually forming a circle? You could see the shape clearly?" Jason was leaning forward more to see her better.

"Uh-huh, yep." Vicky was still gazing into his eyes. "Can I just ask what your interest in all this is, Jason?"

Harding looked like a rabbit trapped in the headlights of an oncoming juggernaut. "It's… It's important that I know all there is to know about it."

He would say no more, and Vicky didn't feel like

digging for the information. The mystery of Jason Harding would keep for a little while longer.

"Okay, if it's that important, maybe you'd like to see for yourself."

"How?" asked a puzzled Harding.

Vicky tapped the camera now located between Tobe's legs. Tobe shot her a horrified glance.

"Vicky, I don't think we should... No offence, Mr Harding, but I haven't had a chance to look at it myself yet."

"You were there, Tobe," Vicky reminded him. "You saw it live. Just spin the tape back a bit and play it for Jason."

"Vicky, I really think—"

"Go on, do it for me." Tobe looked like he would rather disembowel himself, but in the end he turned the camera on and pressed rewind. The technician stopped the tape instinctively after a couple of seconds, knowing full well that Harding would only see the tail-end of the show. Tobe handed him the lens. Harding wasn't exactly excited, but that's how he came across. In actual fact it was more a nervous tension than anything.

"Just look into here," Tobe said. Harding lowered his head as the cameraman pressed play.

Inside on the small black and white playback screen he watched a rerun of his most terrifying nightmare unfold.

\*\*\*

Dr Benjamin Hopkins was busy.

Then again, he couldn't remember a day when he hadn't been busy here at St August's. Okay, the place was no inner-city hospital with stabbings and drug overdoses every five minutes, but it had its moments. Even on a relatively quiet day like today there was always scope for a few surprises. There he'd been, in his office, trying to catch up on a mountain of paperwork, having left the department in the capable hands of his junior doctors, when Charge Nurse Leo Mountford knocked on his door. The rest of it had been a blur. Running out into reception, the exchange with Frank Dexter, wheeling the patients inside.

The two lifeboat men were in no immediate danger, he'd ascertained that straight away. Wayne Gough had indeed broken a couple of ribs and was even now waiting in one of the side cubicles before being taken up to X-ray. And his superior, Coxswain Phil Holmes, had come to on the stretcher beside him moments after entering the department, seemingly none the worse for his ordeal. He was disorientated, as was only to be expected if what Frank had told him was true, but his injuries on the face of it were far from life-threatening. He was looked over all the same, then booked in for a CAT scan as soon as possible. Just to make sure.

No, the really serious cases were the four rescued fishermen Frank and his mates had brought in, soaked to the skin and turning blue. Basic life support had been given at the scene, but now the medics were bagging the casualties, cutting off their clothes and getting the saline and adrenaline in.

His juniors, the Senior House Officers on duty, Lisa Brookes and Nick Laurie, supported Ben. Their titles made them sound like high-ranking doctors, but in actual fact they'd been thrown in at the deep end, both having only served a few weeks of their six month rotation down here. That said, they were very capable emergency physicians – two of the best rookies Ben had ever seen if truth be known (although he'd never admit that in their company; it didn't do to let your ego get in the way of your job this early). But whether or not that would be enough today...

All three of them were trying to establish airways, the young and the more experienced working side by side while Leo and his nurses flitted about, frantically responding to commands and medical jargon.

Ben's patient, an older man than the rest – probably the father if it was a family business – was stiff as a board. He checked again for a pulse, rubber against cool flesh. Nothing. The man's mouth was still full of water, and despite several attempts to suction it out, it just kept coming back again.

"His lungs must be full of that crap," said Ben. "He's drowning on the inside." Yet he wasn't in as bad a shape as some of the others. The first ones Ben had seen were covered in thick algae, a slimy mantle running from forehead to chin.

Ben continued his own CPR, but could still get no breath sounds. As much of the liquid as they brought up, the man would replace it in seconds, spewing out gallons of the stuff until his own face was glistening too. The nurse nearest to his mouth stopped the suction for a minute. It was no good, Ben would have to use the defibrillator to get the heart going again first, then think about how to sort his airway afterwards; a tracheotomy, like as not. Brain damage was at the forefront of his mind. No oxygen could get to the brain, but if the heart had stopped then there was no way to pump that oxygen around the body anyway.

The paddles were charging, and Ben was just about to shock the patient when he noticed something. As the man's mouth filled up with saliva and saltwater again, his chest rose a fraction of an inch. The nurse was moving forward to try the suction again, and he shouted:

"No! Wait a second."

Ben put his stethoscope to the man's left breast and

listened closely. There was a faint echo of a beat accompanied by some gurgled breathing noises.

"Jesus wept," Ben whispered.

He'd been going about this the wrong way. They had to get some *more* fluid into the man, as much as he would take.

Because right now it was the only thing keeping him alive.

\*\*\*

When Rob Woodhead stepped into the Casualty waiting room he saw his three friends at the desk. Frank was talking to the stern-looking woman on the other side and she was tapping information into the hospital database, obviously details about what had happened and who they'd brought in.

"It's Rob!" said Keith. Sean and Frank glanced back. The crew was all together again, and while that didn't mean things would suddenly start to happen any quicker, it was somehow comforting. If only two more of their number were out here with them instead of in there being treated… *If only Phil was up and about*, thought Rob. *We could all use a few of his words of wisdom about now.*

"Any news?" He could tell by their downcast faces that they were still in the dark.

"Not heard a thing, mate," Frank replied. "Ben Hopkins took 'em through not long ago." Then he carried on telling the receptionist what she needed to know.

"I still can't believe what happened today," Sean broke in. "Can you?"

Rob shook his head. "I don't think it's caught up with any of us yet. Wait till the adrenaline drains away."

Keith rubbed his head. "It was the damnedest thing I've ever seen."

"I'm not just talking about that cloud, neither," said Sean. "What the hell was the matter with Lou and the others? I've seen drownings before but nothing compared to this. It was just like their faces were... I don't know what to call it."

"Whatever's wrong, it's out of our hands for now." Rob went quiet for a moment. "Has anyone contacted the families? I mean Wayne and Phil's. All of Lou's family was aboard that boat this morning."

"Hospital's been trying, but they can't get through," Keith said with a sigh. "I wanted to ring Mel on the payphone, but that's stuffed as well."

"Don't forget about the Coastguard and RNLI headquarters," Sean reminded them.

Rob nodded. "When I left, Elliot was going to try and phone them from the station." *But what if the lines are still down there, too?* Rob wondered. *What a fucking time for BT to be playing silly beggars.* It was always happening around here, though, this kind of thing. They were only a small place, not a priority for the phone companies or the electricity people. Rob could remember a time when he was a boy and the power had been out for almost a week in the middle of summer. In winter you expect it; snow, ice and what have you. But not at the height of the season. They were quick enough to send out the bills, mind. Regular as clockwork when they wanted something from you. It was another story when something went wrong. Dawn was always saying that—

Suddenly Rob stiffened, frozen with panic.

*Dawn!*

He'd forgotten all about Dawn, her father and the lighthouse. There was a clear view from that white monolith down to the lifeboat launch. And Stanley Keets just loved to stand at the top, peering out. Ready to report back. Dawn would have been there when the helicopter exploded. She'd have heard the bang, seen the black smoke. With Stanley's help she'd put two and two together, wondering whether he was out there or not, probably half out of her mind with worry. Dawn hated this part of his life. It was the only thing they didn't see eye to eye on. Rob grimaced at the thought of Stanley Keets fuelling the fire:

*"He's more interested in playing the hero than putting you first, love."*

Rob had to see her, explain what had happened. How he couldn't let this shout pass. He had to—

"Gentlemen." Rob was dragged back to the here and now by the kindly voice of Charge Nurse Leo Mountford. He stood before them in his white coat down to his knees, wearing a stethoscope around his neck like a fashion accessory. His bald head glinted in the artificial light, two patches of downy hair at either temple the only remnants of a once thick bushland that lived on his head ten years ago. He held out his hand. "I think you'd probably be more comfortable in the Relatives' Room.

"You're probably going to need to sit down."

\*\*\*

Lily's BMW arrived at the car park of St August's a few minutes after Rob had deposited his bike.

Harding was still playing the footage over and over in his mind, matching it to the images from his dream, from his painting. He imagined being there, close enough to reach out and touch that wrathful cloud, that freezing rain. The churning and bubbling waters at the bottom, whipped round like the maelstrom it was. The thought numbed his entire body, chilling him to the core. Somebody was saying something, but he didn't catch it.

"Sorry, what?"

"I said we've arrived, Jason." Lily was opening her car door and Vicky, in the back, was following her lead.

Harding shook himself. Like a dog after a bath, he tried to shrug off the droplets of doom clinging to him. It didn't work. Tobe was waiting for him to get out so he could alight on the A&E entrance side. Much easier than walking all the way around from Vicky's side.

Harding went to help Matt out of the front, but the man was already on his feet, vehemently refusing such offers of kindness.

Jason was glaring at the hospital now; memories of that fateful day were flooding back. There was absolutely no way he could follow these people inside.

Vicky joined him, as he looked sideways at the building. It was older than the one he was thinking about, but it was a hospital just the same.

"Thank you, Lily. And thanks Jason. I don't know what we would have done without you," Vicky said. Then she did something so totally spontaneous, she even looked shocked herself. Vicky raised herself up and kissed Harding on the cheek, her lips lightly brushing his skin.

In the time it took him to blink twice she was already retreating, halfway through the door with her male colleagues in tow, both of whom were casting bitter looks back at him as they went.

"Right," said Lily. "That's that, then. I'll drop you off at home and I really must be—"

"I don't think we should just abandon them, Lily." Harding could feel the hotness in that cheek, which was probably turning scarlet. "They're strangers here."

He was walking towards the entrance before she could

say another word, and by the time she did it was too late.

"But Jason, dear," she called out after him, though he wasn't really listening. "So are we."

## Chapter Seventeen
### Fate

He couldn't believe how lucky he'd been, and on his day off at that.

Dennis Owen would wipe the floor with the rest of them this week. Forget all those usual crocks of shite about council does this, vandals do that. This was real news. Action, excitement, human interest. It had it all! He was destined to make the front page with it because nothing this spectacular could ever happen between now and the Wednesday deadline. Hell, nothing as spectacular as this had occurred in decades around here. And he just happened to be passing on his way to his sister's house in Sable when he saw the crowds converging. He missed the launch but saw enough when they came back. It was serendipity, fate, karma. Okay, maybe not karma after the amount of people he'd screwed over in his life, but it was certainly something spiritual. Hell, how about that! There *was* some higher power guiding his destiny and, as usual, Dennis couldn't wait to exploit the fact, this time by snagging the story for the *Hambleton Echo*.

# The Wet

But why stop there? he told himself. He'd not seen any other reporters on the scene. No one asking questions or taking pictures like he had. Only those people with bloody stupid little cameras, like the ones you get inside Christmas crackers. To his knowledge he'd been the first and last one at Angels Landing this morning, probably because it was the weekend – although Dennis imagined somebody would have contacted the papers by now; some greedy scrote desperate to turn their tip-off into easy money. And no TV crews either. They always kept tabs on the emergency services, didn't they? Even on a Saturday. Strange.

Ah well, their loss was his massive gain. He'd be able to sell not only his story, naturally, but his pictures too. Pictures that were close to his heart, as they were in a roll of film located in his top shirt pocket. Dennis wouldn't let it out of his sight until he'd developed the strip personally down in the *Echo*'s darkrooms. It paid to be an all-rounder and no mistake. This way Dennis didn't have to rely on anyone else to do the processing. Someone who could cock it up or, worse still, ask for a cut of the profits just to keep their mouths shut. No, Dennis would handle it himself.

That's where he was speeding off to right now. No time like the present. With a bit of luck (a bit *more* luck) he might have the story sewn up before lunchtime, so he could start touting it round on the Internet and by fax. Only snippets at first, you understand. A synopsis to whet the appetite and loosen the purse strings. Sylvia would forgive him if he didn't see her today; he'd buy her something nice with the proceeds. Pay for a new TV or one of those aquariums she was always talking about. (Dennis couldn't understand why anyone who lived in a fishing village would want to keep fish as pets. If you wanted to see fish, just go down to the harbour and watch the boats unloading, that was his advice.) He wasn't all bad. At least, not where family was concerned.

Dennis Owen travelled along lower Haven's Point Road, past the farmhouse, the fields and trees on the edge of the land, past the lighthouse a bit further down, stuck out there on the rocks near the bottom like a pale digit giving the finger to the sea. His head was spinning, his mind reeling with the thrill of it all.

*You'll be the toast of the town – or the envy. And with a by-line in one of the dailies under your belt, no one will ever dare call you "Small Fry" again.*

Dennis tightened his grip on the wheel. That name still hurt after all these years. Children could be so cruel. They'd probably forgotten all about it by now, incidents in the playground, taunts at the bus stop because of his height. That day in the toilets when Tommy Crocker had kicked in the cubicle door and run off with his trousers and pants, leaving poor old Dennis to walk down the hall with just his bag to cover himself.

*"Small Fry! Small Fry! Small Fry!"*

They'd all forgotten by now. But he would never forget. Each face was burned into his memory like a series of firebrands. He could see them all now, laughing and pointing, snatching the bag away and throwing it over the rooftops. It made a change from throwing it into the road.

How could he ever forget his formative years? They'd forged him into the man he was today. Distrustful, deceitful, dishonest; unable to even look at a member of the opposite sex, let alone forge any kind of meaningful relationship with one.

Oh, but he'd show them once and for all. Every day he'd lived and breathed on Earth had been leading up to this point. Finally his own boat had come in, and Dennis Owen would no longer be a nobody working on a backwater hick's rag. He'd be grudgingly respected amongst his peers, and he could imagine the looks on those kids' faces – now grown – when they saw his name in every tabloid and broadsheet in every newsagents across the land. At last, he would be *somebody*.

And Dennis Owen was right. He would at last become a somebody this weekend, but not in the way he suspected. Not in a way he could have dreamed of, even after a million years of guessing.

Fate was guiding him that day for another reason altogether.

\*\*\*

Stanley Keets watched the tiny car drive past from the square window of his lighthouse. It was the only vehicle trundling along lower Haven's Point Road. On its own, just as he would be if he didn't have Dawn. That was justification enough for what he was doing, surely? It wasn't selfishness, not at all. If he managed to split Dawn and Woodhead up, that young good-for-nothing upstart would soon find another girl to sniff around; bloody hell, the thought of his little girl and that ape together drove him spare. And Dawn, well Dawn would have her father, wouldn't she.

So what happens when you're dead and buried, Stanley Keets? What happens to your beloved daughter then? A picture of Dawn as an old, lonely spinster wearing black lace and mourning for her lost parent broke into his mind. He shoved it away, burying it with all the speed of a backed-up grave digger.

He moved away from the window and walked over to Dawn on the couch. She was nursing the brandy he'd poured for her to calm those shattered nerves. Another reason why she was well shut of Woodhead.

"Is... is it Rob?" she asked, her voice rising and falling.

Stanley shook his head. "No, love. Just a car going by. Looks like he's making for Hambleton." He watched her head droop as her hopes were again dashed. Dawn had been in a terrible state after the explosion and he'd brought her downstairs more or less straight away. It was bad enough for her not knowing whether Rob was out there at all, but the loud bang, the blast had added another dimension to her fears. Any normal father would have been comforting his child, telling her everything was going to be all right. Reminding her that there were more lifeboat men than Rob in Sable, that he wasn't necessarily out on the rescue – regardless of the fact they both knew exactly where Rob was. He hardly ever missed a shout; he was one of their *star players*.

But Stanley had chosen a different approach. Calling Woodhead every name under the sun, labelling him inconsiderate (Ha! That was rich) and blind to her feelings. Working Dawn up more. He never even stopped to consider the possibility that Rob might actually be injured or maybe frying in the burning wreckage of the lifeboat. He'd be okay. His sort always was. The ends justified the means by Stanley's reckoning.

"What do you think that was out there, Dad?" Dawn's hands were still trembling; she was having trouble holding the glass. "That noise?"

"I honestly don't know, sweetheart."

"And all that smoke. Something's happened to the boat. To Rob. I just know it. I can *feel* it! What if he's—"

"Hey, hey." Stanley went over and sat beside Dawn, his arm finding its way around her shoulder as she burst into tears again. "No fella's worth getting yourself into this state over." He talked as if Rob had just dumped her for another woman or something. He relished her vulnerability. It was a strange thing, but Stanley could actually believe she'd regressed into her childhood again. An eight-year-old who'd grazed her knee on the lighthouse steps. Who still needed him to protect her from the boogey man living under her bed.

"I have to find out," she mumbled into his chest. Dawn had had no success trying to get through to the station or the hospital. She just kept getting that same robotic voice on the line, "There is a fault. Please call again later…" She apparently couldn't wait for later, could only see one option.

"I'm going to St August's. That's where they'll have taken any casualties. That's if they made it out." Her voice grew very small.

Stanley held Dawn's shoulders and looked her in the eyes. "No, I don't think that's a good idea."

Dawn pulled away momentarily. "Why not?" Now that voice was stronger.

"I just wouldn't like to see you upset."

"What, more upset than I am now? Not possible."

Stanley knew she'd made up her mind about this, and once that happened there was no shifting her. She was like her mother in that respect. He had to play along, show concern.

"All right, all right. If you must. But I'll take you."

"Look Dad, thanks for the offer but there's really no need to—"

"Dawn, you're in no fit state to drive. I said I'll take you, and that's an end to it."

Dawn tipped her head. "Okay, then. Thanks Dad." She hugged him and went to fetch her coat, spirits raised now that she was at least doing something. As opposed to waiting for bad news to find her.

But Stanley was less than pleased about the whole thing. He wished they could just shut out the world and stay in his lighthouse forever. Him and his little girl. They'd be safe here.

And for one brief moment Stanley Keets found himself wishing something else as well. That something really had happened to Rob Woodhead that morning. At least then he would leave them alone to get on with their lives. Dawn would miss him at first, sure. But she'd soon see that her daddy was there for her. He knew what was best.

Then the thoughts were gone; such terrible, terrible thoughts. So bad that by the time Stanley left the lighthouse with his only daughter he'd repressed them almost entirely.

*Almost* entirely.

## Chapter Eighteen
### Depths

"No, I'm sorry. I don't understand this at all."

Rob was standing with his hands on his hips, leathers creaking as Charge Nurse Leo Mountford went through what had happened again.

Wayne and Phil were fine, first of all. That was the good news. Broken ribs and a concussion they could deal with quite easily, as they had done millions of times in the past. But what Leo had told them about the four fishermen was a little harder to swallow. And their treatment so bizarre the Charge Nurse looked like he didn't believe it himself.

"So hang on," said Frank. "You're telling us that they're not breathing, but they're still alive?"

"Not exactly. They *are* breathing, just not in the same way you or I do."

"This is horseshit," snapped Rob. "Either they're breathing or they're not. Which is it? I think we have a right to know. If they're dead, just tell us for Christ's sake!"

Before Leo could say anything else, Ben Hopkins appeared at the Relatives' Room door. His tie hung loosely from his striped shirt and he had his hands in his pockets. Ben exuded a casualness that was meant to put people at their ease. To Rob he just seemed like someone who couldn't be bothered with all this and, given half a chance, would rather be out on the course knocking a little white ball around with a four iron.

"Let me reassure you, they *are* breathing," he said matter-of-factly. "Although at this stage even I'm not sure how."

"What the hell does that mean?"

"Easy, Rob." Frank came up to stand next to him. Emotions were running high. These people meant a great deal to Rob, but he had to let the doctor speak.

"I understand your concern, really I do," said Ben. "Believe me, I'm just as worried about the situation as you are."

Rob muttered something under his breath, but they ignored it. "All I can tell you is what I know for certain at this time. The men you brought in are alive, just. Somehow they managed to survive drowning by... now I know this sounds crazy, but bear with me. They survived by learning, or should I say *remembering*, how to breathe underwater. Their bodies adapted to the environment they found themselves in. How or why, I still don't know."

"I don't get it," Sean moaned from his chair at the back. "If you drown, you die. Right?"

"Ordinarily, yes."

"So what, Lou and his lads have become fish-men with gills. Is that it?" The picture Sean painted was ridiculous, like a character from a comic book. But no one laughed.

"That's not what I'm saying at all. But think about it. We spend months in the womb, in amniotic fluid. How do any of us survive that? It's only when we're born and the doctor or midwife slaps us on the back that we start to breathe the air around us. Somewhere along the line we forget how to do it. What if, by some miracle, Lou Turner and his crew – or rather their bodies – found a way to get back that knowledge? What if sheer panic alone drove them to it, that and the drop in temperature."

Frank's eyes became narrow slits. "Yeah, but if that's the case, how come it hasn't happened before to other drowning victims? They must have gone through the same panic and terror as Lou. Why haven't any of them survived? Why didn't *their* bodies adapt?"

"Okay, now that I don't know either. Remember this is all just speculation," the doctor reminded him. "I've only had chance to give them a cursory examination, after they were… stabilised. My personal theory is this. There's a certain amount of oxygen in water, and contrary to popular belief it's actually easier for our lungs to breathe in liquid than in air. Babies who are born prematurely and their lungs aren't strong enough to cope with breathing air yet, are sometimes given highly oxygenated liquid to keep them alive. I think Lou and the others managed to survive on the minimal amount of oxygen in the sea out there. Who knows, perhaps they were fortunate enough to stumble open a particularly rich patch of ocean. Maybe they were just lucky enough to—"

"Maybe something wanted them to survive," Rob said quietly, a shiver spreading through his bones.

***

It was like stepping into another dimension for Harding. One he'd left behind so long ago, but was always with him, submerged. Bridled sounds and memories floated to the surface of his mind. The voices of patients he'd once seen. The chatter of anxious relatives as they waited for news about their loved ones. The clanking as trolleys went by, on their way to the lift, to other departments.

Harding's joints seized up.

He could see Vicky and Matt at the desk. Tobe sat on one of the waiting room seats with his camera. But his brain was overlaying images on top of them. Vicky became Christine, and he was Matt, looking at himself. Standing at a similar desk demanding to know what—

Shouting. Screaming.

Harding looked up sharply and to his left. A small boy sat between father and mother, the crimson patches on his arms and legs were clearly hurting.

*Alex. Oh Lord in Heaven, it's Alex!*

And he was crying. Crying so very loudly. Harding had to go to him. He blocked out the other people there: the middle-aged woman, angry because she wasn't being taken seriously, no matter how bad her breathing was; the man holding his bruised hand, the thumb almost black now; the fellow with his torn trousers, on his way through to Casualty. Harding saw none of them.

Only Alex. His son, Alex.

He was drawn towards the lad hypnotically, his steps Frankenstein-like. The kid's blond hair (it looked ginger to Harding) and sky blue eyes, now screwed-up and weeping, filled his field of vision. He came up to the youngster and knelt down in front of him.

"What have you been doing to yourself then, young man?" he asked, ruffling the crying boy's hair. "Here, let me have a look."

The parents watched, a little wary of the stranger but thinking nothing of it as yet. They were probably used to people coming up and telling them what a fine boy they had, old ladies they saw on the streets of Sable or whatever.

"Your mother's going to be so upset when she hears about this, Alex." Harding's eyes were dull, lifeless. "She can't stand to see you in... to see you in pain."

Now they were obviously worried. Their son had stopped crying, wiping the tears away from his face. He was frightened of this man who'd called him Alex, when it clearly wasn't his name.

"Mum...?" He turned around, not quite sure how to respond.

"Kieran..." the mother said, concerned.

"What's your game, then, eh?" the father growled at Harding.

He just carried on staring at the man's son.

"Janet, go and fetch security," the dad carried on. "I think there's something wrong with him... you know, upstairs."

"There's no need for that." The suggestion was made calmly, but persuasively. "Come on, Jason. Let's go and see how your friends are doing."

Harding felt somebody press up behind him. He looked over his shoulder and recognised the face of Lily. It was enough to bring him to his senses, back to the present, back from his delusion. The boy's hair was blond, not ginger. Definitely blond. He saw the child for who he really was.

"I'm sorry. I'm so sorry, please—"

"I should think so, too!" barked the mother, Janet, more angry than worried now. "Scaring our little Keiran like that."

"What is he, some kind of perv?" the father asked, addressing Lily.

Jason stood up and backed away. Ever the diplomat,

Lily had a few words with the parents, smoothing things over. Explaining as best she could what had driven Harding to act the way he did. He saw their expressions change from ones of anger and confusion, to those of pity and compassion. Looking at their son with gratitude in their eyes. Thankful they still had him.

Lily led Harding away from the scene. But he couldn't go without glancing back just once at the trio. The boy called Kieran, now over his initial terror, waved to Harding. His tears had all but dried up.

Yet, no matter how hard he tried, the ashen-faced man couldn't bring himself to wave back. At the child he had believed to be his own flesh and blood.

At the child he had waved goodbye to once before.

***

Ben talked to them at length about the treatment, using even more complicated terms and phrases than Leo. Basically, from what Rob could gather, it came down to this: the only way to keep the men alive for the time being was to make sure their lungs didn't dry out. Oxygenated liquid was being delivered to them and they were, for now, breathing "normally". However, they remained in a kind of coma-like state, which was perhaps just as well, because if they did wake up in their present condition the shock might do more harm than good. They would almost certainly gag, maybe even choke to death as they fought against everything they knew to be wrong. At the moment it was instinctual, but once the brain became involved anything could happen. For the moment they were stable, and they should all be grateful for that.

Now it was just a case of monitoring the situation and

trying to get in touch with someone who could help. A specialist or scientist; there was bound to be a lot of interest in the case. As Ben said himself:

"This is virtually unheard of as far as I'm aware, and to be brutally honest with you, I'm a little out of my depth. Scratch that, I'm *totally* out of my depth. But the potential benefits could be amazing."

"Like what?" demanded Rob harshly. "Being able to find the bloody Lost City of Atlantis without diving gear?"

"Don't be so ridiculous." Ben was getting a little tired of this outright hostility, he could see that. It wasn't the doctor's fault this was happening, and he couldn't do anything about it right this minute. Ben was allowing for the fact that Rob had risked his life, that they'd all risked their necks to save these men. But he was only trying to look on the positive side. Jesus, most doctors he knew would be all doom and gloom, airing on the side of caution and reminding them that there was no way these men could still be alive. As it was, Ben didn't seem to have a clue just how they had survived. Didn't appear to believe his own words, all that nonsense about breathing underwater. Was just trying to rationalise this, explain away something that couldn't *be* explained – not by him at any rate. How they could have expelled all that carbon dioxide?

They were lucky to have him, really. The majority of doctors wouldn't have spotted a way to save them as fast as he did – or had the imagination. The men had been drowning, so establish an airway and get all that water up. That's what 99.9% would have done, ignoring the obvious fact that they were actually *breathing* the fucking water, though Christ alone knew how! That small act would have killed them as surely as if he'd put a gun to their heads and pulled the trigger.

"Look, I'm sorry, Doc. I'm just worried, that's all. Lou's like the only family I have left.' Rob collapsed into a chair. He looked like he was deflating, the troubles of the world pressing down on him. "I want them to get better," he said to no one in particular.

"We all do," Ben assured him. "*Of course* we do. But until we can find someone more experienced with... Well, this is the only way to ensure they don't get any worse. And that their brains aren't starved of oxygen in the meantime."

"Ben, can I ask you something?" Frank rose from his own seat and walked into the middle of the room.

"Sure."

"You say that these folk survived because their bodies remembered how to breathe liquid."

"That's one theory, yes. Although what part the sea itself played in all this, I can't tell you."

"Only, okay, let's assume that's right. We've got potentially another couple of men missing out there, presumed drowned. And until about twenty minutes ago, that's what we thought was wrong with Lou and the others." Frank paused for a second, looking round at his crew, each face in turn. Seeing if they'd caught his drift. "So, what if the same thing's happened to them? What if they're under the water somewhere in that state? Out of it, but still alive?"

Ben apparently hadn't considered this. "Theoretically, I suppose—"

"So, we could go out when the storm's blown over – if the bastard ever does – and look for them?" Rob interrupted.

"They could still be alive?" Sean asked, finally catching up with them.

Frank nodded. "Sounds as if it's possible."

"But they could be anywhere." Keith looked uneasy, being the voice of reason, but that was what he always did, bring people back to earth – usually people who did the lottery, saying "told you so" after they inevitably didn't win.

Rob was exactly the opposite, especially when it was something as important as this. Whatever the chance, no matter how wafer slim, he'd take it. "We could do it; I know we could. They're out there right now, just waiting for us to return."

\*\*\*

"What do you mean we can't use the phone?" Vicky's face was flushed now for another reason. Frustration rather than embarrassment at kissing the stranger outside. She'd been aware of raised voices in another section of the waiting room but had been too focussed on all this nonsense to really take any notice. Just your average A&E where she was from.

"It's not that you *can't* use it. It's just that there isn't much point." The receptionist's prissy manner left a lot to be desired. "There's something wrong with the line. I can't do anything about it."

"I'll use the payphone, then."

"Out of order, too, by all accounts."

Why did that seem to give the woman so much satisfaction? "But we need to get a message through to our TV station."

"I'm sorry, that's not my problem. My problem is trying to process the patients for this department. I'll be sure to let you know once they're back, Miss…?"

"West. Victoria West, Creation-Time TV. Miss…?"

The receptionist simply grinned. If she was even the slightest bit intimidated by the notion that Vicky worked for a television station, she didn't show it.

"Take a seat, Miss West. One of the nurses will attend to your friend shortly."

*My friend. Yes, you'd get on very well with him*, thought Vicky. She opened her mouth again, fully intending to say something else, but quickly realised she was wasting her time. The receptionist, her hair still lashed back as if she feared someone might steal it, had cut herself off and was now typing in Matt's information on the computer.

Behind them, Tobe was sat with his eye pressed up against the viewfinder of his camera. When Vicky turned, she wondered if he was taking shots of the waiting room to follow up their report. Background detail for when it came to be strung together – eventually. However, the angle of the camera, pointing half at the floor, told her that he was watching the footage he'd already taken from the chopper. Just as Jason Harding had done on their drive to the hospital.

The very thought of his name was enough to make her smile to herself. No doubt he'd be on his way back to wherever he lived now, mulling over the strange events of this Saturday morning. Remembering the peck she'd given him on the cheek. It shouldn't be too hard to find out his address; it was a small place after all. When this was over, maybe she'd visit him and thank him properly. An impromptu call with a bottle of wine, perhaps? Vicky had yet to discover his secrets, and she was damned if she was going to leave it at that.

*What will he think when he remembers me? That there was a spark, a connection, chemistry?* Not even she could deny it. Had he felt the same?

Then, to her amazement, she was looking at the face of Harding once more. She told herself it was part of the daydream. But no hallucination could ever be this powerful. This real. Not even her panicked retreat back into childhood on the helicopter.

Vicky knew that he'd followed them inside, and the silent question she'd asked herself was answered.

Lily was at his side, though, half supporting him. Harding looked like death warmed up. Was he himself ill? Maybe that was why they'd come in here, and not— Either way, she felt a sudden pang of concern.

Leaving Matt to sit down next to Tobe, she went over to the pair.

"Jason, Lily. I didn't think I'd see you again so soon."

"Neither did I," said the older woman.

"What on earth's the matter with Jason? Is he sick?" Without consciously knowing she was doing it, Vicky slid an arm around the other side of Harding to help him walk. He didn't appear to notice her and said nothing when she grabbed his upper arm.

"It's a long story," Lily moaned.

"I'd like to hear it sometime."

Lily smiled a patronising smile, not unlike the receptionist woman's. It clearly said this was none of her business. And, of course, it wasn't.

Not yet at any rate.


Tobe was glued to the screen. Not even he was prepared for the fantastic shots he'd taken, and he'd been there at the time. So, what would your average audience at home think? There was no two ways about it, this was going to make his career.

That man Harding's reaction in the car was proof, if any were needed. And he'd only seen a short excerpt. His jaw had hung open as he watched, mesmerised by the Rain Circle. Well, it was enough to captivate anyone, even in black and white. He couldn't wait to examine it on a colour monitor, and hopefully he'd get the chance as soon as Vicky called for transport back home.

Or maybe they'd all stay to follow the story through to its conclusion, whatever that might be, sending the footage back, or even editing on site and transmitting it for broadcast. The pictures of the Rain Circle could then be mixed with a live feed once the Outside Broadcast Unit got here. He didn't fancy letting it go so easily, mind, the footage which had nearly cost him his life. That hadn't really sunk in yet. His imminent demise had seemed real enough at the time, but since touchdown it had become some sort of surreal nightmare. It had happened and yet it hadn't. An experience he'd gone through by proxy. His body there, his mind elsewhere. If he didn't have the evidence in his very hands, then he might even be able to convince himself it had never happened at all.

And now Tobe was coming up to the part where they reached the Rain Circle itself. He saw the blackness of the cloud, the singularity – perfect in shape and purpose – pelting the sea with hard, hail-like bullets until it surrendered, presumably. But he also saw something else. Just a quick flash as the RAF helicopter zoomed into frame. Something that made him swallow dryly.

Then it was gone.

Tobe fumbled around for the rewind button. He had to look again, make sure he wasn't imagining things. But someone came and sat beside him, pulling the camera roughly away from his face. It was Matt.

"Can't you leave that thing alone for a minute? You'll go blind." He laughed at his own joke, then winced suddenly at his burnt arm. "Shit!" he hissed through his teeth.

"Matt, what did you do that for? I was just watching the footage we took. I thought I saw…"

"What?" sniffed Matt, blatantly uninterested in

anything he had to say.

"Nothing. So what did Creation-Time say? When are they coming? Are they sending an OB unit?"

"Phones are bollocks'd, aren't they. Couldn't get through." Matt looked around the room. "Fucking pissant place. Nothing works around here." He shifted in the chair, and his eyes came to rest upon Vicky and the people who'd driven him here. Matt sneered, showing no kind of gratitude towards them.

"Vicky's friend's back I see."

Tobe stared at them, too. "Oh Jesus, I thought he'd gone. There's something not quite right about him."

"Nothing wrong with him, Tobe. He knows exactly what he's doing."

"Did you see the way he kept looking at Vic?"

"Yeah. He just wants to get inside her pants, same as the rest of 'em."

*Same as you did*, thought Tobe.

"Been there, done that. And he might not like what he finds," Matt concluded. "Vicky comes with a lot of baggage, I can tell you. No, he might not like what he finds at all…"

## Chapter Nineteen
### Blame

How had he let things get so out of hand?

It hadn't been all his fault, he realised, but it still didn't excuse the way he'd lost his temper like that.

Rob slumped back into one of the padded chairs in the Relatives' Room of St August's Hospital, going over the events of the last half hour in his mind. No matter which way he looked at them, though, he always came to the same conclusion. He'd stuffed up, royally. More than that, he'd be lucky if Dawn ever spoke to him again. He knew how her father was, what he would do to ruin things between them. He wanted his little girl back under lock and key; nothing would please him more than to turn back the clock twenty years or more. Rob knew the routine.

*So why did I play right into his hands?* And just as he thought the day couldn't get any worse as well.

It had all started when he bumped into that damned TV crew again. Them and that blonde woman, Vicky what's-her-face? They had stoked the fire. Unfortunately,

Stanley Keets had been the one to get burnt. Not that he didn't thoroughly deserve it. He'd been on Rob's back from the beginning.

After Dr Ben Hopkins had given his little speech and told them more or less that waiting was the only option, all they could do at this time, Frank told his men that they could head off if they liked. See their families and loved ones, reassure them that everything was all right (as far as the RNLI men were concerned; though Lord knows how the relations of that poor chopper crew would get by. Had they even heard yet?). All the Turners were either at St August's in comas, or out there under the waves with a slim chance of survival – if Ben was right – so there was no family to contact here in Sable. Frank had no family either, so he'd volunteered to let Wayne and Phil's relatives know the score. If they didn't already, if they hadn't found out over the grapevine. Then he would make his way back to the station to sort things out. The lifeboat men would all congregate here at the hospital later, without a doubt; nothing was said out loud, but they all knew. Now was the time for reflection, to let the horrors of that morning sink in. Or perhaps try to forget them.

For his part Rob was going to bike it up to the lighthouse and try to undo some of the damage he knew Dawn's father had inflicted. There was no question in his mind: Stanley Keets was hellbent on poisoning Dawn against him. No one would ever be good enough for her. Certainly not someone like Rob Woodhead. As it turned out the mountain was already on its way here, in a certain pink Suzuki jeep Rob had procured for Dawn.

Rob's mates had filed out of the Relatives' Room, and then out of the Casualty entrance itself. He'd been halfway across reception when he saw them all sat there. The Creation-Time TV crew from earlier. The ones who'd followed them out in the chopper. Now they'd got all their juicy pictures of the tragic episode, they had followed the trail of blood to the local hospital like vultures. The thought of St August's filling up with people from the media, all their colleagues and rivals descending on Sable from the big cities to pick over the bare bones of the story, made him feel nauseous. Already there were two more figures with them, talking to them. A woman who looked very business-like, and a man in a shirt and leather jacket who looked like he'd just seen a ghost.

Rob went straight over, a red rag to a bull.

"Hope you're satisfied," he yelled at their ringleader.

"I'm sorry?" The woman, Vicky, seemed confused.

"You and your fellow thrill-seekers here. Nothing but parasites, the lot of you!"

She gawked at him for at least a minute; the conversation they'd had that morning took place a million years ago. Then something seemed to click. "You're the guy from the lifeboat station."

"Oh, *come on*, you can do better than that!" The patients in the – aptly-named – waiting room raised and turned their heads towards the noise. "You're not telling me it's a coincidence you're here. You followed us to the hospital, just like you followed us out to sea."

"Actually," replied Vicky, going on the offensive, "our pilot was injured when we landed. So, get your facts straight before you come across here shouting the odds."

Matt held up his arm and smirked.

"He probably did it on purpose so's you'd have an excuse to hang around, get past the Casualty door. Poke about a little. Isn't that how you people operate? Look, he's even got his bloody camera with him." Rob jabbed a finger at Tobe.

Vicky kept quiet. Rob bent down so he was face to face with the smaller weatherwoman.

"We think four men died out there today. Another four

are in comas with God knows what wrong with them, two of the crew were hurt in the course of the rescue, and a couple more of the injured are still out there somewhere. I think they've all been through enough without you sticking your nose in, don't you?"

The haggard guy next to her moved round to face Rob. "This is a hospital, there are sick people here."

"Who rattled your cage?"

"I can understand what you're going through, but—"

"You don't understand a thing." Rob had shifted across to stare out this new bloke. It didn't work. When he looked into those eyes he saw fear, but it wasn't Rob the man was frightened of. It was something else.

"I do understand. More than you realise," he answered.

"Jason," said the businesswoman on the other side of him. "Leave it alone. This gentleman's obviously very upset."

"Too right I am!" Rob was on the verge of saying something else to the guy, when a strange feeling came over him. The doors of St August's A&E department were shoved open again, and Dawn Keets was at the entrance. Her eyes were red from crying, her anxious brow furrowed. When she looked over and saw the hunched figure of her boyfriend, relief flooded through her. You could see it changing her physically.

Rob straightened, his argument with the TV people dwindling away. He was half-running to the entrance. Dawn did the same and they met silently in the middle. She extended a hand to touch him, to find out if he was real or merely a figment of her imagination. All her hopes and wishes come true. To her apparent surprise he was solid enough, and he leant in to kiss her where she stood. Rob just needed to hold her, tell her all the things that had been going through his mind…

Then Stanley Keets appeared behind her and the mood was sullied.

"Dawn," he began, "I was just on my way to—"

"Rob, don't." Dawn pulled away from him suddenly, a move heartily encouraged by her father. "I thought you were dead; do you know that? I honestly thought I'd never see you again."

"She's been crying since we heard the... Look at what you've put her through." Stanley's words were grinding against Rob's skull, sparks flying in his imagination.

"You keep out of this. It's between Dawn and me." Rob covered the ground between them in two short steps. "The Turners needed my help; I couldn't just ignore that."

"You could've let me know," said Dawn.

"There wasn't time, and then when we got back I couldn't get through."

"We were supposed to be spending the day together, all three of us."

Rob couldn't believe what he was hearing. This was Stanley Keets' work, stirring her emotions like paint in a tin. Surely she wasn't saying that their lunch at the lighthouse was more important than saving lives?

"What else could I do?"

"You could start by showing a bit of consideration, lad," Stanley chipped in again. Rob felt a twinge of fury. It seemed like he was being punished for trying to do some good. Dawn knew what he was when she agreed to go out with him. "You're a bad seed, Rob Woodhead, and you'll abandon my daughter just like you abandoned your family. Aye, and the Turners too, if I recall rightly."

The rage grew, taking on a life of its own. Rob let down his barriers, allowing it to burst free. Stanley was still talking.

"It's common knowledge that—"

"Dad, no." Dawn had a hand on his forearm.

"I'll have my say, Dawn. This worthless yobbo's not fit to lick your shoes. He's let everyone down he's ever come into contact with and—"

Rob's actions were so quick that not even he was fully aware of them. With his left hand he took Stanley Keets by the scruff of the neck, whilst simultaneously drawing back his right and balling it into a fist. If he'd let fly at that precise moment, Stanley would have found himself in a cubicle. But he hesitated. A small dissenting voice of reason cut through the boiling anger, holding him back at the last instant. Dawn's frantic cries helped snap him out of his trance.

The lifeboat man sensed a presence behind him, then suddenly to the left of him. A shadow: someone dressed in a dark uniform, ready to step in. Rob let Stanley Keets go, holding up both of his hands so the security guard could see. Three seconds earlier and he might have taken them both out – the satisfaction at seeing Keets' nose bloodied and broken an overwhelming temptation. Carefully, he backed off. Dawn's father straightened himself up, the nucleus of a smile on the irate parent's lips.

Rob looked around at the faces in Casualty. The Creation-Time TV people, the gaunt man who'd said he understood all this, the businesswoman. All eyes focused on him.

Then finally Dawn.

"So that's how you get your kicks, is it? Attacking defenceless old men." It was meant to provoke Rob further, but he just dismissed Stanley's taunts.

Dawn shook her head, disappointed at them both. "I think it's probably for the best if we go now," she said.

"Dawn, wait."

"We'll talk later, Rob."

And that was the end of the drama. Dawn and Stanley Keets went away without saying another word. Ben came out to see what all the racket was about, and explained to the security man that it was all right for Rob to stay. The doctor then escorted him back to the Relatives' Room where he told him in no uncertain terms to cool down.

Rob was left to wallow in his own self-pity for a while. As he sat there, he pored over what had been one of the worst days of his life since he left Sable as a young man. In the space of several short hours, he'd gone from ecstatic to miserable, from one end of the scale to the other.

All because of that damned storm-cloud out there. Yes, there was no doubt whatsoever, it had a lot to answer for, that thing.

Maybe more than any of them knew.

## Chapter Twenty
### Hero's Welcome

Melanie Tomkinson sat on the settee biting her nail.

The television was blaring away to itself, a news broadcast about some plane crash abroad. They were bringing the bodies out now. Melanie pressed the standby button and the image collapsed in on itself until the screen went black. She would find no comfort there, nothing to take her mind off things. Only disaster after disaster. Normally she would have been moved by such tragic events, would sit glued to the screen to follow the story. But today she was more bothered about what was happening on her own doorstep.

It had been two hours or more since Keith had called and told her he was heading out to sea. The station was answering an SOS from the Turners' fishing trawler – nice people; she knew them well – and Keith's pager had gone off en route to his workshop.

Of course, he'd been gone this long before, especially if they were out searching for swimmers lost at sea or the like, but never without getting a message back to her somehow. Besides, she had a bad feeling about this one. Something must have happened to—

No! She couldn't allow herself to think like that. Keith was safe and well, she believed he was. Deep down in her heart of hearts she believed it. Had to.

It was always the same when he went out on a shout, however. Keith would let her know beforehand – more often than not a rushed, garbled call from the station (God, sometimes she wished he'd just tell her after the event, when he was back home unharmed). And every time he would say he loved her and there was nothing to worry about; he was an experienced, seasoned lifeboat man. But she knew why he was really phoning her. It wasn't to put her in the picture at all. It was to speak with her. To hear her voice just one more time in case...

Melanie had started to get slightly twitchy at just gone ten. She'd heard that faint bang in the distance that might just have been another rumble of thunder – although something told her it was anything but. By half-past she was quite anxious indeed; she even picked up the phone and was about to call the station, but she thought perhaps he might be trying to get through to her. By eleven she still hadn't heard a thing and was working herself up into a frenzy. That was when she *did* pick up the receiver and start to punch in the station's number. All she got was a recorded message telling her the call had not been recognised. Cursing loudly, she'd replaced the handset and tried again. She was halfway through before she realised the phone wasn't working at all this time. There wasn't even a dial-tone. Her hands were shaking violently as she hung up.

They had been married for almost nine years now, but had known each other for a lot longer – both of them being Sablites born and bred. She remembered the day he'd proposed to her, at that fancy restaurant in Hambleton; getting down on one knee in front of everyone like that! She'd been both embarrassed and flattered at the same time. What a lovely evening.

Yes, she'd done all right for herself, had Mel. The local electrician and TV repairman with a thriving business, the first couple in Sable to get satellite telly no less. Plus, he was gorgeous looking to boot, a rugged bear of a man.

At 33 she still felt the same way. Loved him more now than ever, if anything. The years in between had strengthened and nurtured her feelings for Keith, and vice versa she liked to think. They'd even talked about starting a family soon. Melanie didn't know what she'd do if anything—

The door. Somebody was trying to get in.

When she heard the key in the lock, Melanie knew it was Keith. He was the only person who had a key for one thing, apart from the Kellys next door and they only used it in emergencies. Not even their respective parents had duplicates. Melanie sprang off the couch. Within seconds she was at the door, waiting for it to swing open.

She was shocked to see her husband's appearance. He looked like he'd been in the wars. His hair was all over the shop and was damp with sweat, his clothes were in disarray, and was it her imagination or did he walk with a stoop as he crossed the threshold? Not that any of those details really mattered. He was home. Her Keith was *home*, returned to her at last.

He smiled when he saw her, but it was lacking in its usual warmth. She knew that smile. Something had happened out there. Something terrible.

But Melanie was so pleased to see him she wrapped herself around his frame, almost crushing the wind out of him.

"S-Steady, love. I'm all right. Really."

"Oh Keith. I've been worried sick!" Now came the tears. "The phones are down, I've not heard a thing since you rang me... Where have you been all this time?"

Keith hugged her, then put a finger up to her lips. He wasn't ready to talk about it yet. She could understand that. There would be time for questions later. Time for talking afterwards. Right now they needed each other, more than words could express. They needed to be close. As close as two people could be.

Nothing had to be said. After all their years of marriage they could communicate with looks alone.

They both knew what came next.

Keith closed the front door behind him, and followed Melanie up the stairs.

They were upon each other even before they entered the bedroom, eager, just so delighted to be together. Keith's kisses were wild, fierce, and Melanie responded with a fever, a welcome release of all those hours of pent-up stress. His hands were in her long honey-brown hair, sweeping through it, cupping the back of her head. She was pulling at his shirt, yanking it out of his jeans.

Somehow, they made it to the bed, staggering towards it like Siamese twins joined at the waist, kicking off boots and slippers as they went. Melanie virtually tore the shirt from him. Buttons flew in all directions, bouncing across the carpet and ricocheting off furniture.

Keith reached around and unzipped her skirt. The dark blue material fell away to the floor with a crackle of static. He squeezed her flesh through the champagne-coloured half-slip beneath, the silky-smooth way it slid over her hips and full, rounded buttocks exciting him. He rubbed himself up against her and she moaned softly in his ear.

Melanie undid his jeans and pushed them down. His hardness pressed into her stomach through those thin cotton pants she'd bought him for Christmas last year.

Now Keith was fumbling with the buttons on her blouse, frustrated, desperate to uncover what lay beneath. It wasn't long before it was open and he gazed at the sight of her heaving breasts, threatening to escape from the lacy bra that imprisoned them. He took one in his hand, grappling with the garment until a swollen nipple was exposed. Then he planted his mouth on the sensitive bud.

Melanie squirmed with joy, that familiar warmth spreading through her.

Keith nuzzled between them, his tongue trailing over the flesh, nibbling, licking and sucking. Melanie fell backwards onto the bed, pulling Keith down on top of her, his head still buried in her cleavage. He looked up, a trickle of saliva running from his chin. Then his face was gone.

Keith was moving down her body. He hitched up the underskirt until it was around her midriff and expertly removed her tights and briefs, tossing them to one side. Without hesitation, he lapped at her: spiralling his tongue round, driving her mad with anticipation. She'd always loved that.

Until the time came when they could postpone the moment no longer. He wanted her right now, a desire which had be sated. And she was more than happy to oblige, delighted to celebrate the fact he was alive; that he'd returned to her.

Melanie let out a deep groan as she felt him enter her. She cocked back her head and clenched her teeth, relishing his length as it was thrust in up to the hilt. They became as one: their thoughts, their actions, their longings. Individuality lost in a whirlwind of intense passion. The events of that morning suddenly seemed so far away, so unreal. This was the only reality they knew now, and she was glad of it.

Again Keith worked on her breasts, lavishing them

with kisses and caressing each one in turn. Fondling, cupping, kneading. Keith sailed in and out of his wife. She brought her hands down to his spine, guiding him, helping him to move back and forth. Then Melanie hooked her heels over the back of his thighs, angling herself so that his movements would bring even more waves of pleasure.

The bed rocked beneath their combined weight, springs squeaking in protest, headboard banging against the partition wall. *God, I hope the Kellys are out*, thought Melanie absently, not really caring either way. It was too late to stop. She couldn't hold back even if her life depended on it. Her cries were loud and feral, matching the grunts of her husband.

"A-huh, oh, oh yes, Keith. Just a little more... *Ooh* that's it, just... Hhm. Yeah. Uh-uh. Oh *God!* Oh God, yes..."

*Squeak, squeak, squeak...*

"Uh-*huh!* Don't stop that... Don't... oh-*oh!*"

*Bang, bang, bang...*

"Oh God, I love you, Keith. I love you so, so... Please, please don't... don't stop..."

His forehead was awash with sweat. She could feel rivulets trickling down his back as he ground away on top of her, pumping rhythmically. The cords on his neck stood proud, his brow furrowed. He was speeding up, heading for a climax.

Melanie prepared herself, her own orgasm rushing to meet his.

Keith kissed her full on the mouth, muffling her high-pitched moans. His beard tickled just like it always did, but that only served to arouse her even more. She closed her eyes. Their moisture was mingling together, his back arching. In one last powerful surge he released his seed into her.

Melanie made a guttural sound and held on to his back

more tightly, her fingernails trying to find purchase on the slick skin. She opened her eyes wide, unable to comprehend the power of this experience. This was the best sex they'd ever had – even counting their honeymoon, when they'd been at it like dogs in heat for days. It took her a moment or so to realise why.

For some reason Keith was still firm, his fluid streaming out faster and faster. It was filling her up, swamping her.

Melanie's mouth was sealed over by his lips, and when she attempted to pull away she found she couldn't move. She looked into Keith's eyes. They were covered in a weird glistening membrane. It was getting hard to breathe properly. Melanie felt liquid running down her throat, flowing from her husband's maw.

She began to choke.

Down below the pressure was unbearable. The ecstasy she'd experienced only seconds ago had become a burning agony. It was as though someone had inserted a fire hose into her and turned it on full blast.

Melanie thrashed about on the bed, banging Keith's back with her fists, hopelessly flailing her legs around beneath him. *What the hell was he doing? Couldn't he see she was in pain? Couldn't he see he was... killing her?*

The sweat on his body spread, covering the couple locked in a lethal clinch. His solution was still spurting up into her – *but it was cold, ice cold* – forcing its way deeper and deeper inside, tearing her apart. Melanie wanted to scream but was denied the opportunity, a flurry of sputum clogging up her windpipe.

Everything was misting over. Keith's soaking features, the wetness dripping off his brow and onto her cheeks, the ceiling above him, the top of the window where the sun shined happily through the nets.

Melanie was blacking out, though not before she felt

her neck bursting down the sides and her belly cracking wide open.

A runny substance gushed out across the bedclothes, a thin kind of red colour like diluted cherry cordial.

And Keith relaxed at last, his load finally spent. Slumping down over the glossy form of something that had once been his wife.

\*\*\*

The Seagull was quiet that Saturday lunch-time. In fact, it was almost as dead as the corpses in the graveyard next door. Usually, the pub would catch most of the tourist trade on the first day of any summer weekend. In they'd trot, people in shorts and T-shirts. A pint and maybe a sandwich or ploughman's was just the ticket after a long drive or coach ride. Many would stop off here before moving on to their campsites further up the coast, in Hambleton perhaps. Others might be camping on the outskirts of Sable itself.

It didn't matter to Big Billy Braden as long as his cash register sang.

But today, it wasn't so much singing as sat on the counter whimpering. He looked round at the smattering of regulars that frequented his establishment. It could have been a cold day in November for all the new faces he saw.

Billy leaned on the pumps to survey his "empire". The traditional stone walls and timber beams clashed wildly with the arcade machines in the corner and the pool table, but those paid well – usually – that was the important thing. Seascape paintings and brass ornaments hung over a fire that was thankfully out today and would remain so until the chilly autumn evenings drew in.

# The Wet

Finally, his roaming gaze came to rest on Tina, his new barmaid, who was leaning against the bar filing her nails and chewing spearmint.

She'd been heaven-sent, Tina. As proficient at working the punters as she was at working the pumps. Not all of his customers had approved at first, mostly the women whose husbands spent much of their time in here. Neither had Nell, his wife. But Billy did the hiring and firing around here and he'd chosen wisely this time. The fact that she was an absolute stunner had nothing to do with it as far as he was concerned (and he'd promised Nell the same thing time and again). Tina was good at her job and knew how to handle their clientele – when they had some. It was as simple as that.

So why was he still staring at her so intently now? Why did he like to watch the way her hands pulled a pint, the way she giggled as someone said something to her across the bar. The way her body moved when she walked...

Thank God Nell was at her mother's for the week. She'd skin him alive if she caught him ogling Tina. But Christ, what he wouldn't give for one night, just one night—

No, he had to stop thinking about it or it'd drive him mad. What on earth would she see in him, a 40-something landlord with a beer-belly and tattoos down each hairy arm? He'd been fortunate enough to find Nell, a looker herself in her day. Billy wasn't going to risk it all for a quick grope and a fumble in the toilets after closing time. That's assuming she was even willing.

Tina stopped filing and looked up, aware that his eyes were on her. Billy turned away sharply and pretended to wipe up some non-existent spillage on the counter. He could almost feel Tina grinning to herself but heard her continue filing.

The landlord was extremely grateful when the doors went and he saw a familiar figure amble into The Seagull. Now he had something to take his mind off... off things.

Sean Howard waved to the proprietor and stepped up to the bar. He was licking his lips like he had a raging thirst, eyeing up the lager as he did so. Well, if anyone deserved a drink it was this chap.

"Sean, how goes it? Heard there was a call out this morning," Billy was already lining up a pint: Sean's usual.

"Bad news travels fast. Who'd you hear that from?"

"Me." Sean swung round and came face to face with Michael Croxley, Sable's odd job man. "Rob was just about to fix my van, too. D'you have any idea when he'll be back?"

"No, I don't, sorry. He's at the hospital."

Mike looked shocked. "Oh shit, I didn't mean... I'm always putting my foot in it. Is he okay?"

"Don't worry, Mike. Rob's fine. He's just waiting to hear about Lou Turner and his crew."

Billy was suddenly intrigued. "Why, what happened out there?"

"They were caught in a freak storm. Bastard sunk their trawler. We managed to find all but a couple of 'em. It was a bad do, I don't mind telling you." Sean took a long, hard swig of the amber liquid. "And then there was the chopper."

Mike finished quaffing his own pint and placed the glass on the counter. "Chopper? RAF, you mean?"

Sean nodded. "Aye. Went down not too far from us. Didn't see it myself. Too busy trying to drag those fishermen onto The Jenny."

Billy whistled through his front teeth. "Sounds as if you've been to hell and back, mate."

"You might not be far off there, Billy."

Tina squeezed past Billy at the back, heading for the

gap in the bar. He hesitated far too long before moving out of her way.

"Well, go on then, Sean. What happened next?" asked Mike.

Billy held up his hand. Alf Fletcher had just come in, Sable's oldest living resident, or thereabouts. Billy always gave him preferential treatment. "Just hold on till I've served Alf," he said, sliding sideways to pump out Alf's usual half-pint of bitter.

Mike looked disappointed. It wasn't often that a story like this came along and he was desperate to hear the ins and outs.

"It's okay, I've got to use the... 'you know what' anyway." Sean drained the dregs from his own glass and left the white frothy remnants crawling down the inside. He slapped Mike on the back and exited stage left.


The gents in The Seagull were situated at the foot of a long flight of stairs, just off from the main bar. Sean came round the corner and stood at the top. For a second he felt a bit dizzy. He put a hand to his head, blinking to clear his vision. The stairs stretched down in front of him. *It's all the stress of this morning catching up with me*, he said to himself. *Should have let the docs give me the once-over, as well.* Sean laughed weakly.

He couldn't stand there forever, the pressure on his bladder would make sure of that. God, he'd never needed to take a piss so badly in his life. Carefully, with one hand on the white wall, Sean began his descent.

One step, then another. They seemed to go on and on, winding round and round in a spiral. He knew there were only about nine or ten at most, but he must have counted three times that amount the further down he went.

Finally, he reached the bottom. Sean stretched out and

touched the handle with quivering fingertips. They slipped off the cold metal at first. It took him several attempts to open the blessed door, and when he entered he saw just one other person in the toilet: a man stood relieving himself at a urinal. He looked up briefly to see who'd entered, then turned back to his own task in hand.

Sean knew the man to talk to, but couldn't for the life of him remember his name. Shrugging, he took up a position to the right of the fellow, two urinals down. Men liked their own space when they are performing their ablutions, he'd read it somewhere in a book. It went back to when they were hunters or something and were at their most exposed to attack from animals as they took a leak or a dump.

Sean's dizziness was subsiding. Perhaps it was the lager. He had gulped it down pretty fast. Maybe the alcohol had decided to have a little fun and games with his system. Maybe it was a bad pint? He'd had a few of those in his time, though not lately. Either way, it had gone straight through him and now it wanted out. Sean would be only too happy to oblige.

He unzipped his trousers and blundered around inside for his manhood, which seemed quite content to stay where it was. Sean was having none of it and pulled it roughly out through the hole in his boxers. If he didn't pee soon, his innards might just explode like a popped water balloon. So he waited there for the first long streak of yellow to emerge. He'd closed his eyes and given way to the sensation, letting go as his bladder slowly emptied itself and—

Nothing came out.

*Damn and blast*, thought Sean. *It was all that time I spent getting down those stairs. Held it in too long, and now I can't go at all!*

It was a curious sensation. Wanting to expel it all so

badly, but not being able to coax out a drop. Relax. He had to relax and it would all happen naturally. It was just a matter of waiting.

The other man was finishing up and walking over to the sink behind. Sean had an idea. Listening to the flowing water as it came out of the taps was bound to encourage some kind of movement.

Sean cocked his head, his hearing so acute he could have picked out a pin dropping in a busy subway station. There it was, the first trickles. Then a splashing as it hit the porcelain bowl. Stronger now, the man rubbing his hands in the cascade. A squeeze or two of soap, the gurgle as water was sucked down into the plug-hole. Listen to the running tap as it—

*Yes!* Sean could feel the pressure building, his urine ready to burst free in a gorgeous fountain of gold. And then it happened. Sean started to pee with such a force it was as if he hadn't been in a week or more. A camel couldn't have stored up so much fluid before a long trip through the desert.

Sean began to shake. He looked like an epileptic having a fit.

The other man in the room was now drying his hands in a warm blast of air, his back to Sean. He wasn't aware that anything was wrong until he caught sight of a quaking shape in the mirror which hung over the water basin. He turned, shocked by the sight of Sean's convulsing body.

"Hey, are you all right?" It was the stupid kind of thing everyone says at moments like these, probably just to hear the sound of their own voice; to reassure themselves that they can still speak. It was quite obvious that the man was not "all right". He was about as far from being all right as anyone could possibly be.

The concerned bloke walked towards him, but as he did so the urinal on the wall shattered into a million pieces, showering the room with fragments. He ducked for cover just as a chunk of hard, fired clay slammed into the mirror at the back. Pieces of reflective glass crumbled into the washbasin below.

"Holy crap!" shouted the man, his eyes still glued to Sean.

And he watched as the shaking figure stumbled backwards and a line of thick yellow cut into the wall. It reminded him of a light beam from any number of sci-fi films he'd seen, or that time when James Bond had been strapped to a table and a laser had slowly climbed its way up between his legs...

It sliced into the plaster, digging in deep, and yet the man sensed that it wasn't hot, this deadly streak of piss. There was no steam coming from the rents in the wall. It was simply the incredible force of it that did the damage. The speed at which it was jetting out.

The first man fell over, putting out a hand to steady himself and slicing his palm open on a piece of razor-sharp urinal. An intense stabbing pain caused him to look away for a moment. He saw the blood escaping from his wound and gasped. When he turned his face back towards Sean, he saw that the guy was moving round, or more accurately he was being pulled around; still shaking violently, his eyes like two oversized golf balls with no hint of an iris in either one.

The onlooker's own eyes shifted down. Tiny traces of red now mingled with the urine and the member Sean was gripping so hard was red raw at its bulbous tip. By rights the man's thoughts should have turned to escape, but he was so utterly transfixed by the spectacle taking place in front of him. Obligated somehow to watch until it played itself out. Until it was all over.

But Sean was turning in his direction now.

Finally, the man was snapped out of his stupor by

sheer survival instinct. Like the maniac in front of him, his body acted independently of his mind (which was furiously trying to assimilate these events for future inspection, if there ever was a future). He raised himself up, blocking out the pain in his hand, and stood flush against the wall.

The door was only a few feet away but it might as well have been a thousand. The "laser" had already tracked through the wood vertically, giving it the appearance of one of those saloon-style doors upended on its side. Now it was eating away at the jamb, then the plaster by the entrance. It wasn't going all the way through the wall, he could see that now, but it was tunnelling in deep enough.

Should he slide beneath it like a limbo dancer, and hope for the best? Or run in the opposite direction? Hide in one of the stalls and wait for help to arrive?

Just as he was deciding what to do, the matter was taken out of his hands. Sean toppled sideways and his weapon scythed its way towards the man.

All he saw was a quick flash of yellow before his whole world became one of unwavering, unbelievable torment.


"What the hell was that?" Mike Croxley was barely a third of the way through his next pint, but the scream had broken his concentration.

"What was what?" asked Billy, rummaging through the till for Alf's change.

"Didn't you hear that cry? Sounded as if it came from the below, from the gents."

"Probably some poor sod had a curry last night." Billy handed over the coins and looked longingly across at Tina. She was travelling round the pub collecting the handful of empty glasses left, occasionally bending over to reach them.

"You don't think Sean..."

"Hmmm?" Billy was miles away, or a good few metres at any rate.

"Sean. I didn't think he looked all that well when he came in."

"He's bound to be a bit shaken up, Mike."

"All the same, I think I'll go and see what's keeping him." Mike left his pint on the bar and made the landlord promise to look after it for him. Billy agreed, shaking his head as Mike traipsed down the stairs. Mike worried too much, that was why he was always getting his leg pulled by the regulars. This was probably just another practical joke to wind him up, like the time Graham Cotton told him the cod was off because there were fears it might be radioactive. Billy chuckled. And the daft thing was he always fell for it, no matter how ridiculous the gag.

Sean was probably letting off steam after his ordeal this morning – they do say that laughter is the best medicine. He'd be waiting on the other side of the gents' door to spring out at Mike and frighten him to death. Any minute now there'd be another scream and Mike would come rushing back up the stairs saying: "That wasn't funny, Sean. You could've given me a heart attack!"

Yep, here he came. White as a sheet.

"B-Billy, come quick. There's something wrong with Sean."

Billy laughed. "Mike, he's just having you on, mate."

"No!" There was a hard edge to his denial that made Billy stop and stare. *Think back, have you ever seen Mike in quite such a state? No, never this bad.*

"What's—"

"Come on, you have to come now and see! There's someone else in there, Kevin Ratcliffe, I think, and he's... he's..."

Billy lifted the gate on the bar and went with Mike, calling over his shoulder to Tina: "I'll be back in a minute, love."

As he went down the stairs with his customer it crossed his mind that perhaps Mike was getting his own back. Revenge for all those stunts they'd pulled over the years. All the laughs they'd had at his expense. But was he that good an actor? He looked genuinely scared, as if he'd seen the Creature from the Black Lagoon down there or something.

They arrived at the entrance and Mike opened it with one hand, refusing to go in with Billy.

Once the door was open – there was something wrong with it, but that barely registered – the landlord's mind was only able to feed the scene to him in fragments, like a mother cutting up food for her child. Two halves of a man on the floor; marks on the walls, single jagged lines; and Sean curled up in the corner covered in a weird yellow and red slime.

Hesitating, Billy moved forwards and said: "Sean... Christ, what's—"

Sean moved. Only slightly, but he definitely moved. Billy tried to think of a possible explanation for these events and was drawing a blank. All he knew was he had to help somehow. It was too late for the man split in two (how had that happened? Jesus, just *how* had that happened?) but maybe something could be done for Sean.

"Billy... Billy?" Mike's voice was feeble from behind.

Billy was halfway across the room when Sean began to rise up, turning his face towards the visitor.

And the next sound that came from Billy's lips was that of a dying animal begging to be put out of its misery.

## Chapter Twenty-One
### Burdens

Lily didn't like leaving Harding at the hospital, but she'd waited there quite long enough. She'd spent the whole morning in Sable; in and around the place. It was already longer than she'd anticipated, and she'd seen more than she cared to anyway; including a public brawl in the waiting room, one which Jason had nearly got himself embroiled in. This may have been a Saturday, but she still had appointments to keep, work to chase up. Harding wasn't the only client on her books, even though at times it certainly felt like it.

Stupidly, Lily had mentioned her need to depart within earshot of Victoria West, the young lady Jason Harding seemed so enamoured with. Lily supposed she should be relieved, after all it was about time he found someone else – but was she the right choice?

"You wouldn't by any chance be going near a town or city, would you? Somewhere with a telephone that might actually work?" she'd asked Lily.

What could she say? Of course she was going near a

town or city, where else would she be conducting business, in the middle of a field? Lily had said yes, and that one small word had kept her waiting around even longer. Because she'd promised Vicky she would take Matt with her when he was done here, so he could pass on some sort of video tape or whatever. It was very important footage they'd taken of the storm and it was vital that it should find its way to Creation-Time TV without further delay, she'd explained. Without further delay? Hah, that was a joke!

"You've been marvellous so far putting up with us, but if you could just do this one last thing we'd be eternally grateful."

And so, Lily had seized her opportunity. "Grateful enough to give me some airtime in the future, Miss West?"

"Airtime?"

Lily realised that the woman still didn't know what she did, or what Harding did for that matter.

"To promote clients of mine. Artists, painters, sculptors... I represent them."

Vicky's eyes lit up, something suddenly registering. A memory coming back to her. A report on Creation-Time's art show, she explained. About a new talent to emerge on the scene, a brilliant painter called... J. Harding. That's where she'd seen the face before, a blurry publicity shot used in the programme. A rare photograph of this reclusive artist.

She nodded her head, recalling out loud the works she'd seen. An exhibition? One painting in particular coming back to her, of a sweeping tidal wave, or at least that's what it looked like to her. Blues, whites, greens. Capturing the very nature of the subject, in more ways than one.

"My God, I can't believe it. That's— I *love* art!"

"Most civilised people do," said Lily, thinking back to the incident in Casualty earlier.

"Sure. I mean, I'll definitely see what I can do." Vicky didn't sound all that sure to Lily, as if perhaps she didn't have as much pull there as she made out.

"So, you're an artist, Jason?" the woman said, turning to him.

"For my sins," he replied.

"The only thing is..." Lily interrupted.

"Yes?" answered Vicky.

"How will Jason get home if I leave?"

Harding straightened himself, apparently perplexed that she was talking about him in the third person. "I'll manage."

"You can't walk, it's too far," Lily pointed out. It had taken them a good fifteen minutes in the car, and there was no telling when he'd be done here. "If the phones don't come back on there'll be no way of calling a taxi."

Vicky patted her arm. "Don't worry about it. As soon as Matt calls up our station, they'll send transport. I can give Jason a lift back home." Vicky appeared to be looking forward to the prospect; she certainly wanted Jason to stay with her.

"Even so, I—"

"Listen, it's the least I can do, Lily. You've both been so kind."

At that moment Matt emerged with a dressing on his burns. "Nothing too serious," he told them. "Just like he said." Matt thumbed over at Harding. "First degree. I'll be as good as new in no time."

"I'm sure we'll all look forward to that," Vicky commented with a snigger. Then she took Matt aside and laid out the plan, but not that far away Lily couldn't overhear. He would go with her to the nearest town: Hambleton, Jason had informed them earlier, or maybe even the nearest city, then he had to call up Creation-Time and get them to collect the tape from him. Last, but not least, he had to tell them to get their arses to St August's with an OB unit – whatever that was – so she could do a live report.

"Oh, and we'll need someone to come and look at the chopper, too," she said finally. "Now have you got all that?"

Matt pulled a face. "'Course I have, I'm not an idiot." Vicky looked like she was going to say something about that, but simply shrugged. "What are you going to do now?"

"Well, once again our friend Woodhead has inadvertently given me an idea."

"If it's anything like the last one, I should forget about it."

"Tobe and I will hang around here, see if we can talk to some of the staff. Get the lowdown on the fishermen, or even the lifeboat men he said were injured. They can't all be like that prick in the Relatives' Room." Vicky rubbed the back of her neck. "We need interviews, Matt. Basically, we'll try to find out what's really going on here. The storm-cloud was just the start, I reckon."

"If you're going to be doing interviews, you really ought to have a soundman around. I told you we should have brought the gear from the chopper."

"Matt, look. We'll just have to make do with Tobe's camera mic. Now will you get off, for heaven's sake. Lily's waiting for you."

Vicky pulled him back around and Lily pretended she hadn't been tab-hanging. Moving to give Harding a hug goodbye, getting him to promise to call her.

"He's all yours," Vicky then told Lily, pushing – shoving – Matt forward. It wasn't really a fair exchange, Harding for Matt. But Vicky walked with them both to the entrance to make sure it was completed. Lily stepped out into the sunshine, pausing only briefly to say a curt "Bye" to the presenter.

Matt nodded a silent adieu to Tobe, then stopped in front of Vicky, "I'd like to say it's been fun working with you, Vic—"

"If you do, I'll slap you," she said.

As he strolled out of Casualty, Matt twisted his head round to look at the woman; there was a glint in his eye that betrayed his true feelings. That he actually did care about his co-worker. "Just be careful, Vicky," he said.

Then he went with Lily over to her silver BMW.

***

Vicky returned to find Tobe still fiddling about with his camera, loading up another thirty minute tape. At first he'd been reluctant to let the other tape go, but he gave it up in the end because he realised it was the only way anybody would ever get to see what he'd took; apart from Jason Harding, of course.

The A&E department was pretty empty now that the other patients had either gone in or gone home. It probably had something to do with the fact that no one could get through to St August's either by phone or radio, so no ambulances were speeding off to deal with emergencies. The only cases were those who'd either walked or driven here by car, and even they were quite thin on the ground.

Vicky smiled at Harding as she came back.

"You know, I never did thank you properly for standing up to that ape Woodhead earlier on."

The man's eyes drifted over to the closed off Relatives' Room. "You shouldn't be so hard on him. If what you've told me is anything to go by, he's been through the wringer today. A lot of people have."

"All the same... Listen, are you hungry, Jason?"

"Not really."

"Well, I am. I could eat a horse *and* its rider. What say you and me go in search of the canteen in this place? That's assuming they even have a canteen, and it's not out of order or anything. I'll shout you a coffee."

Harding blinked what looked like tired eyes, probably thinking to himself that caffeine would help. "All right, then. You've convinced me."

Vicky went over to Tobe and explained that they'd be twenty minutes or so. If anything was to happen, he should come and fetch them straight away. Then when they came back, Tobe could pop down and grab a bite while they kept a lookout. The cameraman appeared unsure about letting them go off alone, but in the end said nothing as they left.

Vicky linked arms with Harding. If he had a problem with that, he didn't put up much of a fight. "Right then, let's go and find out where this canteen is, shall we?"

\*\*\*

Tobe sat back as the pair went up to the receptionist to ask directions. His small eyes taking in every movement, including Vicky slipping her arm into that man's. He recorded the moments, like miniature versions of the camera he held in his hands, telling himself he was only looking out for Vicky.

There was just something about Harding, as he'd said before. Something that both scared and angered Tobe at the same time. But there was precious little he could do about it at the moment. For now, all he could do was keep his eyes peeled.

After all, it was what he did best.

\*\*\*

The cafeteria at St August's was, appropriately enough, situated where the old dining hall used to be. Grey, wipeable tables were lined up in rows like desks in an exam: equally spaced apart, but large enough for two or three people to gather around if they breathed in. Though it was still lunch hour at most places of work, there were more members of the public in the canteen than members of staff. They probably had to take their breaks when they could, thought Vicky. The hospital would soon grind to a standstill if doctors and nurses all ate at the same time.

It was self-service, so while Vicky loaded up her brown wood-effect tray, Harding went off to snag a table for them to sit at. Vicky noticed that he picked one that was as far away from the other diners as possible, cutting himself off from them. And he was nervously glancing round; always on guard, alert. Some people would have found these mannerisms strange, but not Vicky. Harding fascinated her. Had done since the moment she'd first met him. Maybe it was that whole tortured artist thing he had going on? Or maybe it was because although she'd only known him a short while, it seemed like centuries. At the same time, she really didn't know anything about him at all. That was the purpose of this exercise, she reminded herself. To get to know the *real* Jason Harding.

For a second Vicky wondered why he had agreed. Why he chose to remain at the hospital with them. The most obvious answer was that he needed to know about the Rain Circle; he'd told them as much in the car. It was very important to him. But Vicky dared to hope there was another – more personal – reason.

She lifted a plate onto her tray. Now she was no longer

in that chopper, she was starving. Fish and chips, with mushy peas (well, she *was* at the seaside), a jam roly-poly for afterwards, plus a couple of chocolate bars. To hell with diets today, she needed comfort food and by God she was going to have it! Vicky rounded her selection off with two cups of coffee, along with the obligatory sachets of sugar and tubs of usually foul-tasting milk that required a degree in safe-cracking to open.

She paid for it all at the end, giving the lady at the till an apologetic smile when she discovered she had nothing smaller than notes in her purse. Harding saw she was having trouble with the tray and responded immediately, coming over to help her carry it, the dessert bowl precariously near the edge.

"How much do I owe you for the coffee?" he asked.

"Told you, my treat for all you've done."

"I haven't done anything, really. Lily was the one with the car."

"You don't drive yourself?" Vicky enquired.

"Used to. Not any more."

They arrived at the table together and put the tray down. Harding waited for her to sit before taking his coffee and positioning himself directly opposite her. "Like I said before, don't worry about getting home," she reminded him. "I'll sort something out as soon as Creation-Time sends a team."

Harding didn't seem bothered either way, but offered his thanks, nonetheless.

"So," said Vicky, digging into her fish as best she could with the plastic cutlery provided, "how did you come to be living here in Sable, Jason? From your accent I'd say you weren't born around these parts." Down south, London way, Vicky had decided.

"No, no I wasn't." That was all he said by way of confirmation.

*You've got your work cut out for you this time, my girl*, Vicky said to herself. But his reluctance, his apparent shyness, only made her more determined.

"I can certainly see the attraction for a painter, though. All that scenery, you must be in your element."

Harding just stared at her, so hard it made Vicky feel slightly uncomfortable. He seemed to notice her unease and took a sip of the coffee, black and unsweetened.

"Okay, I'm with you. I don't go a bundle on small talk, either," said Vicky. "Let's cut to the chase, then. You're wondering about me, and the feeling's mutual, Jason, I can assure you. So here's my story, for what it's worth. I was born in Broadborough, brought up by my mother. I've never known my father and quite frankly I never want to know him – he walked out on Mum when she was only nineteen, leaving a little present for her which arrived nine months later." Vicky touched her chest with her hand. "She didn't even consider abortion, although no one would have blamed her if she had. Her parents – my grandparents – would have nothing to do with her once they knew. They still won't. But that's Mum through and through, always putting others first. In this case, moi.

"She managed to survive on welfare for a while, then got hooked up with another loser when I was only five. That didn't last, either. Just long enough for my little sister, Caroline, to be conceived. I know this doesn't paint her in a very good light, but she wasn't... Mum just made some bad choices, that's all."

Harding nodded, looking down at his coffee. Vicky went on.

"She worked like a demon after that. I think she finally figured out that she couldn't rely on anyone but herself. Mum put food on the table and clothes on our backs. She sacrificed a lot to look after us; she didn't have to, and she never once complained. Okay, maybe a few times, but then we were a bit of a handful." Vicky twirled a chip around on her fork.

Harding leaned forward, more interested by the second. "So you have a sister. What does she do now?"

Vicky searched the mushy peas for answers, and said at last, "Caroline's dead, Jason. She was killed by a hit and run driver twelve years ago."

Harding swallowed. "I'm so sorry. I didn't know."

"How would you?" There was a tinge of bitterness to her voice she couldn't keep out. "After... After it happened, Mum was devastated. They never caught the person who did it, you see. The bastard's still out there somewhere, carrying on as if nothing..."

"I doubt that very much."

"No, it's easy for him – oh yeah it was definitely a him – he never knew Caroline. She was just something that rolled over the bonnet of his car one day. But I can't block it out that easily."

Harding rested his elbows on the table. "Block it out? You saw the accident yourself?"

Vicky dropped the plastic fork on her plate. "She never blamed me for what happened that day, you know. Mum, I mean."

"Why should she blame you?"

"Because I was supposed to be looking after her. It was what I did, what I always did. Big sis. Except I wasn't there for her when it counted." Vicky stopped for a second, but Harding didn't fill the gap. Instead he waited for her to go on in her own time. "It was my job to keep an eye on her while Mum was out cleaning, or at the launderette. But like most fifteen-year-olds, all I thought about was myself. It was near the end of the school holidays, the sun was out for a change so we went to the park. I met up with some friends down there and we got chatting. I can't even remember what about now, isn't that crazy? It must have been important: it cost my sister her life.

"Next thing I know Caroline's gone. Running across the grass, then out onto the open road. She'd seen the ice cream van pull up and wanted a cornet, I suppose. She was mad on ice cream, our Caroline. I started shouting at her, calling out for her to stop. I don't know if she heard me or just didn't want to. And then I was sprinting past the park, over the playing field. But I-I wasn't fast enough. There was a white blur, I remember that, and short-cropped hair, bare arms clutching a steering wheel. Caroline was standing there one minute... The next she'd vanished. When I got there I found the car had knocked her almost thirty, forty feet down the road. The scumbag hadn't even tried to brake, he just carried on going. Christ knows what speed he was doing, and in a built-up area at that, but... Well, nobody saw a thing, of course. No number plates, no descriptions. Do you know how many white cars there are in Broadborough alone?"

"No," admitted Harding.

"No, neither do I... It's just..." Vicky was aware that she'd let her guard down. Told Harding more than she'd meant to. Why was that? She'd never really opened up to anyone about Caroline before, nobody – no men – she'd been close enough to before. She hadn't even discussed it with her mother much, the subject matter too painful. It felt weird, talking about this with a complete and utter stranger. But at the same time it felt right. The most natural thing in the world. Somehow she felt like she could share anything with him.

"It must have been very tough for you." Harding was genuinely sympathetic, his words ladled with understanding.

"Yes," said Vicky, "it was. I went off the rails there for a while. Nearly ended up in trouble with the law. Till Mum sorted me out, got me to buckle down. I'm all she's

# The Wet

got left, and she made me realise that." She pushed her fish and chips to one side, half-eaten, and turned her attention to the pudding. "I don't know why I'm telling you all this, I barely know you."

"Sometimes... sometimes it helps to talk things over with someone who's not involved." Harding drank from the coffee cup again.

"You believe that?"

"Not really, but a person I used to know did. Somebody who helped me one time."

Vicky consumed a dollop of the roly-poly, savouring the sugary taste. Harding wore a glazed expression. He was somewhere else, thinking about something else. Vicky wanted to know what it was.

"Jason, can I ask you something?"

He flickered back to reality. "Of course."

"Who are you? I mean who are you *really*?"

"I don't know what you mean."

Vicky reached over and placed her hand on his arm. "You weren't always Jason Harding the artist. Something happened to you once, I can see the pain in your eyes."

He looked like he wanted to run away, leave the table and make a dash for the door. But something was holding him fast. Like he couldn't hide from Vicky. A kindred spirit?

"Up until a few years ago I was a doctor. Only a GP, but I spent a fair amount of time in places like these." He waved his free hand around.

Vicky fought to keep the excitement out of her expression. He was opening up to her, as she had done to him, and the feeling was incredible.

"That explains the reaction you had when you came into Casualty," she said. It also explained how he'd known about Matt's burns. "So what happened to make you quit?"

Harding tried to pull back, but she kept her hand were

it was. "Did somebody die, Jason? One of your patients?"

"In a way, yes."

"Someone close to you?"

"Yes." He was nearly there, she could feel it. Just one more step. "My son."

Vicky drew in a sharp breath. "Your *son*? Oh my God, how awful."

"He drowned. A boating accident. I-I couldn't save him." Harding's eyes were tearing up. This was clearly difficult for him. Vicky suddenly felt guilty.

"You don't have to go on, not if you don't want to."

"No, no. I want to, Vicky." It was the first time he'd said her name out loud, and it tripped off his tongue as if he was meant to say it, to keep saying it over and over. "Alex was only six when he died. We were on a lake and he... he fell in. I dived in after him but couldn't... find him. It was too murky. By the time I did, it was too late. I tried to... revive him, but..." His voice was low, the sobs heart-wrenching. Vicky recognised the signs.

"And you blame yourself, even though everyone else keeps on telling you it wasn't your fault, right?"

Harding pressed the heel of his hand to his eye, wiping away the tears. "It *was* my fault. Maybe if I hadn't hesitated before jumping in after him? Or if I'd put him off, told him no when he wanted to go out there. He'd have been upset, but at least he'd still be alive. Maybe if—"

"Maybe if I'd been paying more attention to Caroline. Maybe if we hadn't gone to the park that day and stayed at home watching the TV. Maybe if I'd shouted louder, run faster," said Vicky. "I've been there, Jason. The what ifs never stop, do they?"

"No."

"But when all's said and done, it was out of our hands. We can't control everything that happens. It's questionable whether we can control *anything* that happens. And we certainly can't see into the future."

Harding was only half-listening. "I lost everything that day. My practice, my wife and family. My sanity."

Vicky cocked her head.

"Oh, that's right. You went off the rails, I went round the bend." The attempt at humour was wildly out of character and fell straight between the cracks of the conversation. "I had a breakdown shortly after Alex's death."

Vicky rubbed his arm, gentle, soothing strokes.

"That's where the painting came in. Dr McKenzie – ah, he was my psychiatrist – used it as part of my therapy. I was always keen on drawing and painting at school. At one point it was a toss up which one I would do for a living. The doctor won, I'm afraid, for all the good it did me, and I settled for snatching a few hours here and there with my easel. McKenzie encouraged me to set down my feelings, to express my fears visually. Mostly about the water and... you know."

"Did it help?"

Harding placed his hand on hers, his tears gradually drying. "In a strange sort of way it did, yes. It definitely helped with the nightmares. Through my oils I felt as if I could get some kind of handle on the dreams. Capture my personal demons, so to speak. As it turns out a few people seemed to like them."

"More than a few. Me included."

Harding appeared surprised.

Vicky smiled. "As I said, it was on that Creation-Time arts programme. They were very good, from what I remember."

"That side of it's not really important," he said with a sigh. "Only in the sense that I'm keeping Alex's memory alive."

"Everyone has to earn a crust, Jason."

"You sound just like Lily." She wasn't sure whether to take it as a compliment or not. "The point is," he continued, "it helped me get over the ordeal. I was doing okay, not great, but okay – until this week."

Vicky felt his hand trembling on top of hers. "It's all right, Jason," she assured him.

"No, it's not. The nightmares came back, really terrifying dreams. Worse even than the ones after— So I started to paint them again, putting down what I saw on the canvas, just like McKenzie told me."

His grip on her hand tightened, but she said nothing.

"It didn't work this time. All it seemed to do was make them stronger, more intense. Last night I thought I was going to die. It actually felt like I was drowning in my own bed, can you believe that?"

"A dream always feels real when you're in it," offered Vicky.

"What about when you wake up?" Harding's head turned to one side, mouth open as if he was taking in a deep breath. When he turned back again, he said: "Look, this is going to sound pretty strange, but I swear it's the truth."

Vicky nodded once to show that she was behind him.

"In the dreams I'm caught up in a storm, battered by the rain, swept away by the currents it creates. I can see it quite clearly, even now. I don't fully understand it, but somehow, I feel connected to the thing." Vicky could see where this was heading, and she didn't like it one bit. "I saw your Rain Circle, as you call it, before it appeared this morning, Vicky. Jesus, I've even begun painting it at home."

"That's... that's impossible, Jason. Surely it must be some kind of coincidence. One storm's pretty much like another."

"You said yourself that this one is unusual; easily recognisable, wouldn't you say? Trust me, it's the same one, and that's what really scares me."

Vicky felt her heartbeat quicken. She knew he was telling her the truth, incredible as it may sound. "But how could—?"

"I don't know. Perhaps it was a premonition. I've never really believed in that kind of rubbish, but it makes you wonder. One thing I do know for sure…" He looked deep into her eyes again.

"It's evil, Vicky. Evil through and through."


They walked back to the waiting room together, a newfound closeness between them. Confidences had been entered into, secrets and burdens shared that afternoon. Neither knew what would come of this, but they didn't really care. Harding's revelations had shocked Vicky, more than she let on, but she was grateful he'd opened up to her. They'd continued talking afterwards, Vicky filling in the blanks about how she came to be here: her studies, her first breaks in the TV business. And Harding had done likewise, sometimes going off on a tangent, but always giving her more to go on. More pieces of his own enigmatic puzzle. He talked freely to her now, like an old friend… or lover. Nothing resembling the tight-lipped man from before.

Harding and Vicky were like two survivors from a shipwreck who'd found each other in spite of the odds. Both clinging to the debris – and each other – treading water and waiting for the sharks to start circling.

As they wandered down the corridor, Vicky asked another question that had been preying on her mind.

"Why did you choose this place, Jason? Why Sable? I would have thought it was difficult enough to recover without moving to a home by the sea."

Harding thought for a moment. "I suppose I wanted to confront my fears head-on. I don't really know."

"You seem to know a bit about the area, Jason."

"A little. Just what I've read in local books and such."

Vicky turned to him. "So why the name? Sable strikes me as a very odd choice for an idyllic seaside village."

"As far as I know, I think it's down to the colour of the sands or something. That grey-brown tint they have along this part of the coast. Almost black."

Vicky grinned and said, "Oh," as if getting the punchline of a joke for the first time. Colour, that made sense. As a painter, Jason's mind was always going to go there.

"Why did you think it was odd?" asked a puzzled Harding, waiting for a response.

"It's just that, well, I've always taken the word to mean something else."

"What?"

Vicky was thinking about the fur, used traditionally as mourning garments. They carried connotations of evil, the devil. But what she actually said was:

"To me, Jason, Sable means darkness.

"It's always meant the dark."

## Chapter Twenty-Two
### The Messenger

Coxswain Phil Holmes lived in a house on the very edge of Sable.

He resided there with his elderly mother, Georgina, having been a bachelor all his life. Frank remembered him saying one time that it was going to stay that way, as well. A bad experience early on had sworn him off women for all eternity. But he never talked much about this. Phil was an intensely private person even when you got to know him.

Thankfully he hadn't missed out on the joys of "parenthood", thanks to his brother, John. Phil had been like a second father to John's kid, and it nearly broke his heart when young Jenny had been diagnosed with sugar diabetes. But Phil had helped his brother and sister-in-law get over the initial trepidation and fear of this disease (all they could hear were the warnings: could lead to blindness or possible amputations later in life). He'd convinced them to listen to what the doctors were saying, that it was manageable and she could lead a perfectly normal life if she was sensible. He'd even spent time with Jenny, working on her diet and injections.

People had a tendency to panic; it was human nature. This was one of the reasons why Frank had to be tactful here. He didn't want a repeat performance of what had happened at the Gough house. Wayne's girlfriend and parents going absolutely berserk before he could even tell them the lad was fine, just a couple of broken ribs and one hoary old tale to tell.

He would have to make it clear to Mrs Holmes right from the outset that her son was okay, recovering nicely in hospital with a slight headache. It could have been much worse. Frank recalled the piece of rotor that had crashed through the window at the front of the boat. Phil's prone form on the floor...

Yes, it could have been much, *much* worse.

After telling her all about it, he'd offer to run her to the hospital himself, stopping off along the way to let Phil's brother know, of course. The family didn't live too far away, thank goodness. Finally, when all that was done, he'd head back to the station to try and concoct a report about what had happened, filling in time sheets and the like. All nice and neat.

Except for the life of him he didn't know what he was going to put. He still didn't understand what he'd been through, what they'd all been through a few hours earlier. More importantly, what had happened to the four men they'd rescued.

Phil would know what to write. He'd filled in tons of reports like that (okay, maybe not *quite* like that) being the only member of the crew who was a full-timer. The boat was, quite literally, his life. He'd spend every waking hour down at the station checking her out, polishing her up and waxing, often taking Jenny down there to have a look round her namesake; she was just as interested in it all as

The Wet

her old uncle. The rest of the crew had other commitments and could only usually spare Sundays or days off.

Yes, he was one of the old breed was Phil, and his family was very proud of him. *They'll have even more reason to be proud when they hear what went on today*, Frank said to himself. There would probably even be a Bronze medal for gallantry in it for him.

As Frank's blue Astra turned the corner, he was in for a pleasant surprise. Phil's brother was at the house, car parked outside on the road. That would save him a bit of time. He might even get back to the hospital himself later to see how the fishermen were doing, and to have a word with Wayne and Phil if they were up to it.

Frank pulled up behind the other car and got out, slamming the door shut with a bang.

The front door was open before he was halfway up the drive. John had come out when he heard the engine. It was a rare thing for Mrs Holmes to have visitors of an afternoon. *He probably thought it was Phil returning*, reasoned Frank.

"Er, hello… Frank isn't it?" John held out his hand, a worried look on his face. "You're one of Phil's friends from the lifeboat."

Frank nodded. "Now before you get too worked up, John, your brother's fine." Frank could see the relief flooding through him as he pumped his hand.

"So, what's wrong? Where is he?"

"Is your mum – Phil's mum – in? Only I'd rather tell this story just the once."

"Yeah, sure. Come in. Do you want a cup of tea? Kettle's just boiled."

In spite the circumstances, Frank smiled. "Do you know, that's the best news I've heard all day."

"Mum? Mum, we've got a visitor."

John introduced Frank to his mother, and then his wife, Amanda. Ten year-old Jenny was out the back playing in the garden with her dog.

"Like I was just saying to John outside, Mrs Holmes, there really is nothing to worry about." Frank sat down on one of the high-backed chairs that flanked the huge window in the living room.

The white-haired lady eased back in her own seat. Her face was quite smooth. So much so that Frank would never have believed her to be pushing eighty. There was usually a twinkle in her eyes that came from being young at heart, but today it seemed less vital.

"Something's happened to Philip," she said.

"Well, yes and no."

John brought the tea pot and cups in on a tray and placed them on the coffee table. A big hand-crocheted mat prevented it from scratching the wood.

"You see," began Frank, "we had a call out this morning. Some fishermen were in trouble. They got caught up in a storm at sea. Only when we got there, it was worse than we thought. There was no sign of the boat, and the conditions were rough to say the least. Anyway, we spotted some of the men in the water and went to rescue them."

John, now sat on the couch, was clenching and unclenching his fists, even though Frank had assured him his brother was all right. Amanda poured the tea which had now brewed.

"How do you take it?" she asked Frank.

"Oh, white please. No sugar... Right, so, that's when we ran into difficulties. The storm was rocking the lifeboat from side to side, and Phil was steering her from the inside."

"The Jenny," said Mrs Holmes senior, smiling.

Frank nodded. "The next thing we knew she was out of control and heading towards the storm. When I went into the cabin, I found Phil was unconscious. Now, like I said before there's no need to worry. He's all right now, just a mild concussion so Ben Hopkins says at St August's. We managed to get The Jenny back home and took him straight there." Frank deliberately omitted the part about the Search & Rescue helicopter and the rotor-blade crashing through the front of their boat. He didn't think they could cope with too much information like that at once.

Amanda handed Frank a cup of steaming brown liquid. "So, Philip's at the hospital?"

"Yeah, I just left there a short while ago. He came to not long after we arrived, but the doctors sent him up for a CAT scan just to make sure. As far as I'm aware he's just got a bit of a bump on his head."

John edged forward. "Why did nobody contact us when it happened, Frank?"

"I don't know about here, but all the phones are out at St August's. Something wrong with the lines."

Amanda went round the back of the settee and picked up the phone, one of those old-fashioned kinds which was resting on the sideboard. "I keep getting a computerised message when I try to dial."

"Yep, it's same at the hospital. Must be a general fault. I bet the whole of Sable's down." Frank slurped from the china cup, holding the saucer beneath to catch any drops. The warm nectar eased itself down his throat. Without pausing to think, he smacked his lips. He'd never realised tea could taste so good. And Frank suddenly noticed how hungry he was, too. What with all the drama he'd missed out on lunch completely. Any minute now his stomach would start to rumble as loud as that thunder cloud out at sea.

"Well, we certainly appreciate you coming out here to tell us, Frank." John seemed more at ease now that he'd heard the "entire" story.

"What I was going to suggest was that I drive you to the hospital, Mrs Holmes—"

"Please, dear. Call me Georgina."

"Georgina... but no doubt you'll be going up there yourselves now, John?"

"Oh, yes. Yes we will."

"Right then, I'll head for the station and see if I can sort out the paperwork." Frank had another drink of the tea, enough to see him through the car journey to Angels Landing.

But the last mouthful went down the wrong way. He stood up, coughing and spluttering.

*God, this hasn't happened to me since I was in short trousers*, he thought. *That'll teach me to gulp down my tea.* Frank would have laughed at his own foolishness, except for the fact that he couldn't catch his breath. His throat was sore from the coughing, and it felt like there was an obstruction in his windpipe.

John rushed over to him. With hands the size of table tennis paddles, he slapped Frank on the back. Frank wanted to tell him to stop. That it wasn't helping. But there was no way he could possibly speak. He heard Amanda shouting at her husband.

"He's going blue, he's going blue!"

*They're panicking again*, said a distant voice in Frank's head.

He was hacking, trying to bring up the blockage. And all the time he was choking he thought about the irony of the situation, that he'd survived untold dangers this morning during the rescue only to die drinking a cup of mother Holmes' tea. It was absurd. He couldn't go out like this...

Or maybe that was it. He'd cheated death by coming back from that storm. Lord knows they all should have died out there, just like those RAF men: him, Rob, Wayne, Sean, Keith and Phil. Perhaps *Death* had decided to get his own back. Was he lurking around even now? Ready with his scythe poised saying: "You're only delaying the inevitable, Frank Dexter. Your time ran out today. Morning, afternoon, it's all the same to me. One way or another, you're mine!"

John's final slap brought the obstruction up. Frank marvelled at the ball of shiny brown mess that slavered from his lips. The tea he'd drunk had somehow clotted together inside his throat and now it was dangling on strands of his own spit.

But that didn't matter. It was over, he could breathe again.

The brown goo began climbing back up, using his spittle as a kind of pulley system. Both Frank and John observed this grotesque display and neither did anything to stop it. Then it suddenly sprang up and splattered over Frank's face.

His hands were up too, tugging at the stuff, trying to peel it off while John just stood there, his mouth working up and down.

Amanda screamed for the both of them.

"What is it? What's happened?" This was Georgina, who couldn't see because Amanda was in front of her.

Frank looked like he was wearing a strange Halloween mask. He'd become the Mud-Monster, no longer human in any true sense of the word. The dirty liquid was rippling over his scalp.

He'd been able to breathe for all of ten seconds before the supply was cut off again. Frank was coughing for a second time, the tea worming its way into his mouth, to the back of his throat and beyond. He tottered around the room, unable to see where he was going. Frank crashed into the TV, then the sideboard, knocking the phone onto the floor with a clatter.

"John!" Amanda shrieked. "Do something."

Sadly there was nothing John *could* do. Deep down he knew that, so he didn't even try. Frank, on the other hand, did plenty.

No longer was he writhing about beneath the tight mud pack. Now he was just squatting on the floor, head bowed. He seemed to be breathing again, his back convulsing. And when he whipped his head back, Amanda could swear that he was looking straight at her, regardless of the fact his eyes were obscured.

Frank's back legs tensed, the swelling muscles twitching.

John saw what he had in mind and leapt across the room. He missed Frank by a mile as the man sprang forwards at John's wife. Frank cast his arms out wide like a bird, his hands a pink blur.

Except when he pounced on Amanda, she saw that those same hands were actually liquefying, the fingers losing their coherence. And with all the strength of a full-grown gorilla, Frank closed them around her head, through the skull.

Then he plunged them into the grey matter of her brain.

## Chapter Twenty-Three
### Catch-up

Tobe had been checking over his camera for the umpteenth time and waiting for Vicky to get back with her creepy "boyfriend" when he noticed the door of the Relatives' Room was ajar.

Before he knew it, that Woodhead bloke, the one who'd had such a go at them earlier – not to mention almost cleaning some poor old sod's clock at the entrance – was out and about. Obviously he'd been cooling down in there since the incident, but Tobe figured it wouldn't take much to set him off again. God, he prayed there would be no more trouble. Tobe was on his own now and was hopeless at confrontations. Besides, he'd stand no chance against the black-haired giant; the most he could hope for was that some of the blows would glance off him.

Tobe squashed himself up in the seat, trying to make himself invisible, willing Woodhead to look in the other direction. He was amazed when his tactics actually seemed to work. Tobe blew a huge sigh of relief when Woodhead walked right by him to talk to the severe-looking woman at reception.

The usually stern lady listened to what he had to say, responding with nods and shakes of the head. Tobe strained to hear, but only caught snatches of the conversation. He heard the name Hopkins mentioned a few times, and then Woodhead smiled at the receptionist. She returned the smile coyly, then disappeared into the back. Tobe thought about going to find Vicky; she'd said to let her know if anything else developed.

However, right now he reckoned it was probably safer to stay where he was and not draw attention to himself. He didn't fancy shelling out for a new camera – who knew where Woodhead might stick it! – nor being treated in this very hospital for multiple head injuries after the lifeboat man had done his worst.

So he just sat there and kept his head down as another man came out to speak with Woodhead.

\*\*\*

"So they've been moved?" said Rob.

"Yes. Only up to the ICU. We can monitor them better from there. But I'm afraid there's still no change. Leo's shift ended a few minutes ago, and he's volunteered to call for help when he gets back home. With a bit of luck, we might get a specialist out here by tonight." Charge Nurse Leo Mountford lived on the far side of Hambleton where the phones were almost certain to be working.

Ben was more than a bit annoyed at being called out here again to see to Rob. He still had a stack of paperwork to get through, and with the new arrivals his job had just got that much more difficult. The RLNI man's devotion was commendable, and Ben realised that these were people he knew. But even so, the man should learn to wait until the doctor was able to see him. He'd promised to keep Rob updated, and that's what he'd do. What else could the guy ask for?

Rob answered the unspoken question with: "Can I see them?"

"Not right now, Rob. You'll only upset yourself further."

"Okay then, what about Wayne or Phil? Any chance of talking to them?" Rob was adamant. He needed to do something constructive apparently, even if it was only speaking to his colleagues about the rescue.

"They're both up on the wards right now. Maybe you—"

"Please, doc." He put on his best puppy dog face.

Ben gave up. At least if Rob was on the upper floor he wouldn't be getting into fights in their Casualty department. "Okay, then. I suppose it can't do any harm. Wayne's parents are already up there."

Rob beamed. "Thanks. I appreciate it." Ben told him where the patients could be found and watched him bound off to the lift.

"Listen, don't go tiring them out," he called after the man. "D'you hear?"

Rob stuck his thumb up as the lift doors closed around him. Benjamin Hopkins shook his head and began walking back to his office.

\*\*\*

From the hillside next to St August's, the stranger watched.

This was where the victims had been brought after

they were taken from the lifeboat. He could see the bike in the car park, the one that rescuer had driven past him. The one he'd tailed so discretely. They still had no idea what was going on. No idea at all of the trouble they were in.

He stared with wide eyes at the hospital below.

His enemies would know where he was now, and soon they would come, if they weren't around already. The man couldn't see the storm-cloud from here – *his* storm-cloud – but it was still out there almost kissing the sea. He could sense it. The cloud would stay there until it had done what it set out to do, what it was told to do.

All this was merely a diversion, or an accident – he hadn't decided which. *It* knew they were coming too, so a surprise was being prepared. Nothing could be allowed to stand in the way.

He hated himself for it, but he could feel the excitement building. It wouldn't be long now. He'd stay here till then. Waiting for the opportunity to present itself.

Then, like a guest at a masquerade ball, he would reveal himself.

Even if it was the last thing he ever did.

\*\*\*

It was nearly half-two by the time Vicky and Harding rejoined Tobe in the waiting room. Side by side they'd appeared, as close as two people could get without holding hands. Tobe felt a twinge of jealousy. Now that Matt was out of the picture he had thought— Shit, she'd only known the man for a few hours and yet their body language spoke volumes.

He'd been watching her since the meeting on the beach. The lingering looks in Harding's direction, that kiss in the car park outside, the cosy little lunch date. Vicky was attracted to him, it was bloody obvious. To the cameraman he seemed like an oddball, though. A real cold fish, who was more interested in the storm than anything else. Of course, that all might have changed now. Tobe would've given his left arm to know what they'd been discussing.

"Anything happen, Tobe?" Vicky asked as she approached him.

"Depends on what you mean. Your mate Woodhead's been on the prowl again. Went upstairs a short while ago."

Harding sat down a few seats away from Tobe. The cameraman looked sideways at him, fighting the urge to curl his lip.

"I bet you fifty quid he was going to see those fishermen, or his friends who were injured. I'd like to be a fly on the wall up there." Vicky rolled her eyes to the tall ceiling.

"We'd never get past security with the camera."

"I know, but a girl can dream, can't she?"

*So can a boy*, thought Tobe. *So can I.*

"Right, so we stick around and wait for the OBU to show up, then. Or for something more interesting to happen." Vicky dropped into the chair beside Harding. "You can go for a break now if you like, Tobe. Canteen's just down there, turn right, go along the corridor and then right again. You can't miss it."

Tobe was hesitant, in two minds about leaving the couple alone again. They'd only just got back! In the end, however, his growling stomach won. It had always been his first love, food. Never ignored you, never stood you up, never told you it just wanted to be friends.

As he walked away, he turned back once to see if Vicky was watching him. She wasn't. Inhaling deeply, Tobe held the camera to his chest and followed his nose to the canteen.

\*\*\*

Wayne and Phil had been placed together on the same ward, along with three other men Rob didn't recognise. Both would be staying in overnight for observation.

"Just a precaution," stated the matron on duty, a woman with a kindly face and a slight frame. "They should be fine tomorrow, touch wood." She brushed the door jamb with her fingers. Rob was encouraged to see that in this technological age, there was still a certain amount of room for blind faith. And at least she hadn't said they'd be "right as rain" in no time. That particular phrase was enough to turn Rob's stomach after everything he'd witnessed.

Wayne's family clamoured round the boy, almost to the point of suffocation. His girlfriend, a young girl with a ponytail, was perched on the bed next to him, her arm draped around his shoulders. Mum and Dad were on seats at either side, pressing close to the mattress; Mum no doubt wishing she could climb on the bed as well.

Rob's youthful crewmate, torso all strapped up, gave him a wave when he came in. Wayne said something to his family, and they rose as one to greet Rob, all smiles and arm-claps. Wayne's girlfriend even planted a smacker on his lips.

"Wayne's been telling us all about how you saved him, Rob," said the lad's mother.

"I can't thank you enough," chirped the girlfriend.

"There's a pint at The Seagull with your name on it, son," bellowed the father.

Embarrassed, Rob smiled and thanked them, saying

he was glad to help. But it was nice to be popular on today of all days. He just wished he could have done more for the others…

Eventually, Rob managed to extricate himself from the bosom of Wayne's family, leaving them to fuss over their hero once more. He went over to the facing bed where his Coxswain, Phil Holmes, was sitting up, too, hands folded across his chest. His family hadn't arrived yet, so he was more than pleased to have company.

"I think they're planning on making you an honorary Gough," he said, laughing, as Rob sat down on an orange plastic chair. "You should see your face, lad."

"Yeah." Rob could imagine the colour of his cheeks. "So how are you, Chief?"

"I'm just about going mad cooped up like this, I don't mind telling you."

"You've only been here a few hours," Rob said.

"Aye, but it seems like forever. You know what I'm like, Rob. I have to be up and about." Phil rolled over a bit so he could see his friend better. "But between you and me the sister there is worse than Genghis Khan. I daren't set foot out of bed." Rob raised his eyebrows. "Don't let that face fool you, she can be a vixen right enough."

Rob chuckled. "How did the scan go?"

"Like being in a bloody coffin for forty minutes. *Christ!* I kept telling them I was fine, but they wouldn't listen."

"They're just playing it safe. You *were* out for the count back there."

"So they tell me." Phil looked worried by this. "I don't remember a thing after we hit the storm. There was a bright light, I think, and… no, it's gone. Is The Jenny all right?"

"Some damage to the cabin windows where—" Rob stopped himself short, not knowing if he should mention the rotor-blade that had hit the boat; it'd been removed, but was still a reminder of the close call... Hopkins' final words to him were ringing in his ears. "It's nothing too serious, but she'll have to go away for repairs."

Phil winced. When something happened to The Jenny he took it personally, like he would if anything happened to the real Jenny. "But we got the fishermen out of the water, right?"

"Right."

Phil studied Rob's face closely. "Not all of them, though. I can tell. How many?"

"Four."

"Shit!"

"We got Lou, David, George Turner, oh and Harry Dale. There are two still missing, Brian Turner and whoever else Lou set on for that trip."

"Probably Josh Bramwell, he was keen to do some work for the Turners last time I saw him. How are the others doing?"

Rob passed on what he knew, which wasn't much. He tried to paraphrase what Leo and Ben had said, but gave up after the first couple of sentences, and explained it all as best he could himself. Throughout his monologue Phil looked at him with increasing suspicion.

"Maybe I hit my head harder than I thought," he said when Rob was finished. "It sounded like you were telling me those men were breathing underwater."

"Er... not exactly, at least I don't think so. It's a bit complicated, something to do with premature babies and oxygenated water." Rob poked his tongue out of the side of his mouth. "Probably best if you wait for Ben to drop by."

"Right enough, I'll do that. But it all sounds like one big pile of manure to me."

Rob rocked back on the chair legs. "I don't know what to believe anymore, Chief. All I know is that in one morning I've seen four friends wind up in comas, with a couple more folk still out there somewhere – probably dead. Two of my shipmates have been injured in the rescue attempt, and my girlfriend is more or less accusing me of being selfish for going out on the call in the first place instead of playing happy families with her old man up at the lighthouse."

"This is Stanley Keets we're talking about, I presume." Phil grabbed a glass of water from his bedside table and took a sip. "I wouldn't worry about that too much. He's always been the same, cleaved to his daughter when his wife walked out on him."

"I nearly hit him when he walked into A&E, you know."

Phil brought the glass to his lips again, but pulled it away without drinking. "You *nearly* hit him, eh?"

"Yeah. He was saying things about my family and…" Rob left it there.

"I admire your restraint, son. Listen, when I get out of here I'll go and have a word with his lass."

"Dawn."

"Dawn, aye. Explain the situation. Stanley Keets or no Stanley Keets, I guarantee you she'll be back in your arms again before you know it."

Rob snorted. "Somehow I don't think so. She's not too keen on the lifeboat. Dawn worries about me. It's only natural, I know, but…"

"Puts a strain on relationships." Phil spoke like a man with experience. "Some people can handle it, others… Doesn't help matters when there's someone around sticking his oar in at every turn, if you'll pardon the expression."

"I think, well actually I *know* she wants me to quit."

"I see." Phil rolled onto his back and looked up at the ceiling. "And will you, Rob?"

This time Rob didn't answer. He just stared up at that same spot above them as if the cracks in the paintwork held the key to the meaning of life itself.

## Chapter Twenty-Four
### Lost and Found

Harding was safe and warm, his face turned to the glowing circle in the sky. What's more he was content, untroubled by the day's events, by thoughts he shouldn't even be having. There was no need for thinking here. Harding could simply lay back and relax, enjoy the tranquility of this place; a place where no harm could possibly come to him.

A hand crawled across his chest, rubbing, kneading the skin beneath his shirt. He found that his own arm was stretched out on the ground – the freshly-cut grass – pinned down by a comforting weight beside him. He pulled the body closer to his own, looking over at the face pressed into his side, chin resting on his ribcage.

Christine smiled up at Harding, her hand now snaking down his torso. It tickled him but he didn't push her away. Moments like this were meant to be cherished. Savoured.

Slowly, she dragged herself up until their lips touched. The sweet smell and taste of her was like honey. Harding reached around Christine with both hands. He would hold on to her like this for all eternity, and never let go.

The kiss seemed to last for hours; who knows, maybe it did. In this special place, anything was possible. Time didn't exist and things would be played out exactly as they should be. Harding brushed a strand of hair out of her face as she broke off.

A strand of *blonde* hair.

What had happened to all those gorgeous ginger locks? The ones he loved so much, the ones he'd buried his hands in more times than he could recall. But that wasn't the only strange thing. The freckles had disappeared from around Christine's nose and cheeks. Granted, they weren't prominent like some people's, but he knew they were there. And now he was aware of their absence.

"Happy?" the woman asked him.

Harding squinted. Even Christine's voice had changed. Then he realised that this wasn't Christine Harding at all. It wasn't the woman he'd married almost twenty years ago, when they were both still in their teens.

It was Victoria West.

"Are you happy, Jason?" she asked him a second time.

"You know I am," he answered softly. They kissed again, this time more intensely. Jason Harding gave himself to her utterly; so completely he feared he would lose his own identity, his very soul. His body responded to her easily, as if it was used to her touch.

Harding allowed himself to drift away, safe in the knowledge that he was with Vicky. It was time to face up to his feelings. Feelings he'd tried to ignore, but which were too strong to suppress. Vicky had always been here, somehow he'd known that all along. He would overcome the guilt, the torment, to be with her. She made everything all right. Harding was complete.

He loved Vicky.

The very thought made him giddy, but it was true. He could say it now without hindrance.

"I love you."

"I love you too, Dad."

Harding struggled to his senses. Vicky was gone, and the ground beneath him was hard. It rocked from side to side as he looked this way and that. Opposite, his son, Alex – with that same flame-coloured hair of his mother's – was watching him quizzically. Harding gripped the wooden sides of the boat that curved upwards around him. A small rowing boat built for just two or three.

No, not again. "Vicky. VICKEEEE!" He screamed out her name. Why did she have to leave him now? He didn't know if he could face this alone. Not this time.

"Dad? Dad, what's wrong?" Alex was getting up out of his seat, a thin strip of wood just wide enough to sit on.

"Alex, no. Stay where you are." Harding had a warning hand out, but his son didn't see the danger. "Alex, please. You have to sit back down. It's very important that you do it. Do it now!"

Alex started to lower himself, frightened by his father's reaction. "O-Okay, Dad."

Good, Alex was sitting again. Maybe Harding *could* change things this time. Perhaps it didn't have to happen like it did before. At that moment he was convinced he could stop it. That he had an uncanny mystical ability to turn back time, erase this disaster and start again, like rubbing out graphite pencil marks on a sketch pad.

But suddenly the boat struck that rock, a jagged grey monstrosity sticking up out of the lake: that's how Harding remembered it in his mind, though in reality he suspected it was little more than on oversized stone lurking beneath the water. In any event, the hard knock was sufficient to jerk the boat sideways. Harding's outstretched arms were ready as always. He wasn't finished yet; he was prepared for this moment. After playing it over so many times, how could he be anything but?

Yet he was always too late. He never made it to the other side of the boat in time. Alex was tipped into the cold lake, same as before. Harding stood uselessly by in the tiny vessel as his son was sucked under, swallowed by moistened jaws; the surface sealing itself over straight away.

He was trapped.

Harding experienced about a million different emotions all at once. They prevented him from acting. Paralysed him.

Only when he heard the shouting from the bank did he do something. Harding jumped into the water after Alex. It wasn't that he couldn't swim at all. He could, and so could Alex; they'd made sure of that, his loving parents. It was just that he couldn't swim on that particular day.

Harding sank like he was made of lead.

The lake hadn't looked all that deep from the bank, but now that he was actually immersed in the damned thing, it seemed to be a bottomless chasm filled with putrid water. There was no end to it, and he couldn't see a thing past three inches. Bubbles of air, huge bubbles the size of tennis balls, shot past his face. They came from his open mouth, which was even now drawing in the rancid slime that was the essence of the lake.

The doctor's part of his brain was furiously yelling warnings about poison and pollution, but the father bit was more concerned with another, more important thing.

Harding's arms were swinging about, dragged back in waves of dense liquid. By chance his hand struck something soft, but it flew past too quickly for him to grab hold. Harding kicked his legs and propelled himself in the direction of the object. He reached out and— Yes, he had it in his hands!

But it was only relatively small, and it felt rubbery to the touch. Harding realised he was cradling an old wellington boot in his arms, no doubt dislodged from its resting place at the bottom of the lake by his mad scramble to save his son.

Then something hit him in the stomach. Winded, Harding let out even more of the air he'd been preserving. Thankfully he had enough of his wits about him to keep hold of this torpedo. He ran his fingers briskly over the surface. It was hard and round like a bowling ball.

Or a child's skull.

*Alex.*

Harding clutched the boy to him with one hand, bringing an arm around him. With the other he scooped at the water, attempting to claw his way to the surface. With all his might he kicked away from the bed of the lake, wherever it was, holding his fragile charge at his side. Swimming for the both of them.

It was obvious that Alex was no longer breathing. Harding was having difficulty himself, and his lungs were much larger. Add that to the fact that Alex fell into the water first and there was only one conclusion.

Harding beat this logic into submission with his own diminishing hope. His child wasn't dead yet. Alex still had a chance. Once they were on dry land he could get him breathing again. He was a doctor for Christsakes! He'd read about it in medical journals, seen programmes on the telly, where drowning victims had survived their ordeals even after long periods of time.

If only he could find the surface, break that film of liquid. But it was nowhere in sight.

Then Harding heard the noise. A patter; *pitter-patter*. Rain drumming constantly against the lake. A spring shower. He'd use the sound to guide himself upwards, to pinpoint their means of escape. They both needed air, and soon.

The same thing as before, Harding gulped down rank torrents of lake water. He swallowed until he felt certain he would vomit. The sound of the downpour was louder, accompanied by the *thud-thudding* of rumbling thunder.

His face pushed through the boundary separating lake from sky. It took him by surprise, but he could feel the trickles of rain running down his forehead, diving off his eyebrows like miniature bungee jumpers. Harding could breathe again, and if *he* could, then so might his son.

Another boom of thunder. Harding raised his head. The black storm-cloud was above him, unleashing its deadly load. A screen of solid drizzle slid down in front, cutting him off from the outside world, from the bank, and from any help he could give Alex.

In the rain, Harding saw something. He wasn't sure at first, but then he could make out the shape quite clearly. It was borne of water and yet *was* the water. Harding tried to swim away from it, the rain punching him full in the face now. He witnessed drops of his own blood blending with the lake, carried away on the swirls.

Harding had to get his son away from here. He knew what that thing wanted. To take from him that which he held most dear – along with his sanity for good measure. Harding wouldn't let it happen. Not this time.

Except, as he glanced down at the small form he clung on to, carried in his arms like a stuffed toy, he realised it was too late.

Alex's skin was being scoured off his face, pieces of bone jutting through the gaps. His eyes were so much jelly, running away in the rain. Skeletal arms rested on the top of the lake. Lifeless. Dead. Tufts of sodden ginger hair were falling out of his head in silty clumps.

Harding let go of the cadaver. A current took it away from him almost immediately, and he watched the decomposing thing that he'd once called "Al" and "Troop" and "Captain Mayhem" disappear beneath the curtain of freezing hard H2O.

He wept. He cried out. Nothing could change what had already happened. His son was dead. It was a certainty he had to live with.

Or did he?

Here came the sweeping arc of the Rain Circle, as Vicky had named it. The ends of it raking the lake (or was it a sea now?) like a sharpened comb.

Harding decided. No more struggling, no more longing for escape. He would accept his fate willingly, gladly even. For right now oblivion seemed like a welcome alternative to his living hell.

He waited for it to pass over him, through him. Tearing him up in strips like a piece of paper. Harding waited for the laughter to come. The laughter that sounded so very much like thunder.

*Get ready. Here it is.*

Harding started to scream. He felt the full force of it on his body, pelting him. The end was in sight. He would see Alex again in another, less cruel place.

Just a few more seconds of pain. And he looked up...


...into the eyes of Victoria West.

"You came back for me," he mumbled.

"Jason. Jason, wake up!" Vicky was shaking him as he slowly came to. "You were having a bad dream."

Harding looked mystified for a moment, wondering how he could have dropped off like that. Vicky held him at the shoulders and was taken aback when he suddenly closed his arms around her. The embrace felt good to both of them. Natural almost.

"You were squirming around on the chair. I didn't know what to do." She could feel his whole body trembling, his warm breath on her neck coming in short bursts. Vicky decided not to tell him he'd been shouting out her name.

"I saw…"

"It's okay now. Really, it's okay." Vicky brushed the back of his head in a soothing motion and found that his hair was damp with sweat. Eventually she felt the quaking subside. They reluctantly pulled apart, though Vicky cupped his hands in her own.

"Tell me about it. If you want to, that is."

"No, it's all right, Vicky."

She squeezed his knuckles, her skin closing over the bone. "Was it the same as before? Did you see your son?"

Harding confirmed her suspicions.

"I had dreams like that for years after Caroline died. It's the mind's way of coping with loss, I suppose."

"This is different. They're so… I can't describe it."

"Real?"

"Yes. And you were there, Vicky. At the start."

Vicky edged even closer to Harding. "Was *it* there, too? The Rain Circle?"

Harding nodded. "It was, yes. And it was laughing at me. In my dream it's alive, and it's laughing at me."

She shook her head. "It's only a dream, Jason."

"Was it?"

"Jason, you're scaring me."

Before Harding could say any more, Tobe returned from his lunch, camera still held before him like a talisman to ward off evil. It was never far away from his person. The cameraman looked down at their interlaced hands, seemed like he was about to say something, but sat down at the side of Vicky instead.

It was obvious the stocky man didn't like Harding,

Vicky could tell. But Jason spoke to her colleague regardless.

"Let me ask you something," he said, leaning over Vicky.

"Tobe," the fellow reminded him, still glowering.

"Tobe. You had a chance to look at that footage of the Rain Circle before it went off to your station, didn't you?"

Tobe shrugged. "Sure, while we were waiting for Matt to be seen. So what?"

"Did you notice anything out of the ordinary?"

"Jason, we've been through this already," said Vicky.

"Please. I just need to hear what... Tobe has to say."

"I don't know what you're talking about." Tobe's scowl was evaporating, his expression more bewildered than anything.

"Were there any patterns on the video, anything inside the Rain Circle itself, perhaps?"

Tobe frowned, eyes rolling around as if he was trying to remember.

"There *was* something, wasn't there?"

"Yeah, but it's so stupid. It might just have been a trick of the light, a flash of lightning across the rain."

Now it was Harding's turn to glare. "Just tell me what you saw."

Tobe composed himself, placing the camera across his knees. "Well, if you really must know, I thought I saw... It was—"

"Yes?" asked Vicky herself.

"You saw a face, didn't you?" Harding's eyes narrowed.

Astonished, Vicky looked from Harding to Tobe. And as soon as the cameraman said yes, she realised that Harding was right.

He was right, and deep down she'd known it all along.

## Chapter Twenty-Five
### Intensive Care

Fiona Long pressed her face up against the glass window of the ICU. Inside were four patients hooked up to all manner of monitors. They looked asleep, but there was something very wrong about that slumber: their faces glassy with perspiration, feverish at best.

She hadn't believed it when Beth had told her about them. Four fishermen brought in to Casualty that morning, their lungs full of seawater – and yet they were still breathing. Not only that, but it was the water that had kept them alive so far. It was what was keeping them alive right now. Fiona had jumped at the chance to see for herself, being something of a fan of the unexplained. She had all the books at home: mysterious this, wonders of that. Legends, mythologies and whatever. From frogs and fish dropping out of the sky, to UFOs and Stonehenge, Fiona lapped it all up. Her friends thought she was quite mad, of course. She was a nurse, and nurses were supposed to believe in science and medicine and stuff. But for Fiona it was an escape from her everyday life, from having to tell people that their relatives had just died, or they had some debilitating illness. Her hobby had to be as far removed from all that as possible, or at least that was the general idea. She never thought the two worlds would collide like this. Not in her hospital.

"See, what did I tell you?" said Beth Spencer, her dark-skinned face a reflection in the glass.

"So, what d'you have to do?" asked Fiona.

"Just keep an eye on them. Call for assistance if they wake up."

"Wow." Fiona misted up the window with her breath.

"You want to take a look? Go ahead. I'll keep an eye out at the door, and if matron comes down the corridor, I'll just say one of the doctors sent you to check up on me or something."

Fiona grinned. "What, because they were too hungover to come themselves?" she added cheekily. She knew what most of the physicians were like at St August's. If she were ever ill, she'd insist on being driven somewhere – anywhere – else. There was no way on Earth she'd let them operate on her here, that was for sure. Half the surgeons were practically blind from playing with themselves in their offices – mirror in one hand, todger in the other ("Oh I do so love you, doctor." "Not as much as I love *you*, doctor!"). All right, so she might be a little biased after what had happened with Mal, sorry Dr Malcolm Oakes, but she wasn't stupid. She had eyes and ears.

But then matron wasn't stupid, either. She would never swallow that line. If Fiona was caught wagging off again she'd go ballistic this time. Still, it might just be worth the risk. "Oh, I don't know."

"Look, it's up to you. Just get a move on if you're going."

Soon there would be experts swarming all over this place, thought Fiona, taking samples and running tests. She wouldn't be able to get anywhere near. This was the best chance she'd ever have to take a look, and Fiona made her mind up to grab it with both hands.

The nurse looked left and right. All clear. In she went.

Fiona felt a buzz like she'd never felt before. She smoothed down her light blue uniform and walked into the room, pretending she was here on some urgent medical matter or another. This was clearly wrong, ogling these men like animals at the zoo, but it was also very exciting.

Just what was the matter with them, though? That was the question. Had some underwater organism taken up residence in their bodies? Was it even now keeping them alive in some sort of symbiotic relationship? Naw, too far-fetched. Too *Star Trek*, Fiona told herself.

Even so, she couldn't help jumping to bizarre conclusions. It was in her nature.

The patient in the bed nearest to her was older than the rest, as far as she could tell. She stepped closer, peering into the man's mouth. Beth had been telling the truth all right, it was full of liquid and looked like an organic well. It bubbled as the man's chest rose and fell.

The heart monitor showed a steady beat, the electronic line peaking, then diving. A *bip, bip, bip*, echoed around the room. Blood pressure: 120 over 80. In every other regard he was perfectly healthy. It was the oddest thing she'd ever seen.

Fiona gazed down the length of the bed and noticed straps around his wrists and ankles. Purely a precautionary measure. The men were in no way dangerous, but if they should suddenly wake up and find that their throats were full of liquid, well... It was for their own safety as much as anything else.

But what would happen when they did eventually

wake up? Fiona asked herself. Would they just spew up all that goo in their systems, the doctors beating them on the backs to get them breathing air again? Or would they have to live in a tank for the rest of their lives like six-foot fish?

(That blasted imagination of hers again!)

Or maybe they'd be able to breathe on land as well as underwater, like that man in the TV series from the '70s, that bloke from *Dallas*, she'd forgotten his name. It wasn't important, it was all fantasy anyway.

The reality was probably much more mundane, and heartbreaking. Fiona doubted whether they'd ever wake again, and even if they did who's to say what state their brains would be in? She believed that miracles could happen, but this was pushing it.

Fiona moved across to the next bed. The patient she was looking at now was quite attractive. That was to say, he would be once he was towelled off. No one looks their best when they've just been shipwrecked, trawler-wrecked, or whatever the correct terminology was. He looked a lot like the older man, too. Father and son, most likely.

In front of her the young man's heart monitor started to rise and fall much quicker, the pure green line shooting up at intervals. The *bip, bip, bip* of his machine now a *bi-bip, bi-bip, bi-bip*.

*Can he sense that I'm here?* thought Fiona. Often coma patients could hear visitors talking or could tell when someone was in the room. This was a different case, but the same might be true.

Fiona went to the foot of the bed to look at his chart, returning with it still in her hand. "It's all right," she scanned the paper for a name, "David. I'm Nurse Long."

Was he going to wake up? If so, she'd probably better fetch Beth and get the hell out of there. But something stopped Fiona from doing that. A curiosity, perhaps. She wanted to know what they'd been through. Wanted to hear their tale.

"You've been in an accident, while you were out fishing this morning. But you're safe now. You're at St August's hospital and we're going to take care of you," she said, her voice almost a whisper.

The monitor began to beep much faster. Too fast. Something was wrong (more wrong?)

Fiona caught movement out of the corner of her eye. David's arm was twitching.

*Oh no! Oh God, no. I knew I shouldn't have come in here, I just knew it. Now I'm going to get in so much trouble, I'm going to—*

Both arms were twitching. Fiona looked more closely. No, not twitching. Swelling up, at the wrists.

Fiona dropped the chart. The metal clanged against the floor, but she didn't hear it. It was far away, somewhere else.

She stumbled backwards, never taking her eyes off those wrists. The straps were creaking, splitting down the seams. Fiona put both hands to her mouth. As a nurse she'd seen all kinds of things, but nothing could compare to this. David's arms were now as thick as telegraph poles and expanding rapidly.

*Snap!* One wrist was free.
*Snap!* Now the other.
Beth. She had to get Beth!

Fiona couldn't move. Her body belonged to someone else, and her mouth opened to shout for help, but nothing came out.

*Any minute now, he'll wake up and start to gag*, she thought. *But Christ Almighty, what's* happening *to him?*

David woke up. He turned and fixed her with eyes that were no longer brown, or green, or blue. Eyes layered with a thick coat of… of something that looked very much like raw egg white. It dripped out of each corner and trickled down his face. Transparent, but so viscous it dulled the pupils themselves.

He opened and closed his mouth now, water spilling out over his chin and soaking the hospital gown he was wearing. And his face seemed to erupt with sweat. Like flowers blooming, each bead popped up on the surface of his skin, one on top of the other until there was a full bed of "plants".

When he breathed in he sounded like someone with bronchitis, just ten times worse. His only oxygen coming from the liquid still inside his lungs.

Fiona broke free of her trance, retreating once more. Desperate to get away from this and back to normality. She no longer craved the unexplained – let the experts deal with it. Right now she'd settle for putting her feet up and watching a soap.

She backed up further, then ran into an obstacle. The adjoining bed.

Fiona turned her head to the left and saw that the two men in the facing beds were rising; exactly like David. She had to make for the door. Fiona didn't know why, but something told her it would be the end of her if she stayed.

Then the arm came from behind, wrapping itself around her neck. The old man from the first bed took hold of Fiona. Her hands came up to free the grip, but it was too strong, the bulging forearm pressing against her windpipe, crushing it.

David broke free of his ankle straps and stood up. Fiona watched, petrified, as he tramped towards her.

She wanted to say to them: "Stop, *please*. I only want to help you."

But they didn't need, or want, her help. They wanted something else entirely.

David smiled as he stepped up to Fiona. Then reality seemed to melt all around her.

"Come on, come on," Beth said impatiently, glancing up and down the corridor again. What was keeping her friend? Surely it didn't take that long to just look over some fishermen in comas.

There was a bumping noise from inside the ICU.

Beth whirled around and looked through the window. She could see figures. The patients were up and about. But no sign of Fiona.

Hardly believing what she'd observed, the second nurse opened the door and dashed in, ready to help the men back to their beds and push the button on the wall for help.

However, as soon as the door was wide, Beth could see something wasn't right. The men looked... abnormal, their faces—

And when Beth came into the room proper, she almost slipped sideways. She dropped her gaze to the puddle of syrupy grue spreading out over the floor, and to the remains of the nurse's uniform floating on top.

Beth Spencer screamed at the top of her voice.

## Chapter Twenty-Six
### Impact

Thanks to the marvellous acoustics in what had once been Fairbanks House, the screams nurse Beth Spencer made could be heard in most parts of the hospital, echoing down corridors, travelling at speed up and down air vents. High and low it came.

They heard it in the Geriatric Department, in Orthopaedics and on the wards. An agonising shriek so filled with terror, it made everyone it came into contact with shudder involuntarily. It actually hurt the ears at first, such was its intensity, and although St August's had witnessed its fair share of howling patients in the past, none had ever cried out because their lives were in danger – not directly, anyway. And certainly not because the scene they were witnessing was so hideous and bizarre that it defied all logical explanation.

It was just such a scream that reached the ears of Vicky, Tobe and Harding in the A&E waiting room. They exchanged horrified glances. The "something interesting" Vicky had spoken of earlier looked like it had arrived. As a security man dressed in black ran to the lift, barking something into his walkie-talkie, she jumped up and tugged at Tobe's arm.

"Come on, bring the camera," said Vicky.

"Where're we going?"

"To see what the hell that racket was."

Tobe looked like he would be content if he never found out what the hell it was, but he followed, nonetheless.

Harding remained seated.

"Jason, are you coming?" Vicky was almost at the stairs and called over her shoulder.

Harding shook his head. He couldn't go. Surely after all he'd told her she understood that. Just being in a hospital again made him sick to his stomach. If he was to go up to the wards… And that yell, it sounded too much like Christine's when he'd dragged his boy to the riverbank. The scream of a woman who knew her baby was gone and never coming back. A scream full of horror, despair and lost hope.

"All right, it's up to you." A disappointed Vicky charged up the stairs, followed closely by the puffing shape of Tobe, still messing with his camera. They had to hurry; the lift was already ascending.

"Hey, hey! Where d'you think you're going?" shouted the woman from reception, who had been momentarily distracted by the noise.

It was too late. Vicky and Tobe were already gone. Harding watched as their feet disappeared behind the railings at the top, heading almost certainly into danger. The woman he'd said he loved in his dream, even though she was a stranger to him. The person he'd felt bonded to in ways he couldn't explain.

Yet still he could not move from that orange plastic seat in the waiting room.

***

"Jesus! What was that?"

Phil was up in the bed, twisting round. Rob was rising, too, and at the glass window of the ward in no time at all.

"What is it, Rob?" Wayne and his family were all gaping at him. "What's going on?"

"I don't know. Can't see a damned thing from this angle. Hold on, I'll go and take a look."

Phil started to get out of bed and Rob pointed at him. "Whoa, Chief. You're not going anywhere. Hopkins'd have my guts for garters. It's probably just one of the patients getting over-excited or something."

Phil sat on the edge of his bed and sighed. Probably realising he couldn't keep up with Rob anyway – and he still looked a little woozy, if the truth be told – so he waved him on. But they both knew it was more than just a hysterical patient somewhere in the hospital. All the lifeboat men in that room recognised the sound of a person in trouble when they heard one.

After an hour or more sat in the chair by Phil's bed, Rob felt stiff and tired. His shoulder was aching where he'd pulled Wayne up from the side of The Jenny. The muscles all bunched up and tense. But the more he moved about, the less it hurt. He let the thought of that scream take his mind off things, something to focus on other than the state of his love life or the rescue at sea. His boots squeaked on the shiny floor as he tried to gauge where the sound had come from.

He chose to turn right.

Rob sprinted past wards where men and women were stirring, wondering what on Earth was going on. Baffled faces appeared at entranceways and windows, doctors and nurses stood about not knowing exactly what to do.

Rob ran on, through a set of double doors, past the sign that announced in white block capitals on a blue background: INTENSIVE CARE.

\*\*\*

Vicky and Tobe chased after the security man. She managed to make it to the top of the stairs just as the lift doors closed again and saw the bulky figure trotting off down a corridor. Tobe was miles behind. She couldn't wait for him, couldn't risk losing their guide.

Vicky began running along the same length of hospital. Tobe's head rose above the last of the steps. "Try and keep up, Tobe," she called as she drove on.

"You... try running... with... this," gasped Tobe breathlessly, the camera merely a convenient excuse for his lack of velocity. But Vicky barely heard him. She was too busy keeping her target in sight: the black-uniformed figure up ahead.

The man looked back.

Vicky ducked behind a column in the wall, Tobe trailing her at the rear. "Please don't let him see us," she whispered over and over to herself, like the mantra of a religious order.

Cautiously, she peered round the column. The security man had vanished.

"Bugger!"

"What's up," grunted Tobe, finally reaching her.

"We lost him."

The spot where she'd seen the man last was a T-junction of sorts. He could have gone one of two ways, left or right. Vicky jogged up the aisle and turned the corner. She didn't spot the shape until it was too late, and by that time it had knocked her to the ground.

Vicky saw stars as the lumbering form towered over her...

\*\*\*

Meredith Patterson had been a security man for nigh on seven years now, ever since his "retirement" from the force – in his early forties, due to a small dispute with one of his superiors over the handling of a prisoner.

And in all that time, both as a copper and hired muscle, he'd never known anyone to cry out that loud. Whoever was doing it was in real trouble. Maybe there was a rapist or a psychopath loose on the upper floors. With no way to contact his former colleagues in time, Meredith and his small band of security men – three in total – were all that stood between the patients and whatever was roaming the hospital, causing all the uproar.

"Ctzzzz... Pat... Pat?" The walkie-talkie crackled into life once more and Meredith depressed the switch on the side.

"Go ahead, Graeme." Meredith was speaking to Graeme Bowler, his second-in-command, in charge of the east and south wings. He was a good man, but prone to panic in crisis situations – not really an advantage in this line of work.

"The screams... fzzzzz... from... czzzzz." What the fuck was the matter with these things? thought Meredith; they'd been acting up all day. He managed to catch one word in a sea of static: "ICU." Then there was a shattering of glass in the background.

"Graeme? Graeme, please respond." The radio fizzled and popped, then cut out completely.

ICU. That was only minutes away from his position. Meredith drew his baton and charged off up the hall.

\*\*\*

The shadow filling the space above her seemed huge, menacing, distorted.

"Tobe..." Vicky called out weakly.

A hand reached out and closed around her forearm. It pulled her up effortlessly. Her legs were unsteady, her head spinning from the fall, but she tried to make out who had hold of her.

There was no mistaking that jet-black hair, or those roguish good looks.

"You stupid twat. Why don't you watch where you're going?" she snapped, anger taking over.

Rob Woodhead made no attempt to apologise.

Tobe joined Vicky and raised his eyebrows at the man. "Are... are you all right, Vicky?"

"Yeah, I think so. No thanks to this clod, though. He just knocked the wind out of me, that's all."

Tobe saw the way Rob was eyeing him up and down, the grimace when he clocked the camera. Slowly, Tobe eased himself behind Vicky, putting her in the firing line if there was any trouble.

# The Wet

"If you're up here for a story, you can just turn around and piss off back where you came from," barked Rob.

"We heard the screams. Thought we could help," retorted Vicky.

"Yeah, right."

"Well, I don't know about you, but I want to find out what's going on around here."

"And splash it all over the tea-time news!"

Vicky was fed up with this. "Look, Woodhead. Just what is your problem with us? Or have you got a problem with *me*, is that it? I don't need this kind of abuse. I've got a soundman who sees me right on that score!" She began striding down the corridor, choosing the right path because it was where Rob had been heading. Obviously there was nothing down the way he'd just come.

"I don't like the way you lot barge in and feed off other people's misery," Rob shouted after her.

Vicky rounded on him suddenly, taking him a bit by surprise. "Oh no, there's more too it than that. This is personal for you, isn't it? Besides, you don't know a thing about me. I don't feed off *anyone's* misery. In fact, until today I was interviewing people for—"

"Hold it." Rob was looking down at her feet. Vicky had been so caught up in the argument she hadn't noticed that she was walking in puddles of water. No, they weren't puddles as such. It was more like when you have a burst pipe and the water invades your house, or if you live next to a river and it bursts its banks, water seeping in under doors, ruining carpets and wallpaper.

"Someone's left a tap running," said Tobe.

"It's coming from this direction." Rob splashed through the spillage, tracing the direction of the current. Vicky and Tobe were hot on his heels, the camera loaded and ready. When in doubt, it was always best to leave it going.

Rob took two steps, bringing him round the next corner, and shrank back, almost knocking Vicky over again.

"You stupid—" she started, then saw something shoot past them and slam up against the wall.

Vicky barely had time to register the security man's pained face – the guy they'd been following, definitely – or his dark uniform, before his body exploded across the lime-green plaster, splattering it a deep red.

He was carried on a wave of white foam, which held him there for a second before dispersing to let him slide to the floor. His baton came clattering down the corridor after him and stopped just shy of his feet.

The three of them gaped at this grotesque frame. His head now looked like a watermelon dropped from a great height. From his limbs dripped skin that was like a wet coat of paint. Eyes that had been round and bulging as he was catapulted through the air now resembled fried eggs oozing down his cheeks.

Vicky felt the bile rising in her throat. The semi-digested meal she'd eaten with Harding all set for an encore performance. Tobe hid behind his camera, detaching himself from it all the only way he knew how: by filming it, pretending he was watching it in some nice, safe editing suite back at Creation-Time.

Rob wrenched his eyes from the dead man, and turned the corner fully.

Vicky tried to pull him back, but he shrugged her off.

"Wait, where are you..." There was no point in continuing. Rob had moved on. Vicky took a deep breath and went after him, cursing her own stupidity and ambition, as she had done in the chopper that morning – before promising she wouldn't put herself in a situation such as that one again. So much for promises.

When she stepped out into the open corridor, Vicky saw what she saw.

But she no longer believed the evidence of her own sight.

# Part Three
**Dark Waters**

"Human beings were invented by water as a device for transporting itself from one place to another…"

*Another Roadside Attraction*, Tom Robbins

## Chapter Twenty-Seven
### Sable

The ripples grew in strength and number, until they became tiny waves of a sort. Then these pushed further and yet further outwards…

***

There was something wrong in the quiet seaside village of Sable. Something very wrong indeed. Everyone could feel it. The delicate balance the inhabitants enjoyed on a day-to-day basis had been upset.

The older residents recognised the signs – the last time there had been an atmosphere like this was when Hitler tried to invade these shores – but others knew in their own way, deep down in their souls.

It wasn't simply a feeling, however. You only had to look around, peek through the net curtains to see that no one was venturing out. The streets were empty, regardless of the fact it was a Saturday: a shopping day. No cars were on the narrow roads through the village.

It was as quiet as quiet could be.

And for the first time since Sable had been a mere settlement in the Middle Ages, when there used to be a tavern instead of a pub, The Seagull was all closed up at the weekend. No doubt about it, something had happened – was still happening – inside.

Mr and Mrs Kelly could feel the strangeness settling over Sable, too. More than most probably. And if either of them had cared to go upstairs for a moment, upon entering the main bedroom they would have seen the dark patch on the far wall – the adjoining wall – as large as an old master. The diamond-effect wallpaper peeling off in soggy strips. If they *had* seen this, perhaps they would've assumed that they had rising damp, or that there was something fundamentally wrong with the structure of their house. Or would they run at the thought of what was on the other side of that wall, what was making its way through from the other side?

From the Tomkinson's side?

Then there was the thing emerging from old mother Holmes' place, cursing itself for its lack of restraint. For not curbing the killer instinct that had gripped it, a thirst for revenge as the madness clouded its mind. There would be time for all that later, it reminded itself. For the time being it must find others. It needed these people, the good people of Sable, and would use them accordingly.

After all, they were only flesh and blood.

## Chapter Twenty-Eight
### Confrontation

Victoria West stood paralysed with fear.

Rob had halted a little way up the corridor, gazing down the other end at the devastating display. The wall of the Intensive Care Unit had been totally blown away as if a bomb had exploded inside. Bits of wood and glass jutted out around its wrecked frame, the rest of the partition – plaster and stone – was mixed into the watery-red stream flowing down the corridor itself.

"I-I never heard an explosion," said Vicky, more to herself than to Rob.

"That's because there wasn't one."

Rob started walking again, leaving Vicky well behind. As he came closer, he noticed there was a hole in the adjacent wall as well. It looked like a boulder had rumbled through the ICU and continued on into another part of the hospital, with nothing and no one getting in its way. Rob recalled the security man flying past him on a jet of water. The Turners and Harry Dale were in the ICU, Ben had told him. Their lungs full of liquid. This was no coincidence.

Judging the area to be relatively safe, Rob stepped up to examine the destruction. The holes were seeping with wetness, and thick, slimy globules dangled here and there.

"Woodhead! Behind you!"

Instinctively Rob jumped, turning as he did so. At first he couldn't see what Vicky was warning him about. Then he looked down.

It crawled out of the shattered ICU on all fours. Rob grimaced as it straightened itself, kneeling before him. Its dark skin was shrivelled like a prune, hands in an imploring gesture. Two eyes the shape of full moons shone out of its face, the only part of its visage to escape the wrinkling. Whatever it was wore a blue dress, hanging from it like rags on a scarecrow. Rob spotted a white tag on its chest and mouthed the name "Spencer".

Vicky had journeyed up the corridor now, but kept her distance from Rob and the creature that looked very much like a wizened mummy, only it was far from dusty and dry.

It opened a flat mouth to speak, lips that had once been full, now horribly deflated. "Help... must..." the thing breathed, minute traces of blood escaping with each word.

"My God!" whispered Vicky, suddenly realising there was no threat. This had once been a young, vibrant human being. A nurse at St August's. The thought filled her with dismay.

"We'll fetch a doctor. You'll be okay," Rob told her, but his assurances sounded ridiculous even to him. What could a doctor do for her? She was beyond anyone's help, all shrivelled up like she'd been in the bath for ten years.

Nurse Spencer seemed to acknowledge this herself, and tried to laugh. Rob and Vicky looked on, dumbfounded, as she hobbled on her knees and her eyes went back into her skull.

With a last-ditch groan, the woman fell forward onto the floor, the puddles splashing up around her. Rob went over, to feel for a pulse perhaps, or to carry her somewhere? He had no idea where. But it was far too late. Already she was melting into the ground, shedding her shrinking skin like a snake. Soon there was nothing left but her uniform.

Vicky put a hand to her mouth.

"Did I miss anything?" asked Tobe, sidling up to her, camera on his shoulder. The next thing they knew, Vicky had vomited up her lunch all over his shoes.

\*\*\*

"Did you hear that?"

Mick Barron quizzed the man in the next bed along. Douglas Walker, his plastered leg suspended before him in mid-air, tilted his head. "Hear what?"

"That!" Mick waited again, giving Douglas a chance to redeem himself, to use those massive ears strapped to the side of his head. It was a puzzle really that someone with such enormous lugholes as Douglas should be as deaf as he was. Mick had lost count of the amount of times he'd had to repeat himself during their time together on the ward. Playing Scrabble or Monopoly was a nightmare ("What was that word again, Mick?" "How much did you say I owe?"). Trust him to get lumbered with someone like that.

"I can't hear nothing," Douglas informed him.

"Are you sure you're not in here to have your ears syringed?"

"My what?"

"And I don't suppose you heard that screaming earlier either, did you?"

Douglas looked vacantly at his ward-mate.

"Forget it. It's not important." Mick listened again. Yes, there it was, the faint rumbling noise. It was coming from behind him. Getting up out of bed, he put on the hideous green dressing gown his wife had packed for him and eased into his slippers. Stuff Matron, it had been three days since the op. If her hospital wasn't so full of weird sounds and lunatics screeching the place down, he wouldn't be up at all now, would he?

Perhaps the rumbling meant they were in for a summer storm? After several days of sunshine Sable was pushing its luck a bit. But Mick could see no darkening of the sky outside. The massive window at the far end of the ward showed only blue.

"Where are you going?" asked Douglas.

"For a walk."

"What?"

"I said I'm going to the chippy, d'you want anything?"

A mystified Douglas shook his head.

Mick looked around. One or two of the other patients had noticed the noise as well and were muttering to each other. Only Douglas, it seemed, was happily oblivious to the banging. Louder with each passing second.

Mick had taken a few short steps when the cracks appeared in the wall. They zig-zagged down from top to bottom, over Douglas' bed.

"Douglas," he roared, preparing to run across.

"What?" asked the man, cupping a hand to his ear.

Then the stonework bowed inwards and Douglas disappeared beneath a giant wrecking ball of water.

Crushed completely flat under the pressure.

\*\*\*

Tobe wiped down his shoes with some spare tissues he had in his pocket. Vicky's heaving had eventually subsided and she was busy apologising to the cameraman, more embarrassed because she'd lost control than anything. Although, given the circumstances...

Raised voices and anguished cries drifted up the corridor, distracting the group. Vicky tugged at Tobe's shirt and the pair of them went off to check them out. When they turned the corner yet again, a red smear on the facing wall the only remnant of the security guard they'd originally followed, they saw patients falling over themselves to escape into the hallway.

"Get the camera ready," said Vicky, composing herself, wiping away the last specks of sick from around her mouth with her sweater sleeve. "Tobe?"

Her colleague was watching those folk as they filled the hallway, the expressions on their faces ones of pure terror. They'd personally witnessed a lot today and Tobe didn't look convinced that he wanted to witness any more. But he nodded and tagged along.

The ward nearest to them was in turmoil. Vicky squeezed in through the door just as a bed hit the wall on the far side, its castors spinning in the air. Sunlight from the big window made it impossible to see what was happening at first, but as her eyes adjusted she glimpsed shapes moving around in the room. Tobe bent down, filming on one knee, half-hiding behind Vicky again.

A patient wearing a green dressing gown and hiding under one of the beds chose that moment to break cover. He barely got to his feet before something travelled straight through him like an arrow. It punctured his back and exited at his chest with a splatter of scarlet. The water blast dissolved, leaving a gaping chasm in the man, froth bubbling around its edges. He collapsed forwards with a grunt, hands up as if he was in a bank raid.

Vicky shielded her eyes, trying to make sense of what was happening. One of the figures was lowering its arm, but she could see no hand at the end of it.

"Vic, I don't think we should be here," Tobe implored.

Part of her agreed with him. Part of her wanted to run away from all this madness and hide. But another part, a stronger part, needed to know what had done this. And why. It wasn't just the rapidly-developing TV journalist inside her that needed to know, either – although that's what Woodhead would say. No, she wanted to understand for herself. Her brain craved an explanation for the security man, the ICU, the nurse. The cloud? The Rain Circle... (Oh there was a connection all right!) Now this. It was only natural to want answers. Only human. She just hoped she lived long enough to uncover them.

And almost as one, the four figures noticed them, turning slowly to face Vicky and Tobe. She saw them clearly for the first time, the abhorrence of their nature. Skin gleamed like polished silver, faces, arms; everything but the hospital gowns that they wore – which were sticking to torsos and thighs, black with sweat or other bodily juices. They appeared bald, though Vicky could tell it was just a case of their hair being slicked back, glued to their distended heads. None of them had eyes as far as she could make out, yet they all looked directly at her. Looked through her, even. Mouths were wide but far from empty. They were gummed up with a blend of saliva and something Vicky couldn't identify.

They all took a step towards her, their stance reminding her of zombies from those old Italian horror films, the ones she used to love when she was a teenager. However, these men were not dead, simply... changed. And she felt certain there was intelligence behind their actions.

"David! Lou!"

Vicky snapped round in the direction of the voice. So did the four "men" ahead of her. Rob Woodhead was at the mashed hole in the wall, the breach created to gain entrance. He'd followed their path of vandalism from the ICU right through to this ward.

They regarded him oddly, half-recognising him.

"It's me, Rob. Rob Woodhead," he confirmed.

*Christ Almighty*, thought Vicky. *Doesn't he realise these are the people responsible for all this? Maybe he does. Perhaps he's the only one who can get through to them.* It was reminiscent of a hostage situation, with Rob attempting to talk the gunmen into laying down their arms.

"You know me. Think. Try to remember," said Rob. "You've got to come with me now. We need to let the doctors take a look at you." He spoke in hushed tones, calmly, with his hands out in front of him. A true negotiator, showing them they had nothing to fear; there were no concealed weapons. At the same time he was working his way through the hole, inching closer to them. They were listening to him, all four of them. The room was quiet for several seconds.

Then the silence was broken by a sudden whirring and beeping. Tobe's camera had chosen that particular moment to act up. He opened his free eye, the one not jammed up against the lens, swivelled it right to the camera, then glanced over at the four fishermen.

They raised their arms, four sets of two. Vicky could do nothing but watch, Tobe below her on one knee doing the same.

The first jets broke free. The water started to form a ring around the men's hands, then gushed energetically forwards.

Towards *them*.

Vicky braced herself for the inevitable strike of the water cannons. She'd seen what one of them could do, but all of those combined? There'd be nothing left of her or Tobe. Not even a red smear to remember them by.

In her final moments she thought of Jason Harding. A revelation struck her, a realisation. She knew without a shadow of a doubt that she was in love with him now. There could be no other explanation for the intensity of her feelings. They were meant to be together, they'd been *thrown* together for that purpose. And now something so bizarre she could barely believe it was happening would keep them apart forever. It didn't seem fair, after they'd only just found each other. Another tragedy in a long line.

All she could feel was regret, sorrow and pity.

For herself and for what might have been.

\*\*\*

For the third time that day, Dr Benjamin Hopkins' peace was disturbed.

He'd been settling down to his paperwork again – a can of diet coke his only sustenance – when he'd heard the screams. As if these weren't enough, the other shouts coming from the wards above and the stomping of feet directly overhead guaranteed he wouldn't get any more charts done or reports filled in that afternoon.

He was on his way out to reception, and from there to the lift, when they entered the car park. Through the glass of the double doors he saw the vans and cars arrive. Some were camouflaged, others ordinary everyday vehicles.

"What's going on, Nina?" he enquired of the receptionist, who was also watching them pull in.

"I have no idea."

Then the door of the lead van opened, and a grey-blue shape hopped out.

***

Everything seemed to occur at half its normal speed.

First Tobe dropped heavily sideways. Then Vicky was aware of hands grabbing her, before momentum carried her in the opposite direction to her cameraman. She landed by the NHS bed that had been thrown across the room.

Behind her she felt, rather than saw or heard, the doorway being decimated. There was a weight on top of her, pressing down on her body. She strained to twist round, to find out who had saved them.

Two eyes stared back at her, a face inches away from her own. Jason Harding was shielding her from the debris as best he could. It was only when the fine mist cleared that the full force of the blast was driven home to her. Just as the fishermen had wrecked St August's ICU and powered their way through the upper floor of the hospital, so now they had totally destroyed a section of corridor as well as the ward's entranceway. If Vicky and Tobe had been in its path…

Vicky coughed at the masonry dust still falling.

"Are you all right?" Harding asked quickly.

"Yes, I think so." More coughing.

Harding snatched a look sideways at Tobe, who he must have knocked out of the way. The man appeared dazed but at least he was alive.

The fishermen were searching around for any sign of their victims, heads pivoting left and right in unison. It wasn't long before their vision settled on Harding, his back and shoulders sticking up above the bed.

"They've seen us," he told Vicky. Now it was his turn to search around, for something – anything – he could use against them.

Meanwhile Woodhead had slipped through the hole in all the confusion and was now at the rear of the men as they edged closer to Harding's position. Friends or no, he looked like he was going to try and stop them before they did any more damage – or killed any more people? One bedside table was miraculously intact, and Rob pulled out the top draw, emptying the contents – a paperback book, a handkerchief, a comb – onto the floor. He headed for the biggest figure, the oldest one – maybe their leader, captain? The one he'd called Lou? – who still had his back to the lifeboat man.

Woodhead took the draw by the handle and hefted it around.

Before the wooden box could hit its target though, the older guy raised his arm and blew it clean out of Rob's hand with a blast of compressed liquid. Rob dived for cover, knowing full well that the next shot would be aimed at him.

The party advanced on Harding in a spearhead formation, a younger man at the front. Closer and closer until he became focused on Harding, so focused that nobody noticed Vicky crawling to the left-hand wall, the only one apart from the window side that was still intact.

Harding spun over, a sitting duck – literally. He cocked his head, as if wondering whether there was somebody – *something* – else inside that body, watching him, scrutinising him. A sense of being observed...

"Hey!" yelled Vicky to his left.

The guy at the front glanced sideways at the woman, paying her little or no mind. She could do nothing to him. Not now.

Or so he assumed...

Vicky broke the seal on the fire extinguisher and brought the two clips together. She pointed the nozzle at the figure and sprayed him in a white shower. It went in his face, in his mouth, in his eyes – or what could be seen of them. Vicky held the red cannister up like a trophy, her aim remarkably accurate.

The fisherman staggered backwards, the dripping ends of his arms now morphing back into hands as he wiped the foam away. The extinguisher emptied itself quickly, and there were still three more fishermen coming at them. The wounded member of their quartet keeled over, writhing in agony, unable to stop the lather from invading his form. Vicky thought for one insane moment that it might be enough to deter the others, but they kept on, raising their arms again, ignoring their comrade and gearing up to fire once more.

Suddenly they stopped. They had Vicky and Harding in their sights, but the trio turned to each other as if sharing some private joke, or responding to a silent signal. Vicky couldn't believe it when they backtracked to the window.

Leaving the fallen man behind, they took a run at the glass. The older one first, then his remaining crew. With a loud crash they broke through, shards of glass sprinkling around them, some of which landed on the inside, some in the car park down below.

Rob emerged from under cover and went over to the broken window, rubbing his face. Vicky joined him, looking down. She saw the men on the concrete floor down below, quite clearly dead, or at the very least fatally injured. The lifeboat man was shaking his head.

"Wait, look... *Jesus!*" said Vicky.

The captain – Lou – was twitching; spasming might be more appropriate. The other two followed suit, and a minute later they were getting to their feet, shaking off the glass that clung to them.

"That's... That's just not—"

"Make sure someone sees to David." Rob was already climbing out through the window, nodding back towards the felled sailor behind them – in a room which now looked more like a battlefield than a hospital ward.

"Wait, Woodhead!" Vicky was wasting her breath. He was already clambering down the trellis on the side of the building. "Idiot," she added under her breath.

"Who did he mean?" asked Harding, getting up.

Vicky came back to join him. "I assume he means that thing over there. I think those were the men he rescued this morning."

Harding walked over to the prone body. "So the Rain Circle did this?"

Vicky frowned and gave a shrug.

"David", as Woodhead had called him, was perfectly still now, eerily so in fact. Harding crouched by the fellow. *Once the doctor...* thought Vicky. Jason reached out to touch the body.

"Get away from that man. Now!"

The stern order came from nowhere, delivered in an equally abrupt tone. Vicky peered round to see a bunch of people entering the ward, stepping over the rubble, wading through a reservoir of water and collapsed masonry. Each one was kitted out in full environment suit – grey-blue in colour – complete with glass face mask and respirator.

But this wasn't what surprised her the most. The lead figure, the one who'd told Harding to step away, was also brandishing a pistol.

And it was pointing in their direction.

## Chapter Twenty-Nine
### New Arrivals

Rob Woodhead wasn't afraid of heights. But that didn't mean he liked them, either.

He'd heard someone say once that you shouldn't look down when you're climbing a mountain. However, when you're climbing down from the second floor of a hospital on the outside, clinging to the trellis and to an exterior so old it should have received a telegram from the Queen, it was probably a good idea to look where you're going every once in a while. If Rob should fall he doubted very much that he'd be getting up again like the men he was chasing. His friends, hell his *family* more like.

To take his mind off the drop, Rob wracked his brains about what he'd just seen. About what could be the matter with Lou, David and the others. Something out at sea had done this to them, that much was certain. Maybe they'd ingested some kind of natural aquatic drug, a stimulant. That would explain the way they looked, why they'd gone berserk, and their incredibly high pain threshold. The three fishermen could have broken every bone in their bodies jumping from the window above him and not even realise it yet. *So how do you rationalise the other things you saw, Rob?* his voice of reason spoke up. What would account for the stuff they'd done, the way their hands... *transformed* like that? Rob had seen the holes they'd made in St August's walls, not to mention the blast that killed one of the patients; he was trying to forget about the nurse and the security man, and God alone knew how many others. But it wasn't Lou and his lads who were doing this. How could they? It was impossible!

Something was *making* them do these things. But were those people he'd known all his life still in there somewhere, just beneath the surface, desperate to escape? He'd almost got through to them, he was sure of it. If it hadn't been for Vicky West and co...

All Rob knew was that he had to get them back so Ben, or those experts he'd mentioned, could examine them. Quite how he intended to do this when any one of the three were capable of killing him in an instant he hadn't figured out yet. One thing at a time, and right now his "thing" was to get down the side of this fucking hospital without breaking his neck.

It seemed to take forever, and he nearly lost his footing once or twice, but inevitably the ground came up to meet him. The fishermen had a bit of a head start on Rob, but he ran round the corner after them.

There was no sign of the men. They'd vanished without a trace.

Maybe it would have been quicker to take the stairs or the lift. But then he really would have lost them. Least this way he was tracing their steps, going in the same direction as Lou.

The ambulance pulled out of the bay, almost running Rob over. Inside, in the driver and passenger seats, were Lou and George. In the back, presumably, was the other fisherman, Harry – the hired hand. Rob sped alongside and grabbed at the door handle, but Lou swerved the white vehicle round, shaking off their pursuer. Thankfully, because it had never made it above five mph, Rob landed on his feet. He was searching for his Vincent even before the ambulance disappeared round the corner. And there it was, right where he'd left it. A shining vision in the car park.

Rob fished out his keys, located in a pocket in his leather trousers. He didn't have time to fetch his helmet from the Relatives' Room in A&E, so he gunned the engine and kicked off. Ambulances were fast, but his Vincent was faster – and much more manoeuvrable.

It was as he rode to the front of St August's that he heard the first cracks of gunfire.

\*\*\*

"I said get away from that man!" barked the stranger, his pistol levelled at Harding's head.

Another suited guy came up to stand next to him. "Please do as he says." His voice was just as firm, with an upper-class lilt, but Harding detected a certain warmth there. "It really is for your own good."

Harding couldn't see the faces behind those clear fronts, the sunlight streaming in and glinting off the reflective surfaces. Therefore, he couldn't judge the earnestness of either person. He did as he was told, all the same; the gun was incentive enough.

Getting up, he eased his way to the right of the body but refused to raise his hands. Tobe was still on the floor, shuffling away from the newcomers. Vicky remained where she was, looking worriedly from the gun to Harding.

"What's going on here? Who are you people?" she demanded, her manner somewhere between confusion and anger.

The second bloke put his gloved hand on the armed man's shoulder. Reluctantly the pistol was lowered, but not entirely.

"Please excuse the Colonel. He just didn't want you touching that body. It's not safe," said the man with the pristine accent. "My name is Fuller."

"And you're what? Army?"

Fuller was about to answer when a third man, this one dressed in a shirt and tie with a stethoscope hanging round his neck, pushed his way through to the front.

He gaped at the ward in disbelief, one hand on his hip, the other over his mouth. The doctor said something under his breath that nobody caught.

"We've been brought by Dr Hopkins here," said Fuller, moving away from his companions. "It seems he has quite a problem on his hands."

"So where were you guys five minutes ago when all hell was breaking loose in here?" Vicky asked. "We could have used your *help* then."

"I apologise, but who exactly is 'we'?" Fuller gestured at the three of them.

"Victoria West, Tobe Howell from Creation-Time TV," Vicky said proudly.

"I see."

Vicky looked uncomfortable, as if she could feel Fuller's eyes on her through his facemask. "A-And this is Jason Harding," she added quickly.

"Harding? I know that name from somewhere, don't I?"

He stayed silent, just watching it all play out – and happy that the gun was no longer levelled at him.

"Professor?" This was the Colonel again, his tone just

as gruff as before. "The victim?"

"Of course, of course."

"You're a *professor*?" Vicky said.

"Professor Edward Fuller, biophysicist – amongst other things – at your service." He tried to sound glib, but under the circumstances didn't quite pull it off.

Fuller bent down and had a look at the sailor Woodhead had called David, the soles of his rubber boots squeaking on the floor. The professor turned the body over so that the white foam on the face was exposed. "Interesting. Who did this?"

"I did," Vicky admitted. "Is— is he dead?"

"I think so, yes. The chemicals in the spray seem to have reacted with… ah, um…"

"With what?" Harding spoke up for the first time.

Fuller looked back at the Colonel. "Tell your men to take him downstairs where I can do a proper examination. Oh, and the other corpse, too." Without hesitation four suited men stepped up and headed for David and the dead patient, the hole in his chest weeping blood.

"There are some more bodies down the hall, well not really bodies anymore…" Vicky struggled to find the words and gave up. "Plus, there are three more just like him," she pointed to David, who was being lifted up off the floor, "outside."

"We'll see to it," said the Colonel.

"I bet you will," Vicky spat. "Look, it's pretty obvious – at least to me – that you've come here to do more than just help. So, what's the deal?"

"You're quite right, Miss West."

"Fuller—"

"No, she deserves to know. They all do. This," the professor waved a hand around the room, "this gives them the *right* to know. Miss West. Victoria." He was staring at her again, unflinchingly, in a way Harding really hated. "If this is what we suspect, and quite frankly I don't see how it could be anything else, then we're dealing with a communicable disease so frightening the consequences do not bear thinking about. I'm afraid St August's Hospital will have to be placed under quarantine.

"And so will you."

\*\*\*

Rob spotted the build-up of cars, vans, lorries and other vehicles in the driveway, grey-suited men flitting about in between. He also saw the spark of muzzle fire as said men let loose with their automatic weapons.

Their intentions were clear. To stop the ambulance from leaving, and use as much force as necessary to do so.

It weaved erratically from side to side, accelerating to no more than ten or fifteen mph. Bullet holes peppered the flank. No one was going anywhere until these men said so. Now they were aiming for the wheels, the petrol tank. They wanted to stop the escaping ambulance all right, even if it meant killing everyone inside it.

Rob couldn't let that happen. He hadn't gone through all that crap on The Jenny just so these lunatics could kill the people they'd rescued; people who might yet be saved, be cured. He refused to let them down this time.

Revving up the Vincent, Rob drove it towards the first set of men. With all the noise the soldiers were making they never heard the black charger approaching. Rob steered it as close as he could to the men without actually hitting them. Alarmed, the suited figures scattered, a couple actually falling backwards as Rob skirted past; threatening to run them over, plough into them like a bowling ball knocking over pins.

Once he was in front of the stationary obstacles, Rob checked his mirrors. The soldiers were too stunned to fire at him, but he slipped in and out of their vehicles just in case they were tempted. Surely they wouldn't shoot at their own troops?

Then he was out the other side, searching for the ambulance. Rob prayed to God he'd done the right thing, that he could bring back the three fishermen alive. But back where? To this hospital? Christ, there were folk with guns here! To another one maybe, far away from Sable?

If he couldn't, then he might as well have let the figures in grey do their worst.

## Chapter Thirty
### Fact-Finding

"So what do we think? Germ warfare?"

Vicky stood in the corner of one of the upstairs offices, a temporary home for Harding, Tobe and herself. "Why else would the military get involved?"

Tobe sat on a leather chair behind the oak desk, arms folded, lost now without his camera – which the Colonel's men had confiscated. He looked rather like a scared but silly child who'd had his security blanket snatched away.

There was a small window in the office which overlooked the south side of the hospital, all hilly terrain. Not much of a view, and yet Harding stared out through the glass, seemingly captivated.

"I mean we all heard that shooting outside, right? They must have been trying to stop those... those things from escaping. Either them or Woodhead. You mark my words this is no manmade disease we're talking about here." For the last five minutes or so Vicky had been trying to bring order to her thoughts. Talking it all through out loud. It wasn't helping. "But what I'd really like to know is what this has got to do with our so-called Rain Circle?"

"Who says it's got anything to do with it?" Tobe broke in.

"What, you're suggesting that this village is just a magnet for weird things like this? They *have* to be connected. It's too much of a coincidence. Also, that's where the fishermen were picked up."

"Fuller said—"

"I heard what Fuller said. Can't you see he's been ferried in to calm things down? To try and put a lid on this? You want to know what I think? The cloud is some kind of delivery system and they're using Sable as a testing ground."

"No way, Vic." Tobe sat up straight. "It's a populated area. They wouldn't do that."

"Who wouldn't, Tobe?" Hands on her hips, Vicky waited for an answer then drove home her argument. "We don't even know who these guys are. They could be terrorists or something. Nowadays anyone can get hold of a gun and call himself 'Colonel'."

"Be careful he doesn't hear you say that, Miss West." Vicky hadn't even noticed the door open, but there he was: Professor Edward Fuller, inside the room, sans helmet.

He was a well-groomed gentleman, handsome in an elegant, old-fashioned way. He had a roman nose and prominent eyebrows. His hair – a silvery blond that must have been golden in earlier years – was curly but thinning. Small patches of scalp could be seen at a number of points through the twisted follicles. Again, when he spoke it was with the air of a well-educated Brit. The kind who might be seen giving scientific lectures on the television in the early hours of the morning or speaking at expensive after dinner functions.

"Why's that, Professor? Is he going to shoot us with

that pop-gun of his?"

Fuller looked at her, the same scrutiny she'd been subjected to earlier. "Whilst I agree that the Colonel's methods are somewhat... over the top, shall we say, he was only acting in the best interests of your friend. I'm quite sure of that."

Harding turned his back on the window, the light pulling a cloak over him.

"The disease is transmitted by touch, you see." Fuller made to shut the door and Vicky caught a glimpse of another suited man outside through the crack; he was cradling a black object in his arms, across his chest. She took it to be a rifle. "As far as we can tell."

"And we're all okay?" Tobe asked.

"Well, we'll have to run some more tests to be on the safe side." Each of them had had a swab in their mouths and a blood sample taken before being brought here. "But you're not running around attacking anyone so that's a positive sign."

"Then we can go?" asked Vicky.

"Once you've answered a few questions, Miss West. You're not under arrest or anything." Fuller smiled.

"And will you answer some of ours?" Vicky tapped her fingers against her hips.

"If I can. But first of all I need to know if any of you have seen this man." Fuller produced a folded photograph from his pocket, a passport-sized snap blown up to around A5. He handed it to Vicky. The subject looked startled, probably because of the flash, his eyes wide, his thick neck and square face taking up most of the frame. But it was to his neatly-trimmed beard that the eyes were immediately drawn, dark and foreboding.

Vicky shook her head. "Never seen him before in my life. Who is he?"

Fuller side-stepped the question. "It's a very good

likeness, are you quite sure?"

"Positive."

Fuller took the picture from her, his gloved hands briefly touching her own, and then handed it to Harding at the back. "How about you, Mr Harding?"

He scanned the photo. "No, I haven't seen him."

"All right." Fuller finally handed it to Tobe. "Ring any bells, Mr Howell?"

"No, sorry."

"That's okay." Fuller pocketed the photo again.

"Professor?" Vicky came up behind him. "You didn't answer my question. Who is he?"

Fuller turned to her. "His name is Darville, and he is the man responsible for all this."

Vicky shook her head. "How?"

Fuller looked nervously over to the door. "I'm afraid I can't answer that at this time, but trust me when I say I'm here to help. To put an end to all this."

Before Vicky could pursue the matter, Fuller was over by that door. "I'll return in a short while. In the meantime if there's anything you need – refreshments, tea, coffee, food – just knock on the door and tell the man outside."

*The guard*, thought Vicky.

Fuller exited without another word, as quietly as he'd come in. If they hadn't been watching him go they might have assumed he was still in the room with them somewhere. In a sense he was; his presence remained long after he'd departed.

"Maybe we should knock on the door and ask for the Colonel. Get to the bottom of this right now," Vicky suggested.

"I don't think you ought to piss that guy off, Vic," Tobe whined.

"Your friend's right." Harding came around the desk, his eyes on the door.

"I just want to know if this is on the level," Vicky replied. "Are they really here to help, or to cover something up?"

\*\*\*

The Colonel watched the tape through a third time.

It was only a monochrome image but he could see well enough: the security man smeared against the wall, the pandemonium in the hospital hallways, the skirmish with the fishermen – or at least some of it, the camerawork was more than a little shaky at the end, and understandably so.

The Colonel hadn't been expecting this.

Oh, he'd come prepared all right, Fuller had made sure of that, but only to keep on top of Sable and its people for a few days until the mess could be sorted out or they could locate their missing teammate. But the Colonel hadn't expected the exposure to do this. Sure, it had sent Darville insane, but...

The Colonel had seen some pretty weird shit in his time – like a man being tortured with acid, his flesh burning away until he talked, the effects of chemical weapons, anthrax and the like – in his line of work it was an occupational hazard. But this was in a different league altogether. What those men were doing was not only beyond all known laws of physics, it was beyond the Colonel's own laws of reality. And that was never a good thing as far as he was concerned.

To top it all off, three of the bastards had escaped, along with some git on a bike who'd tried to run over his troops. The Colonel had ordered a vehicle to go after them, search and destroy if necessary. He couldn't risk this thing spreading any further.

Fuller joined him in the corridor.

"Where the fuck have you been?" the Colonel growled. His hood was down also, and he fixed the professor with an evil eye, bloodshot and beady.

"I… I was just talking to our three guests from your tape. They haven't seen Darville."

"Right. But he's here, isn't he?"

Fuller nodded. "I'd stake my reputation on it."

The Colonel laughed gruffly. "Your reputation won't be worth shit at the end of this, Professor. According to Dr Hopkins those fishermen were brought in this morning by a lifeboat crew. Now, he didn't touch the specimens directly, thank God for latex, but he can't vouch for anyone else."

Fuller bit his lip. "Are those lifeboat men still in the hospital?"

"Two of them are here, on one of the wards. The stupid fucker let the others go home."

"He wasn't to know."

The Colonel spat on the floor by Fuller's boot. "If they should start to display symptoms or come into contact with anyone…"

Fuller looked down at the spittle. "I know."

"I don't think you do, Fuller. Take a good look at the footage that cameraman shot, and then imagine what would happen with say twenty or thirty of those things on the loose. Holy shit, even a hundred!" He offloaded the camera onto Fuller, then prodded him hard in the chest. "You didn't tell me this was going to happen."

"I didn't know. Nobody could have predicted what Darville was going to do. What he was going to unleash. We needed to be ready. *I* needed to gather my equipment."

"Well, you and your equipment'd better come up with something ASAP." The Colonel took out a pack of cigarettes and lit one up. He blew the first puff in Fuller's face. "Otherwise, it won't just be Sable that goes up in smoke. D'you get my drift?"

Fuller said that he did, and promptly walked away with the camera. His coughing could be heard down the length of the corridor as he walked away.

## Chapter Thirty-One
### The Chase

The ambulance was speeding up the narrow country lanes, but Rob soon had it in sight. Strangely it was heading back towards Angels Landing and Sable, instead of in the direction of Hambleton and freedom. But then, why should there be any logic to what they were doing? It was obvious that the fishermen weren't responsible for their own actions – Rob had known Lou and the boys a lifetime, and they would never willingly hurt a fly, let alone devastate an entire hospital ward – which meant they were wild cards, loose cannons, driven crazy by whatever they'd picked up in the sea: a disease, a parasite, something Rob couldn't explain. All Ben Hopkins' clever speeches about how they'd survived had been rubbish. The fishermen were being *kept* alive, as Rob had said right from the off.

Kept alive for a reason.

Rob accelerated, not bothering to hold back the Vincent this time, and not considering the hazard of oncoming traffic that might – foolishly – try to drive round the ambulance. As he rode he thought also of the men with guns back in the hospital yard, the grey-suited figures still at the forefront of his mind. Guns in Sable? And automatics as far as Rob could tell. It was obvious that they were there for the fishermen, but none of it made any sense. All Rob knew was that they were trying to stop the ambulance at any cost. There was no mistaking their intentions, either; they were shooting to kill. Except these men *were* thinking clearly. They knew exactly what they were doing, and that made their actions indefensible.

Or did it?

The more Rob pondered this, the more he could see it from their side. If they were military as he suspected (some of the vehicles he'd weaved around were camouflaged, but none had markings) then they were probably under orders to stop the fishermen no matter what. And who could really blame them? They weren't emotionally attached to Lou and co. Didn't have a history with them like he did. All the soldiers were trying to do was contain a threat. Stop the "enemy" from getting away and doing even more damage. It made sense, despite all of Rob's arguments to the contrary. If he were in their position, might he not do the same? There were times in the Navy when he'd had to do things he hadn't agreed with, but he'd done them all the same. He'd obeyed his superiors. What was the difference here?

The Vincent's engine rocketed her along, almost catching up with the white blob in front; hardly a graceful mode of transport like his, but it couldn't half shift. Designed to get to injured people as fast as possible. For the first time since leaving St August's car park, Rob looked in his mirrors. He didn't know what made him do it, instinct maybe, but he was glad that he did because there was another van coming up behind, a blue one. Although it was a good distance behind him at the moment, it wouldn't stay that way for long. Rob just caught a streak of grey behind the windscreen. It was supposed to look like any ordinary van on the road, but the way they were driving smacked of professionalism. Of training. His "friends" from the hospital weren't going to let it go, not that he thought for one minute that they would. When they caught up, the fishermen would either be subdued or put down, and he'd most likely be placed under arrest.

If he was going to do something, it had to be now. If he could bring an end to this calmly perhaps there wouldn't be any need for more shooting. More bloodshed. Rob pulled up behind the ambulance, now doing around fifty, then manoeuvred alongside them in the tiny gap between vehicle and embankment. Stones and dust flew up in a plume behind the bike as its tyres gripped the road.

Rob steadied the Vincent. The wind playing with his dark hair reminded him of his absent helmet, but he couldn't think of that right now. Tensing his left arm, he took his right hand off the handlebars and beat on the side of the ambulance with his palm. Rob could see George in the passenger seat, but the man didn't take any notice. He tried shouting out but could barely be heard above the roar of the motors. The Vincent lurched and slipped to one side. Rob immediately brought his hand back to help with the steering. Gritting his teeth, he nosed the bike forwards until it was about level with the passenger door. Again, he banged on the metal of the ambulance's side, this time with his fist. The fisherman did look now. He fixed Rob with a gaze that froze his blood, the man's face seemingly melting, runny juices gushing over forehead, cheeks: that open mouth. Distracted, Rob didn't notice the ambulance swerving over into his space, attempting to run him off the road. He pushed away from its flank, wobbling slightly but holding his course.

The ambulance cut him up a second time, catching the

Vincent's rear tyre. The effect was to send the bike wildly out of control. Rob bore down on the handlebars, determination alone keeping him on the road.

He saw the dip a fraction of a second before the Vincent hit it. Rob's front wheel dropped, knocking his ride violently sideways and onto the embankment. The slope and gravity dragged him downwards. Rob knew he had to slow himself, but the brakes weren't working. The Vincent tipped over on its side, wheels spinning in the air. Rob was thrown clear, hands up in front of his face as he flew headlong over the grass. He landed on his shoulder and whipped round, his body cartwheeling, his bike doing the same just off to the left of him.

Rob heard a crunching noise and couldn't tell whether it came from him or the Vincent. He saw greens, then blues and whites, then greens again. A sickening merry-go-round as the field and sky spun in every direction. Soft as the grass was, it still hurt as Rob struck it. Greens and blues and whites, and greens and blues and—

Black.

***

The driver of the pursuing van saw the bike flip over the side of the road but did nothing. He couldn't stop, he had to catch up with the ambulance. Changing gear, he belted up the lane after it. Whoever was driving the thing was having difficulty steering it seemed, and that gave them just the opportunity they were looking for.

Gloved fingers tightened over the steering wheel. The PVC-type material of the suit made his skin itch, but he didn't complain. He looked over to his travelling companion, who was even now loading up a magazine of rounds. They hadn't been told what to expect, only that there would be resistance. And above all else, if they couldn't bring the subjects back the mission would revert to one of a search and destroy rather than apprehension.

The back of the ambulance loomed in front of him. With a hand signal, his finger pointing downwards, the man's partner indicated that he was going to take out the tyres. Once that was done, the ambulance would be forced to stop, and they'd release the lock on the back of their own van where the rest of their squad was housed. It would then be a matter of detaining the subjects and "escorting" them to the hospital, calling back along the way to pick up the rogue motorcyclist.

The passenger lowered his electric window and leaned out. The sooner this was over with the better. Less chance of bumping into anyone else on the road and having to explain what was going on (the cover story, not the official line – mainly because they didn't know what the official brief was). He sat on the bottom part of the open window, legs hooked around the seat-belt inside. The soldier brought his weapon up and prepared to fire.

Suddenly the back doors of the ambulance swung wide open. Both men stared at the interior of the vehicle, a matter of metres away. There was one person standing in the frame, keeping his balance in spite of the uneven terrain. He wore a hospital gown, darker than most and refusing to flap in the breeze. Sticking to him…

The driver of the van blinked behind his face-plate, the glass steaming up as his breathing increased. He should pull back. Something was about to happen, something really bad.

There was a bright flash to the left of him as the gunner fired his first shots. One of the ambulance's tyres exploded in a ball of air and flames. The guy in the back of the ambulance hardly shifted at all. He simply raised an arm, the bicep bulging as he did so.

*Has he... Yes, he has a weapon!* the driver said to himself, but he could see no signs of a gun. The man's hand seemed to disappear as the ambulance limped along the road, now on three wheels. The driver tried to warn his colleague, reaching across to tap his leg, both his eyes still focussed on the ambulance.

A weird ball, or a ring, encircled the man's hand and forearm – a bubble filled with frothing fluid. The blast took them all by surprise, even after they'd witnessed its build up. Instead of the bullets he'd been expecting, and which he'd been shown how to avoid on courses, the driver was confronted with a streak of water which shattered his windscreen completely and tore through the van itself.

The driver heard screams as the jet shot into the rear of the van, ripping apart the troops waiting to spring into action. It then exited through the van's back doors as powerfully as it had entered through the front.

The soldier who was hanging out of the passenger window felt himself slipping outside, his leg no longer wrapped round the seat-belt (his leg no longer existed anymore – carried away by the full force of the squall). He tumbled back, and out of the window, hitting the road hard. There was a momentary spasm of pain, either from the fall or the bleeding stump of his leg, but then it was all over. He rolled under the van, the back wheel crushing him, running cleanly over his chest and squashing his heart flat against his backbone. A tangled mix of grey and red emerged from under the exhaust pipe, coming to rest eventually in the middle of the road.

The driver had a knee-jerk reaction to the blast – literally. His foot slammed down on the accelerator in panic, sending the van slap-bang into the back of the ambulance. The front crumpled up immediately, attaching itself clumsily to the vehicle it had been chasing. The water beam cut out as the "patient" was beaten back by the collision. The pair of vehicles carried on like this for a few seconds, in a makeshift convoy, then the ambulance veered off to the right. As soon as it hit the embankment it rolled over on its side, taking the blue van with it.

Within seconds the flaming back wheel of the ambulance had become a fireball that climbed up to the ambulance's petrol tank. The driver, hanging by the seat-belt, glass face-plate cracked like crazy paving, his head bleeding profusely, tried to open the door of his Transit. It wouldn't shift. He leaned against the padding, now buckled inwards, pressing the handle-lock. All he could see was the fire raging through the missing windshield. He knew he didn't have long to get out.

Undoing his seat-belt, the soldier shifted round and put his feet up against the door, now above him. He gave it a swift kick. It moved, only the tiniest bit, but it moved. Again he kicked. The door finally gave, creaking open on its busted hinges. Using the belt as a climbing rope, he pulled himself up and out of the van. Now he was standing upright on the side of the vehicle, the flames licking up all around. If he was going to jump, it had to be now. He bent his legs and...

The driver was leaping, away from the two vans cruelly coupled together, away from his poor unfortunate colleagues trapped inside, probably all dead. He was going to be all right, and as soon as he hit the ground he'd start running in case the whole thing exploded.

His mind caught up, the nerve endings on his back working overtime, registering the severe burns as his suit stuck to him. And he realised he wasn't jumping at all, he was being carried upwards on a plume of pure white heat, his body blistering, turning black. Would he ever fall back down to earth? Or was he doomed to remain up here forever in agony? It felt like the latter to him, an eternity of suffering. Of heat and pain.

But by the time the driver hit the ground, a charcoaled lump that still burned brightly like a bonfire, he was already dead.

## Chapter Thirty-Two
### Interviews

The Colonel drew a curtain around Wayne Gough's bed. Wayne looked the man up and down, the intense eyes, the severe haircut – almost, but not quite bald – the prominent Adam's Apple that bobbed up and down just above the neck of the grey environment suit. The visitor smiled, but it wasn't something he was used to doing.

Taking a seat by the bed, the one Wayne's mother had occupied earlier, he said: "Mr Gough? Mr Wayne Gough?"

"Yeah." Wayne felt more than a bit intimidated by the fellow, but found the courage to ask: "What's going on around here? Where did those men take my family?"

"There's been an 'incident', sir," the Colonel told him, as if it were a minor thing. "My men and I are looking into the problem. As for your family, we've just moved them down the hall while I have a talk with you. Nothing to worry about."

"Your men had guns," said Wayne. It wasn't an

accusation, merely a statement of fact. "Has this got anything to do with that screaming we heard earlier? That swab thing, the bloods that were taken?"

The Colonel coughed. "Look, Wayne, I have to ask you some questions regarding the rescue you and your men undertook this morning. I've already spoken with your Coxswain back there, Philip…"

"Holmes," Wayne finished for him. "Phil."

"Right, but he can't remember much about it. Seems he was knocked unconscious at the wheel of your ship."

"Boat," Wayne corrected, then when the Colonel looked puzzled: "It's a life*boat*. Not a ship."

The Colonel nodded. "Anyway, he can't tell me what I need to know, which is what happened out there."

"Am I in some sort of trouble?"

"No, of course not. Just tell me everything you remember about the rescue. Don't leave out a thing, no matter how trivial you think it might be."

\*\*\*

"There really isn't that much to tell."

Harding sat facing Professor Fuller in the office, Vicky and Tobe having been ushered away somewhere else – not quite at gunpoint, but very nearly. He needed a drink, badly.

"Anything you could tell me might help."

"Like I said before, I noticed the storm-cloud when I woke this morning. It was quite far away, hanging over the horizon, but I could see it plainly enough." Harding laced his fingers together. "Then when my agent, Lily, arrived I got her to take me to Angels Landing so I could get a better view."

"Why was that?" Fuller poked his tongue out of the corner of his mouth. "You were interested in the cloud?"

"I suppose so."

"Yes. And then what happened?"

"I noticed Vicky... Miss West's chopper on the way there. They were having difficulties. I later discovered she'd been out filming the cloud."

Fuller reached for a case out of one of his leg-pockets. Inside were a pair of thin, frameless glasses which he put on to look through the notes in front of him. "The, ah... the Rain Circle? Am I right. That is what Miss West Christened it, is it not?"

"That's correct."

"You then brought her pilot back here for treatment. Did Miss West tell you anything about the Rain Circle at all?"

"Only that it was unusual. She's something of an expert, I understand."

"Quite so, I've been examining her records. A qualified meteorologist, did you know that?"

"How did you get hold of her records?"

"The Colonel had a background search carried out. A... deep dive, as they say. He was faxed the results not long ago."

Harding's brow furrowed. "The phones are back up and running then?"

Fuller paused, a little flummoxed by the question. "He has his own private lines of communication, Mr Harding. The Colonel is not beholden to the whims of BT or Cable and Wireless."

"And did you run a 'background search' on me?" Harding had been observing the professor ever since he entered the room, taking everything in. His actions, his speech, his manner. Looking for something which would give the game away, whatever the game happened to be.

Fuller was a lot more personable than the Colonel – for one thing he had a name! – Harding had to give him that, but it only made him more suspicious in his eyes. He didn't dislike the man, but he didn't trust him either. And the way he leered over Vicky... Harding had no right to feel jealous (*so why do you?*) but he couldn't help himself. It was more to do with what the man held back. He had all the makings of a classical actor – Harding could imagine him treading the boards, reciting Shakespeare. Those guys made the best villains in movies, didn't they? He hoped he was wrong, for all their sakes.

"You don't trust me, do you?" Fuller said, a question to deflect a question.

"Have you given me any reason to, Professor?"

"Certainly. I've told you what little I know at this stage, that the disease is transmitted by touch and that we could be looking at a major contamination unless we—"

"Yes, you've told us all that. But you still haven't explained where the virus *came* from, what it has to do with the Rain Circle, and how that man – Darville, wasn't it? – how he came to be carrying it in the first place."

Fuller sighed. "I'm afraid I can't tell you anything more than I have done. The Colonel..."

Harding narrowed his eyes. "Even if it meant we could help? If you've checked up on me, you'll know by now that I used to be a doctor, and I've never seen a disease of any kind that can do those sorts of things to a human being."

"Not in your experience. But then, your experience is somewhat limited, isn't it?" Fuller replied cooly. "You haven't worked in the field for years, *Mr* Harding, and even when you did you were only a common or garden GP. How many cases of rare diseases did you treat in your time as a practising physician?"

Harding scowled, the words cutting deep. "None, but

I read journals. I studied papers. Be straight with me Professor, is this some kind of genetic thing?"

"I'm not at liberty to say."

Harding leant back in the chair. "Do you have a cure?"

"I want you to think back to the wards, Mr Harding. Is there anything—"

"Do you?"

"—anything more you can tell us about what happened?" The professor took off his glasses again and placed them on the table. "Think back, even the slightest piece of information could be vital."

\*\*\*

"Look, I'm not saying another word until you let me use a phone. And don't tell me they're still not working; I know you boys have your ways and means."

Vicky West sat, legs crossed, with her hands clasping her knee. She was in what appeared to be an upstairs waiting room, where relatives usually sit just before visiting hour. She was alone in the room with the Colonel, who walked from left to right in front of her, reading papers on a clipboard. There were no windows in the room and the artificial light above glinted off the soldier's forehead.

"Miss West, according to your colleague's statement – that's a Mr Tobe Howell, a cameraman for CreationTime – you deliberately flew out into the middle of a dangerous rescue mission just so you could take pictures for your station. Is that correct?"

"It's a free country."

"Ah, but don't you think that it's a bit of a coincidence that an RAF Search and Rescue helicopter just happened to blow up while you were out there?"

Vicky gaped at him in disbelief. "We had nothing to do with that!"

"Oh no? Funny though, isn't it?"

"So's what happened to the fishermen that were rescued, only I don't see anyone laughing here Colonel."

The brutish man bent down, his face so close she could see every line, every wrinkle. His breath was foul when he opened his mouth to speak. "If I were you I'd start co-operating, Miss West, or you could find yourself in a lot of hot water."

As nervous as she was inside, Vicky remained calm on the outside. She'd never liked bullies, this kind especially. "Which branch of the military are you and your personnel with exactly, Colonel?"

"That's got nothing to do with you."

"I just want to make sure I get all my facts straight before I report this little fiasco."

The Colonel laughed in her face, a globule of spit landing on her chin. "You're not *going* to be reporting any of this, Miss West."

When he moved away, Vicky wiped her chin and shivered. "Why not? Fuller said we could go as soon as it was safe. How're you going to stop me from talking?" Vicky knew it was a stupid thing to ask, especially in light of the Colonel's volatile nature, but it just slipped out.

The Colonel didn't answer her, but he did rest his hand on his pistol – now residing in a holster at his hip.

"People know I'm here," said Vicky. "You can't hide the truth, Colonel."

"Do you know what I think? Nobody knows you're here, Miss West, otherwise we wouldn't be sat in this room having such a nice cosy chat. You stumbled onto this by accident. You're not a reporter, you're a fucking weatherwoman for fuck's sake! Hardly Lois Lane."

"My station will know soon enough. The footage from this morning's on its way to them right now."

The Colonel lit up a cigarette, tossing the match on the floor near her feet. "Tell me what happened after you heard the screaming on the upper floor, Miss West."

***

The Colonel met up with Fuller after the interviews, downstairs in the morgue. Both now had their hoods up, their face-masks back on.

Two bodies were laid out before them, both naked: one David Turner, the other the patient with a gaping hole in his chest. Fuller was taking a scraping from the wound.

"I couldn't have done much better with a pump-action shotgun," commented the Colonel.

"No, it's quite remarkable."

"It's worrying. That's what it is. I've still not heard back from the unit that went after his buddies." The Colonel was about to tap David on the head when Fuller grabbed his arm. The military man pulled it away, angrily.

"You've kept us hanging on far too long, Professor. We have all the information we need. No more preparation. I think it's high time I sent some troops into Sable itself. Dr Hopkins has kindly provided us with addresses for the lifeboat men who returned home. Now, maybe we'll get lucky and none of them'll have contracted this..." The Colonel scrabbled around for a description and failed miserably. "The two upstairs certainly seem okay. We'll do a house to house, possibly even an evacuation so you can check them all out here. We'll stick to the cover story, say there's a gas leak in the area. That'll put the wind up them and make them more willing to come along quietly. Then we can get around to this, what did West call it…? Rain Circle? That is if we can find the bloody thing. It's still not showing up on our satellites."

"The rescue workers seemed to find it easily enough."

"I realise that."

"What about Darville? He's still on the loose."

"We'll find him."

"He's dangerous."

"So am I. Remember that, Professor."

Fuller turned away sharply, continuing his work. He heard the Colonel's heavy footsteps tailing off.

Neither man said goodbye.

## Chapter Thirty-Three
### Encounters

It was a strange sensation, sort of like swimming through tar.

The blackness was comforting; oblivion a welcome release. Somehow, he knew which direction to take, guided by a soft voice, one he recognised instantly. The person who'd told him all those tall tales when he was little, about the sea, about Sable.

About life.

On his knee, bouncing up and down. It was his first real memory. Couldn't have been more than two or three. A big giant holding him, looking down on him. But the face was kind, and in that grip he felt safe, secure. Like nothing could hurt him. Ever.

Rob Woodhead saw that face again, attached to the voice calling out to him.

He was in a hospital room at St August's, that had been blown apart by... something. Rob couldn't quite remember. There was a gaping hole where the windows used to be and beds upended all around. Except one. The one with his dad in.

"Rob," his father said in greeting.

He looked nothing like the last time Rob had seen him, weak and at death's door. Here he was in his prime, sat up in the bed, smiling.

"Dad? Is that you?"

"Yeah, it's me. Come over here and let me have a look at you, son. It's been too long."

Rob didn't exactly walk, as *willed* himself over to the bed.

"Nasty business, all this," said Mr Woodhead Sr. "Lou and his lot."

"How did you—"

"You'd be surprised." His father grinned. Rob hadn't noticed before – his later memories of his dad tainted by sorrow and regret – but it was *his* grin. The one he used to get his own way, or charm himself out of trouble. Usually.

"Dad, I'm sorry... I..."

"Rob, you don't have to explain. I already know. It's me who should be apologising to you." The man pulled back his covers and stood up next to Rob. Instead of hospital apparel, he wore his fishing clothes: heavy woollen sweater Rob's mum had made for him, his old, faded trousers and his pair of trusty boots. He placed his hands on Rob's shoulders, the grip firm. "You only get one life, son. I'm glad that you did what you wanted to do with it. I just wish I could have been more of a part of it."

"So do I, Dad. So do I."

"I read all the letters you sent your mother; did you know that? Got her to tell me everything you said when you rang, though I was too blasted stubborn to get on the phone myself. I was proud of you, son. Still am."

Rob looked at him sideways. "Is this a dream, Dad?"

"No. At least I don't think so."

"Then I'm dead?"

"No, you're not dead," he said with a laugh. "It's not your time yet. Don't ask me to explain all this because I can't, but I've been allowed to see you. To warn you."

"Who? Who's allowed you to see me?"

"I can't tell you that, either. You're just going to have to trust me on this one."

"Okay."

"You're the only person who can help them, Rob. Lou and his boys. And the others."

"The others?"

"But you can't do it on your own. I know it, you know it. You feel responsible for what happened, but it's not your fault. Whatever you do, you have to remember that."

Rob shook his head, confused. "You're not making any sense, Dad."

"When the time comes, you'll know what to do." His father hugged him tight, clapping his back. "Now go, Rob. People are dying. You have to go!"

Rob put his arms around his father and saw a boy standing behind them. The kid couldn't have been more than six or seven, and had striking ginger hair – complete with freckles. The child put his finger to his lips, then the whole ward collapsed in a tidal wave of water. It fell over the child, over Rob's dad and himself. Rob was immersed in seconds, losing his grip on his father. And he thought he saw... something there. A face? But his mind was turning over like a key in an ignition. There was another strange sensation: a feeling.

An aching.

A heaviness over his eyes, something hard touching his right temple. His pupils flickered. Once, twice.

Then he was awake.

Rob's vision was blurred. He saw shapes merging together. Something very dark several metres away. Rob blinked, screwing up his eyes tight. And tried again. He was lying on his right-hand side, his face resting on the ground, against the grass.

The black blob turned out to be his Vincent, lying nearby in sympathy.

Rob's leathers creaked when he tried to move, roll onto his front. He felt like he'd been in a wrecker's yard crusher, just like the cars he saw when he went to scrounge for parts. Every single bone in his body cried out, but especially in his shoulder, which had already taken a battering earlier on in the day.

Rob put his hands flat out on the grass. He looked like a rusty gym instructor attempting to do press-ups, and not succeeding. With an effort, Rob got his knees underneath him. There was blood on the grass below him, and he checked his torso for wounds. Also, nothing.

Then he felt a trickle down his cheek and put his hand to his face. It came away bright red. There was a cut above his right eye that ran across and then down. It didn't feel like a clean cut, but rather a crude breaking of the skin due to his fall. Rob fished around in his pocket for a tissue and stemmed the bleeding as best he could.

Thankfully the rest of him seemed pretty much intact, which was more than could be said for his bike. Rob got up, swayed for a moment, then staggered over to the wreck. It had half-buried itself in some long grass, but the damage was all-too visible. The Vincent's handlebars were bent, as were both the mudguards. Her wheels were buckled, too, spokes sticking out at angles to the wheels. It wasn't unfixable – Rob had never come across such a machine – but it was far from being rideable either.

Snatches of the "dream" came back to Rob, gradually, in bits. His father, the ward, the boy with the ginger hair. He'd been thinking about his father just that morning, and as for the hospital ward, well that explained itself, didn't it? But who was the young kid he'd seen? Not himself at that age; Rob's own hair had always been as black as night. Possibly someone he'd known at school, and forgotten? The mind can dredge up all sorts of rubbish when you're unconscious.

The question was, what would he do now? For some reason Rob needed to see Dawn. He needed to get to the lighthouse as soon as he possibly could, and if that meant walking, then that's what he'd do.

But first... First he had to climb up this damned embankment and try to get his bearings.

Rob looked back down the road where he'd come from. After twenty minutes of walking – stopping every few minutes or so to let the aching subside – he seemed no nearer Haven Point than when he set off. What would only take him five, maybe ten minutes by Vincent, was going to take him considerably longer on foot.

The walk gave him even more time to think. To wonder. What had happened to the fishermen he'd been chasing? And where had they been heading? Back to Sable? To Angels Landing? Back to the sea? Wherever it was they'd probably reached the place ages ago in the ambulance. That is, if the blue Transit behind hadn't caught up with them first.

*People are dying...*

He could be worrying about nothing. The fishermen might all be dead now, riddled with bullets and carted off back to St August's. End of story.

But first things first, he'd get to the lighthouse, fix himself up, slap some antiseptic on his cut. He definitely couldn't go back to the hospital after what he'd done. Best to keep his head down and try to figure out what was going on around here. Stanley wouldn't be best pleased to see him, but his daughter would. Rob had seen the way she'd reacted at the hospital before Stanley came in, so pleased to see him, glad that he was all right. Half the worries about the lifeboat had been planted in her mind by her overbearing father; although if she ever found out the truth of what occurred that morning, she'd go spare. The man was only looking out for her, and Rob could respect that – if he had a daughter he'd like as not be just the same. But he had to be made to realise that Rob was no threat. How could he be when he felt the way he did about Dawn?

He didn't want to cut Stanley out of her life; far from it. If anyone could understand the importance of family, it was him. He'd gone for years without seeing his mum and dad. No way did he want that to happen with the woman he loved. Once they'd all calmed down, they could talk it through. If it was really what she wanted, he'd even jack the lifeboat in. After what he'd been through today, no one could really blame him, could they? But these were things that would have to wait until—

Rob had been so lost in his own thoughts he almost tripped over the thing in the road. How had he missed it? Rob asked himself, as big as it was. An ashen face gaped up at him from behind a clear mask. The man's chest had been completely flattened and his grey-blue PVC suit was covered in dried blood. Rob's eyes were drawn to the crumpled part of the body, then down further, past the waist. It looked almost as if the part of his leg just below the knee had been bent underneath him, but then Rob noticed the tears in the suit there, the pieces of flesh dangling out and whiteness of bone. This poor man had had the lower portion of his leg ripped clean off. It wasn't too hard to work out how.

There was a trail of watery redness, now dried into the road, which ran away from the corpse. Rob followed it along, perhaps another five minutes or so. There was a black smear on the asphalt and tiny bits of rubber. The marks continued on for a bit, then led off the side of the road. Swallowing dryly, Rob leaned over the embankment.

The two vans lying there at the bottom looked like a huge felled monster, their blackened husks still smoking and alive with flames at certain spots. The driver's door of what had once been the blue Transit was wide open, as was the back, and Rob saw a number of dingy, undefined shapes inside – just large enough to be people. Soldiers. Another was about fifteen, twenty feet away, blown clear by the explosion it appeared.

The glass windscreen of the ambulance had melted on the left-hand side – now the base, as it was tipped over. There was an opening at the other where the roof had buckled outwards. It was wide enough for two people to climb through, he noted. He saw no burnt bodies in either the passenger or the driver's seats of the ambulance.

But what about the back?

Rob was about to climb down the embankment when he heard the sound of engines on the road – coming from the direction he'd just travelled. Quickly he hobbled across to a bush at the top of the grassy hillock and hid behind it. Rob didn't have to wait long before he saw vans, jeeps, and cars approaching. Again, some sported a camouflaged pattern, some were civilian make like the Transit. They were the vehicles he'd driven through to escape back at the hospital. They'd obviously come out looking for their comrades-in-arms when nobody reported back. The rumbling stopped as they pulled up, one after the other.

From the lead vehicle – a cream-coloured van – Rob watched two grey-suited soldiers emerge and point at the crash site. There was a conflab; Rob saw the first man talking into the radio headset inside his hood that ran from ear to chin, and the other nodding his head, then shaking it and pointing again. When this was over the first man went back along the line of vans and such, having a word with each driver in turn. The next thing, all but the first two vehicles in the convoy pulled out and drove off down the road. Rob counted around twelve in total.

Now only the cream van and a black jeep remained behind, with about seven men milling around them. They brought out their weapons, the same ones Rob had seen at the hospital, automatics (Rob couldn't be certain from that distance, but they looked like MP5s). The man from the first car, Rob assumed he was in command of the group, thrust his arm forward, jabbing at the air with his gloved finger. The signal to move out.

Rob crouched down further behind the bush. It wasn't ideal cover. If they found him here he'd be arrested, maybe; certainly held for questioning. The only thing in his favour was the fact that they were focused on the burning vehicles, possibly to the exclusion of everything else. Rob recalled his basic training from the Navy. Keeping himself as low as he could, he watched them pass by.

Luck seemed to be with him for the time being. Not one of them noticed him.

He risked another peek. The soldiers were about thirty metres away, heading for the ambulance. His heart was pounding, he could feel it pressing against his ribs. The blood throbbing in his ears, over his cut eye.

There was a loud shout which startled him.

Something was stepping out of the damaged ambulance, from the back. It pulled itself over the smashed and bubbled front of the Transit where the two vehicles were joined together, a horrifying sight. A charred figure, hissing as black liquid flowed over it. Steam rose as the monster's "natural" juices touched the red-hot parts of its body, cooling it down.

There wasn't much of its face left now, and what little

Rob could see was covered in crackling flaps of skin which ran with a mixture of pus and stringy saliva.

Three of the soldiers had taken up a defensive stance on the ground, on their knees, rifles raised at the gruesome character. Others were approaching, though careful not to get too close.

Rob heard the leader shout: "Please step away from the vehicle with your hands raised!" There was a hitch in the voice, fear beneath all the bravado. It was a surreal episode, the soldiers almost like policemen who'd pulled a driver over for speeding.

The figure just turned its head towards them. If it had had eyes it would have looked vacantly at them, taking about as much notice as a dog does of a tick.

Until the tick bites.

Rob watched as the "person" – who used to be Harry Dale – came at them, arms held up in front of him. There was no doubt about it, the crash had definitely injured him (the way he lurched over the bonnet of the Transit, legs partially withered) but he – it – showed no signs of relenting.

A dark water blast shot from its arm, knocking one of the upright soldiers off his feet. The man screamed, that substance burrowing through his suit. The fisherman targeted another trooper, this time the shot having more of a kick. That poor sod was thrown across the embankment, a massive hole materialising where his stomach used to be. Pieces of severed intestine flew out as he landed, raining down on the green grass like sausage meat.

"Fire!" The group's leader bellowed the order and his men couldn't wait to obey it. Even before the last part of the word was uttered, a soldier on the ground let off a spray of bullets.

The fisherman was punched backwards by the swathe of hot lead, dancing like a marionette. He tossed and turned, but still didn't go down. Where the projectiles hit him, tiny fountains spurted out, but not of blood. The fisherman was leaking.

Rob didn't hang around to witness the outcome of the fight. Harry was beyond saving, hardly human anymore. His priority was to get to the lighthouse now, and the only way to do that was in one of the vehicles nearby.

He didn't bother crawling; the men wouldn't have seen him if he'd been painted sky blue with pink dots and blowing a trumpet. They were far too busy tackling the fisherman.

Rob limped up to the cream van, the gunfire raging below him. Climbing quickly into the driver's seat, he looked back to see Harry on the offensive again. Another one of the soldiers was doused in an oil-like jet, his body disintegrating like the nurse back at St August's. Rob eased the door closed and realised there were no keys in the ignition.

"Dammnit!" He reached around underneath and pulled away the lower section of the steering column.

Rob brushed the two wires together that would make the van start. The engine grunted to life first time, barely audible above the gunfire. He slipped off the handbrake, placed his foot on the clutch, then shoved the gearstick into first. Bringing the clutch up, Rob pressed down on the accelerator. The van kangarooed to start with, Rob familiarising himself with the thing as he went.

Soon it was coasting along, Rob working his way up through the gears. He wiped his forehead with the back of his hand. Sweat and blood worked their way into the cracks of his skin. Rob took one look in the side mirror. He could just see the occasional flash of rifle fire and a grey suit every now and again. He wondered who would win the battle, and a twinge of guilt and helplessness ran through him. Partly because he'd left those men to face

God-knows-what. And partly because he hadn't been able to help the very monster those soldiers were facing.

Turning his attention back to the road, Rob drove the van on towards Haven Point and the lighthouse.

## Chapter Thirty-Four
### Observations

The main bulk of the troops had pulled out.

From his hiding place in the hills, still unnoticed, the stranger known as Darville observed the exodus. He'd seen them all arrive, naturally. He recognised the Colonel and Fuller straight away, regardless of the fact they were both wearing chemical warfare suits. He should know them by now, they'd all worked together for long enough.

He pitied the Colonel. The man just didn't have a clue, trying to contain this. It couldn't be done – not by him anyway. Too much had been set in motion already. Darville had seen the window smash, the men jumping out. The men who'd been taken from the sea.

From where they belonged.

An accident, but it suited their purpose quite nicely. It was only a matter of time now, and if the Colonel and his lot could be stalled…

But he'd waited. He couldn't just walk in there, not with all those soldiers about. Couldn't risk bumping into

Fuller prematurely or being taken into custody (not that he wouldn't put up a fight first). Fuller, ah poor naïve Fuller. His old friend. Darville smiled, recalling their last few days together before his own escape. The professor thought that he'd had him, but Darville was smarter than that. Fuller was probably wondering where he was right now.

"I'm closer than you think, Edward," Darville said. "Much closer than you think."

Now that the soldiers had departed, or at least a fair few of them, Darville would work his way down to the hospital. To make his move.

Only then could he begin to stop them.

## Chapter Thirty-Five
### The Battle

The time was quarter past five when the cavalcade approached Sable. Vans following jeeps, following cars and people carriers, plus a huge lorry for evacuation purposes. Were it not for the camouflaged patterns on some of the vehicles one might have mistaken the stream of traffic for those long-lost summer holidaymakers Billy Braden had been expecting that Saturday lunch-time. The grey-blue environment suits and shiny black weaponry were also clues as to the procession's true identity.

The soldiers had not stopped at the lighthouse, nor any of the cottages by Angels Landing or those on the clifftops themselves. They'd made straight for the village. For Sable, as per their instructions, issued personally by the Colonel; and no one disobeyed the Colonel. Sable was to be investigated first, then on the way back any stragglers could be mopped up. And any houses marked on their maps with a cross were priorities – these being the abodes of the men involved in the sea rescue that morning.

The house of one Robert Woodhead was first up, and although it was searched thoroughly they could find no trace of the owner, suspected to have escaped from the hospital just as they arrived; one or two of the men had a particular score to settle with the biker. But it was a long shot anyway and none of the soldiers who broke in expected to find him sat watching TV and eating a sandwich.

Next up was the home of Coxswain Philip Holmes and his ageing mother. Phil was at the hospital "under observation" – and not by the doctors – however the house was still to be checked as Frank Dexter could well have paid it a visit after he left St August's. He'd told Wayne Gough's family that he was on his way there next.

This time the team that went in did find something. Evidence of a struggle, and the remains of three adult humans – one of whom was still in an armchair facing the window. Trained as they were, even the most hardened veterans found the state of those bodies upsetting. Although none would admit to it; they just got on with bagging them for later examination. But they were even more stunned to find a little girl hiding outside in the garden shed, shaking and crying.

"It's all right, love. We won't hurt you," the soldier who discovered her had said. "What's your name?"

"J-Jenny," she replied. "Jenny Holmes."

Jenny had been taken back to the convoy to sit in a silver people carrier with one of the female officers, Lt Lowe; her immediate superior thought that Jenny might be more responsive to a woman, as cliched as that was. And, it had to be said, Lt Lowe couldn't help warming to the brave little girl. After some careful questioning she managed to coax the story out of her, about how the car had come to her granny's house – she heard it but took hardly any notice; she was too busy playing with her dog

Brad to be bothered.

But then a little while later she'd heard funny noises coming from the house, and so Jenny had peeped through the window to find out what was going on.

The young girl started to shake as she recounted what had happened, how the "funny man" had hurt her daddy, how he'd changed Daddy's face somehow so that it no longer looked like him anymore. She didn't see what it did to Mummy or Gran, the chair turned away from her, but she knew it had to be bad.

And when she looked round, she'd seen Brad barking at the back door. Before she could stop him, he'd scratched his way inside.

"There was a growling noise," continued Jenny, "and then a yelping."

She hadn't been able to look after that. Jenny had run away and hidden in the shed to wait for her Uncle Phil to come home. He'd know what to do, how to get rid of the funny man and help her parents.

Lt Lowe had taken off her face-mask at that point – strictly against regulations – and hugged the child to her, Jenny's face pressed against her chest. All she could think about were the remains in that house and how Jenny would never see her folks again.

"You did the right thing, baby," Lowe told her softly. "You're safe now. And you'll see your Uncle Phil real soon."

"Promise?"

"I promise."

But all the time Lowe was wondering what effect this would have on Jenny. If she'd ever get over this, ever be able to sleep again without having nightmares or wetting the bed. What had happened here today would affect her greatly in the short term, that much was obvious, but it would also haunt her as a grown-up as well, putting the hex on her relationships and maybe even her working life, too. The one bright spot was that Philip Holmes was alive and well back at St August's, and in time perhaps the wounds would heal. Perhaps.

The convoy continued on into Sable where they found the streets to be deserted. The patchwork houses made up of different coloured bricks looked vacant, still and empty. Some of the troops jumped out to knock on doors, ready with the official line about a gas leak. Yet no one answered. Not one person came out and when they pressed up against the windows, the soldiers could see no signs of life. Short of searching every single house there wasn't much more they could do but move on.

Past the ancient church with its massive cross on the top and the double graveyard, they came into what was referred to on the map as the centre of Sable. On one side was a typical pub, The Seagull, its double doors shut tight against the outside. No regulars coming and going. A bit further up was a shop, the usual kind you get in almost every seaside village selling everything from papers to buckets and spades, to hammers and gas tanks. Although the door was wide open this looked vacant as well.

"I don't get it, sir," said the driver of the lead vehicle – a turquoise van – to his sergeant sitting to the left of him. "Where is everyone?"

"No cars, no people. This place is like a ghost town."

The order was passed to halt and the whole convoy, doing about ten miles an hour, ground down. Doors opened – side doors, back doors, sliding doors – and infantry poured out. They took up defensive, but non-threatening, positions around the convoy. If the Sablites were hiding out of fear, just like Jenny, they didn't want to alarm them further.

Slowly, the troops advanced through the middle of town on foot. Lt Lowe remained with her charge in the people carrier, watching them go. She began to wonder whether she ought to have gone back to the hospital with the girl. At least her uncle was there.

"Where are they going?" asked Jenny. "To look for the funny man?"

Lowe wiped the window with her elbow. "They're going to warn people about him, honey."

Jenny was still clinging to the Lt's body, afraid to let go. But much of the terror had gone from her voice. "What if he's out there somewhere, though?"

"Don't worry. My friends can handle him."

Her charge relaxed a bit more, snuggling up to Lowe. If the truth be told she was glad of the excuse to stay in here rather than venturing out into that territory.


Four of the suited figures went to peruse The Seagull – it seemed as good a place as any to start. They knocked on the door first, but when nobody answered the men kicked down the wooden obstruction.

At the exact moment that door flew inwards, all four of them vanished.

Troops covering from the rear were powerless to help as a breath-taking flood of beer, blood and water crashed into their colleagues, knocking them off their feet and into the middle of the road. The four felled soldiers, their PVC attire shiny and lustrous, struggled to stand up, rifles at the ready, trained on the open doorway.

By the side of the small park more of the soldiers spun round when they heard a loud bubbling noise coming from the pond. The knee-high fence encircling it was sucked under the ground as water spread from beneath. Then a great geyser erupted twenty feet into the air. It danced in the late afternoon sun, shimmering with pretty colours.

Radio communication jumped from one body to the

next, reporting in and asking what they should do. No one seemed to know; not the regular servicemen, and certainly not the officers. No one could have imagined this scenario. But it was about to get a hell of a lot stranger.

The ground at their feet trembled violently. Cracks appeared to the left and right, spouting deadly fountains from the sewer system. Those poor soldiers who happened to be standing on a split in the road or street at the time, were either rocketed upwards to land as crumpled and battered masses or obliterated on the spot – the force of the surge shredding them to pieces.

None of the infantry saw where they came from. One minute the streets and roads were clear, apart from the prominent pistons of liquid, the next they were full of people. And the crowds strode forwards with a purpose, through the jets coming out of the ground. They came from all sides at once, trapping the convoy, cutting off their escape route.

At least ten soldiers died before the order was given to fire, and the lead vehicle, the turquoise van with the sergeant and driver inside, was blown easily over onto its side.


Lt Lowe couldn't believe what she was seeing.

From the people carrier near the back she was still afforded a good view of the carnage, and the clamour was deafening.

She pulled Jenny closer; it wasn't clear who needed comforting the most. Despite the ruckus all around them, the little girl lay peacefully in her arms. Probably nervous exhaustion, the Lt reasoned. But no. Something was wrong, Lowe could sense it. She craned her head. Jenny looked asleep. She shook her and called out her name. No response.

It was as she checked the child's neck for a pulse that Lowe noticed her unusual necklace, partially hidden by the T-Shirt, but also the blanket they'd wrapped her in. It wasn't like any jewellery she'd seen before. Not fancy or decorative, but functional. Placed there for a reason, and around the neck instead of the wrist so Jenny would never take it off or lose it. The necklace told Lowe all she needed to know, and explained instantly why Jenny had gone limp in her arms.

"Just hold on. Hold on, baby," Lowe whispered as she set the girl down on the seat and began hunting for the emergency medical kit in the front. If Jenny didn't get a shot of insulin and soon, then it wouldn't matter what happened outside.

Because that brave little girl would be dead.

The sickening thing that had once been called Sean Howard "surfed" out of the entrance to The Seagull, followed closely by some of the establishment's regulars, Mike Croxley and old Alf Fletcher included. The four soldiers they were heading for depressed their triggers and a volley of hot metal winged its way towards the Sablites.

The fact that they had been normal villagers just a few short hours ago meant nothing to the hardened veterans. They were the enemy, pure and simple. And they were attacking.

Round after round whizzed past their bodies, riding on a crest out of the pub. Some shots even found their mark, sinking with an awful squelching sound into soaking flesh. But still they advanced.

Sean was the first to reach the soldiers and he snatched the rifle out of the commander's hands. Casting the smoking weapon aside, he seized the guy by the arms, forcing him to his knees. Sean's hands slipped through the

PVC covering and melded with the skin and bone underneath. The soldier tried to break free as his arms and upper body bulged inside the suit. There was a soft popping sound, and the clear faceplate was coated red.

A shot rang past Sean's gruesome features, and he turned to throw the lifeless soldier at the gunman who was to blame. They were both carried back and into a wall, bodies broken and twisted.

The other two soldiers involved in the fight were dispatched just as easily. Ex-barmaid, Tina, delighted in ramming her hand right through one infantryman's chest, while the other soldier was pummelled by Alf, a new-found strength coursing through him, all arthritic pains forgotten. The old man's veins bulged as he picked up the trooper, then snapped him over muscular legs like so much brittle wood.

On the far side of the village centre, the man who'd been Keith Tomkinson and his crewmate Frank Dexter had met up. They bathed in the chaos they'd created, their offspring swarming over the men with guns, taking them systematically apart. Now they saw the wisdom of sparing these villagers rather than quenching their own insatiable blood-lust. They needed cannon fodder; an army to combat *this* army. To buy them some time. Frank and Keith had obeyed.

From the third van down the line came a furious *rat-tat-tat-tat* of a mounted chain-gun. It was positioned on the top and a soldier was standing up through the sunroof to operate it, another crouching by his side, feeding the hungry machine with ammunition. One, two villagers were spectacularly cut down by the fire.

Frank and Keith pointed their "hands" at the ground, propelling themselves up and over the war zone on a fountain of water. The lifeboat men landed on the van, Frank at the back, Keith crashing onto the bonnet. The chain-gun pivoted downwards, and its operator got ready to discharge the load into Keith. Before he could do anything else, Frank pulled him out through the sunroof. The gun drooped uselessly as he took hold of the man's shoulders. Frank's hands became indistinct once more, a flash of soda and foam, then he plunged them deep into the soldier on either side, through the pectoral, trapezius and deltoid muscles, slicing through bones like a hot knife through butter, altering molecules along the way. Down he went to meet at the groin, until the soldier was in three parts, the PVC glistening with redness.

The gunner's aide tried to jump from the top of the van, unwilling to share the same fate, but he slipped on the metallic surface, his boots finding no grip on the river of vital fluid now washing over the vehicle. Keith was up and on top of him in an instant. The tough, trained military man gazed up at Keith's dripping face, and felt his bladder empty itself inside his suit. Keith seemed to sense this release, perhaps the warmth building up in the frightened man's loins alerting him, or maybe he knew on another level. Either way he smiled and this alone was enough to freeze the soldier to the spot.

Keith placed his mockery of a hand on the soldier's stomach and pushed. Now it was inside the suit, dipping into the hot, trickling urine. And the trooper could feel his own bodily waste rising, turning against him, slithering over him like a thousand tiny eels. Over his chest, crawling up his vest, under his arm-pits, and up through his neck-seal into his mask. He did move now, motivated by the strong smell of his own piss. Keith pulled out his hand and shifted it up to help pin the soldier's arms down. The yellow liquid climbed with a will all of its own, pumping into the mask, seeking out any orifices it could find: mouth, nostrils, ears. The soldier heaved at the taste, drowning in his own secretions. Soon the mask was full up, the umber fluid bubbling against the glass. After a few spasmodic jerks, the soldier gave up and died.

Rising, Keith joined Frank on the roof. The lifeboat men exchanged glances, then directed their arms towards the van. Four tremendous jets bit into the roof, completely flooding it in seconds. The pair jumped lithely down off the vehicle before it swelled up and burst, the effect as lethal as a hand grenade going off in its belly.


Lt Lowe ignored the explosion down the line from her vehicle. She was concentrating on unwrapping the sterile syringe and drawing off a quantity of insulin to administer this to Jenny. Consulting the medical handbook, she stepped up to the unconscious little girl, praying that she had the right dosage, that she wouldn't cock this up.

*And how are you going to get her out of here after you've given her the injection?* she thought. *One crisis at a time, Lowe. One at a time!*

She'd never really pictured herself as the maternal kind. Perhaps one day, when Mr Right came along (not that she met many "right" men in her line of work; more like Mr Right Now. "And what do you do?", "I'm sorry, I can't tell you that... It's classified!"). But Jenny had awakened that instinct inside, tugging at her heartstrings. The need to protect her, to save her, was overwhelming. Totally beyond her control.

Lowe looked around for a vein to use, a thin stripe of blue that would carry the medicine into Jenny's system. She found one at last, then remembered to tap the air bubbles out of the syringe; it was something they always seemed to do on TV. Another swift prayer and Lowe guided the needle point in, pressing the end inwards, sending the clear drug on its way.

There was more shooting outside. Lowe saw a grey

body fly past the opposite window, unable to tell who it was. There were so many out there she didn't recognise individuals anymore. Lowe turned her attention back to the battle going on in the people carrier.

Jenny flinched as the needle came out, her closed eyelids fluttering.

*Is that a good sign?* Lowe wondered. *Oh please let her wake up now... please, please God...*

Lowe could see Jenny's hand opening and closing, her arm moving, twitching. Precious life-signs. Did it really work that fast, insulin? Lowe had never known anyone with diabetes, so she didn't have a clue. She was just glad she hadn't been too late, that Jenny was still with her.

Leaning over, Lowe inspected the arm where the puncture wound was. It looked sore, inflamed. She knew that it took much longer for people with diabetes to heal, could that be the reason? No, stupid. The needle must have been faulty or something, they were meant to be sterile but—

Lowe turned the arm over in her gloved hands. Now it was weeping.

"Oh Christ!" Lowe was in a panic, not knowing what to do next. Should she apply antiseptic? Dress the wound and hope for the best? *What?* She couldn't exactly ask for help – and the wagon was jammed in tight, the convoy nose to tail. She should try and contact St August's, get some proper advice. Yes, that's what she'd—

Then it happened.

As Lowe hovered over Jenny's arm, the prick there spat something into her face. The female soldier only had a brief moment before it spattered onto her cheeks and brow, but she could have sworn that stuff was the insulin she'd just administered, darkened slightly by Jenny's blood – but almost definitely the same medicine. Jenny's body was rejecting it in a most disturbing way, like a toddler getting rid of a spoonful of baby food it didn't care for.

Shocked, Lowe recoiled, wiping away the mess, trying to prevent it from getting into her eyes. Too late, it was everywhere – including that one place, blinding her temporarily. Stinging, making her eyes run.

Lowe pressed her eyelids shut, rubbing at the balls through them. That just made things worse. Thinking fast, she put her hand out, feeling for her water flask and unscrewing the lid. Lowe splashed it into her face, forcing herself to open her eyes, to wash out the chemicals.

Through a blurred fog she saw Jenny sitting up on the seat, looking at her with childlike wonder, head cocked slightly. Lowe blinked away more of the insulin, trying to discern the girl's features. But they wouldn't – or couldn't – come into focus. However, it wasn't her own lack of vision that was the problem. Jenny's face wasn't the same. It was changing, eyebrows stooping, meeting in the middle, an odd gleaming quality affecting her skin. And where there had been big, round, innocent pupils before, now there was a dense but translucent scum – giving Jenny the appearance of a blind girl. A poor, pitiful blind girl.

Except now Lowe realised it was herself who should be pitied. Had she been tricked, or had the effects of Jenny's encounter with the "funny man" finally taken their toll? For he had seen her at the window, Lowe was certain of that. He had passed this thing on to her. She would have been better off dying with her parents, her granny. Dying as Lowe was about to do in a few seconds.

"Jenny... no..."

Already she could sense the build up, feel the energy involved in Jenny's metamorphosis, her preparation.

From the outside, if anyone had been taking notice, all that could be seen was a coat of redness plastering the window before being suddenly washed away by a cool blast of running water...

"Fall back!"

Someone gave the order, it didn't matter who – it probably wasn't even an official command, just a lowly private with more common sense than his superiors. And though they tried to do so, men and women were dropping like the proverbial flies. Gunfire was drowned out – quite literally – by the opposition. Those soldiers who were merely injured, sprawled out over the pavement, could see the after-effects of the attack, the sneak attack none of them had been prepared for. They could see the remains of wrecked vehicles, the devastated Sable streets. And they knew they hadn't really stood a chance against this new foe.

One or two of the soldiers in their final few seconds on Earth, actually asked themselves the question...

What would?

## Chapter Thirty-Six
### Discoveries

Rob swung the van onto the drive that led to Haven Point lighthouse. There was Dawn's pink Suzuki, "The Love Mobile". He hadn't realised how much he needed to see her face until now, how much he needed to feel her arms around him. Screw Stanley Keets!

He pulled up on the other side of the white tower, so that his van wouldn't be seen from the road. With a bit of luck anybody who came looking for him would just pass on by. With a bit of luck.

The only problem was that luck seemed to be in short supply today. Actually, he couldn't remember a day that had been so unlucky in his entire life. Or as draining. A sit down and a stiff drink would be like being in Heaven after what he'd been through.

Rob nearly fell out of the driver's seat, his muscles contracting, telling him to take it easy. He couldn't oblige them yet. Willpower alone saw him round to the door, every step a punishment. Rob felt a strange sense of danger, of impending doom, but he didn't know why. He lifted a hand to knock, but with the first rap it swung inwards.

The door was already open.

\*\*\*

Harding, Vicky and Tobe had been reunited after their interrogations, back in the first office with a guard on the door.

Harding hadn't known whether to hug Vicky when he saw her, but she took the decision out of his hands, wrapping herself around him. Tobe slumped down in the leather chair behind the desk.

"Are you all right?" she asked Harding.

"Fine. I could do with a glass of whiskey, but apart from that..."

Vicky smiled. "What did they ask you?"

"All kinds of things about today, about the Rain Circle. About *you*."

"Yeah, I don't think they like me very much. Story of my life."

"I heard engines outside, did you?"

Vicky nodded, her blonde hair falling over her face. "Troops pulling out. I think we're in the middle of something really nasty here. Something no one was meant to see."

"I say we just sit tight and wait until they say we can go," offered Tobe.

"Look, you don't seriously think they'll just let us all leave after what we've seen here today, do you?" Vicky was amazed at her cameraman. "We work for a TV company for goodness sakes!"

Tobe sat bolt upright in the chair. "What are you

talking about, Vic?"

Vicky didn't even dignify that with an answer. She could tell Harding was on her wavelength.

"We have to get you out of here, and soon," Harding told her.

"I don't know if it's escaped your attention, but those are serious people out there. They've got guns," Tobe argued.

"All the more reason not to stick around," answered Vicky.

"Matt'll be here soon with an OB unit," Tobe reminded her.

"Will he?" Vicky didn't look so sure. "When I mentioned that to the Colonel he didn't even flinch."

There was a knock at the door and Vicky spun around to see Fuller push his way into the room.

"Sorry to interrupt, but I have to speak with you urgently," he said, closing the door and lowering his voice so the guard outside couldn't hear. "Miss West, Mr Howell, I'm afraid that if you don't come with me now you could both be dead within the hour."

\*\*\*

Rob pushed the door open even further with his fingers. It creaked loudly on its hinges.

Stanley Keets was a stickler for security. Whether out or in he always kept his lighthouse locked up tight. It made sense when you thought about it; the number of hours he spent up the top leaning on that blasted rail. Even if he saw a stranger approaching, he wouldn't be able to get down in time to stop them gaining entry.

If his sixth sense hadn't warned Rob, then this was a

dead giveaway that something was amiss. The inside was dark and cold, a complete contrast to the sunny world outside. Rob crept into the entrance, resisting the urge to call out Dawn's name.

He'd only been here a couple of times, to pick Dawn up when they were going out somewhere, and even then he'd only stayed for a few minutes while she grabbed her coat or whatever, Stanley usually looking daggers at him as he sat in the living room. Rob listened at the curving stairway for any sound of voices.

Nothing.

Cautiously, and with a great fear welling inside, he started up the stairs. His body cried out again, but he ignored the pain. He had to get up there. One foot after the other, he climbed, hand on the wooden rail for support. He was nearing the living room now. Blood from the cut over his eye was dripping down his cheek. *God knows what I must look like*, he thought, trying to take his mind off the palpable dread in the air.

His head came up and into the living room itself. He couldn't believe what he was seeing ahead of him. The place was a mess: sofa upturned, ornaments lay smashed on the floor, the coffee table across the other side of the room, reared up against the rounded wall. It looked just like a mini-tornado had swept through the room. It looked just like the hospital ward back at St August's.

*Oh Jesus, no...*

Rob climbed higher, the sense of danger building.

He heard somebody rush at him from behind. They'd been waiting for Rob to clear the stairs. He rounded and stepped out of the way just in time, as something sharp whizzed past the side of his face.

\*\*\*

"*What?*"

Vicky was visibly shaken by the news. It was one thing to suspect you might be silenced, permanently, but quite another for someone to tell you it for certain.

"Please, lower your voice. The guard outside will hear." Fuller came further into the office, away from the door, away from the ears of the guard. Once more his hood was down so he could talk face to face. "I'm afraid that if you don't come away with me now, something terrible will happen to you."

Tobe had risen by now, leaving the chair behind him. "But... but you... can't—"

"*I'm* not going to do anything, Mr Howell. But I have my doubts about the Colonel. He's been acting very irrationally. I don't know what he might do. As we speak, troops are already making their way into Sable itself. He's talking about evacuating the villagers, bringing them back here. I dread to think what he'd do if any of them resisted, or if he discovers the infection has spread." Fuller shook his head. "This is all getting out of hand."

"Wait, back up a second," Vicky broke in. "You're saying he's going to execute us?"

"No... I... I don't know. He's capable of anything, the Colonel. I think he blames me for what happened here. You see, I needed time to prepare. I didn't want us to come before we were ready."

Harding still held Vicky and he could feel her heartbeat quickening inside her chest. "So, you weren't called in by anybody here at all!" he said.

Fuller hung his head, then shook it. "No, no we weren't. We – that is the Colonel – guessed what was happening as soon as he intercepted the emergency call to the coastguard. It was a simple matter for him to 'shut down' the area." The professor walked over to Vicky and took her by the elbow. "But look, we're wasting time. We have to get you out of here."

This time Harding did react, slapping the man's gloved hand away. "She's not going anywhere with you."

Fuller seemed shocked, then his eyes misted up. Harding thought he was about to start blubbering. "Please listen, if you come with me now I'll talk to your station, grant you an exclusive interview – the works. Hell, it'll be the only way *I'll* make it out of this alive."

Vicky patted Harding's arm and turned towards the professor. "All right, I believe you. But first you have to tell us what all this is really about."

\*\*\*

There was a whistling noise as the fire axe flew past Rob's head.

It sparked against the stone wall of the lighthouse before landing on the carpeted floor of the living room. Rob stepped forward, fist raised. Then he stopped when he recognised his assailant.

A dishevelled Stanley Keets was before him, his white hair wild, his eyes out on stalks.

"For fuck's sake, what're you…" Rob's words died in his throat as his vision moved downwards. It settled on Stanley's left arm, which was bright red. Blood ran from a lesion at the shoulder, leaving the appendage limp. His right hand, the one he'd used to swing the fire axe – which normally resided on hooks at the top of the stairs – was still in a gripping position, in spite of the fact that the "weapon" had slid out of his grasp when he attacked.

The whole thing was like a bizarre reconstruction of

the hospital scene that had played out earlier. Rob's fist raised; almost, but not quite, striking Stanley. The older man standing there and waiting for it to land. Except this time both of them looked like they'd been in the wars, and had the battle scars to prove it.

"Stanley...?" said Rob, but the other man didn't reply. "Stanley!" Louder, more forceful. "What happened to you? Where's Dawn?"

A flicker of awareness in Stanley's eyes. "W-Woodhead? Is that you?"

"Yes, Stanley. What happened here?"

"I thought you were one... one of them."

Rob looked around the room. "Who, Stanley?"

"They... were hurt, burnt. I let them in. Oh God, but their faces..."

"How long ago, Stanley? Are they still here?"

Rob could get no more sense out of the fellow. It was obvious he'd been in contact with the fishermen from the crash. Lou and George. They'd headed for the nearest building, in bad shape, probably dying – although that hadn't stopped Harry Dale from making a mess of those soldiers. Rob's thoughts turned again to Dawn.

Picking up the discarded axe, he left Stanley where he was and headed across the room, glancing over at the small toilet, which was empty. Then on to the kitchen. The door was closed, so Rob nudged it open with his toe. He held the axe with both hands, cursing himself for not picking up the soldier's pistol back on the road. But he'd been in too much of a hurry to get away.

The kitchen was clear, as well. Rob tightened his grip on the axe handle and made his way outside, back to the stairs.

***

"It's a long story, Miss West, and we really haven't got time right now. Suffice to say that it all started with Darville, the man whose photo I showed you earlier. He used to work at our facility until he... escaped. He killed two technicians and one of the guards."

"But why?" asked Tobe. "Why's he spreading this virus?"

"And what has it got to do with our Rain Circle?" Vicky added.

"I don't *know* why he's doing this. That's what I hoped to find out here, but... As I said Miss West, we really haven't got much time. If we're to leave we should do so now while most of the Colonel's people are gone. I'll explain everything when we're safe."

"All right then, let's go." Vicky pulled Harding along and Tobe dashed to the door.

Fuller barred their way; he seemed anxious. "I'm afraid I can only manage to smuggle two of you out. Tell the guard I'm taking you for more questions, or maybe an examination." His eyes seemed to light up at the thought of giving Vicky a physical. "But he'll definitely become suspicious if I march out with all three of you."

"Oh brilliant!" said Tobe. "Just bleeding brilliant."

Harding looked at Vicky. "You and Tobe get going. I'll be okay here."

Vicky pressed herself up against him. "No way. I'm not leaving you, Jason."

"They're not going to do anything to me. I'm only a lowly painter."

"No, I can't—"

Fuller coughed. "Time's running out. We have to leave now."

"Please, Vicky. I want you to be safe."

"Once we're away and you've made contact with your station we can come back for Mr Harding. The Colonel will do nothing if he thinks the media are involved."

"Come on Vicky, he's told you he'll come back." Tobe was chomping at the bit.

"I don't give a toss; I'm not going anywhere without Jason."

Harding pulled Vicky round to face him. "Go," he said softly, a gleam in his eyes like she'd never seen before. Something passed between them, an understanding or an emotion far greater than that. She knew she'd see him again soon. "I don't want to be responsible for any more deaths, Vicky. Especially yours. I couldn't bear it."

Vicky nodded. "I—"

Harding bent his head low and kissed her, stemming the flow of her sentence. Vicky was stunned to start with, then returned the kiss, closing her eyes and forgetting about everything else but his lips. It was even better than she'd imagined. But reluctantly, inevitably, they had to break it off.

"Thank God for that," said Tobe, face sour. "So can we go now, d'you think?"

\*\*\*

Rob mounted the stairs again, up towards the next level of the lighthouse.

He quietened his breathing slightly, aware that he was making too much noise. If the fishermen were still around, he didn't want to tip them off that he was coming. Surprise was about all he had at the moment, and even with that he didn't know what kind of chance he stood against *them*. Rob was still determined to take those folk alive if he could; they were in a weakened condition, just like the one at the crash-site – Stanley Keets was testament to that. He was lucky to be alive.

But where was Dawn? He'd checked her room, the one just above the living room – it had been completely empty. Untouched as far as he could discern.

Rob had got nothing from her father, just gibberings about being knocked across the living room. Hopefully she'd had the time and the wherewithal to find a hiding place. There was only one way to find out.

Rob reached the next floor, axe poised, head turning from side to side, checking behind him first this time. Up here was the master bedroom – Stanley's – and a bathroom. He knew because he'd had to come up and wash on one of the few occasions he'd visited, fresh from the garage.

This bedroom was also deserted, and no mess in here either. Again, no struggle had taken place in the room, it seemed. But there were dark footprints on the polished wooden floor, leading off in the direction of the bathroom. Rob heard a faint sizzling sound. No, it was more like a hissing... The shower was on.

He headed straight across to the bathroom door, which was shut. Hefting the axe in his left hand, he took the doorknob in his right.

Rob turned it.

Upon opening the door, he walked in. The shower curtain was pulled across, pellets of spray bouncing against the material, water spilling over from the full bath beneath. Cautiously, Rob edged forwards, axe ready. He took hold of a corner of the curtain, then pulled it back. The water hit him immediately, drenching his leather jacket and trousers. Rob swung his weapon and it connected with the head of the shower, knocking it sideways so that the beads struck the tiled wall. There was nobody there.

Leastways, nobody stood up.

Rob heard a splashing and looked down into the full, overflowing bath.

And the face that looked back at him through the clear film was no longer human in any true sense of the word.

\*\*\*

Fuller, Tobe and Vicky had got past the guard with very little trouble. He knew that the professor was authorised to do what he liked with "prisoners" (it wasn't a word any of them used, but if it walked like a duck…).

The tricky part would be getting out of the hospital itself.

"There are sentries posted at every main entrance and exit," explained Fuller. "My car's just outside, but we need to get past them first."

"How do you propose we do that?" asked Vicky, struggling to keep up as he walked briskly down the corridor, on the lookout for any sign of the Colonel.

"We'll take the lift down to the morgue to start with, there's a fire exit in there."

"I won't ask what you've been doing in the morgue," Vicky said.

"Best not to," he replied sheepishly.

The trio made it to the lift without being seen, except for a couple of patrolmen who both nodded to Fuller but didn't detain him. They were used to seeing the man flitting about the place by now, and probably had no idea who the people with him were.

The metal doors clunked. No one spoke as they descended. Vicky was looking at the professor, trying to weigh him up. Wondering whether he would really go back for Harding or not. He seemed far more interested in saving his own skin than anything, and to do that he needed Creation-Time. He needed *them*, Tobe and her. Harding was inconsequential.

But as soon as they were out of the area, Vicky would personally make sure that police, camera crews, the works, were swarming around this place.

The Colonel wouldn't dare do anything then.

\*\*\*

He'd seen this before back at the ambulance, but Rob still froze at the spectacle of the charcoaled fisherman. There was enough of the face left to make a reasonable identification, though if Rob hadn't known this man forever it might have been hard. Lou Turner's body was ravaged by burns and angry pustules which glowed grey under the rippling surface of the bathwater. Yet even as Rob watched he could see the tissues knitting themselves together, the skin healing gradually. The bed of liquid he was immersed in was restoring him, piecing him back together. The shower's spray giving him back the energy and vigour he lacked. His – its – eyes were caked over with tangled blackness, but now it opened both lids to reveal glimmering pools of dark matter underneath. This creature saw, but not through the eyes of a man. It was wondering what the disruption was, why the fountain had been deflected. Why its rejuvenation had been disturbed.

Rob didn't know what to do next. Surely he couldn't reason with Lou in this state. Maybe he'd just kidded himself that he got through to them back at St August's, that he saw a semblance of humanity left inside. But the urge to help was as great as ever.

# The Wet

Lou started to rise, to almost levitate himself out of the bath. Water slopped clumsily onto the floor, running over the bathroom mats and saturating them completely. The fisherman lifted one of his hands and Rob gaped at the metamorphosis up close. The fingers, the bones and muscles quivered, shivering until there was nothing left of them but a bubbling mass of whiteness. Lou was preparing to strike, his target lined up.

Sheer survival instinct took over. Rob brought the axe down sharply at an angle, cutting a swathe through Lou's wrist. The metal passed right through what remained of his flesh, almost as if it weren't there, but it was enough to redirect the blast that followed. Instead of hitting Rob full in the chest as was the intention, the burst ate its way into the tiles behind him, shattering them and shrouding Rob in a hail of ceramic splinters.

With all the effort he could muster, Rob shoved the axe head forward, smacking the fisherman full in the face. The blow glanced off him, and with his other arm Lou tried to knock the weapon out of Rob's grasp.

Lou was strong, *very* strong, but still weakened by the crash. Unfortunately, so was Rob, the legacy of his fall from the Vincent sending agonising shockwaves through his entire body. Eventually, Rob stepped back, taking the axe with him. This unbalanced Lou and he wobbled sideways out of the bath.

Wasting no time, Rob hefted the axe and struck the side of Lou's head with the edge. This time the fisherman was fazed, enough for Rob to bring a knee up into his stomach. There was a gurgling sound and Lou heaved up a deluge of murky grey slime which seemed to slide across the floor with a life of its own.

Horrified, Rob swung the axe one last time, smashing it against the back of Lou's skull. He sank to the floor with a sputter, sprawling out over the mess he'd made. The body was motionless. Rob kicked it with the toe of his boot. It didn't move.

He backed away from the scene, clutching the axe.

Slowly, Rob retreated, out into the bedroom, nearly to the stairs. He couldn't tear his eyes away from the body. *Jesus, what have I done! Lou…*

It was then that he heard the sound of crying echoing down from above.

\*\*\*

It was cold in the morgue, as was only to be expected. Fuller led Tobe and Vicky past the bodies on the examining tables, illuminated by overhead florescent lights. Both were split open from neck to abdomen, their organs exposed – some of them removed. The top half of David Turner's head was missing, the insides scooped out and placed in a bowl next to it.

Tobe went pale, hand to his mouth. But after all she'd seen that afternoon nothing was about to shock Vicky.

"Your handiwork, Professor?" she asked Fuller.

"Hmmm? Oh, yes. I was trying to establish exactly how the chemicals in the extinguisher did what they did to him."

Vicky was again trying to keep up. "And what did you find?"

"Nothing conclusive. Besides, it was always my intention to cure these people, not kill them. I'll leave that entirely in the Colonel's capable hands." They reached the door, a red rectangle with a metal bar across it. "The morgue is below ground, where the wine cellar used to be when this was a house," Fuller turned to tell them. "I studied the plans when we got here. There was a fire some years ago, so they take every precaution now. The steps lead up into the car park from here I believe."

He pushed on the bar and sunlight flooded in, eclipsing the artificial lights in the morgue. "Come on, this way."

Vicky and Tobe went with him up the fire escape steps, concrete ones put in when the exit was created. They took them directly up into the car park. Fuller looked around, then suddenly ducked down.

"What is it?" whispered Tobe.

"One of the Colonel's men on patrol," Fuller replied in hushed tones. "I don't think he saw me."

"Even if we get to your car without being seen," Vicky began, "he's bound to spot us if we drive straight past him."

"I've thought of that." The professor pointed to the grassland surrounding the hospital on three of its four sides. "There are more ways out of here than through the front gate, Miss West."

Vicky loathed the way he kept looking at her, like she was his meal ticket out of this. Perhaps he was thinking about the money he might make when it was all over: book rights, exclusive interviews, special appearances. Then again, if the Colonel was as well connected as Fuller made out, would the man be able to stay alive long enough to enjoy any of it? Would any of them for that matter?

"He's still going to hear the engine, though, isn't he?" For once Tobe had a point.

"We'll have to wait until he goes round the front and just risk it," said Fuller, smiling unevenly back at them.

\*\*\*

Rob followed the crying. There was no mistaking it. A woman's.

Dawn's.

Though he was still unsteady on his feet, he took the final lot of stairs to the top two at a time, leaving the memories of Lou behind with his corpse. The crying came louder, filled with fear. The axe felt heavy in his hands but comforting. It had already proved its worth.

Rob surfaced, coming out onto the balcony that skirted the building. Out where the light shone at night or in fog. The glass warped his reflection, tripling it, quadrupling it. There were dark shapes moving on the other side of the glass, round the corner. The wind blew Rob's hair as he came out into the open, hugging the railings attached to the walkway.

The crying had dulled to a whimpering noise. He prayed he wasn't too late.

Rob kept low but moved fast, springing round the curved bend as quickly as he could, axe slung over one shoulder, poised, ready to strike.

There, gripping the metal railing and looking out over the seascape, was the last known survivor of the wreck – George Turner. On the floor some feet away was Dawn, curled virtually into a ball, knees pulled under her, crying into her chest.

Rob pulled back behind the light. Now he had the lay of the land he could plan what to do next. It didn't look like Dawn had been harmed; she was just very, very scared. Probably escaped right up here when the fishermen broke in, up and up – perhaps chased? – but this one had found her. Why hadn't he attacked her as they had done her father? Might George be reasoned with after all? Was there some humanity left in there? Or perhaps he just didn't see her as a threat. No, that wasn't it. Rob had seen them kill indiscriminately back at the hospital. There had to be another reason.

Then it came to him. Of course, it was so obvious it was staring him in the face. The crying. That was why he'd paused. Dawn's weeping was the only thing keeping her alive. He couldn't openly savage someone who was crying tears of sorrow. For some reason it had stayed his hand. And bought her some time. Now it was up to Rob to get her out of this.

At the back of his mind the same thoughts of guilt were there, telling him he'd killed Lou and was about to murder the last of his sons. But he also remembered what his dad had said – *what his subconscious had said?* He'd know how to save them. What if the only way to do that was to end their suffering?

In any event he had to do something before the fisherman changed his – its – mind. For the moment the sea was holding its gaze. If he could just creep up behind… Right, now. *Go now!*

Rob let out a couple of breaths. Closed his eyes.

Then turned the corner…

\*\*\*

The soldier finished his tour of the car park and returned to the front of the building.

Fuller shot out from under cover the second he'd cleared the corner, with Vicky and Tobe following close behind. They all kept low, but Vicky wondered what would happen if someone should choose that moment to peer out from behind one of the hospital windows. Before she could think about it any more they were at their destination. Fuller opened up his vehicle and told them to quickly get inside. There was no telling how long they had before the guard came back.

Tobe climbed into the front and Vicky hauled herself into the back. Fuller took the driver's seat. Once the doors were all shut, as quietly as possible, he started the engine.

Fuller pulled away from his parking spot.

"That was a close call," Tobe said, but he appeared happy now they were finally getting away from this place, from the guns, from the people who shot water out of their hands – for pity's sake! – from the Colonel. From it all.

"We're not out of this yet," Fuller reminded him.

The professor was heading for the fenced off grass verge. The only way to escape was through it. "Hold on tight," he said, driving straight for the obstruction.

Vicky held onto the underside of her seat as the wire fence collapsed around them, scratching paintwork and making screeching noises along the length of the vehicle. As she brought her hand up again, Vicky felt something sticky on her fingers. And for the first time since getting in she noticed the terrible smell, so bad now it was overpowering her.

Vicky bent down to look below her seat. There was something wedged between the rear of Fuller's chair and the base of the back seat. It lay on the floor, squabs of crusty redness all over it. Vicky thought she saw bits of clothing, trousers... Overalls? And part of a head. *There's a fucking dead body in here with me!* She screwed up her face and Fuller must have noticed it in the rear-view.

"Is something wrong, Miss West?" he asked her, continuing to drive over the grassy dunes.

As calmly as she could Vicky shook her head, one hand snaking round the door handle. It was locked from the inside.

"What's that stink?" Tobe asked, finally noticing the pungent aroma of death.

"Oh, I'm sorry about that. I haven't had a chance to

clean up since yesterday. The sun does tend to take its toll, doesn't it? The drive back here didn't help matters, either."

Tobe had absolutely no idea what Fuller was talking about but nodded as if he agreed wholeheartedly. Then he spoilt it all by asking: "Why're we going in the wrong direction, Professor?"

Fuller turned to him, and Tobe finally saw the glassy texture of his eyes rippling. The professor opened his mouth wide as if in pain, a terrifying rictus. It opened still further until Vicky was sure she'd hear bones crack, but there was nothing. She shouted out from the back seat, but the cameraman was lost. Taking in each and every detail of those last few seconds, the circular spiral of juices gathering in Fuller's orifice, silky threads escaping to splatter across his cheeks. The narrowing of the man's eyebrows in concentration, the effort great for him. But not too great.

And the torrent of ghastly saliva that emerged from the professor's mouth at speeds a Grand Prix racer would have been proud of, cannoning first into Tobe's nose – breaking it and snapping it sideways – then into his very face, reappearing again seconds later on the other side where it broke through the passenger window, too.

There was silence for a moment, before Vicky's shouts turned to screams.

But the red Land Rover continued on its journey across the grassland undeterred.

\*\*\*

When Rob rounded the corner again, the fisherman was gone.

Softly, he padded forwards. Dawn was still on the

floor. She looked up, blinking tears out of her eyes.

"Rob—" Her voice was choked with emotion. He put a finger to his lips, glancing left and right for the burnt figure.

"No! Rob, watch out!" Her eyes moved past him, over his shoulder.

Rob didn't look back. Instead he flung himself down as low as he possibly could. Something whipped over the top of his head. Not wind, but rather a jet of filthy water. The metal rail ahead of them on the bend simply disappeared. One minute it was there, the next gone; totally obliterated by the blast, leaving a gap in the bars.

Rob rolled over. George Turner had circled around behind *him*. Now the thing was staggering towards Rob. Its face, though devastated by fire and whatever inhabited him, somehow managed to sneer.

Rob suddenly remembered he was still holding the axe. Before the fisherman could "shoot" again he dug it into the man's legs, keeping hold of it with just one hand. The head bit deep into thigh muscle that hadn't had time to heal. George tottered backwards, taking the axe with him, lodged in his leg.

Rob scrambled to his feet and found Dawn.

"Are you all right?" he asked her.

Too shocked to talk she just tipped her head.

"Dawn, you're gonna have to go round and try to make it to the steps."

This time she spoke up. "No Rob I—"

"We haven't got time to argue about this, do it. *Now!*"

Rob helped her up and gestured for her to go. She finally did, but turned back just in time to see the axe fly through the air and hit Rob in the back. Thankfully only the handle connected with his body, but it was enough to send him crashing to the ground once more, the wind forced out of him.

Dawn screamed loudly, racing back.

Rob shook his head, his vision blurring again. He tried to speak, to tell Dawn to run, but facedown he could only manage a grunt.

Dawn got hold of him under the arms, in an effort to stand him back up. She wasn't strong enough and Rob was at the wrong angle.

The monstrous fisherman approached again. He held up his hands, but nothing happened. No blasts of lethal spray. The last one had taken too much out of him, and the wound in his leg was still gushing red-blackness.

Now he shambled towards them, hands still raised with the intention of grabbing hold of Dawn – physical contact the only option left to him. He was two metres away and closing the gap. Closer, closer. Dawn saw the shadow fall over them.

Stepping past Rob, the thing lurched forwards, but she let go and pulled back. His hands clutched at air as she moved away. Dawn's tears had dried up, all cried out. Now she was focussed on luring the creature away from her boyfriend. And it worked. The lumbering mass of burnt meat came after her. She hadn't thought about what to do next, though. The stairway was right round the other side…

Dawn retreated, the fisherman following awkwardly, disfigured face gleaming.

Rob fought to push himself up. It was useless. His arms were rebelling against him, going numb, muscles finally giving in. *No, I've come this far…* Yet he could do nothing but watch as the terrifying figure suddenly sprang and caught up with Dawn.

It moved so quickly at the end she had no time to get out of its way. It grabbed her flailing arms by the wrists, dragging her closer, spinning with her. Then it let go of her right arm and took her by the throat. Dawn gagged as she was lifted up off the platform.

Something suddenly hit the fisherman from the back. Had charged at him, presumably having come up the stairs and round the side.

"Let my little girl go!" yelled Stanley Keets from behind.

"Daa... dad?" coughed Dawn as the grip loosened around her neck.

Stanley raked at his foe's back and neck with the nails on his one good hand. A gash opened, spilling vast amounts of unclotted blood.

The fisherman toppled round and smacked Stanley with the back of his hand. Dawn's father fell, but only to his knees. In seconds he was up again and attacking like a madman. He concentrated on the arm that held Dawn, trying to free her.

If the creature felt any pain whatsoever it certainly didn't show it. Again Stanley was struck, but held on this time. The three of them were locked together in some sort of strange dance, jumbled, spinning round, all coated in the fisherman's seeping juices.

Rob saw what was going to happen next but was powerless to prevent it.

"Stanley, watch out!" he called.

It was too late. The fisherman put a foot backwards into thin air. He tilted sideways, then was falling through the hole in the railings. Dawn was clawing at the hand, but it held her tightly. Stanley snatched at Dawn's T-shirt. Over they all went, losing balance, pulled back by the thing that had once been George Turner.

Rob looked on, horrified, as they all vanished. With his last ounce of strength, he made it to the edge. Rob was just in time to see a bulky shape with six arms and six legs plunge down the side of the lighthouse...

Then splash into the sea so far below.

## Chapter Thirty-Seven
### Intruder

Harding paced up and down within the confines of the small office. Once or twice, he wondered what had happened to the doctor it belonged to. Was he being interviewed now just like they had been – surely not for this length of time? More likely he'd been one of the first to die in whatever happened here earlier. Harding was having difficulty remembering it in any great detail. Even when he'd been asked to relate it all to Fuller, he'd found it impossible to recall with any accuracy. It was a blur, an impossible sequence of events starting with his dream last night and then waking up to find that storm-cloud watching him. The one from his painting.

The only thing he could remember properly was those men's faces, how horribly distorted they'd been. That and the oh-so timely intervention of the Colonel.

Was he really as dangerous as Fuller made out? The professor certainly seemed scared, afraid for his life. So much so that he was willing to speak to the media to save himself, and Vicky as well. Fuller certainly believed

Vicky's life was in jeopardy, so the big secret must be worth killing for. (*A secret the professor knows.*) And so many had died here already...

As he paced, Harding began to have doubts about what he'd done, letting Vicky go off like that. He'd thought it was the only way to guarantee her safety – it didn't matter what happened to him. But was she really safe in Fuller's hands? Harding remembered what he'd thought during the interview, how good an actor Fuller would make. What if he'd been acting then, trying to break up the group without a fuss? All a performance? His fear of the Colonel, it was a convincing turn, but... Perhaps he was taking them off somewhere, to the facility he'd mentioned, and he wanted to—

There was a noise outside in the corridor. A commotion. Boots running on the squeaking floor. Harding stopped pacing and went over to the door. He put his ear against the wood.

Someone was shouting out orders. They sounded in a panic. *They've been caught*, thought Harding. *They've been caught by the Colonel, trying to escape...*

All the blood drained out of his face, and he raised his fist, about to knock on the polished oak.

When the door suddenly opened.

A man came in backwards, his broad build filling the doorway. He was dragging the slumped body of the guard inside. He noticed Harding standing next to the wall. When he turned, Harding recognised his face. The closely cropped beard, the bulky neck and shoulders. It was the same man Fuller had shown him a picture of. The man who'd instigated the killing. The man they'd called Darville.

Darville finished pulling the soldier in and closed the door. Then he picked up the guard's rifle.

"Keep quiet," he rasped. As husky as his voice was,

Harding detected a trace of an accent. Foreign, European. He couldn't place it yet. "You understand?"

Harding backed away, his hands up in the air. He nodded curtly.

"Good." Darville opened the door a crack and peered out, the rifle still waving in Harding's direction, though lowering with each passing second. Harding thought about rushing forward and grabbing the weapon, but before he could do anything about it Darville shut the door and brought the gun up again.

"Don't," he warned.

Holding the rifle in one hand he proceeded to drag the soldier into the middle of the room by the scruff of the neck. "They have passed by, for now." He looked Harding up and down. "I don't know you. You're not one of the Colonel's—"

"But I know *you*," Harding broke in. *That was stupid. Very stupid.*

"Did I say you could talk?"

Harding shook his head.

"I ask the questions. You answer. Clear?"

Harding nodded again.

"Fuller. Where is he?"

Harding said nothing.

"I can tell that you know."

"What do you want with him?"

"You think I'm here to kill him?" Darville laughed hoarsely. "Or maybe I kill you first, eh?"

"Like you murdered him?" Harding pointed to the guard.

"He is not dead. He will just wake up with a nasty headache. What has Fuller told you about me? That I am the Devil himself?" Darville walked towards Harding. "If that is so, then he was describing himself, not me."

"I don't believe you."

Darville sighed. He had a wild look in his eye as he raised the rifle. Harding stiffened, ready for the bullets to pound into him. Darville put the gun down on the desk and jumped forwards. He placed his hands on both sides of Harding's skull, digging in. "If I wanted to kill you, you would be dead by now."

Harding struggled against him, but the man's strength was incredible.

"And this is how I would do it, crushing your head like a grapefruit, yes?" Darville let go of Harding. There was still pressure where his fingers had been. "But I cannot do that. Only Fuller can do that."

Harding clutched his head, gasping for air. "What… what are you talking about? You're the cause of all this, you're infected—"

"Do you not see it yet? Fuller is the one. All this is *his* doing, though I would not call him 'infected'." Darville studied Harding's face. "I know you are an intelligent man. I can see it, you realise I am right."

"No…" But Darville was correct. Harding knew he was telling the truth. He knew instinctively that he could trust this man; which was more than could be said for Fuller.

"You can see I am no killer."

"Fuller, he… he's gone. And he's taken my friends with him."

"Gone? Gone where?"

Harding gaped at him. "Out of Sable, to contact the TV station. He said he was frightened of what the Colonel would do."

"No, no. Fuller would never leave this area. Not now. But there is some truth to the last part." Darville rubbed his chin. "The Colonel is the only one who can harm him, that's why he's been – how you say? – sticking close to the man."

"We have to tell him, then," said Harding. "If we hurry, we can—"

"You do not understand. The Colonel thinks the same as you; Fuller has told him the same lies. His men are searching for me right now. One of them saw me in the corridor. If the Colonel gets hold of me, he will either shoot me on the spot, or lock me away before I can explain. And even then, I doubt he will listen. By that time, it will be too late."

Harding stepped up to Darville. "Too late?"

"Fuller has something in mind. All this is leading somewhere, but I don't know where. All I know is I must stop him before it goes too far." Darville grabbed Harding by the arms. "You believe me now, eh?"

"I-I don't know what to believe."

"Say it!"

"Yes. Yes, I think I do."

"Then there is only one thing for it. We must find Fuller ourselves and pray that your friends are still alive. Because if they are with him, then they do not have much time left at all…"

## Chapter Thirty-Eight
### Hidden

The red Land Rover sneaked into the stretch of woodland, crunching its way over dead branches on the ground, trampling grass and earth and wildlife. The driver didn't seem to care. This was not his domain anyway. Not yet. This was somewhere he used to live but now didn't belong. On dry land. But here was the thing that would ferry him back to his new home; the *promised* land. His mission completed.

The big four-wheel drive returned to the spot it had visited the day before, while its owner was still on leave. The incident with Darville had shaken him up and the Colonel had "graciously" given him a little time off. Time to plan, to find a suitable location. He'd recognised Sable as the place as soon as he got close. This was where it had begun so many years ago, and this was the place where it would end.

Things had come full circle.

Tyres gripped the ground as he braked sharply. The trailer was here, covered in a sheet of camouflaged tarpaulin. If it was up to him, he would simply find the nearest beach and wade into the sea. His offspring had everything under control at the village (they were capable of fighting another two or three battalions if it came to it – not that it would – and soon they would need to stall for time no longer). Unfortunately, his "guest" could not breathe underwater as well as he. She had not been altered, and that was how she must remain. For now.

He turned around to look at the woman there on the back seat. It had all been too much for her. Vicky lay across the leather, hair over her face. It was perhaps just as well. The being who was once known as Fuller opened the driver's door and leapt out, leaving the putrefying body of Tobe Howell behind. He'd been so keen to come along, and the professor knew Vicky would be more willing to go with him if Howell agreed as well. To gain his freedom. Well, now he'd been granted the ultimate freedom.

Clenching the tarpaulin in his fist, he concentrated. It would have been so easy to just rip it off, but that would hardly test his skills. He needed to constantly extend himself, use the abilities he'd been given since the transition. Those first painful hours came back to him, writhing in agony at his home... Then they were gone. Reflections of another life, another time.

His hand quivered, then appeared to dissolve into the material of the tarpaulin. It became sodden, the dampness spreading, changing the molecular structure of the cloth. Until at last the whole sheet melted away like so much snow in a heat wave. He then took the trailer by the socket and lifted it round to hook it onto the Land Rover's towing bracket. Now all he needed was to find a clear enough runway. Somewhere to give the plane space to take off (yes, the professor's private income and flying experience had come in very handy indeed – *it* had chosen well...). Strictly speaking this was only a one-man craft, but with a few adjustments they'd both be able to squeeze in.

The trailer attached, he made his way back to the driver's seat. It would not be long now; this he knew for certain. Just as his own strength grew, so too did the one whom he served. He knew this because they were one and the same. Joined forever.

Smiling, he opened the door and climbed in. The engine roared into life. Birds settling down on the trees above took flight as the red Land Rover disappeared further into the woodland.

Then it was gone.

# Part Four
## The Wet

"Water, water, everywhere,
Nor any drop to drink."

> *The Ancient Mariner*, Samuel Taylor Coleridge.

## Chapter Thirty-Nine
### Whatever Happened to Lily and Matt?

And the waves grew bigger, rising almost to the height of a small house. Gushing and frothing on their way, destroying everything in their path...

\*\*\*

The room was no larger than her bathroom at home. Smaller if the truth be known, lined with coffee-coloured walls. Thin material, but it might as well have been steel bars. Lily wasn't going anywhere.

One tiny window let in streaky sunlight, as much as the trees would allow, but was too high to see out of. She hadn't seen a soul for ages, since she first entered the portakabin, since she'd originally been questioned. But she didn't complain, didn't bang on the door and demand to be set free. It wasn't like her to do nothing, not when there was work to be done, appointments to be kept. No, it wasn't like her at all.

But there was a simple enough explanation for her change in character. She was scared. She'd seen the way they handled Matt and knew that obstinacy would get her nowhere in a hurry. She dreaded to think what they'd do to the TV man if he kept up with the smart comments. Then again, what did she care? He was an obnoxious foul-mouthed oaf anyway. She didn't even know him really and for the half a day or so she had known him she'd spent most of the time wishing she'd never clapped eyes on the bloke. That and wondering why he wasn't put down at birth.

If only she hadn't come up here this morning, stupid ideas about dragging Jason to the gallery function in her head. She knew he'd say no before she set off, so why did she bother?

Because she cared, that's why.

In the old days – the good old days? – clients had been just that: clients. She did her job, took her percentage and drifted around at the openings enjoying free wine. Simple. Faces, names in a book. Nothing more, nothing less. As she'd grown older she'd noticed things about them. Started to worry a little more about each one, shared in their successes and been there when things took a downturn. It wasn't just about the money anymore, although that was the main reason she existed. It was about what made her happy.

Then, of course, Jason had come along. He was a real mess to begin with, but she'd helped him along. Provided the extra support he needed when he still lived in the city. It wasn't anything to do with his work – he had the makings of an artistic genius, yes, there was no disputing that – but she also liked him as a person and couldn't bear to see him suffer. When he'd told her he was moving to the coast she'd tried to talk him out of it to begin with. But

# The Wet

he'd told her it was something he just had to do, that he'd been thinking about it for some time. He'd even been out and got all the bumf, visited a few nice, quiet places until he found one that felt right.

"Why do you want to go, Jason? Surely living by the sea will be a constant reminder."

He'd listened to what she had to say, all her arguments, and countered with his own. Stating that it was time he faced his fears and moved on, that it would be good for his painting, for inspiration – appealing to the agent side of her, no doubt.

"Plus there's that old saying," he'd told her one night after a glass or two of the hard stuff. "Keep your friends close, but your enemies even closer."

She hadn't known what he was talking about at the time. Even now it still seemed a bizarre thing to come out with. The only drawback was that he wouldn't be able to keep his best friend as close as he'd like. Lily had appreciated that, mainly because she could see his affection for her was real. She could hear the sincerity in his voice. He really was going to miss her. But not half as much as she'd miss him.

She'd never really had a best friend the whole of her adult life – always too busy, she supposed. Oh, she had pals, acquaintances, a few family members dotted about the place who crawled round on birthdays – if they could be bothered to remember – and at Christmas time to get their presents. But Jason was different. Special. She was proud to be not only his agent, but also his friend.

Having said that, if he were here right now she'd cheerfully throttle him for getting her into this fix. He'd been the one who wanted to go to whats-it-called? Angels Pass? Point? Landing, that was it, Landing... Who'd spotted the chopper in distress. Or perhaps that should be damsel, although she'd turned out to be nothing of the kind. The one who'd gone to the hospital with her and her crew: Vicky West. Ah, Vicky. Vicky and Jason Harding...

Lily couldn't fail to notice the way they looked at each other. Only an idiot would've missed the obvious attraction. She should feel happy for him; after all hadn't she been trying to fix him up with her PA Rhona for months now, telling him he should forget about Christine and find someone new? But Vicky, well that was a different kettle of piranhas altogether. He needed stability and she doubted whether the word was in Vicky's vocabulary. Lily just hoped she wouldn't hurt him; he'd had enough of that in his life.

*My God, what am I doing*, she thought. *I should be worrying about myself, not Jason's love life.*

But you only had to look at this predicament to realise just how *unstable* Vicky's world really was. Even the people she mixed with were disaster magnets, Matt especially with that mouth of his.

She recalled trying to start a conversation with him after they left the hospital.

"It must be quite exciting, I imagine, what you do. Television and everything. I mean, I have contacts in that area but—"

"It's as exciting as watching paint dry." Had that been a sly dig at her clients? No, she didn't believe he had the wit. "Today's been the most eventful day in my career." *What a career that must have been*, thought Lily. "And we all nearly got killed because of it. I say give me interviews with boring as shit windsurfers anytime. Least you know where you stand."

"Yes, but—"

"But nothing. Look, no offence. I think you're a wonderful human being and everything, but my arm's killing me and I'm just about all talked out. I appreciate the lift and everything – let's just leave it at that, though, yeah?"

So, she did. Small talk was merely a force of habit for her, but she knew enough to realise when she was flogging a dead horse. She'd kept her mouth shut the rest of the journey, which, as it turned out, was remarkably short.

Ten, perhaps fifteen minutes out from St August's on the road to Hambleton, they came across a queue of three cars waiting at a set of traffic lights – the kind workmen use for temporary hold-ups. Except these lights never changed. They remained permanently on red as the BMW pulled up behind the last of the vehicles.

Lily waited patiently, drumming her fingers on the wheel. She sat up in the seat, then brought down her window and leaned out. She could see men in yellow hard hats, but that was all. After a few more minutes passed by, a man in the lead car got out and walked towards the lights. His intention: to find out what was going on and how long they'd have to wait.

He came back not long afterwards with one of the men in hard hats. The pair exchanged words, then the driver got back in the car and did a four-point turn, before driving off in the direction he'd just come from. Mr Hard Hat came down the line of traffic next, speaking with each driver in turn. The other two cars in front reluctantly did the same thing, this time easing forward into the space left by the first car and doing a U-turn.

"What's his problem?" grumbled Matt.

"I don't know, but I suspect we're about to find out."

The worker in his bright hat and grey jumpsuit approached, leaning in through the open window of the BMW. Lily removed her glasses as he spoke.

"Hi, sorry to inconvenience you folks but there's a problem with some of the gas pipes up ahead. Could be a leak. Very dangerous."

"What?" Matt groaned. "You're joking!"

"I'm sorry, I'm going to have to ask you to turn back."

Lily gripped the wheel tighter. "Isn't there some way to get through? It's important."

"I understand, but like I said it's too dangerous. There's no safe way, I'm afraid." His eyes were everywhere at once, shifty, scanning their faces, the inside of their car; never once meeting Lily's own. They widened when he saw the video tape on Matt's lap. "Maybe if you tell me where you're going and why, I can see what we could arrange."

"We're going to London to visit the fucking Queen," Matt informed him. The man's eyes narrowed.

"I apologise for my friend," said Lily, rolling her eyes. "I'm actually very late for an appointment in Manchester. Here's my card." Lily took a business card from the tray in front of the gear stick. She didn't travel anywhere without a few spares. You never knew when you were going to bump into a potential client – or buyer. He read it through thoroughly, taking in all the information.

"And what about him?" The workman jabbed a finger at Matt.

"Oh he's—"

"He's sick of all this bullshit, that's what he is!" Matt snapped. "Listen mate, I work for Creation-Time TV, and I've got an urgent package to deliver to them, so if you'd just let us through…"

"I see. Well, that changes everything." The guy waved over to some of his colleagues.

"See?" said Matt with a smirk. "You've just got to know how to handle the plebs. We'll get through now; their bosses'll be frightened of bad publicity."

Mr Hard Hat turned back to them. "If you'll just step out of the car, both of you, we'll have this all settled in no time."

"Out of the car? What the hell are you talking about?"

Matt's face was turning red, due more to embarrassment than anger Lily suspected. "Just make some space for us and we'll be on our way."

Lily saw the other men trotting over. A couple had the same kind of outfits as this man. For the first time she noticed that none of them had company insignias on the jumpsuits.

"Step out of the car, please," he said again. Lily could tell he wasn't going to ask a third time.

She opened her door. The hard hat man held it for her. Matt stayed put. The workman's friends came up alongside the passenger door and wrenched it wide. The hinges creaked.

"Hey, what're you doing? I'm not going any—" Matt was "helped" out of the BMW. Lily twisted round in time to see one of the workers glance about, then drive his fist into Matt's stomach. The soundman crumpled up against the car, coughing hoarsely.

"Self-defence," said his attacker as if it was the most normal thing in the world. Maybe it was to him. "He was hysterical, threatening us. You all saw that, didn't you?" His colleagues concurred with him.

"You fucking... I'll get you for—" Matt's croaky utterance was cut off by a kick to his spleen, delivered with just enough force to hurt but not cause lasting damage. Then the thug reached inside the BMW and retrieved the tape from the front seat where Matt had dropped it.

Following this, neither Lily nor Matt had resisted. The men had walked them past the lights – there was a small hole next to the road for show, a pickaxe and shovel reared up inside, but nothing that should have held up any traffic. Yet Lily saw cars being turned back from the other side as well. It was almost as if Sable had been isolated from the rest of the world by these people, whoever they were. But why? Maybe there was a leak after all, or some other danger, and they'd just reacted to Matt like that because he was being clever with them? Whatever the reason the measures were very effective. Nothing in, nothing out.

So, what did they want with them now?

Lily and Matt had been bundled into a van with a blue flame painted on the side – and off they went. Lily thought about asking them questions but decided against it; she just hoped Matt had the good sense to keep it zipped, too.

From here they were taken to the portakabin inside some woodland or other down the road. Out of sight, out of mind? It was a seemingly inoffensive structure on wheels, so it was obviously mobile. Just the sort of place from which a gas leak operation might be directed.

The pair were ushered inside to a waiting area. They sat down in a corner with one or two other visitors. Lily recognised one of them straight away. She'd seen the bald man not long ago back at the hospital. A nurse or something, she seemed to recall. What was *he* doing here? He was talking with a smaller guy who barely covered the seat beneath him. Lily, glancing continually over her shoulder at the men who'd brought her in, introduced herself and Matt.

"I'm Dennis Owen," he told her. His eyes sparkled when he shook Lily's hand. "I'm a reporter for the *Hambleton Echo*. Very pleased to meet you, Lily. And this is…"

"Leo Mountford, charge nurse at St August's. But we've met already, haven't we. How's the arm? Burn wasn't it?"

Matt snorted.

"Has anyone got any idea what's happening?" asked Lily, lowering her voice.

"Haven't a clue," Leo said. "Something about a gas leak."

Now it was Dennis' turn to snort. Lily gazed at his

face, and he caught her looking at him. The man smiled and Lily blushed slightly. "I don't think any of us really believe that, do we?" he said. "I've been trying to tell him there's something else going on here. For a start they confiscated my roll of film."

"What was on it?" asked Lily.

"Pictures of that storm this morning, and the RNLI men coming back in. I *was* on my way back to the office to develop it when…"

Lily recalled the workman's interest when Matt mentioned Creation-Time. And the way he looked when he saw the tape in the car. She wondered where it was now. "So you've been here since this morning?"

"Since just before lunch." Dennis smiled again at her. "Then of course Leo arrived a little while later. He's a good conversationalist, but not much to look at."

Lily wasn't slow to pick up on the veiled compliment intended for her.

"I haven't found out anything yet, but I'm going to. I'm hoping to dig a little deeper here and—"

"Do you think that's wise?"

"Probably not, but it's my nature to snoop."

Lily smiled nervously back.

"They can't keep us locked up like this," Matt said suddenly, his eyes still red from his beating.

"Ah, but they're not *keeping* us here, are they Leo?" Dennis turned to his companion for confirmation.

"No, we're free to go at any time they keep telling us. But you try it and see what happens."

"We're stuck here. They know it and we know it," said Dennis, winking. "It's just a matter of waiting to see what they want from us."

But regardless of what he was saying, Lily could see the journalist was in his element. He no longer cared about the missing photos because he'd stumbled upon something bigger now. A conspiracy even? She felt frightened for him but didn't know why.

They'd talked for a bit longer and then the interviews had started. Each of them taken to a separate "room" in the portakabin. A fresh-faced young man had escorted her, telling her not to worry as he sat her down. Then he'd stayed inside by the door as Lily was questioned by a brutish-looking guy. One after the other, the interrogator rattled off things he wanted to know: about her movements during the day; her job; even about her personal life. She'd noticed the younger man flinch once or twice as the interrogator shouted, pressuring her to remember every detail she could. Lily herself had almost burst into tears, but refused to give him the satisfaction. Instead, she'd looked imploringly at the guard, his eyes telling her that he could do nothing for the poor woman.

Finally, after what must have been an hour or more (Lily's watch had been taken from her at the start, along with her phone and other possessions), she'd been left alone in the room.

Her cell.

By now her afternoon appointments would have given up on her. Rhona would be wondering where she was. If only she'd told her she was visiting Jason, but she'd felt it her duty to keep quiet – certain writers working for the broadsheets would have paid a tidy sum to find out where he lived now. Besides, Rhona would have wanted to come along. She was potty about Jason.

No, it was the only way to keep his location a secret, to protect him. Not that anyone would be able to find this place if they tried. Even with Jason's extra help, his garbled directions over the phone, she'd had a hell of a job.

As a consequence nobody knew where she was, or even where to start looking for her if she went missing. Lily sat on the chair provided, with her head in her hands, contemplating her fate. She found herself wondering what questions they'd asked Matt, Leo… Dennis. What was Jason doing right now? Probably still making eyes at Vicky.

But most of all she wondered how she'd gotten into all this, and if there was any way out.

## Chapter Forty
**Aquarius**

Harding liked to think he was a pretty good judge of character.

Which was why it had been so frustrating to be proved wrong about Darville. And why he was so angry with himself for letting Vicky and Tobe go with Fuller.

The bearded foreigner had showed him the way he'd got into St August's, through an entrance in the ambulance bay and up the stairs. Of course, he'd had to deal with the sentry on guard first.

"And how did you manage that?" Harding enquired. "These blokes have guns."

"I know how to – how you say over here? – handle myself," was all he would disclose.

Darville led him up to the hills overlooking the hospital, where he'd parked his Volvo – well, not actually *his*. One that he'd "borrowed" for a short time. It made him more difficult to trace.

Harding told him everything that had happened so far, how he'd seen the cloud that morning, how he'd taken Vicky and her crew to the hospital, the business on the wards (Darville didn't seem the least bit surprised by this), right up to the arrival of the Colonel and Fuller. As they drove away, though, Harding had demanded an explanation from him, starting with who he was.

"My name is Marcel Darville," he told him, keeping one eye on the uneven route ahead. "I was born in Belgium, my mother's country, but as my father was of American origin I spent the latter part of my childhood there. Still managed to retain the accent, however, as you might have noticed? Something to remember mamma by.

"I was a bright boy, some might even have called me a prodigy, yet I would cringe at the word. My interest in ecology, nature and the world around me – in addition to a very insightful tutor at Yale – determined my chosen career in the natural sciences. And ever since I was sixteen, eh, I've dreamed of the day when…" He paused, silence filled the car.

"Go on," prompted Harding.

"I can see the images now. Those pictures on the television set of the famines of the 1970s, into the '80s. The droughts. They affected me forever, you understand? I am sorry my friend, I do not yet know your name."

"Jason."

"Ah, Jason, the leader of the Argonauts. I should have guessed. It was my all-time favourite classical story; did you know that?" How could he have possibly known? Harding feared the man was drifting off topic, but he needn't have worried. "And like the hero from that story, I too was in search of a Golden Fleece. A means to end drought and ultimately famine as well. An end to the suffering, Jason. You understand, no?"

Harding was starting to, little by little. "You're talking about controlling the weather. Manipulation, inducing rainfall?"

"In a manner of speaking."

"So that thing out there belongs to you?"

"No, no, no. True, my area of expertise is cloud seeding, but I did not create that... monstrosity hanging over the ocean. My research has been used, perverted. I suspect by the man you call Fuller, or what is left of him."

Harding breathed in deeply. "And where *does* Fuller fit into all this? Where does the Colonel for that matter?"

"In good time I shall come to him, but first you must believe me when I say our intentions were pure. We were only trying to do good. It is important to me."

"I... I believe you."

Darville relaxed somewhat at the wheel. "Thank you, Jason. It means a great deal, especially after all that has happened. To find someone who— But now to your first question. I came into contact with Edward Fuller almost ten years ago now. We were both attending a conference in Boston concerning the fate of our planet. Global warming, the Rain Forests. I am sure you are familiar with this type of thing, eh? He was giving a speech on the importance of purifying water for third world countries. Needless to say, the topic intrigued me. A noble cause, yes? I made it my aim to meet with him and so at one of the buffet lunches I introduced myself. I have never met a more intelligent professional as Edward, so dedicated to the cause of humanity."

Harding detected a note of reverence in the man's tone. Of admiration and strong friendship.

"He came from a rich family, but left his homeland at an early age to pursue his own interests. We found on that day our goals were compatible ones. Just as I had the idea to prevent droughts by creating rainfall where there was none before, it was Edward's belief that this precipitation, and indeed all water, could be controlled, directed and purified. That flooding could be prevented by this means, introducing his 'smart' water into the eco-system. We were both working on the same problem but from different angles. Together we might eventually save lives, bring water to the needy. Think of the potential! No more Tucsons, no more Ulaanbaatars. And those most in need would have as much or as little water as they desired. Not to mention the hydro-electrical benefits."

Harding wrinkled his nose. "You sought to control nature itself."

"We preferred to think of it as harnessing her energy, just as one might focus the rays of the sun to generate power."

"It's not the same thing *at all*. We don't switch the sun off and on when it suits us or control the intensity of its rays."

Darville glanced over at him, then carried on with his story. "In any event, this was our intention. We pooled resources. Two heads are better than the one, at least we can agree on that, eh?"

Harding said nothing.

"Edward's fortune alone wasn't enough to keep the project alive, though, and I am hardly a wealthy man. All I could offer was my knowledge. So, we sought outside funding. I cannot tell you the number of organisations and corporations that turned us down, even after examining our preliminary findings. They were either not interested in the preservation of human life, or they were not willing to waste their money on what they thought was pure science fiction."

"Let me guess, this is where the Colonel comes in?"

"No, not yet. Not for a long time actually." Darville coughed dryly. "Just when we were becoming despondent, disillusioned, we were approached by a man offering support. He had heard of our efforts and was keen to listen to our ideas for the future. He said he was a representative of a group who could help us. They would provide the facilities we needed, and fund our research. No questions asked. Naturally we were thrilled, but we still had to know more about his employers before we said yes. That was when they invited us to meet with their board at a large office block in New York city; oh, they have branches in every major country you care to name, Jason. They convinced us of their own humanitarian drive, outlining what they wanted from the project. All they would ask for was the chance to sell our services to those governments who could afford it. Would the USA itself not pay for help with the storms they keep experiencing rather than pay three, four times as much to repair the damage? To the poorer ones we would offer our help for free. We were very adamant about that. It was the perfect solution.

"Do not misunderstand me, we both had reservations. But as Edward pointed out, we could not forge ahead without their sponsorship. In the end we relented. The group would provide us with a private facility in which to operate and give us all the backup we required. As Edward was becoming homesick for England by this time, it was agreed that we should work from these shores."

"So, what happened then?" Harding asked. "What went wrong?"

"Not a thing, my friend. Indeed, things at Aquarius went very well."

Harding looked puzzled.

"Aquarius was our nickname for the project. The water-carrier." Darville forced a smile that looked more like a grimace. "A bad joke... So, we worked on our own problems with just enough staff to support us, and this continued for many years. If anything, by the end things were going *too* well. Last summer another representative visited, informing us that we needed protection. I think the business with your GM food scared them a little. If the public found out what we were doing before we had a chance to prove ourselves... Also, he told us that there was interest from certain other quarters. Would you believe that a couple of the organisations we'd initially asked to help were now looking to step in? *Hah!* They no longer thought it was science fiction, eh? They wanted the glory for themselves. One man even came to my home to proposition me, warning me that the group I was involved with was dangerous. That they would sell the research to the highest bidder once it was completed, possibly even use it as a weapon! It was a preposterous idea, or at least I thought so at the time. Now I am not so sure.

"But anyway, the result of all this was a series of security measures taken at the facility, to protect us from such people. And the man chosen to head the team, you have already met, Jason."

"The Colonel."

"They did not hinder us or our work, and only a few operatives were ever posted at the facility itself, but I think we all felt safer for their presence. Believe it or not, I was actually on quite good terms with the Colonel when he did visit, before I... had to leave."

Harding tensed up. He had a feeling he already knew the rest of the tale but had to ask regardless. "And why *did* you leave, Darville?"

"It was not through choice, certainly." The bearded man changed down gears to make it up a steepish hill. "Not when we were so close to the end. After all that time..." He took a moment to compose himself, then said, "Edward had been experimenting with a new protein-rich solution he called 'The Wet', bringing him closer than ever before to controlling water production and behavioural patterns. For my part I was also ready. I was actually on my way to see him the morning it happened, to discuss further how to integrate our work for the first series of trials. I-I cannot describe to you what I saw in his laboratory, nor the things Edward did, the impossible things..."

"I think I have a fair idea," Harding assured him.

"Yes, yes. But he was... there was still something of Edward left, you know? He could have killed me, but he did not. He allowed me to escape. To get away from that place. All I can think of is that he must have been exposed to The Wet somehow, perhaps a tear in his glove, I do not know. I walked around in a daze for hours, not knowing what to do. Finally, I returned to my home only to find it staked out by armed men, and the Colonel himself talking to Edward in a car. I knew then that Fuller had laid the blame on me for what had happened. They thought I was the lunatic, the killer. The Colonel and his men were hunting for *me*. They would not listen and even if they did, Fuller would kill them all before they could send for help. He would probably kill me as well this time."

"Why didn't you just go to the authorities?"

"And what would I have told them, Jason? I do not even understand this myself, so how can I explain it to the police? I would be locked up in an institution, eh? No, I decided to try and talk to him alone, to stop him somehow. But I never got the chance. He headed off the next morning and so I trailed him as he searched – for what I did not know – but at least he did not harm anyone. I lost him in the next town, Hambleton, the day before yesterday. I spent all day Friday trying to find him, yes? Then this morning I see the cloud as I drive up towards Sable. I see what he has done and think *my God*, you see? I did not know whether to laugh or cry. My... it works, Jason! The cloud seeding works, and yet in Edward's hands... I reasoned that he would return, if I stayed here long enough. And so I watched and waited. I watched as those fishermen were brought in. My fault, all my fault. I watched as the Colonel arrived at the hospital and I knew then I could not leave this area even if I wanted to. The group will have shut down Sable. Traffic, communications..."

# The Wet

"That's impossible, they can't do that."

"They can and they have, Jason. It is my belief that they have contacts in every sphere, in every walk of life. Perhaps even in the government itself."

Harding gaped at him. "But what about the coastguard report, the RAF crash?"

"All taken care of, I would imagine. However, I suspect the Colonel is running scared. Just as I am. He allowed this 'contagion' to happen, and the group has put much money into our work. It is his neck on the line. And all the time he was hunting for me, the cause was right under his nose. His superiors will not let the situation go on indefinitely. He knows this."

"I just can't believe it."

"Now do you see why I have to find Edward Fuller? He is, was, my friend. If I could talk with him, reason with him… Together we might find a cure for this 'infection'."

"What about my friends? Why did he take *them*? It doesn't make sense. Why not just leave on his own?" Harding was aware that he was clutching his knees, squeezing tight, cutting off the blood supply. His knuckles were white.

"I do not know what to tell you. Only that if he has taken them, and they are still alive, he must have his reasons. But whatever these are, your friends are still in very serious trouble."

"Yes, but—" Harding never had time to finish his sentence because they came upon a bizarre scene ahead, just down from the embankment that led to the main road.

"What has happened here?" Darville questioned, looking out over the scattered bodies and wrecked vehicles. Two appeared to be completely burnt out, husks linked together like overdone sausages in a pan.

"They're wearing chemical suits," stated Harding.

"The Colonel's troops."

As they reared over the next bump it was there in front of them. Darville tried to stop, the Volvo's tyres throwing up dirt and grass, but it was only inches away from the bonnet. There was a dull thud as it connected with the shiny metal and Harding braced himself. A gruesome blend of charred flesh and pus-like liquid decorated the windscreen. The tyres finally bit, skidding them sideways before bringing them to a halt.

Darville's door was open in a flash and he came round the front of the car. Harding pursued, eyes remaining on the windscreen. There was a vaguely human shape sprawled over the front of the vehicle.

"What did we hit?" Harding asked quickly.

"Possibly the one who did all this." Darville surveyed the damage around him. "They must have been trying to stop him… It."

"More death and destruction," said Harding. "Mother Nature's revenge."

Darville pretended not to hear him. He walked down to the grey-suited men, the prone shapes missing limbs. Chests and heads covered in gore; machine guns scattered about – just useless ornaments now. He bowed his head in silence, then started to walk back up to their car.

Darville whirled around when he heard a hissing sound at his feet. One man, his face-mask cracked and open at the mouth, was attempting to move, to speak.

The Belgian bent down over him.

"Careful!" shouted Harding.

The injured man squinted with his one good eye, the other dangling loosely by his cheek, jarred from its socket by the blast that had floored him. He let out a stream of breath. Darville just caught the last thing he would ever say.

"God have mercy."

## Chapter Forty-One
### Revenge

He didn't know how long he'd stood there. Maybe minutes, maybe hours. Time had lost all meaning for Rob.

He just stared down through the gap in the railings, letting the wind sway him. If it pulled him just a little further, nearer to the edge then— He would follow them over, share their fate.

The decision would be taken out of his hands.

He'd thought about stepping over for as long as he remained there, but just couldn't bring himself to make the final effort. So he merely watched the water breaking over the rocks below, imagining what it must have felt like to fall from this height and—

It must have been instant. No suffering. That was saved for those left behind. For him. Rob hoped Stanley was happy now. He'd finally got his wish; Dawn would be his forever and he wouldn't have to worry about some thick mechanic whisking her off to have his wicked way with her. She'd remain his little girl for all of eternity.

Amen.

Rob held his breath and moved forwards. *Just a couple more steps, that's all. Then you'll see Dawn again. Be with her again.*

His left foot dangled over the drop. If only he could have got to her in time. If only she'd run when he told her to, instead of trying to save him.

"I'm not important," Rob wailed. Why couldn't she see that?

Because she loved him. Because his wellbeing meant more to her than life itself, just as hers meant the same to him. If he could have sacrificed himself for her, wouldn't he have done it and sod the consequences? Wasn't that what he'd been trying to do at the time? He wasn't thinking about how she'd feel if he was killed. It was the furthest thing from his mind. All that had mattered to him was getting Dawn out of there.

Now she was gone, leaving him with the memories of her. The way she looked, the way she smelt, the way she'd giggle whenever he did or said something funny. The way her skin felt when she responded to his touch – only that morning, the last time they'd been together.

Why did she have to die?

And the honest truth was, she *didn't* have to. Someone was responsible for all this, for the Turners, for Dawn. That alone kept him from following her over the side of the lighthouse right that minute.

He withdrew his trembling foot.

"Coward," he said softly to himself.

Then he turned, picked up the axe, and went to the stairs. He began down them in a sort of trance, not really knowing where he was or where he was going. Rob was spiralling downwards in more ways than one. He tripped a few times on the stone but picked himself up and carried on. Past the bathroom where Lou Turner laid his head, past the bedrooms, past the kitchen and living area, which was turned upside down, and further to the door, which he flung wide open.

The thought occurred to him that perhaps he'd find the bodies down here somewhere on the rocks, that there may be some chance they were still alive. *Or Dawn, just Dawn. God help me, you can take the rest if you send her back to me!*

But he knew before he got there that the waters had taken them. Swept them away to goodness knows where. There wasn't a sign of them.

He limped around, hobbling away from the place without realising he was even doing it.

His body taking over, taking him anywhere but here.

\*\*\*

The Volvo lurched and spluttered before coming to a complete standstill.

"What's wrong?" asked Harding. "We're nowhere near…"

"I don't know." Darville was shaking the steering wheel as if that might persuade it to keep going, as if his momentum alone could drive the car forwards.

Harding got out and went round to the front. He touched the red-hot bonnet, cautiously opening it up. A cloud of steam greeted him. After a moment Darville joined him.

"I know nothing about motor cars," said the bearded fellow.

"I know a little less than that. But at a guess I'd say… we're out of water."

Darville couldn't help laughing. Leaning up against

the side of the Volvo he clapped his thigh. To his surprise, Harding smiled too. Their mirth was borne more out of a sense of frustration, or the ridiculous nature of their dilemma , than anything genuinely funny. Indeed, the situation couldn't be more grave. If they couldn't get to the boat hire place – the first part of a rudimentary plan they'd come up with – in time...

"There is never a good mechanic around when you need one, eh?" Darville chuckled.

"No," said Harding. "Well, I suppose we start walking then."

"I suppose so," answered Darville with a nod.

They headed off in the direction of the lighthouse at Haven Point. Harding reasoned that even if the phones were still cut off – and if everything Darville had told him was true that was a distinct possibility – they might at least be able to lay their hands on another mode of transportation. Who knows, maybe they kept a boat there themselves? Neither of them had thought about what would happen when they actually *found* a boat. Darville had never sailed in his life before and Harding wasn't keen to repeat his experience on the water. But they'd deal with that when the time came.

It was obvious now where Fuller had gone, so they had to follow. It was as simple as that.

The pair hadn't gone far when Harding spotted a black shadow in the distance. It was shuffling along the road at a slow pace, too small to be anything other than a person. At first he thought it might be like the thing they'd seen back near the embankment, another one of the escaped fishermen. But as they drew closer he could see it was just a man. A man who'd been through Hell.

His leathers were dirty and torn in a couple of places and his head was caked in dried blood. He was holding himself like he was freezing cold, an arm wrapped around

# The Wet

his torso. The face looked familiar, and Harding searched his mind for a memory. Sure enough it supplied one. The guy who'd argued with Vicky back at the hospital, the man she'd called Woodhead. One of the rescuers.

Harding ran towards him.

"Hey, where are you going?" Darville yelled after him, starting to jog himself.

"I know him," Harding called over his shoulder.

Harding stopped a few yards away from the broken man. He appeared not to even see him. Woodhead just stared through him, perhaps convinced he was a mirage. Harding recognised that look on his face and paused.

"Do you remember me?" he asked, stepping nearer. "From the hospital?"

Woodhead continued to gape at him.

"What's happened to you?"

Darville came up alongside and the bloke seemed to snap awake. "I've seen you before," he mumbled. "This morning, you were there…"

"The man on the bike!"

"You… you were watching the storm-cloud."

"Yes, I am to blame for its existence."

Woodhead's eyes narrowed, and from behind him he produced an axe. Harding didn't even see him move, but the next instant he was swinging this at the Belgian.. Darville managed to dodge the blow luckily, slapping the weapon out of his hand. But Woodhead attacked next with his fists, the first punch flooring the big man. He crashed to the grass, Woodhead on top of him. "Fucking murderer!" he screamed.

Harding went to pull him back, but the lifeboat man just shrugged him off, his strength, fuelled by anger and adrenaline, taking Harding by surprise. His fist pounded into Darville's face again, but this time the burly man turned and avoided most of the blow. He brought up his knee, sending Woodhead tumbling over him. They both crawled around, facing each other. Woodhead threw another punch, but this time Darville was ready. He caught his opponent's fist in his hand, knuckles smacking into his palm, and struck Woodhead with a single swipe to the chin. The man fell sideways. Now it was Darville pinning *him* down. Woodhead couldn't move under his bulk. Watching him, Harding soon understood how the scientist had taken down those soldiers.

The guy spat at Darville. "It's all your fault."

"It's not what you think, Woodhead. He's here to help," Harding told him.

"Dawn's dead because of you!"

*Dawn*, thought Harding. *The woman from St August's. The one who came in with the older man. Woodhead's girlfriend?*

"Calm yourself," said Darville.

"Tell us what happened," added Harding.

And so he did. Rob Woodhead explained what had happened to him since he left the hospital. The chase on the road, the crash, the fight between one of the fishermen and those troops, the horrific discoveries he'd made at the lighthouse. Finally, the deaths of Stanley, Dawn and what his friend George Turner had become.

They listened quietly, and then Harding spoke. "Darville's not to blame. Yes, his research helped to create the storm, but he didn't unleash it." Harding related what he knew, the bare bones of what the bearded man had told him. Rob seemed to settle down a bit, taking it all in, though Harding wasn't sure he believed it. He wasn't sure he quite believed it himself. Next Harding filled him in about St August's and Fuller.

"So where's this bastard now?"

"Out there, we think," said Harding.

"What makes you so sure?"

Darville stared at him again. "We are not. But where would you start looking?"

"The storm has some kind of significance for him. It's the focal point for everything that's happened here," Harding explained, placing a hand on Darville's shoulder.

"Okay. Let me up."

Darville and Harding exchanged nervous glances.

"You want to go out there and so do I. Let me up and I'll take you."

"How?" asked Darville.

"The Jenny."

Harding pulled on Darville's shoulder and the big man stood. Holding out his hand, Harding helped Rob to rise as well. Then the man started walking off in the direction he'd just come from, but not before stooping to pick up the axe again.

"Where are we going?" asked Harding, catching him up.

"To Angels Landing."

Harding finally twigged. The lifeboat.

"We're not going to walk all that way. There isn't time."

"No, we're not going to walk all that way," Rob confirmed.

He led them to the cream van round the back of the lighthouse. It was bigger than the Volvo, and what's more Woodhead could get it started.

Rob was climbing into the driver's seat, when Harding stopped him.

"You're in no fit state," he said. "Trust me, I used to be a doctor."

For just a fraction of a second Harding thought there would be an argument, but Rob nodded, relenting without a fuss. Deep down he knew Harding was right, and besides he needed to conserve all his energy for piloting The Jenny.

Darville took the silver handle of the back door and opened it for him. His mouth hung open. Inside, opposite a wooden bench, spare chemical suits were hung up. And welded to the back of the front seats was a rifle rack containing machine guns and hand pistols. Underneath the bench, Darville found some green holdalls. He whistled when he saw the pineapple-shaped objects inside.

"I think we can do a little better than your axe, eh?" he said.

Rob swore under his breath. "I-I never thought to check in here," he stammered. The man had gone wandering into the lighthouse, gone up against those things armed only with a fire-axe, when all the time this arsenal was right under his nose. If only he'd checked, or even just turned around and looked over the back of his seat… Maybe he could have saved his girlfriend? But he'd been in such a hurry to get inside, to see her again. He'd had no way of knowing the nightmare that awaited him.

"So, at least now we go prepared, yes," said Darville holding up one of the grenades.

*But prepared for what?* thought Harding. *Prepared for what?*

## Chapter Forty-Two
### Cold Blood

The Colonel slammed the door to the interview room behind him.

He'd taken up residence in here since they arrived, and it seemed like as good a place as any to be alone. And right now he needed to be on his own. It was all going to shit! He'd listened to Fuller – hell, he knew more about this than any of them – but now he'd gone missing. Along with that bitch West and her two friends.

There had been a possible sighting of Darville, and two guards were down. Could it be that he'd kidnapped them all? Jesus, why would he do that? Break in here just to do that? The man was fucking crazy, he reminded himself. Why do crazy people do anything?

As if all that wasn't bad enough, he'd lost contact with his forces on the road and in Sable. He had no idea what the fuck was going on! But you could bet your life it wasn't good. The Colonel punched a wall, ripping the material of his glove. His knuckles bled.

"Bastard!" he shouted.

Time was running out. If he didn't get a handle on all this soon… What? What would happen next? He knew damned well what would happen. He hadn't sent an official report in to "the powers that be" for days, and the last one had been promising all was well. It wouldn't be hard to put it together soon, realise where he'd gone—

There was a knock at the door.

"Go away."

Again the knock. What if it was them now? His superiors? What if they'd cottoned on? He couldn't just leave them outside. He had to reassure them. Buy some time.

The Colonel opened the door. Standing there was one of his own men, and Dr Benjamin Hopkins, the A&E physician. He breathed a sigh of relief.

"What is it?"

"Sir, he was demanding to see you."

The Colonel nodded and let Hopkins in. "That'll be all," he told the subordinate.

"Aye, sir."

"Before you start, you should know this isn't a good time, doctor."

Hopkins strode into the centre of the room, fuming. "Colonel, I've been appointed spokesperson on behalf of the hospital, and we want some answers."

*I knew it was a mistake to put 'em all together*, thought the Colonel. *Should've separated the staff. Stupid! Stupid! Stupid! Another mistake…*

"I'm afraid I can't give you any, Doctor."

"Can't, or *won't*." Ben watched the Colonel as the man circled him, hands behind his back. "I feel partly responsible for all this. I mean, it was me who let you all in."

*Just who does this prick think he is? Let them in?* "Don't feel bad, you couldn't have stopped us." The

Colonel grinned coldly.

"There are a lot of frightened people out there, Colonel. And after what I saw of the ward—"

"I've already told you once. You saw nothing, Doctor."

"You *wish!*"

"I *know.*"

Hopkins carried on regardless. "If we're dealing with a virus of some kind, as you seem to be suggesting, and it may have been passed on to the lifeboat men that left St August's, we should be alerting the police, the Local Health Authority, the WHO—"

"Don't worry about all that. It's in hand."

"In hand?" The doctor was getting more and more agitated. "And how long are you going to keep us here? I have a wife at home who's—"

"Shut up."

"What did you say?" Hopkins wasn't used to being spoken to like that, probably thought a man in his position demanded respect. "I want access to a telephone. I want to speak to—"

"Shut up," said the Colonel again.

"Look, I've had just about enough of—"

"I said *shut the fuck up!*" The Colonel took Hopkins by the collar and pushed him up against the wall. "You're not in charge here anymore. I am!"

The doctor's eyes bulged as the Colonel brought up a forearm and pressed it against his neck. With his other hand, he drew the automatic from its holster and shoved it halfway up the man's nose.

"I call the shots now," said the Colonel, and guffawed.

Hopkins gasped for air, clutching at the madman's wrist. Probably wondering if insanity was one of the signs? Did the Colonel have the disease?

The doctor brought up his knee, catching the Colonel

between the legs. He let go of Hopkins' neck and bent over wheezing. The doctor slid down the wall, rubbing his throat.

"Shouldn't... shouldn't have.... done..." the Colonel spluttered.

Hopkins made a dash for the door. He had his hand on the knob, ready to step outside, to tell the soldier who'd brought him here all about the Colonel—

There was a loud bang, and then Hopkins paused, reaching around and touching the back of his skull. He was attempting to turn, but instead his legs buckled, and his face struck the door with a gruesome *thunk!*

The Colonel walked over, pulling his head back by the hair to look at the exit wound marring Hopkins' brow, the red-hot gun barrel close by.

"Physician, heal thyself," said the Colonel.

Then he let the head drop again. The shaven-headed man holstered his weapon and reached for his cigarettes. Clamping one between his teeth, he lit up. He inhaled its menthol flavour, letting the excess smoke escape from his lips.

He glanced at the body once more and shook his head. He had tried to warn the doctor. This wasn't a good time for him.

Not a good time at all.

## Chapter Forty-Three
### Angels Return

The van squeezed down the tight track towards Angels Landing, towards the lifeboat station. Darville was behind the wheel, Harding by his side and Rob in the back. He was still subdued, but the anger he'd displayed earlier had gone for the present. It was as if he was saving it all up for the task ahead.

Harding twisted round and looked at the man. With dried blood across his forehead and dirt smearing his skin he resembled a refugee from a war film. A survivor of the Somme. There was that same glazed look on his face, caused by post-traumatic stress. Harding had seen that expression before. When he'd looked in the mirror. Of hope lost and bitterness, of doubt and betrayal. Perhaps the two of them were more alike than they cared to admit. Or at least they were right this minute.

Both of them were driven by one thing. The thought of that cloud. For Woodhead it would be a return visit. For him, the first encounter. No amount of video footage could compare with the real thing. Harding felt his hands begin to tremble.

And they both had a purpose in common. Retribution. Woodhead for the death of his girlfriend, Harding for the abduction of the woman he loved.

*She could be dead already, just like...*

No! He couldn't think like that. As Darville had said, if Fuller took the trouble to kidnap Tobe, kidnap Vicky, he must have had a reason. Harding remembered the way he'd looked at her; what was he doing to her right now? The idea drove him crazy.

Harding turned back and focussed on the way ahead. On the choppy seas out there. On the large black shape over the horizon. It had increased its size since this morning several-fold. Still in the same position, but bigger. A lot bigger. Maybe it was getting closer? Or gaining in power? Or both?

But that's where his friends were. Where *Vicky* was, he'd bet everything he owned on it. And that's where they had to go to save her.

Darville jerked the wheel and bounced them into the car park. He braked a little too suddenly and Harding was shaken from his thoughts.

"So this is it," said Harding.

"The time has come," Darville replied.

Harding got out and went round the back. Rob seemed to come alive when the doors were opened. He slid along the wooden seat on the side of the van's interior, machine gun in his hand. He took another one from the rack and offered it to Harding.

"I wouldn't know what to do with it."

"Suit yourself," snapped Rob.

Harding climbed inside to reach for one of the grey chemical suits hanging from a peg. Now this he would need. He untied his laces and kicked off his shoes. Then he shrugged off his jacket. Bending down in the back of the van, he shoved his right foot into the suit and sat on the bench beside Rob. With the left leg in, he pulled on a pair of rubber boots, sealing the tops up with tape. He followed this procedure with the arms of the suit, sealing up the gloves at the wrists and left the helmet-hood dangling for the time being.

Rob got out, taking with him two of the holdalls. He wandered off in the direction of the hut.

"He's not suiting up?" asked Darville as he came round to the back.

"Guess not."

"He's still mad with me, I think."

"You can hardly blame him."

"No, that is true."

Darville dressed in silence, then the thickset Belgian grabbed a rifle for himself and a Glock handgun, complete with holster. He unzipped the pockets on the side of the suit and shovelled in spare clips of ammo.

They shut the van up, leaving it alone in the car park. By the time they arrived at the back entrance to the station, Rob was already inside with the lights on. Harding noted the broken lock – everyone from that morning had long-since departed – but didn't ask how he'd done it.

Stepping through, Harding asked Darville something that had been on his mind all the way there. "If the Colonel's men couldn't take that… thing by the road, what chance do we stand against Fuller?"

Darville pinched his bottom lip with his front teeth, then answered: "I do not know. But we have to try. There is no one else."

"You still think you'll be able to get through to him?"

"I did once before. There is a battle going on inside, I think. The Edward Fuller I knew wanted only to help mankind. I cannot accept that he is gone forever."

"Well, accept it," Rob said with a snarl, coming back

through. He had on his yellow RNLI waterproofs. "I looked those two in the eye back at the lighthouse. Men *I* used to know. Men I grew up with in Sable. But there was nothing left of them. They were... something else."

Darville shook his head.

"You don't believe me? It's true. You and this Fuller character really fucked them up good."

"Is she seaworthy?" asked Harding, changing the subject; he didn't want a repeat performance of what had happened earlier.

Rob followed his gaze. "The Jenny? She's banged up, but she'll get us there." He went back through into the main section of the hut. Harding and Darville trailed him.

The scientist spotted the wrecked front-part of the cabin. "How will you drive it?"

"From the top. The wind'll be getting up, but I'll manage."

"What about when we reach the Rain Circle?" asked Harding.

"The what?"

Harding realised that he'd never heard the term. Vicky's name for the phenomenon. "The storm, what will you do when we get there?"

"Play it by ear." Rob ran his hand along the hull. Had it been only that morning since he'd steered her back to Angels Landing? Since they rescued those fishermen who'd done so much damage?

"How do we open the doors?" This was Darville.

Rob went over to the office and rooted around in a drawer. He threw the man a set of keys. "Biggest one unlocks 'em."

Darville exited through the side door, leaving Rob and Harding alone.

"When this is all over, he's next," Rob spat.

Harding got out of his way as he walked to the back

of the boat. He didn't particularly care for the man, but he could understand what he was going through. The need to blame somebody. In a way Woodhead was lucky; Darville and Fuller were prime candidates. He'd had no one to blame for Alex's death but himself.

Rob tossed his bag on board. He stepped back, a little unsteady, but knocked away Harding's hand. *He should be resting up*, thought Harding, *not driving us out over the ocean in a battered lifeboat.* But right now, Rob was the only hope they had. Of seeing Vicky again, of putting a stop to whatever was happening. Of turning the clock back.

Harding handed him the other bags they'd brought, just as the doors to the slipway were undone. Darville pulled each one back, letting in the early evening sunlight and the cool breeze off the sea. Rob told Harding to go and help the man with the doors.

When he was out of sight, Rob went over to a cubby hole at the back of the station, where all his tools and the like were stored. He gathered together what he needed and quickly started loading them on board. A little extra insurance.

He'd just finished stowing all this in the rear of the boat as the two men came back in.

"Right," said Harding. "What now?"

Rob leaned over the edge and grinned his famous grin, only it didn't look quite as charming as usual. If anything, it was downright scary.

"Now…" he told them. "Now we can launch."

## Chapter Forty-Four
### The Horde

The battle of Sable had taken a great deal out of them. The soldiers had fought valiantly, if not fearlessly. But in the end they fell. One by one they were exterminated. Now there was nothing left of the troops, only vague puddles shimmering on the roads, on the streets. The vehicles they'd arrived in were in a similar condition. Ripped out wrecks, twisted hunks of metal. The army of meat sent against them now quashed.

They needed to rest. Keith and Frank directed the operation, as they had done the rebirth of the village. Some Sablites returned underground to the sewers to soak up every available drop of sustenance. Others went back to their homes to wallow in baths, to turn on showers, sink taps. To rebuild themselves.

Bullet-wounds disappeared, the gaping red holes filling out again not with skin, but with layers of filmy wetness. The same was true of cuts and bruised flesh, massaged back to health by the healing power of H2O.

Naturally, there were a number beyond all help. Those

shot at point blank range or torn asunder by grenades: missing heads, vital organs, legs. Those bodies could not go on, but their essences could. Standing over one such victim, Sean had shown them the way. He'd placed his hands on the skin and sucked out all but the bones through his pores. It rejoined the group now, its consciousness a part of the whole once more. Not one of the fallen was wasted. All were put to good use.

Readying for the time ahead.

The army may have been vanquished, but its leader was still out there. And he could send more troops against them. He had to be stopped. They had to prevent that from happening.

After they had rested they would take to the roads. Those who could drive would use their own cars, carrying with them those who could not. They'd pursue this leader to his base, wipe out all his kind, and then wait for the glorious dawn. Because it didn't matter what happened after tonight.

The new age was already upon them.

## Chapter Forty-Five
### Three Men in a Boat

Now they were about to set off, it all seemed suddenly so real. And Harding didn't know whether he could go through with it.

He'd never been on the water since the day—

He thought he could do it, but now his legs were buckling as he walked to the ladder. Harding went to put his foot on the first rung and froze up.

"What's the matter?" Rob shouted down.

"I-I don't know if I can…"

"You get seasick, that it?"

"No, it's just that…"

Rob studied his face. The man was white as snow. A phobia? He'd picked a fine time to let them know about it.

"Come on, we have to get going. While it's still light out."

Darville came up behind him. "You are scared of what lies ahead?"

Harding laughed weakly. "Of what lies behind," he replied.

"I don't understand."

"For fuck's sake, let's get moving here!" Rob's impatience was returning. He was eager to get going.

"Wait, can't you see there is something wrong?" Darville argued.

"I don't give a shit. Now, either he gets on board or stays behind. It's as simple as that. What's it going to be?"

Gritting his teeth, Harding placed his foot on the first step, then the next. Darville remained below, his intention to knock out the pin and then climb aboard. Shaking, Harding made it to the top. Sweat had gathered on his upper lip and he licked it away.

Darville picked up the hammer Rob had shown him and walked around to the back of the vessel. There was the pin that held it in position, stopping it from running down the slipway.

"Ready?" he called out.

"Ready," came Rob's curt answer.

Darville struck the pin with a clang. It released The Jenny first time. He ran around and started up her side, the boat scraping its way along the guiders. Glad of the distraction, Harding helped him aboard as Rob took his place at the wheel. The Jenny picked up momentum, then dipped sharply. There was a lurch downwards like a roller-coaster ride and then it struck the water. Darville and Harding clung on to the side of the vessel for support. Rob hardly flinched.

The engines rumbled into life, Rob bringing back the throttle.

They were away.

Harding glanced down at the blueness chopping by. He felt ill, being as close to that substance as this, and had to fight the building nausea. Darville looked concerned again.

"You really do get seasick, eh?"

Harding just nodded. It was simpler to let him think that, and anyway there was an element of truth to it. The motion of the boat was enough to induce sickness if you weren't used to it. Especially tonight. The ocean was rougher than ever, and the high winds constantly battered the trio.

Rob stood upright against the wheel, half using it for balance. He looked out over the mass of brine, but his attention was fixed on the storm-cloud. It hadn't moved its position all day. Rob had erected the radar antenna, more out of habit than anything. He didn't need it to find his way to the cloud. Again, that feeling of dread took him over, his uncanny sixth sense warning him to turn back. For the first time in his life, he disregarded it. Rob already knew there was danger out there. He also knew that he had to go no matter what happened. It didn't concern him anymore. Nothing did.

A picture of Dawn's face entered his mind, as clear as a television signal.

As it had done all those hours ago when he still had a life, the cloud stared into his very soul. A malevolent black eye gaping at him. The eye of death itself, for that's all it had brought. Death and destruction. That morning he'd had the strangest feeling it was alive somehow, but he'd put it down to his imagination. Now, after all he'd seen, after all he'd been told, he was positive that was true. It *was* alive and what's more, he was going out there to kill it.

Rob glared at the cloud in the distance. "I'm coming back," he whispered under his breath. "D'you hear me, you son of a bitch? I'm coming back for *you*."

## Chapter Forty-Six
### The Approach

They could all feel it.
The air was charged with power.
The wind incredibly strong.

The sea was rocking The Jenny to and fro. Darkness was falling. The sun blotted out by the growing cloud, dusk approaching. Darville and Harding made their way towards the bow of the boat. The Belgian scientist was mesmerised.

"I never dreamed… From the shore it seemed so… Less…"

"Yeah, and it's only getting bigger," shouted Harding.

"No, that's impossible."

"How's it feel to finally meet your creation?" Rob barked down from above them. He scowled at Darville.

"This does not belong to me anymore," the man responded. "It is a distortion of my work."

The cloud eclipsed everything else on the horizon, bright flashes of lightning sparking here and there. The thunder was loud in their ears, even above the crashing waves. Harding watched the way it spun the water at its base, in exactly the same way he'd spun the oil paint on his canvas. This was *his* maelstrom as much as anyone's.

He backed away and went round to the steps. The going was tough but he held on, pulling himself along until he came up beside Rob.

"So, we're here," Harding hollered. "What happens now?"

Rob turned to face him. "Well, I don't intend to stay out here all night."

"We're going in?"

Rob nodded. "Get him into the cabin, I'll be there in a minute."

Harding had trouble swallowing. He looked once more at the cloud, and then went down again to fetch Darville, dragging him by the arm. The pair of them collected the bags from on deck and bent to get into the cabin. There was no window anymore and rain and breakers washed through onto a smashed control deck. What was left of the inside wheel hung down like a loose button on a shirt.

"He's going to drive us though, isn't he?" Darville didn't have to shout as loudly in here, and his voice cracked halfway through the sentence.

"Yes." Harding edged as far away from the damaged part of the cabin as possible.

A moment later, the door opened again, letting in wind and rain. Rob stepped through the gap, blankets in his hand. Pivoting, he slammed the door shut behind. "We use these to wrap round people we rescue," he explained, giving one of the big sheets to both Darville and Harding.

Harding wasn't that cold, and was about to say so when he grasped what Rob had in mind. The sailor went to the back and squatted down, pressing himself up against the side of the cabin and placing a bag between his legs. His machine gun was resting over his knees. Harding got down next to him and motioned for Darville to do the same. They pulled the blankets up to their chins.

"I left her on full speed; we should ram it at any moment."

Turbulence suddenly bucked The Jenny, lifting all three men off the floor. They curled themselves into a ball, the blankets inching up higher. Wind and splashes of rain blew in through the broken windows, barely reaching them. Harding and Darville drew their hoods over, the clear face-masks steaming up. Harding screwed up his eyes. When he opened them again all he could see was a solid wall of rain lashing down. Then The Jenny struck the Rain Circle. There was a terrifying thumping noise as the boat was pummelled.

And then everything went crazy.

\*\*\*

A string of vehicles emerged from the sleepy seaside village of Sable. A mirror image of the ones that had trundled in some time ago. Cars of all shapes and sizes, packed with people. The burger van, which had done such a roaring trade at Angels Landing, was there, as was Big Billy Braden's old Jag – with Tina at the wheel (she'd always wanted to drive it) and Rodney Twain the fish 'n' chip king in a white Lada.

At the front rode an orange-red Escort, a silver Proton and a blue Astra estate. The three lifeboat men, the founding fathers of this new Sable, led the pack.

Their destination was St August's hospital.

The time of reckoning was at hand.

## Chapter Forty-Seven
### The Visions

Harding had visited this place before. Many times – and twice in the last twenty-four hours. It was his dreamscape. His own private hell.

Except now he was there with Darville and Rob Woodhead.

They were sitting in a boat, a rowing boat, sailing out over the lake. The water was calm, relaxing almost. But Harding was quick to recognise the deceit. It was a killer. It had taken his son away from him.

Darville stood up to place a hand on Harding's shoulder. Immediately he started to sway. The lake beneath them was tipping the boat. Harding snapped his head round in time to see the thickset man tumble over the side. There was a big splash, soaking Rob and Harding.

Then the boat was capsizing, pitching them all into the damp, dark depths. Harding felt the cold liquid taking him, again. Rob tried to swim but the water was thick like treacle. Darville disappeared into the inky blackness, a flurry of bubbles all that remained.

Harding concentrated. Resisting the fear that touched him with icy fingers; with wet, icy fingers. He couldn't breathe, but he knew now it was all an illusion. All in his mind, a warped reflection of what happened on that day when—

Christ, it seemed so real.

And the laughing he heard, was that in his head, too?

Harding didn't care anymore. He surrendered to oblivion once more.

\*\*\*

Darville awoke to find himself back at the facility.

The last thing he remembered was drowning, falling ever downwards until his lungs had burst with the lack of oxygen. But now he was safe. He lifted his head from the desk. It had just been a nightmare. All a horrible nightmare. He'd been overworking lately, staying up until the small hours. Maybe that was why he'd dropped off here. Also filling out requisition orders wasn't the most riveting of jobs.

Yet his work was progressing apace and if his calculations were correct soon they would be able to test their theories. He and his partner.

Then they would bring water to drought-ridden areas, prevent the flooding that plagued so much of this world. Bring life where there was only death. Hope where there was desperation.

He had a meeting scheduled with Fuller that morning. Darville looked at his watch, he was already late. Grabbing his jacket from the back of the chair, he left his office and dashed down the corridor to the stairs. The labs were only one floor down. That's where he would find his good friend. Fuller was just as much of a workaholic as him, especially lately, now they were on the verge of a breakthrough.

Darville nodded to members of staff as he ran towards the lab. The place would be sealed off, and he'd have to wait for Fuller outside. But he could at least let him know he was here – use the intercom system or tap on the glass partition.

The burly Belgian turned the corner and—

Reality collapsed around his ears.

The lab door was wide open. Something was very wrong inside. He saw red patches on the walls, a lab coat tossed onto the floor in a puddle of gooey slime. Darville ventured further in. There had been an accident here, that much was obvious. He should call for help, ring the alarm. But instead he walked on.

"Edward? Edward, are you there?" It didn't sound like his own voice.

He heard a mumbling sound. It was coming from the far corner. There glass glittered over tables where test tubes had been smashed. He stepped closer, saw a pair of feet sticking out from behind the table.

Darville peered around it and saw a stooped figure in white bending over the body. The figure turned. It was Fuller, but at the same time not him.

The professor had his hand buried deep inside one of his assistants, up to the elbow. His face was covered in perspiration, so much so that it looked like he'd just been swimming at the local pool.

Darville gagged.

"Marcel…" gurgled Fuller through gritted teeth. "I can't control… it…"

Darville went to assist him, but stopped. Something changed in Fuller's eyes. They turned a milky colour and his face rippled, skin undulating. He raised his free hand, then clenched it. What happened next was impossible. Fluid spouted from Fuller's appendage. It missed Darville, but took a chunk out of one of the tables.

Fuller raised himself up, his other arm squelching as it slipped out of the dead technician. He began to shake.

"Edward!" cried Darville. "What is—"

Fuller's face turned grotesque, feral. His shoulders hunched, and as Darville watched, the blood along the man's arm absorbed itself into his body. The professor shook again, jerking his head from side to side.

"Marcel, go now... I'm not strong enough..."

"You have to fight this," pleaded Darville. His mind was spinning.

"I can't. It's too... You don't understand..." Fuller aimed at him again, this time point blank. There was no way he could miss. But the man held fire. "Go, Marcel... *please...*" He was holding off the spray, Darville could see that.

Behind him someone entered the lab. "Professor Fuller, you're..." The mousy-haired woman screamed. Fuller shifted round and released a deluge into her. One minute she was standing there, the next she'd vanished in a splash of white and red.

Darville raced to the door. He had to alert security. But as he fell into the corridor he saw soldiers already heading towards him, the woman's screams attracting them.

Fuller was behind, shouting to the guards, telling them to stop Darville at all costs. They raised their weapons and called for the Belgian to halt. He barely heard them; he just had to get out of there, away from that lab...

Gunfire sparked off the walls as he fled through the rear entrance and outside. Sirens wailed. Darville made for the wall at the back. It was high, but somehow he made it over the top. There was more shouting, more gunfire. He ignored it.

Darville jumped over to the other side, falling a good distance down a slope and landing in a river that shouldn't even have been there. He didn't remember a river flowing beside the facility, but nevertheless it carried him along. And as it did he heard the sound of throaty laughter in his ears.

\*\*\*

Rob Woodhead was walking through the centre of Sable.

He couldn't believe what he was seeing. The ravaged streets and roads, cracks and holes everywhere he looked. Not just that, but overturned vans, vehicles that looked like they'd been crushed flat. And the shop fronts, The Seagull…

What in Heaven's name had happened here?

Rob heard a noise, a swishing sound. He pivoted and came face-to-face with Frank Dexter.

"Holy shit, Frank! What's going on?"

Frank gawked at him, craning his neck.

Another sound to his left, and Rob swung round again. Sean Howard with a pint in his hand. And another noise. To his right was Keith Tomkinson. Keith had something in his arms, slung over them. A body dressed all in white and silken bows. The face of his wife Melanie dangled down over the crook of his elbow.

"Sean? Keith… You're scaring me. What's happened to Sable?" Rob was panicking now.

The material of Melanie's wedding dress turned scarlet, her face like raw liver. Keith dropped the disgusting bundle at Rob's feet, and he saw the woman

# The Wet

disperse over the ground. Flatten out and pool around him.

Keith smirked.

More people flocked around Rob. People he knew: customers; friends. The good folk of Sable. Soon he was surrounded by them. Keith, Frank and Sean came closer, pawing at him. The dripping hands pulling him down. Down to the ground so the crowds could descend upon him.

His father was there, too. He stood with the villagers but didn't push along with them. He simply watched Rob submerging beneath the swell. At his side was the ginger-haired boy.

The crowds pressed down on him, and he realised they were no longer solid anymore. Each body was liquifying over him, choking him, becoming a sea themselves. One that was rapidly drowning him.

There was laughter. It came from everywhere and nowhere at once. At first Rob thought it was in his head.

But then the watery hordes formed a face. A mouth, a nose, eyes... And it was the face that was laughing. So hard and so long.

As Rob resigned himself to his fate.

## Chapter Forty-Eight
### Inside the Maelstrom

Harding pulled back the blanket that was covering him.

All was quiet. The lifeboat had come to a standstill. He shook the men on either side of him. Darville and Rob Woodhead roused themselves sleepily.

"What happened?" asked Darville. "Where are we?"

"Something was inside my head," said Rob. "I could feel it."

Harding nodded, getting to his feet. The boat had stopped swaying, the floor of the cabin perfectly inert. It didn't even feel like they were on the water anymore. Had they run aground somewhere? Drifted off course while they were asleep and hit land further down the coast?

Rob and Darville stood up and looked out through the gap the broken window had left. It was too dark to see anything clearly. Remarkably, the inside of the cabin was fairly dry, the rain having passed directly over the top of them.

"The eye of the storm?" Darville whispered.

Harding's mouth hung open. Could it be? Were they actually *inside* the Rain Circle itself? Grabbing their bags, the three men passed through the cabin door and stepped up on deck. Outside it was even blacker, but surely night hadn't fallen so quickly. Or had they been unconscious for that long?

Rob went over to the searchlight and powered it up. He swung it around and they followed the tubular beam with fascination. To the side of them was the wall of rain they'd passed through, but it seemed so much gentler. The cascade was noiseless now, no thunderous gushing, no pounding in their ears. The light pointed above them. Harding put a hand out to Darville.

"I see it," said the man.

They were directly beneath the cloud. Its rolling blackness cut off the natural light from outside. Now and again a flash of lightning would streak across it, illuminating the contours.

"Jesus," mumbled Rob. "Are we still dreaming?"

Neither one of his companions answered.

The searchlight pulled round under Rob's guidance, tracing the length and shape of the storm. The walls were indeed curved, like Stanley Keets' lighthouse; the rain falling precisely, leaving a circular space inside. The space they now occupied, roughly half the size of a good playing field. Rob tilted the beam and it caught something white.

A thin rectangular shape some forty or fifty metres away from them, jutting out of the dark. Rob caressed the lines of it with his light and came to a cone-like protuberance. There, sticking out of the water, actually joined with the surface as far as they could see, was a small plane. It looked like it was suspended in a pot of glue, half of it breaking through the top. There were shadowy shapes in the cockpit. The landing had certainly not been a smooth one.

Harding and Darville exchanged glances, both knowing it belonged to Fuller.

"It must have been how he seeded the cloud," Darville said eventually.

*But where is he now? Still inside the cockpit, dead?* thought Harding.

As if to answer his question The Jenny's searchlight came upon a figure in the distance. It was swimming towards them, just the head and arms visible. But as it came closer they saw it wasn't moving its arms at all. There was none of the usual thrashing about connected with swimming. No splashes of water. Rather the figure seemed to be gaining height. Now his torso could be seen.

Closer, and it became apparent that the man – for it was definitely a man, they could all tell that – was rising *out* of the water. He walked across, covering the distance between him and The Jenny. Harding and Darville knew who it was even before he spoke.

"My dear friends," Fuller intoned. "I've been expecting you. Welcome to the temple.

"Welcome to both the end and the beginning."

## Chapter Forty-Nine
### The Siege

They arrived quietly and took up positions around the hospital.

The few guards on patrol tried to stop them, with predictable results. Freeing themselves from the confines of their vehicles, they surrounded the building. Not one word was spoken. Each and every villager knew what was at stake. What they must do.

Frank was the first to fire, followed closely by the other "founders". They chipped away pieces of St August's bit by bit. Piece by piece. Then the deluge began.

They all opened up at once.

\*\*\*

Wayne and his family huddled together on the ward, reunited.

"What's happening?" asked his petrified mother.

He couldn't answer her. Wayne just held his girlfriend's hand tightly and for the second time that day, he prayed.

Nearby, his chief Phil Holmes also felt the vibrations.

Stumbling to the window, he saw the ring of people around the hospital, shooting some kind of water cannons up at the building. He ducked back when one of the blasts came too close.

\*\*\*

From the interview room, the Colonel looked on.

Knowing now that his army had been wiped out, he felt no pity. Only pride. They'd died in his service. Under his command. What more could he have asked for?

But now the time had come to give up the game.

He took out his laptop and tapped in a code word. He typed out his final report. It didn't matter either way now. His finger hovered over the send button. Then it was done.

The Colonel kicked the body of Dr Benjamin Hopkins out of his way and opened the door. As he strode down the shaking corridors of the hospital, he brought up his chemical hood, took out his pistol, and chuckled.

In the lift he pressed the ground floor button.

## Chapter Fifty
### Of Man and God

"Is that him?" Rob cried out. "Is that the motherfucker who's done this?"

Fuller drew nearer to them over the calm waters, chuckling to himself. His thinning, curly hair was tossed back, his face a sickening veil of secretions. "And still they do not understand."

"I understand all right!" Rob brought up the machine gun at his side.

"Woodhead, wait—"

Darville's pleas were cut off by a chattering burst which deafened both Harding and himself.

Fuller held up both of his hands, flat out as if he was pushing against some invisible object they could not see. A disc of translucent liquid swirled around his palms, growing in size until it shielded his head and upper body. The bullets whined and whinnied as they ricocheted off the barrier. Fuller might as well have been standing behind a foot of concrete for all the effect they had.

Rob's eyebrows met in the middle; he screamed as he fired. It went on until his magazine was empty and even then he kept depressing the trigger, an empty clicking his only reward.

Fuller lowered his hands. The shield evaporated instantly.

"I – we – might have expected such a display." Fuller's voice was icy clear.

Darville came to the edge of the boat, his hands gripping the rail. "What has become of you, Edward?"

Fuller squinted at his former partner. "If you are asking if this is really me, then the answer is yes, Marcel. I am Edward Fuller."

"Not the person I know. Not my closest friend and colleague."

"Granted. I am not *quite* the man I used to be, as you can see." Fuller lifted a hand to his face and cackled. It was a laugh they all recognised, Harding especially, but filtered through the throat of this man. "I am rejoined. I am one."

"One of what?"

"Merely... One."

"You're ill, Edward. Your experiments, do you not remember? You have created something... a virus spread through the water, and you have passed it on to—"

Fuller's laughing came louder. Rob pulled out his empty magazine and loaded another.

"Is that what you still believe? My 'tampering' created a virus?"

"That's what *you* told us," Harding pointed out.

"Ah yes, Mr Harding. But I thought Marcel was brighter than that. I thought he might be able to see the bigger picture."

"The Edward Fuller I once knew was a God-fearing man. He would never have harmed another intentionally," Darville contended.

"No, that's correct. But I have met my God, Marcel, and he disagrees."

"Your god?"

"*The* God. Our creator. He is a part of me now, and He is an angry, vengeful God!"

"What are you talking about?"

"We are all his subjects. We are all here because of Him. He alone can deliver us. He is all-powerful."

Darville turned back to Harding. "It has sent him over the edge. I fear there may be no reasoning with him."

Fuller strode forward, angered by Darville's outburst. "You dare to— Of all people I thought you would understand. I see I was wrong. I did not create a virus, Marcel. I reawakened something that had lain dormant for millions and millions of years. Something we left behind."

"Our creator?" Darville sounded sceptical.

"Exactly. Once we were all together. Joined in spirit and mind. A whole. But then we separated ourselves from the very thing that nurtured us. We took to the land, turned our backs on the oceans. And the Creator was weakened because of it. Our minds are still joined to Him even today, albeit tenuously. Every time we thirst, each time we need to cleanse ourselves, we turn to Him. Why do we travel so far to be near the sea, why do we find it so relaxing, why do we fill pools with His essence and submerge ourselves in His glory? In an effort to return to what we once were. We are creatures of the water, Marcel, you must see that. Trace memories remain, search your souls and you will find the truth." His hands were stretching out, reaching for them. "Are we not, after all, walking sacks of liquid? Do we not start out in our mothers' wombs, floating in amniotic fluid? Is not our world made up of His being? He is a part of everything, from the tiniest insect up to the largest creatures on Earth, from the forests in Africa to the snow-capped mountains in the Antarctic. This world belongs to *Him* and He has returned to claim it."

"Are you seriously suggesting that God is water?" Harding sniped.

"No, Mr Harding, He is so much more than that. Haven't you been listening to me?"

"*He's* not my God," said Harding.

"Oh really? He exists, though. He is not some fantasy concocted by your ancestors. Even the Bible acknowledges Him, but He did not merely *move* upon the face of the water. Think about the story of Noah; the parting of the Red Sea; the ritual of baptism; Jesus turning the water into wine…" Fuller cast his head downwards. "You only have to look at what I am doing right now." To emphasise his point, Fuller walked around in a circle on the sea.

"You're no Messiah," Rob cried. "You and your god, you're homicidal maniacs!"

Fuller stared at him. "I am the Son, whatever you choose to think. I was the first He touched."

"*Used*," chipped in Darville.

"No. I admit, I resisted at first, before I knew the whole story. I was… frightened. Needlessly, I hasten to add. Soon I was glad to do His bidding, to prepare this place for Him, for the consolidation, because I realised what an honour it was. What happened to the fishermen and their boat was unfortunate, but they sailed too close to the temple. He wasn't ready yet. And of course when the Colonel learned of the temple's whereabouts, steps had to be taken to combat the brute. So my Lord used the fishermen to his advantage. To spread Himself through His own creations; it is His right after all. Nothing could stand in the way of the consolidation. The time away from Him has made us – you – savage. No longer beings of thought and belief. He is displeased with his offspring. With the flesh. The sooner we are back in His care, the better."

"And is it any less savage to kill people in cold blood?" Harding asked him.

"You don't understand. To destroy the flesh is to free the spirit, to return it to the place where it once dwelled. No one truly dies at His hands."

Rob was close to tears. "Horseshit!'

"Is it?"

The patch of ocean inside the Rain Circle glowed. It became brighter, absorbing the tiny searchlight. Harding could see heads below the surface of the water, all around Fuller. The professor lifted his hands, calling them up. A handful of figures emerged. One was wearing a harness and an RAF uniform, the winchman from the Sea King chopper; another was wearing a jumper full of holes and khaki trousers, obviously a fisherman; the same went for the third, only he had waders on; the fourth figure was horribly scarred, burned – a twin of the one they'd seen beside the road; the fifth and sixth were a man and a woman. The pair who'd arrived at St August's earlier to see Rob.

"Dawn! Stanley, George… Brian!" Rob dropped his gun and leapt down from his position at the searchlight. Darville and Harding grabbed him, stopped him from rushing forward.

"It's a trick, Woodhead. Remember, he can get inside your mind." Harding moved aside to avoid Rob's elbow. "Listen to me!"

"I am not the one inside your mind," stated Fuller. "And this is no trick…

It is the will of God!"

## Chapter Fifty-One
### Time to Go

"Come on, time to go."

The voice startled Lily. It was the man who'd interviewed her before.

"Where to?"

"Never mind that, just move."

His timbre frightened her so much she couldn't move. "Please, I don't know what this is—"

The man came in and grabbed her roughly by the arm. Lily cried out as he manhandled her from the "cell" and into the portakabin's foyer. The others were there: Leo, Dennis, Matt, and a few more people she didn't recognise; a man on his own and a couple, the woman heavily made up. They were being held now at gunpoint by several men dressed in jumpsuits. Despite this, Matt was still kicking up a foul-mouthed fuss. The workman she'd spoken to on the road was present, too, as was the younger man who'd sat in on her interrogation. He seemed uncomfortable with what was going on.

"Now, outside. All of you!" ordered the swine behind

# The Wet

Lily. Not only was he the chief interviewer, but he also appeared to be in charge. The small band of people obeyed, traipsing down the steps at the door and out into the open air once more. For Lily it was something of a relief to be out of there.

"Where are you taking us?" Dennis demanded.

"Who rattled your cage, pipsqueak?" the workman said with a sneer.

"Just keep moving and no-one will get hurt," said the interrogator.

Lily didn't believe that for a second. Again, she wondered how on earth she'd gotten into this mess.

"Here?" said one of the jumpsuit men after they'd marched over to the grassland by the two black cars.

"I'm not sure about this," the young soldier spoke up, his voice quivering.

"Orders is orders."

"Here'll do, then we can—"

One man broke from the pack and started to run. He didn't get far.

There was a sudden bang and he dropped over sideways.

"No!" someone screamed.

Then there was confusion. Lily turned around to see the man and woman go down the same way, and the young soldier from her cell wrestling with one of the jumpsuited men. Matt got up and went for the fellow directly behind, the interrogator, charging him and bringing him down with a rugby tackle. There were more shots fired.

Blood on the grass. She didn't know who it belonged to…

Lily stumbled backwards. She saw Matt struggling with the interrogator, grunting loudly. The next thing, he was slumping over him as if drunk, head lolling loosely. The interrogator knocked him off with his knee, and Lily saw a knife-handle jutting out of Matt's chest, a bloom of redness spreading across.

The young soldier disarmed a couple of his comrades before a bullet twirled him around. Dennis punched one of the guards in the face and got a kick in the stomach for his trouble.

Lily could do nothing but watch, horrified. She'd never seen anything like this before in her life, except perhaps on TV. But this was real, happening right in front of her.

And the man who'd just stabbed Matt was rising. The interrogator brought out his gun, aimed it at her and pulled the trigger.

\*\*\*

The Colonel found six of his men downstairs in reception. They were firing at the attackers, using the entranceway as cover.

"You men, with me," he told them.

The Colonel passed through the smashed doors of the Casualty Department, the same ones he'd strode through when he got here. His men stayed where they were. There was fear in their eyes.

"Didn't you hear what I said?" he bellowed, glancing back.

If they did, none of them replied. He considered returning for a moment, teaching them a lesson. But instead he carried on walking outside.

He marched confidently into the open, standing tall, holding his gun in front of him and glaring at the people who'd done this. Who'd undermined him.

The water blasts paused for a moment as the Sablites

observed him.

The Colonel raised his gun at the nearest one and fired. His target, a woman in her mid-thirties wearing a soaking dress, took the shot in her belly. She keeled over.

"See?" shouted the Colonel back to his men. "There's nothing to be afraid of."

But when he looked again at the woman, he saw her getting to her feet, taking her place in the circle. When she opened her mouth, the Colonel saw her spit the bullet out onto the ground.

"Shit the bed!" He fired again, indiscriminately this time, random targets. Not one of them went down and stayed down. Three men broke free of the circle and approached him.

The missing lifeboat men: Frank, Keith and Sean.

"You think I'm scared of you freaks? You wouldn't be here if it weren't for us. I'm not fucking scared," the Colonel said with a snort. They said nothing back. They merely moved closer. The Colonel pointed his gun first at Frank, then Sean, then Keith. Tracking their movements.

Then someone had hold of his left arm. Keith.

"Let go of me!" the Colonel grunted, but there was no threat to his words, no edge of conviction.

Keith's fingers dug their way inside his suit. The Colonel felt his veins come alive, slivers of blood and water pumping up to his shoulder and his neck, stretching the skin taut.

The Colonel brought up his gun arm, but there was a hand at that side, too. Sean held him tightly. He fought the grip, no longer trying to aim at Keith, but desperate to bring the gun up to his own head. To end this now.

The firearm fell out of his useless grasp, clattering to the car park floor.

More pain, this time from Sean's side. Going up his right arm.

The Colonel gritted his teeth. Every movement was amplified, every nerve ending red-hot. Frank placed his hand on the Colonel's chest. It sank inside, through the suit, through the meat and bone. The Colonel made a strangled gargling sound as he felt himself filling up with juices from the torso downwards. Only his head was left intact so he could experience this first-hand. The suit was ripping down the sides as he billowed outwards. Now his legs were distended, bent out of shape and five times their normal size. Bones melted away.

The Colonel could feel the pressure building. Something had to give.

And it did.

His body suddenly popped. Guts and blood sprayed everywhere, covering the car park. The Colonel's head, still very much whole, very much alive inside the hooded helmet, dropped to the ground beside the remnants of his once-muscular physique.

He mouthed something, and then closed his eyes.

\*\*\*

The interrogator depressed the trigger.

But the bullet never made it to Lily.

Dennis Owen threw himself in the way, taking the full force. Lily let out a terrible wail. "Dennis! Oh-my-God-*Dennis!*"

He fell into her arms as the interrogator prepared to fire again. Then suddenly that man was toppling over. Lily saw the fresh-faced soldier from her cell clutching at his former comrade's boots. The wounded lad clambered over his superior and they wrestled with the gun. Its barrel disappeared from view for a moment and there was a deadening *thunk*. The young soldier rolled off and Lily watched smoke rise from a hole in the interrogator's side.

There was only one jumpsuited man left now, the one who'd first stopped them at the traffic lights, and he ran for it, climbing into a black car and pulling away.

Leo went over to the guy who'd made a run for it and came back shaking his head. Then he examined Matt. He too was dead. The heavily made-up woman was still alive, but her travelling companion was not so lucky. The young soldier was next; he was clutching at his shoulder.

"Let me have a look at that," Leo offered. He tore open the shirt to see that the bullet had passed right through. "Keep some pressure on this."

"Moss," said the soldier. "Travis Moss."

"Right Travis, just hold this here and you should be okay till we can get to a hospital."

Moss nodded.

Leo went over to Lily. She was cradling Dennis' head in her lap. He was quite obviously deceased.

"Why? Why did he do that?" she blurted.

Leo crouched down beside her. "I-I don't know."

"He…"

"Look, we have to get going. There's one car left, and we have two people with gunshot wounds. One might need surgery."

Lily didn't hear him.

"Lily," said Leo in his best nurse-patient tone of voice. "Please, there's nothing we can do for him now. It's time to go."

Leo put his arm around her and pulled her up. As she was led to the car she kept looking round at Dennis. Then Leo placed her in the front seat and went back to help Moss and the girl.

## Chapter Fifty-Two
### The Consolidation

Rob shrugged off the two men holding him and jumped overboard. He landed on the water but didn't sink down. Instead, it felt solid beneath his feet. He was able to move forward, go to Dawn. He'd seen her, Stanley and George fall from the top of the lighthouse, yet somehow they'd survived.

Or had they? Had they died and been brought back to life? It didn't matter, either way. They were here, along with Brian Turner *and* Josh Bramwell. The lost fishermen, the ones he'd failed to find. It was really them.

Dawn was smiling, arms wide.

*"I guarantee you she'll be back in your arms again before you know it."* Phil's words to him at the hospital.

Brian was nodding his head contentedly. Even Stanley seemed pleased to see Rob...

That was when the first alarm bells rang. Stanley Keets, no matter what he'd been through, would never be happy to see him. The lifeboat man paused, slowing up his approach. Dawn was disappointed by this; she beckoned for him to come over.

"She's waiting for you, Rob." Fuller was baring his teeth as he spoke.

That did it. Rob started to back away, aware that this wasn't right. He could see nothing in Dawn's eyes. None of the love they'd shared. The orbs were empty, hollow. Lifeless.

No, not lifeless. Filled with something else.

Hatred.

The group formed a semi-circle, holding hands. Fuller stepped back behind them. All six figures rolled back their eyes and shook.

"They must not be allowed to interfere," shouted Fuller.

Then it happened. The waters rose about them, transforming each person. Their bodies became slick amalgamations of liquid and flesh, though more of the former than the latter. They bulged, swelling up, and joined together, controlling the forces at their disposal.

The blast was colossal.

Rob just about had time to drop to the "ground" before it swept over him, missing by millimetres. It struck The Jenny, breaking her in two. Darville was thrown over the rail and landed badly on the surface of the sea, his rifle spinning out of his hands. Harding stumbled on the deck and fell sideways as the section he was on tipped up.

Rob dragged himself backwards as best he could. The "people" ahead of him were getting ready to fire again.

"Harding," he called back over his shoulder. "Toss me one of the bags."

Disoriented, Harding scrabbled around on the deck. His hands found the material of one bag, and he flung it down to the lifeboat man.

Rob opened the sacking up and took out a grenade. They hadn't changed that much since his own time in service. He pulled the pin and dropped it back in the bag, which contained about a dozen or so more. Then threw the package as hard as he could. It landed near the group, but not as close as Rob would have liked. He took off in the opposite direction, counting down the seconds.

The explosion was spectacular. A boom, followed by yellow and white lights, and the whole area around them seemed to go up. Rob instinctively ducked, hands over his head. Harding shielded his eyes from the glare. When he looked down again, he saw that Darville was gone.

He spotted him moments later, skirting around the side of the Rain Circle, avoiding the smoking crater in the middle. Grabbing something cylindrical and red from the deck, Harding clambered down the side of the boat and went after him. Darville was going for Fuller, and Fuller was the only one who knew where Tobe and Vicky were.

Rob hauled himself up, glancing across at them. The two men vanished behind a plume of smoke. He was about to go after them himself when he noticed something moving in the crater. Dawn and Stanley were the first to arise, followed quickly by the others. Rob forgot all about Darville and Harding. But he remembered what he'd come here to do. The lifeboat man jogged back to The Jenny. He pulled himself onto the stern, slid down to the rear compartment. Opening it, he took out the objects he'd brought with him.

The smell was strong as he opened the cannisters and began to tip the contents over the side of the boat.

\*\*\*

When Darville found him, Fuller was kneeling before the wall of rain. It looked almost like he was praying.

"Stop!" the bearded man commanded.

He didn't rise; he didn't face Darville.

"Edward, please put an end to this," Darville begged him.

"I cannot. It's too late. When it is over you will see, Marcel. You will see how wonderful His kingdom is. You *all* will." Fuller stood, still with his back to Darville, and went over to the small plane he'd piloted here. Opening the door, he took out a body, head lolling back in the crook of his arm.

"Vicky!" Harding shouted, catching up with Darville. "What have you done to her?"

"She has been chosen to complete the circle," Fuller said, matter-of-factly. Of Tobe there was no sign… "We will join with them. She and I will initiate the consolidation. Just as one of each sex divided from him, so too will one of each return. To be with Him. Then it will all be over. The union complete, and the rest of our race will follow." Fuller drew himself up. He was taller than before; much taller. His soggy clothes were ripping. When he spoke again, it was in another voice. "There is nothing you can do. This is where it began, in the sea. This is where it must end."

Vicky stirred in his arms. She opened her eyes, her terrified face trying to comprehend where she was.

"*M-Monster*…!" she managed.

"Do not struggle," Fuller told her, lowering his face to hers.

"Noooo!" Harding dashed forward, covering the distance between Fuller and himself. He brought up the red bottle by his side. The extinguisher wasn't as big as the one from St August's, but when he pulled up the lower handle and aimed at Fuller, it sprayed a white froth at him. The professor let out a surprised whine when it stuck to him, and simultaneously let Vicky go. She landed with a bump down at his feet.

Fuller turned his attention to Harding.

He gained even more height, towering over the man. His epidermis was pulled taut, face altering itself. Harding recognised it as the half-glimpsed visage from his dream, from Tobe's tape. The one that frightened him more than anything had ever done before. Fuller was now a living, breathing embodiment of his "God".

He swatted Harding like an insect, slapping him with the back of his hand – which was now the size of a shovel-head. Harding flew through the air for an eternity before landing on the firm ocean waves.

Fuller and his "Lord" were coming together. A hideous pulsating giant of a creature, clothes shredded and falling away. Darville stepped back in amazement, then remembered the Glock. He drew the pistol and worked the trigger.

Nothing happened. The safety was still on. Darville thumbed the switch and let off three rounds. There was no attempt at deflection. The bullets passed cleanly through his old friend's chest, his head, as they would do through water itself. A rumbling laugh like that of thunder greeted Darville's ears.

"Too late," it said.

"Much too late…"

\*\*\*

The group was coalescing.

Rob glanced over to see them slopping together out of the crater, replenishing themselves from the sea beneath. Pale representations of faces he knew flitted about inside the whole and he wondered if these really were the recovered bodies of his friends – of Dawn – or just sick replicas, meant to disturb him. If so, they were doing a bloody good job.

But not that good. The last cannister was almost empty. Rob watched the contents trickle out, every last drop. The water-beast advanced, closing in on The Jenny, the boat's innards exposed by its own blast, engines that would never propel her again could be seen through the sides. It took not a bit of notice.

"Rob..." The voice was thick and phlegmy, but it was unmistakably Dawn's. "Rob... come to usss... we *need* you..."

Rob wiped away tears of sorrow and regret, of anger and frustration.

As the thing climbed up the side of The Jenny, he grabbed another item from the back compartment of the boat. Dawn's face reared up on a length of glistening liquid, and Stanley's came next – always with her, always beside her, even in this altered state.

Rob raised the flare-gun at them. "Dawn..." He couldn't bring himself to fire, his finger poised just above the trigger.

"You... won't do... that," Dawn gurgled, juices dribbling out of her mouth. A long tentacle-like appendage sprouted from the beast and curled around him. Rob couldn't look away from Dawn's face. It hypnotised him. Then the tip of the tentacle pierced his back, picking him up. Rob let out a roar, blood washing down his waterproofs. But somehow he kept his grip on the flare-gun.

"You're right," gasped Rob. "I won't."

He pointed the gun downwards over the side of The Jenny and shot the flare. The petrol and oil he'd dumped earlier set alight – a notion Mike Croxley had put in his head that very morning by almost blowing them to shit.

The fire ran under The Jenny, spreading outwards, covering the surface of the sea and eating into the water creature.

There was a tremendous howl of pain and Dawn's face exploded just feet away from him, the molten fragments landing on the slanting deck near the last two canvas bags. Rob dropped to the deck, the life pouring out of him. His limbs numb.

Stanley reached for his enemy, insubstantial hands snapping open and shut before the flames engulfed him. The last thing Rob saw was the RAF man writhing inside the globulous mass, what remained of Josh Bramwell and George Turner, already burnt to a crisp and turning to lava before his eyes. Brian, the final fisherman, the final Turner, nothing more than a pair of blind eyes peering out…

And his father standing in front of him.

"You did it son," said the fellow, holding out his hand. "Now let's go home."

\*\*\*

Fuller threw back his head as he experienced the effects of the fire.

His children couldn't replenish themselves, the petrol and oil cutting off their access to fresh water. And it drained him physically.

Darville chose that moment to leap at him. Fuller took hold of the Belgian with things that could no longer be called hands. Indeed, Fuller no longer had a human shape. He was more like a huge tower of frogspawn stretching up higher and higher.

"Fight him, Edward!" Darville shouted as he was

lifted thirty, forty feet into the air. The glass of his facemask shattered. The slime encircled him, dragging him in. But instead of struggling, Darville plunged further inside. He jammed his own hands into what had been Fuller's stomach and lost them immediately. The agony was unbearable.

Then he was melding with the Fuller-spawn. He could feel himself slipping away, his own body a part of something else. Yet his mind lived on independently. Darville concentrated on everything he'd ever learned, all the accomplishments of humanity, of the "savage" race – music, poetry, art – his own intentions when he'd started the Aquarius project, all the love he'd ever felt in his life. He fought against the overwhelming abhorrence, stemming the tide of hatred. Distracting The Wet long enough for the fire to consume its temple below the stormcloud.

Fuller's god twisted his consciousness, tempting him, showing him how right this was, how easy it would be to surrender. How only *He* could bring order to the chaos, bring peace to mankind.

Darville resisted with all his might.

***

Harding found himself sinking through the water.

It was losing coherence, no longer stable. Shaking himself, he forced a knee underneath him. He could see Vicky at the foot of the water mountain. He had to get to her before the fire came their way.

Even as he clawed along, he could see Vicky disappearing beneath the waves, the water going back to how it was before. Harding tried to get up, but it was impossible, like standing in quicksand.

And suddenly Vicky was gone.

Harding scanned the surface. He saw no sign of her. Then a hand came up out of the sea. He hesitated. In his mind it was years ago, and it was Alex who was drowning.

No! He couldn't make the same mistake again. He wasn't about to lose Vicky the same way. Harding unzipped his helmet and threw it back. Holding his breath, he dove into the gelatinous ocean just as The Jenny exploded across the way.

\*\*\*

The fire spread quickly.

Carried by the flammable liquid Rob had poured onto the sea, it swept the length of the Rain Circle and even climbed its sides. The heat caused the great fountain that was forming to burst and bubble. It collapsed in upon itself with a tremendous peal.

The black thundercloud above began to disperse, to finally drift apart. The rain stopped falling, the lightning only causing more damage. The temple was no more.

And all the dreams of consolidation went with it.

## Chapter Fifty-Three
### Severed Links

The Sablites shook as if they were being electrocuted.

Their bodies danced about in the circle, before dropping to the ground. Frank, Keith and Sean had their hands out when it struck them down. An immense feeling of loss, their link with the master severed. They fell over on the ground, limbs twitching. Water spilling out from them, no longer tainted.

The soldiers at the door saw their chance to escape and were soon followed by their comrades from inside. They stepped around the remains of their commanding officer, piled into their vehicles, and motored off up the road. In minutes they were but specks on the horizon.

Gradually, people emerged from the hospital, confused and alarmed, but thankful that the shaking had stopped. The damage to St August's looked a lot worse than it actually was, especially from the outside. The old place was built to last. It had survived the fire, and it would survive this.

Medical staff went to the prone bodies surrounding the hospital, recognising faces they knew, no longer distorted by the effects of The Wet. Some were bleeding where the bullet wounds from earlier had caught up with them. The woman who the Colonel had shot in the stomach collapsed, clutching her abdomen.

"Are they all right to, you know… touch?" asked Senior House Officer Nick Laurie.

"Only one way to find out," replied his colleague, Lisa Brookes.

They carried them inside, some on stretchers, some by hand, and did what they were trained to do. It stopped them from thinking about what had happened here today.

Phil Holmes limped down the stairs in time to see some being carried inside, one person after the next. A seemingly endless supply. As one casualty in particular went past, he cried out: "Jenny!"

The little girl stirred, her eyelids fluttering. Phil came alongside and looked down on her just as she woke. "Jenny, love…"

She coughed hard, but smiled at him. "Uncle Phil? Where am I?"

"Don't you worry, sweetheart. You're in safe hands." He stroked her hair, kissing her on the forehead.

"Don't leave me, Uncle Phil."

"I won't, love," he promised. "I'm not going anywhere."

## Chapter Fifty-Four
### Past-Present

Harding could feel the heat even below the surface. It was pitch-black, he waved his hands around in front of his face and trod water. He headed in the direction he'd last seen Vicky. The chemical suit was letting in water at the top, weighing him down, the hood dragging him back. But he strove on.

She had to be somewhere around here…

*Please let me find her, please let—*

Harding was amazed to see a flickering light ahead. It guided him across. There was a figure, a shape. Too small to be Vicky, but he chased it anyway. Harding neared his destination and he heard someone calling to him.

"Dad? Dad are you there?"

Alex! The body belonged to Alex. He opened his mouth to answer and let in a thick tide of salt water.

"Over here, Dad!" The ginger-haired boy was motioning to him, urging him on. "Hurry, Dad!"

Harding kicked and swam, using every muscle in his possession. Thoughts and memories reverberated inside his mind.

*You don't understand...*

He came closer with each kick.

*To destroy the flesh is to free the spirit...*

Hold on, just hold on a little longer.

*To return it to the place where it once dwelled...*

His hands propelled him forward, batting water out of the way.

*No one truly dies...*

And after he'd given up, accepted Alex's death, to see him here.

*No one truly dies at His hands...*

No one.

Harding reached out to his son, his gloved fingers closing over an arm. He pulled with all his might. Had to drag Alex to the surface...

But it wasn't Alex, he realised. It was Vicky. Harding shook his head, looking left and right for his son. The boy had gone, his task completed. Except Harding heard his voice one last time.

"I love you, Dad," he said.

Harding wrapped his arms around Vicky, clasping her so he could drag her upwards. He was running out of air and couldn't see the surface. Harding panicked. It was his dream all over again, except this time it was real. This time there was no way out. He wasn't going to wake up in a cold sweat, and neither was Vicky unless he could—

He was suddenly rising. Harding stopped kicking, puzzled by this strange marvel. It was almost as if they were being carried to freedom on plumes of moisture. And there it was, the thin layer that separated his world from this one. Harding punched through with his head, shaking the water away and coughing.

The fire on the surface some distance away was dying out. Extinguished by the collapsing walls of harmless rain.

Harding turned Vicky around and cupped her head in his hands.

"Vicky? Vicky are you all right?"

There was no response. He wiped matted blonde hair out of her closed eyes and opened her mouth. Harding covered her lips with his own, ready to blow into her lungs. There was no need. He could sense Vicky responding to him, kissing him back. When he finally pulled away from her, Vicky's eyes were open, searching his face for answers he couldn't give.

"Tobe?" asked Harding.

Vicky shook her head solemnly.

They stayed that way for some time, bobbing up and down in the ocean, holding each other and watching the bright rainbow that was forming over the remains of the "temple".

Then Harding noticed something white floating on the sea. They swam over to the bits and pieces of Fuller's plane. The wings were pretty much intact, and so they took one each and slid on top. Using them like surfboards, the pair paddled over to the burnt-out and sinking husk that used to be The Jenny. Harding managed to find a lifebelt for Vicky, part of a stretcher and some lengths of charred rope (once decorative) from the side of the boat floating amongst the wreckage. There was no sign of Rob Woodhead.

They tied the two wings together as best they could. It still let in water down the middle, but it would have to do. Then, taking one final look at the scene behind them, they set off. Both lay out on the makeshift raft, kicking with their feet, and paddling with the stretcher.

They had a long way yet to go, but somehow they both knew they would make it.

Somehow they knew they'd get home.

## Chapter Fifty-Five
### Safe

It was night by the time they reached the cottage.

Vicky was shivering against him, hardly able to walk. Though the swim back had been easier than he imagined, almost as if they'd been guided along, the haul from Hunter's Pass had really taken it out of them.

Faraway sirens shattered the quietness of the night. Tiny blue lights in the distance. Harding realised he'd left the keys in his jacket back in the van at Angels Landing, so he smashed one of the panes of glass in the door to gain entry.

He virtually had to carry Vicky inside, drawing on reserves of strength he never knew he had. Eventually they made it to the bedroom and Harding peeled off her damp clothes. She was barely conscious of what he was doing, not even when he went for a towel and rubbed her down. Only when she sneezed did she open her eyes and mumble something.

"It's okay," said Harding softly, easing her into the bed and pulling the thin sheets over her. He went to the airing cupboard and took out some winter blankets. Then he placed them on top of her, warming her up.

Vicky kissed him on the cheek when he bent over her. "Jason…"

"Go to sleep. We'll talk tomorrow," he told her.

Vicky nodded, too weak to argue.

Harding got out of his own soaking clothes in the half-light from the landing, pulling on a thick pair of sweat pants and a jumper. He stood at the door for a while, watching Vicky sleep, the rise and fall of the blankets as she breathed deeply. They'd both have one hell of a cold, that was for sure, but at least they were still here, alive. Together.

He thought briefly of Rob Woodhead, of Darville and Fuller. Of all the people who had died today.

*No one truly dies…*

Harding turned and hobbled towards the living room to sleep in the chair, remembering the bottle of whiskey he'd been drinking last night. He needed a belt more than he'd ever done in his life. Purely for medicinal purposes, he told himself. Not like the night before, when he'd been drinking to blot out the sorrow.

Tonight, he felt oddly at ease. He didn't know whether it was because he'd seen Alex again, because Alex had helped him. Or because Vicky was with him now. In a sense it didn't really matter, and it wasn't for him to question it. He was grateful whatever the reason.

He wandered into the room, not bothering to turn on the light. He could remember where the bottle was, by the armchair.

But as he stepped inside, he got the feeling that somebody was watching him. Their eyes boring into him. He saw a face in the darkness and jumped. His hand shot out for the light switch—

And Harding found himself looking at his unfinished

painting. The Maelstrom. For a moment he could have sworn... Harding wrinkled his nose. Stepping over to it, he took one last look at its form, its lines so familiar to him (the temple?), before turning it around on the easel. A cross of wood faced him now, the back of the canvas.

Harding went in search of the whiskey and discovered it right where he'd left it. Holding it in one hand, he took a swig. The alcohol warmed his cold bones. He glanced at the arm chair. It no longer held any appeal for him. Maybe Vicky wouldn't mind if he slipped in beside her tonight. Just for tonight.

He ambled slowly to the doorway, turning out the light as he went through it. As he made his way quietly to the bedroom, and climbed in beside Vicky, he craved for sleep to take him.

And it did, almost as soon as his head hit the pillow.

A deep, peaceful sleep.

Devoid of dreams.

# Epilogue
## The Tide

The waters finally calmed themselves as the waves died down, the ripples dispersing naturally.

Though not disappearing altogether. A trace of them remained. Waiting for the next stone to be cast.

\*\*\*

Tuesday: 7.30 am

The old man walked with a stick. It left tiny holes in the sand as he went along, that would be gone by tomorrow. They always were. No trace of his presence from the previous day. But it didn't bother him, he liked the idea of a fresh, clean stretch of sand, unsullied by visitors. He was the first one out here every morning, like the last man alive on Earth. Not a soul in sight. He nodded in satisfaction and congratulated himself again on his choice of retirement spots. Something about being next to the sea...

Stooping, he picked up one of the smooth stones lying on the beach.

Jude, his faithful Collie, chased around his legs in circles, barking loudly.

"All right, girl. All right."

He threw the stone along the beach as hard as he could and the dog bounded after it. A few seconds later she came running back with the off-white object in her jaws. Wagging her tail, Jude dropped the stone at his feet.

"Again?"

Jude barked enthusiastically.

"I'll take that as a yes."

The old man bent once more, strands of grey hair drooping over his eyes. This time he tossed the stone in the direction of the ocean. It landed at the water's edge with a plop, but Jude would find it without any problems. She always did.

In she went, splashing about, fur sticking to her body. Jude loved it.

She sniffed out the stone. But before she could pick it up, Jude noticed something else there. She began to bark, wagging her tail. Cautiously, Jude padded forwards.

It was a strange shape, not entirely human. Bits of it were. Parts of it covered in flesh, other parts in a glistening substance that resembled frogspawn. For days it had drifted down the coast, travelling miles and miles. Aimlessly lapping on the waves. Until the tides had brought it to this place.

Jude went over to the thing and sniffed it.

Then she licked it.

Her tongue tingled slightly and she pulled back.

"Jude? Hey Jude!" The old man laughed to himself every time he said that. "Come on girl, bring the stone.

Bring it!"

Obediently, Jude picked up the stone and started back to her master. The odd incident forgotten now. The strange tingling gone.

She just wanted to play fetch some more.

And maybe, just maybe, splash about again in the sea…

## About the Author

Paul Kane is an award-winning (including the British Fantasy Society's Legends of FantasyCon Award), bestselling writer and editor based in Derbyshire, UK. His short story collections include *Alone (In the Dark)*, *Touching the Flame*, *FunnyBones*, *Peripheral Visions*, *Shadow Writer*, *The Adventures of Dalton Quayle*, *The Butterfly Man and Other Stories*, *The Spaces Between*, *Ghosts*, the British Fantasy Award-nominated *Monsters*, *Shadow Casting*, *Nailbiters*, *Death*, *Disexistence*, *Scary Tales*, *More Monsters*, *Lost Souls*, *The Controllers*, *The Colour of Madness*, *Traumas*, *Darkness & Shadows*, *The Naked Eye*, *Tempting Fate*, *Nailbiters – Hard Bitten*, *Zombies!*, *Even More Monsters* and *Dark Reflections*. His novellas include *The Lazarus Condition*, *RED* and *Pain Cages* (a #1 Amazon bestseller). He is the author of such novels as *Of Darkness and Light*, *The Gemini Factor* and the bestselling *Arrowhead* trilogy (*Arrowhead*, *Broken Arrow* and *Arrowland*, gathered together in the sell-out omnibus edition *Hooded Man*), a post-apocalyptic reworking of the Robin Hood mythology. His latest novels include *Lunar* (which is set to be turned into a feature film), the short YA novel *The Rainbow Man* (as PB Kane), the critically-acclaimed and award-winning *Sherlock Holmes and the Servants of Hell* from Solaris, the sequels to *RED* – *Blood RED* and *Deep RED*, recently collected in an omnibus edition from HellBound Books – *Before*, *Arcana*, *The Storm* and *The Gemini Effect*, plus *Her Last Secret*, *Her Husband's Grave* and *The Family Lie* from HQ/HarperCollins (as PL Kane)

He has also written for comics, most notably for the *Dead Roots* zombie anthology alongside writers such as James Moran (*Torchwood*, *Cockneys vs. Zombies*) and Jason Arnopp (*Doctor Who*, *Friday the 13th*, *The Last Days of Jack Sparks*) and as part of the team turning *Clive Barker's Books of Blood* into motion comics for Seraphim/MadeFire. His stand-alone comic *The Disease*, published by Hellbound Media, was also a 2016 Ghastly Award-nominated title in the "One Shot" category. Paul is co-editor of the anthology *Hellbound Hearts* (Simon & Schuster) – stories based around the mythology that spawned *Hellraiser* – *The Mammoth Book of Body Horror* (Constable & Robinson/Running Press), featuring the likes of Stephen King and James Herbert, *A Carnivàle of Horror* (PS) featuring Ray Bradbury and Joe Hill, *Beyond Rue Morgue* from Titan (stories based around Poe's detective, Dupin), *Exit Wounds* – a crime anthology featuring the likes of Lee Child, Val McDermid, Dennis Lehane and Jeffery Deaver – *Wonderland* (a finalist in the Shirley Jackson Awards), the bestselling *Cursed* and its sequel *Twice Cursed*, *The Other Side of Never* and *In*

*These Hallowed Halls* (the first ever Dark Academia anthology), the last six also from Titan.

His non-fiction books include *The Hellraiser Films and Their Legacy*, *Voices in the Dark* and *Shadow Writer – The Non-Fiction. Vol. 1: Reviews* and *Vol. 2: Articles and Essays*, plus his genre journalism has appeared in the likes of *SFX*, *Fangoria*, *Dreamwatch, Gorezone* and *Rue Morgue*. He also co-wrote the afterword to the PS edition of Stephen King's *Night Shift* collection. Paul has been a Guest at Alt.Fiction five times, was a Guest at the first SFX Weekender, at Thought Bubble in 2011, Derbyshire Literary Festival and Off the Shelf in 2012, Monster Mash and Event Horizon in 2013, Edge-Lit in 2014, HorrorCon, HorrorFest and Grimm Up North in 2015, The Dublin Ghost Story Festival and Sledge-Lit in 2016, IMATS Olympia and Celluloid Screams in 2017, Black Library Live (Warhammer 40k) and The UK Ghost Story Festival in 2019 and 2023, delivered the keynote speech at the 2021 WordCrafter conference, as well as being a panellist at FantasyCon and the World Fantasy Convention, and a fiction judge at the Sci-Fi London Film Festival. He is a former Special Publications Editor of the British Fantasy Society, has served as co-chair for the UK arm of the Horror Writers Association, and was co-chair of ChillerCon UK 2022 in Scarborough.

His work has been optioned for film and television, and his zombie story "Dead Time" was turned into an episode of the Lionsgate/NBC TV series *Fear Itself*, adapted by Steve Niles (*30 Days of Night*) and directed by Darren Lynn Bousman (*SAW II-IV* and *Spiral*). He also scripted *The Opportunity*, which premiered at the Cannes Film Festival, *Wind Chimes* (directed by Brad "*Hallows Eve*" Watson and which sold to TV), *The Weeping Woman* – filmed by award-winning director Mark Steensland, starring Tony-nominated actor Stephen Geoffreys (*Fright*

*Night*) – *Confidence*, directed by award-winning Mike Clarke (*A Hand to Play*, *Paper and Plastic*) which stars Simon Bamford (*Hellraiser*, *Nightbreed*, *Starfish*), and *The Torturer* directed by Joe Manco of Little Spark Films, now streaming in over 100 countries. Loose Canon/Hydra Films have just turned Paul's novelette *Men of the Cloth* into a feature called *Sacrifice* (aka *The Colour of Madness*), starring *Re-Animator* and *You're Next*'s Barbara Crampton. His work for audio includes the full cast drama adaptation of *The Hellbound Heart* for Bafflegab, starring Tom Meeten (*The Ghoul*), Neve McIntosh (*Doctor Who*) and Alice Lowe (*Prevenge*), and the *Robin of Sherwood* adventure *The Red Lord* for Spiteful Puppet/ITV, narrated by Ian Ogilvy (*Return of the Saint*), plus his plays have been performed at FantasyCon and by the Hideout Theatre Company in London. You can find out more at his website www.shadow-writer.co.uk which has featured Guest Writers such as Dean Koontz, Robert Kirkman, Charlaine Harris and Guillermo del Toro.

**http://www.shadow-writer.co.uk**

# OTHER HELLBOUND BOOKS

## The RED Trilogy

Evil takes on many forms -- something Rachael Daniels, an innocent care worker, is about to find out... personally. Something is roaming the streets of the city where she lives, something monstrous with a taste for sweet, red, human blood.
Something that can be anything it wants to be.
Soon, Rachael learns the hard way that not even the friendliest faces can be trusted. As she makes her way across that city one night on an errand of mercy, she quickly discovers the terrifying creature will definitely have no such consideration for her…

Together in one book for the very first time ever, *The RED Trilogy* is a modern, urban reworking of a classic fairy tale, which puts the horror spin on an old favorite. *Blood RED* picks up straight away after the events of *RED*, the first installment, while *Deep RED* throws you into a nightmarish future scenario. If you dare to open these pages, you'll face a terrifying journey into the unknown – courtesy of award winning and #1 bestselling author, Paul Kane (the sellout *Hooded Man, Monsters, Sherlock Holmes and the Servants of Hell*).

Paul Kane

# The Horror Zine's Book of Monsters

With an introduction by Shirley Jackson Award-winner Gemma Files, this outstanding anthology of all things monstrous includes spine-chilling stories from Bentley Little, Simon Clark, Elizabeth Massie, Tim Waggoner, Sumiko Saulson, plus some of the best emerging horror writers working today.

"This anthology gives us a chilling glimpse at the dark and dangerous things prowling in the minds of some of today's best horror writers." – JG Faherty, author of *Ragman* and *Songs in the Key of Death*

"Throughout the pages are creepy tales by up-and-comers who you may have read, plus writers brand new to a horror reader's discerning eye. Embark on a journey to the realm where monsters—familiar or unique—dwell. Highly recommended to horror aficionados obsessed with eldritch fiction—this one's for you!" – Nancy Kilpatrick, author of *Thrones of Blood Series* and *the Darker Passions series*

## **The Toilet Zone: Number Two**
*"Restroom reading at its most terrifying!"*

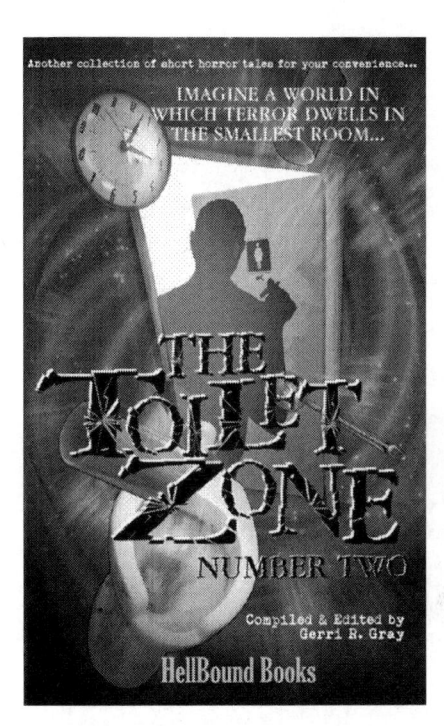

Imagine, if you will, you're traveling through the unknown, hellbound, with no roadmap or stars to guide you. The light fades as you descend into a shadow realm where supernatural terrors make their lair and evil lurks at every turn. Here, dead things don't always stay dead, for this is a world where things that shouldn't be… *are*, and things that should be are not.

In this world, it takes between 2,500 and 4,000 reading words to pay a visit to the smallest, but terrifyingly necessary, room, and stories are written precisely to chill the bones as you wait for nature to make its call.
You open up the book, and one of the 32 tales skulking within its hellish pages chooses you…
It's too late to turn back now. You are about to set foot into another dimension, so best watch out for that signpost up ahead...You've just crossed over into... The Toilet Zone

## TENEBRION

*"The Devil's in the detail."*

Amateur filmmakers inadvertently invoke a demon when they break into an abandoned school to perform and film an authentic Black Mass for their entry into a short movie competition.

Dave Priestley and his crew film in Watsonville elementary school – the site of a horrific tragedy nine years before.

Tenebrion – the malevolent demon of darkness – makes preparations of its own within the dark recesses of Hell. The demon requires a specific set of circumstances and sacrifices to rend a fissure between the worlds and set free its brethren; it has manipulated humans for centuries to put things into place, and the moviemakers are the unfortunate, final pieces of its nefarious puzzle. Priestley, ever the stickler for authenticity and detail, accidentally sets free the denizen of Hell. And while Priestley and his skeptical friends attempt to return Tenebrion to the pit of Hades, it hunts them all down – one by one – for inclusion in its hellish gateway.

## The Horror Writer
*"The most definitive guide into the trials and tribulations of being a horror writer since Stephen King's 'On Writing.'"*

We have assembled some of the very best in the business from whom you can learn so much about the craft of horror writing: Bram Stoker Award© winners, bestselling authors, a President of the Horror Writers' Association, and myriad contemporary horror authors of distinction.

The Horror Writer covers how to connect with your market and carve out a sustainable niche in the independent horror genre, how to tackle the writer's ever-lurking nemesis of productivity, writing good horror stories with powerful, effective scenes, realistic, flowing dialogue and relatable characters without resorting to clichéd jump scares and well-worn gimmicks. Also covered is the delicate subject of handling rejection with good grace, and how to use those inevitable "not quite the right fit for us at this time" letters as an opportunity to hone your craft. Plus... perceptive interviews to provide an intimate peek into the psyche of the horror author and the challenges they work through to bring their nefarious ideas to the page.

And, as if that – and so much more – was not enough, we have for your delectation Ramsey Campbell's beautifully insightful analysis of the tales of HP Lovecraft.

Featuring:
Ramsey Campbell, John Palisano, Chad Lutzke, Lisa Morton, Kenneth W. Cain, Kevin J. Kennedy, Monique Snyman, Scott Nicholson, Lucy A. Snyder, Richard Thomas, Gene O'Neill, Jess Landry, Luke Walker, Stephanie M. Wytovich, Marie O'Regan, Armand Rosamilia, Kevin Lucia, Ben Eads, Kelli Owen, Jasper Bark, and Bret McCormick.

And interviews with: Steve Rasnic Tem, Stephen Graham Jones, David Owain Hughes, Tim Waggoner, and Mort Castle.

**A HellBound Books LLC Publication**

www.hellboundbooks.com

Manufactured by Amazon.ca
Bolton, ON